DEAD END

Chris DiLeo

JOURNALSTONE
YOUR LINK TO ARTIST TALENT

ISBN: 978-1-950305-18-6 (sc)
ISBN: 978-1-950305-19-3 (ebook)
Library of Congress Control Number: 2020934200

First printing edition: March 27, 2020

Cover Design and Layout: Don Noble/Rooster Republic Press
Interior Layout: Lori Michelle
Edited by Sean Leonard
Proofread by Scarlett R. Algee

JournalStone Publishing
3205 Sassafras Trail
Carbondale, Illinois 62901

JournalStone books may be ordered through booksellers or by contacting:
JournalStone | www.journalstone.com

DEAD END

For my father, who left me the books,
and for my mother, who let me read them

"HOME CAN BE A PLACE OF DEATH."

A PLACE OF DEATH

I WAS ELEVEN when I watched my father die.

He ascended the hill behind our house one May morning, slanting forward with purpose along the path where it sloped gradually. At the top, he stopped at the edge. The hill towered over the back deck, dwarfing the house. I enjoyed throwing G.I. Joes off that cliff-like edge, cupping my hands around my mouth to make echoey screams, and watching wide-eyed as the figures fell to clatter and bounce on the lawn.

Dad stretched his arms out at his sides. Blood dribbled off his face. I was in the kitchen at the sliding glass door and he was above me, crucified against a blue sky.

He leaned forward.

And fell.

Mom had already left for work, so it was only me kneeling beside my father, the cold ground wetting my pajamas.

"Dad?"

He was sideways, with his hips warped at an almost-impossible angle. The bloody side of his face lay against the ground. He shook as if freezing.

"Dad?"

His eyes rolled up, completely white—the chalky, milky-yellow white of maggots—and pinkish bile bubbled between his lips. It stank, sharp and acidic. His whole face tightened, and a jagged blue vein bulged in his temple, a crack that might split open his skull.

Woods loomed all around us, thick and so dark it always seemed to be night in there. I never dared to explore any of it, scared of what might be back there, and right then I was sure something watched from the shadows. I felt its hungry stare.

The sun fractured through clouds and the world magnified in startling brightness. My father's fingers trembled in the grass, and he reached toward me with one arm but couldn't lift it very far—bright blood streaked his palm—and I leaned into his hand. He'd never shown me such affection. He was a distant man, something of a stranger to me. The flesh was warm. His fingers tapped Morse code on my cheek.

"Wrong," he said in a throaty gargle. "Wrong, wrong."

"Dad," I said, and could say nothing else. What could I say? We weren't close, but he was my father and I loved him. I was only a little kid.

His hand slipped back to the ground. I tasted salt at the corner of my mouth. His lips parted, and he spoke his dying word, his voice quavering with it.

"Coward."

Thick blood ran from his nose and streamed down through his beard to pool in his ears. His hands twitched, pink vomit oozed over his chin, and he was still.

I was screaming by then, but my voice gave out quickly and I slumped there, sobbing in awful scratchy hiccups, scared to move, not even daring to steal a final hug.

At the bottom of Mullock Road, a school bus's air brakes sighed, and a moment later the engine surged and the bus drove off. Birds chirped, and whatever thing watched me from the woods slipped back into the dark.

Dad's blood dried in crinkly streaks on my cheek.

At the hospital, Mom draped an arm around me and pulled me close so my butt lifted off the hard plastic chair.

"Daddy had a heart attack," Mom said. She sounded quiet, distant. "A heart attack. His heart was sick and stopped beating."

She rested her head on mine. She smelled of baked cookies and sweat.

"His heart stopped," she said. "When people ask, that's what you tell them. His heart stopped. Okay?"

I pictured him on the hill, silhouetted against the vast blue sky. Saw him fall. "Yes, Mommy."

Dad kept repeating his final word, taunting me, judging me: *Coward.*

I wanted his death to mean something, but I was afraid even then of what that something could be.

Every death is meaningless.

PART ONE:
DEATH AND MADNESS

———⚬⚬⚬———

"All that we see or seem is but a dream within a dream."
—Edgar Allan Poe

———⚬⚬⚬———

"It came back. It never left."

CHAPTER 1:
IT CAME BACK

I WAS TWENTY-FIVE and unloading a U-Haul of all the stuff Dani and I had accumulated living together for two years. It was late June in upstate New York, hot and sunny, but my bride-to-be didn't complain once. She was in great shape, though she exercised and did yoga only sporadically, and when she took a breather, I commented that I thought it'd take more than a few heavy boxes to tire her out.

She cocked her head and gave me the death stare she perfected in the classroom. Her Warrenville Wildcats t-shirt pulled tight across her breasts, and made the school mascot's tooth-filled maw stretch wide. We were both English teachers at the high school, had fallen in love as we taught Shakespeare and Poe across the hall from each other, but she was definitely the more attractive.

She flicked hair off her forehead and smiled. "I must be dumbstruck by love," she said in a Scarlett O'Hara voice, "to take such abuse." With her dark hair and big eyes, she even resembled Scarlett.

We kissed.

"Takes more to tire me out than you know," she said.

"Oh, really? Sounds like a challenge."

She smelled of sweat and the day was thickening with humidity and we still had the whole damn truck to unload and somehow squeeze as much as we could into my mom's house, the house I grew up in, but right then she looked so good I pressed my hands to her sweaty back and slid them down to her ass and squeezed. She protested but didn't stop me. I kissed her neck and the spot behind her ear that made her moan, and we stumbled against the truck. We were young, both in our twenties, and our relationship was strongly physical, but we also shared long, wine-fueled, introspective nights full of confessional monologues about our lives, our aspirations, and our fears.

For two English teachers, conversation was also an ideal aphrodisiac.

My right hand hooked over her thigh, and she caught it. "Your mom's inside, Mike."

"She isn't watching."

"You think you're so clever and charming, don't you?"

"I don't know about clever and charming, but people have called me special."

"I'll bet."

We kissed again, and when I grabbed a box of kitchen utensils and turned to the front steps, she slapped my butt. I looked back at her, my eyebrows going up, mouth opening in a parody of shock.

"Making sure you know who's in charge," she said in her best airy Southern accent.

"My ass is in charge?"

"There's that charm," she said.

I carried the box inside up the stairs I'd scaled thousands of times. From my angle, I saw into the kitchen where Mom was baking cookies, a throwback to my youth.

"More stuff for the kitchen," I was saying, "not that you need any."

She stood at the glass door leading onto the deck. The hill rose beyond. As a kid I'd called that hill Mount Munacy (not terribly creative, considering that's my last name) and if I let the memory come, Dad would appear on the cliff edge, shadowed against the sky.

Mom wore green oven mitts that matched the ivy wallpaper, and she was standing at the door, one mitt pressed to the glass, and she was saying something.

"Mom?"

Her head turned toward me, but she had a faraway look in her eyes, receding into her own memory. "It came back," she said, and immediately shook her head. "It never left."

"Mom, what're you—"

Her lips formed a strange, uneven smile that trembled, and she coughed, phlegmy and strained, and coughed again, and then it was an all-out fit, face blooming crimson dots, eyes widening with concern. I dropped the box in my arms, spatulas and flatware jangling, and went to her. Mom took a step, wobbled, and collapsed. I caught her under the arms, but she was too heavy to hold upright, so I eased her down and leaned her against my body.

The coughs wouldn't stop. They rasped in metallic scrapes. I held her, told her it was going to be okay, her body shaking with the coughs as if there were something huge inside her trying to get free. The mitts jiggled off her hands.

I took out my cell, dialed.

Dani called up from the front door, saying something about her favorite ass, but the 9-1-1 operator was in my ear and I was demanding an ambulance and Dani stopped in the kitchen doorway, shirt damp and hair sweat-licked to her temples.

Her face paled.

"Please," I said into the phone. "Hurry."

DEAD END

It was late when we returned from the hospital, but we lay awake in bed, hearts racing, my mind a wound-up coil tightening into a cramping headache.

Dani touched my hand. "It'll be okay."

"Sure," I said, but I'd barely heard her words. What I could hear was my mother's voice, and what she'd said.

It came back. It never left.

CHAPTER 2:
CHRISTIAN SOLDIERS

IT RAINED IN the night, and the ground exhaled steam into the morning. It was to be a quick breakfast and off to the hospital, but when I was halfway done with a bagel and a coffee, the singing started. Church music. I was out on the deck in the morning sun. There was no church nearby, not an official one anyway, yet I was unsurprised when Nedwin Loller appeared around the far side of the property. Years ago, he'd hulked over me, fat bending and folding, and promised my father would get into Heaven if I prayed hard enough.

It is rare when the bigness recalled from childhood is not diminished with age (Mount Munacy had been the Everest of my youth), but with Ned Loller it was magnified. He hefted weight on slow-stomping legs and his purple vestments clutched at his jiggling belly and arms. Beneath a long shroud his shoulders rolled with every grass-flattening, polished black-shoed step.

Behind him, others followed.

A man in a black suit with a pale face took long strides; a skinny black man in a blue button-down shuffled in muddy work boots; a middle-aged man with a shiny bald spot who wore a shirt with a cartoon Jesus on it was almost skipping; a frail woman in a jean skirt tugged along a child of nine or ten, he clumsy in blocky white sneakers; another man in a red-and-black flannel tilted his head into the sun; and a teenage boy in a purple robe to match Loller's marched several feet behind.

They crossed the grass along the side of the house through vapor ghosts and approached Mount Munacy.

Loller sang loudest, face red with strain, and the teenage boy was belting it out too, while the rest of the group added their voices scattered and off-tempo: "Onward, Christian soldiers, marching as to war, with the cross of Jesus going on before."

The man in the flannel glanced at me. I was standing at the closest end of the deck, and my hand came up in a wave.

He squinted and looked away.

Loller lifted a black Bible overhead, while each of his followers held a slim blue book. The little boy clutched one against his chest.

6

The group crossed the lawn and started up the far side of the hill.

They trekked to the top and Loller went to the cliff's edge, and the group formed a half-circle behind him. Loller turned and the sun washed his face to pale sandstone. Light glinted off a large gold cross hung around his neck. His thin hair ruffled in the breeze.

Someone touched my shoulder and I jumped. The last of my coffee sloshed over the cup's rim and speckled the deck floor.

Dani smiled. "Hey."

"Hey."

"What's this, a welcoming party?"

"Depends on your perspective."

"You know those people?"

I pointed. "Ned Loller. Lives in the yellow house at the bottom of the street."

"He a priest?"

"He's something."

Ned's back was to us, but his hands were skyward. The gathered congregation bowed heads into open books.

Dani hooked her hair around one ear and touched my arm. "How are you?"

"I'm okay."

She propped her chin on my shoulder as if I had two heads. "Really? You're okay?"

"A bit stressed."

"God forbid you admit you're stressed. You can be vulnerable with me, you know."

"Yes, dear."

She pushed me playfully and turned me to face her. "I'm serious."

I sighed and draped an arm around her. She nuzzled against me. Her hair was damp and smelled of lilac shampoo. "I'm worried."

"I know. We'll get through it together."

"Funny how things turn out," I said. "Should've stayed in our apartment."

"It'll be okay."

"We came here to save money, but if she doesn't get out—"

"Stop." Dani's hand tensed on my lower back. "You don't know what will happen."

"She didn't look good. You said so yourself."

"I see what you're doing, clever boy."

"Me?"

"Quoting yours truly."

"Was I?"

She stared up at me. "I couldn't do anything. I'm pathetic."

"What were you supposed to do?"

"You were so good, calm and calling 9-1-1. Composed at the hospital."

On the cliff, Ned and his group stumbled into a version of "Amazing Grace." The discordant sounds carried up and away, perhaps God taking mercy on us.

"Didn't do much good," I said.

"You're a better son than you're pretending to be."

"Fortune cookie wisdom?"

"Smartass."

"Again with the ass. Is this a fetish you've never confessed? You know, you can tell me things."

She rolled her eyes as if she were one of her own students and started to say something, but stopped.

"I see that mind of yours working."

"A woman's mind never stops."

"I love you," I said.

"So kiss me already."

We did, and I hugged her tightly. It's a well-worn idea, I guess, but sometimes I ached for her, and I don't mean in a sexual way, and right then with her body against mine and our lips together I felt my heart slow, and the world around us settled like we were in a hot air balloon finally touching ground. Everything might turn out okay. Mom was in poor health, but that didn't mean she was going to die.

Not yet, anyway.

The song on the hill ended and a moment later Ned was speaking, and every few seconds the crowd punctuated his words with a vociferous "Amen," like they were angry at him.

"They sound pissed," I said, and hugged her again.

"Maybe they're jealous of our love," Dani said, and chuckled.

On the hill Ned declared, "Hallelujah! Hallelujah! Christ is risen!"

"When do you want to go?"

I gestured to the hill. "When church lets out."

CHAPTER 3:
SUN-KISSED BELIEVERS

NED AND HIS GATHERING stayed on top of the cliff for another fifteen minutes. They sang more songs and prayed and Ned spoke at length—sermonizing, no doubt—and at the conclusion they opened their blue books and read aloud. I couldn't hear them, so their mouths seemed to move noiselessly, fish gasping on dry land. The cynical part of me found symbolism in that.

The man in the flannel rolled up his sleeves and every few seconds scratched the stubble or the back of his head. He swayed a bit, shifted from foot to foot.

Ned gestured to the woman and she stepped forward. Her son slipped his hand free and baby-stepped closer to the edge. His frumpy suit sagged, and his sneakers were easily two sizes too big.

The woman stopped before Ned, and he cupped their heads in his hands. A blessing, maybe, or a healing.

Ned was unaffiliated with any traditional church, and as far as I knew he wasn't proselytizing anything other than typical, though likely conservative, Christian ideologies, but watching them up there, bodies outlined against a blue sky, Ned's heavy hands pushing down the woman's and the boy's heads, I thought of cultists in movies who wore black and drank blood and sacrificed virgins on candle-lit altars.

Loller stretched his arms to the sky. The others did as well. Perhaps a Satanic yoga cult. They broke into song once more, and Ned led the way down Mount Munacy.

"Lift high the cross," they sang, "the love of Christ proclaim till all the world adore his sacred name."

The boy was watching me, and stumbled in his sneakers. His mom reached out to grab him, but he was falling too quickly, and my arm flinched reflexively. Flannel Man caught the boy's elbow and kept him on his feet.

The boy was safe, except in my mind, where he was falling.

They were soon crossing the lawn again, still singing, and every time they said, "lift high the cross," Ned raised the gold one hanging off his neck.

Ned saw me. His cross glinted sunlight directly into my face.

Talk about symbolism.

Ned headed for the deck stairs, while the others paraded out of sight.

I went to the top of the stairs, but he kept coming up, thumping steps, hand on railing, face blotting red, breath deep and rapid. The last few steps groaned beneath his weight.

"Hello, Mike," he said between breaths.

I stepped back, and his bigness expanded before me. "Ned."

You want your dad to get into Heaven, he'd said to me years ago, *don't you?*

His hand hung between us, and his cheeks bunched around small white teeth. I knew that grin. It was a preacher's grin in a salesman's mouth. *We can be friends,* the doughy face charmed, *believers together in the One True Way, so long as you accept that I know best.*

We shook, his hand a mushy glove of hot flesh.

"How are you, Mike?"

I nodded.

"How is Beatrice?"

"Mom's not great. She's in the hospital."

Ned breathed out a long sigh and settled back into his weight, as if searching for his center of gravity. "I am so sorry to hear that, Mike. Beatrice is wonderful. Always kind. Is it serious?"

"I'm about to head over."

Flesh jiggled around his neck. "I won't keep you."

On Heintz Hill, a motorcycle blared past our dead-end road in a growling scream. Ned's singing congregation was long gone.

"If there is anything I can do, please call."

"Thanks."

"I hope we didn't disturb you. I didn't know about your mother. I would have asked you if I'd known."

"Outdoor church . . . Interesting."

"Your mother graciously allows me to use that hill. There is no spot quite equal to it." His face turned toward the sun. "It's very special. Up there, we are sun-kissed believers. There's a special feeling up there. A blessed one. Magical. Up there, you can find God." His teeth were lost in his mouth. "It is glorious."

My father was crucified against the sky. He fell. I was the only witness.

Daddy had a heart attack.

Ned stared at me, waiting, or trying to read my thoughts, and I was sure he was going to invite me to join his church (*cult*) or at the least, offer to pray with me for my mom's health.

"Anything you need, you let me know. Have a lovely day. God bless."

"You too."

He spared me another handshake and hefted his weight down the steps. It took him a while. I turned to Mount Munacy.

Up there, you can find God.

Or, I knew, you can watch him die.

CHAPTER 4:
HOSPITAL TIME

HOSPITALS KEEP THEIR own time. It is slower, much slower, and it's thick and gelatinous, solidifying around you until you are a clump of fruit suspended in Hospital Time Jell-O.

Mom was in a room by herself on the third floor, and when Dani and I entered to find her propped up in bed but cloaked in a sterile sheet, the TV on but muted, the room smelling of Clorox, we felt that unique hospital time thickening around us.

"How are you?" I asked.

Mom was short, five foot in sneakers, and in the hospital bed she shrank further, a sixty-eight-year-old woman with thin, permed hair and a rounded belly. She looked tired and pale, but tried to make it seem like she was fine, *don't trouble yourself worrying about poor old Mom.*

"Has a doctor been in?"

"This morning," she said.

"And?"

She shrugged. The gesture shrank her even smaller, and I imagined her as an elderly child molded beneath a white sheet.

"Can we get you anything?" Dani asked. She touched Mom's arm.

"Chocolate?"

"Not yet," I said. Dani's expression condemned me as cruel, and Mom's expression judged me as mean. "They didn't say what's wrong with you?"

Mom made an uncertain gesture, hand turning side to side.

"What did they say?"

She opened her mouth, closed it, then looked right at me. "Not much."

"I'll find someone right now."

In the hall, a nurse moved out of view into another room, and down at the nurse's station, two others were talking to visitors. Somewhere a man was groaning, and somewhere else women were laughing, high-pitched and fluttery. From another room stepped a narrow man in a doctor's coat, with a bright blue tie hanging askew from its knot. He looped a stethoscope around his collar.

I crossed the distance and snagged his arm. He gaped at me, afraid and unsure. "My mother is right down there, and I want some information."

"Your mother is . . . "

"Beatrice Munacy."

His eyebrows went up and he gave a little nod, as if he knew my mom well.

"Are you her doctor?"

"I'm the attending."

"What can you tell me?"

He hesitated. "I'll be right with you."

"How long?"

"I'm in the middle of rounds."

"Did you see my mother?"

"I wasn't in earlier when Dr. Schaffer came through. I'm sure he—"

"What did *that* doctor say?"

"You'll have to check with one of the nurses."

At the nurse's station, a woman thunked her pocketbook onto the counter and sighed. "I'll wait," the woman said, and the nurse across from her turned to a computer monitor.

"Look," I said, "is there a diagnosis?"

He adjusted his tie, making it more crooked. "Are you your mom's health proxy?"

My silence satisfied him.

"Is she okay?"

He glanced around, no help in sight. "I'll see what I can do."

"Thanks."

On my way, back a man in a Carhartt t-shirt slowed as we passed. "Don't hold your breath," he said. "Doctors are assholes."

Dani was tucking the sheet around Mom's feet, and I saw something and yanked the sheet back. Her socks were off, her ankles swollen, her feet bruised purplish-brown in places, and dirt-streaked.

"What's this?" I asked. Dirt crusted her untrimmed, yellowing toenails.

Dani pulled the sheet back over them. "They're feet, Mike."

"Why are they dirty?"

Mom didn't look at me. So I was the bad guy for asking questions, for trying to figure out what was going on. That's okay. I could play that role. I did it enough with my students.

"She was in the woods," Dani said.

"What?"

"Don't make a big deal out of it."

I laughed. It sounded almost maniacal. "Why were you in the woods?"

"Relax," Dani said.

I shrugged off her touch. "Will you look at me, Mom?"

She did.

"Why were you in the woods?"

She didn't answer.

"Why were you barefoot? Were you sleepwalking? Delusional?"

It came back. It never left.

"Give it a rest," Dani said.

"I'm just asking."

"Not everyone is scared of the woods," Dani said.

Anger flushed my face, but then Mom finally spoke, her voice soft and introspective: "When I was in the kitchen, standing at the oven, it was the strangest feeling. Like something took over me. Everything fell away."

"You were at the door, looking outside."

"I saw you standing over me."

"You remember what you said?"

"I thought I was dying."

I should've gone to her, hugged her, cried with her. "I'm getting the doctor."

He was at the nurse's station, typing. I slapped my hand on the counter, waited for him to look up.

"You," I said. "*Now.*"

Dumb surprise pushed the doctor to his feet, saving me from a security escort out the lobby doors.

Once in the room he spoke rapidly, perhaps having quickly perused my mom's file and wanting to spill it out before he forgot. "She has diabetes, high blood pressure, COPD, hypothyroidism, renal disease, and CHF."

"What's that?"

"CHF? Congestive heart failure."

"It was just diagnosed?"

The doctor glanced at my mother. Her hands were joined across her waist, gaze downcast like a shamed child. "She's had it for years."

I knew of my mom's health issues, had taken her to numerous doctor appointments, but apparently I didn't know *all* of the issues. "Can it cause sleepwalking?"

"Has she been?"

"No," Dani said.

The doctor looked uncertain, afraid either one of us might attack him. "Okay. The CHF has progressed, but it isn't the immediate concern."

"She's stable, then?"

"Dr. Blatty has been assigned her case. He's a nephrologist." He over-pronounced each syllable of the word.

Dani gave me a look.

"Which is what?" I asked.

"Kidney doctor," Mom said.

"Yes," the doctor said. He adjusted his blue tie and seemed pleased with himself, like he'd taught us something. "That's precisely what he is. Excellent physician."

"When can we talk to him?"

"Soon, I'm sure."

"Right."

The doctor nodded, almost to himself, and left.

I loved my mom, always had, and after my father died our love was the anchor that kept me from drifting. I could have gone off course, given up on school, fallen in with bad kids and drugs and alcohol, but Mom kept me grounded. The past several years since Dani and I had moved into an apartment together, however, strained that love. Instead of keeping me in place during life's tumultuous storms, the anchor was keeping me from finding my own way. I carried it with me, and it took on more and more weight until I could barely lift it. Mom greeted my twice-weekly calls with, "I was beginning to worry, I hadn't heard from you," and concluded with, "When do I get to see you again?" I took her to doctor appointments, did her grocery shopping, ate with her several times a week, but it was always, "I guess I have to schedule another doctor visit to see you again." She hefted guilt as an anchor all its own, and rage helped me carry it. The anger made me feel guilty, of course, and though I didn't want to move back home, financially it was our best option. Two years. Save money, get our own house. Start a family. And in the meantime, maybe being home would make Mom happy.

"You never told me about your kidneys," I said. When she didn't respond, I sighed dramatically. "What else haven't you told me? You have cancer? Are you dying?"

"Mike," Dani said. "Relax."

I appreciated her a moment and felt my irritation ebbing, but then I turned back to my mom, and anger warmed my skin and tightened my chest. "What else don't I know?"

Red-rimmed and glassy, Mom's stare challenged me to be harsher, really unleash on her, let fly accusations and be as cruel as I possibly dared, heft the anchor high in my hands and throw it at my mother who'd raised me into an adult, who only wanted the best for me, who made sacrifices I could never fully appreciate, and who wanted only a little tenderness right now.

"Let's go," I said.

Dani was slow to move, stalling for me to calm, but I went to the door and left.

Dani caught my wrist at the elevator. "Hey." Her fingers found my pulse, squeezed.

"I know, okay?"

"No, it's not okay. Talk to me."

DEAD END

"How long you think she's known?"

"She didn't want to trouble you."

"I doubt that."

"Then what?"

"She thinks ignoring it will make it go away."

"She's your mom, not some child."

I pulled from her grip. "What do you want me to say?"

"The truth."

"My mom's been lying for years, but I'm the one not telling the truth."

I stabbed the elevator button several more times.

She touched my cheek. "Mike, please."

I tried to swallow the words and suddenly couldn't. "I think my mom's dying."

CHAPTER 5:
WHAT'S HIDDEN YOU CAN'T SEE

WE RODE BACK to Mullock without speaking, until we were almost there.

Heintz Hill sloped, as advertised, up in a long, curving hill, matching bi-level homes equidistant on both sides with fresh-cut lawns and maple and willow trees off-center on every other lawn.

It was a warm June day. People should be gardening or tinkering with their cars or strolling on the sidewalk, and kids should be on bikes crisscrossing the road or playing tag or watching the pretty girls in their summer clothes. Instead, the street was quiet, desolate.

Was my whole life ripe with symbolism now?

"I'm sorry I was an asshole," I said finally.

"You can't treat her like that."

"I know." Dani had issues with her own mother, who was off in California with a bunch of new-age healers, her life one of meditation, chakras, and Reiki, whatever that was. They didn't talk at all.

"Whatever issues you have with her, she's your mother and she's not well."

"I know."

"Maybe try something a little more meaningful?"

For a moment, I was pissed—how dare Dani presume to know how I should feel or to what extent I should communicate my feelings, especially considering how she was with her own mother—but she spoke the words in such a perfectly casual, understated way that it caught me off guard and I started laughing.

She joined in.

A man in tight shorts stood beside a prissy poodle pissing along the sidewalk on Heintz Hill.

"Could be a good look for me," I said.

"You mean the pissing poodle?"

"I meant the shorts."

"Your ass isn't that tight," she said, "but you *are* a tight-ass."

We laughed harder, and when I turned onto Mullock, I had to wipe tears from my eyes.

16

DEAD END

"I want you to be honest," Dani said. She turned to me in the car, parked now in the driveway. "It's like there's this whole other you that's hidden, and I want to see it."

"Okay."

"Okay? That's all you have to say?"

"What do you want me to say?" I asked.

"That you're hurting."

I made some sort of ambiguous head nod and body shake, and Dani rightfully stared at me in confusion. "I am. Hurting. Okay?"

"Mike, I'm not trying to pressure you. I love you. We love each other. Right?"

I was a child being scolded. My hands leaped back onto the steering wheel, squeezed.

My mouth opened (to say what, I had no idea), but Dani got out of the car. She swung the door closed hard and went in the house.

CHAPTER 6:
A CLOSED DOOR

DANI WAS IN the hallway bathroom, door closed, the fan whirring out any sound of what she might be doing in there. A bar of light glowed along the door's bottom edge.

I stood in the hallway of the only house I'd ever known. When I was five or six, I would run up and down this hallway as fast as I could. My father would stand in the far doorway and my mother at the opposite end, and I'd sprint from one to the other as they raised their arms and snarled monster sounds at me. I giggled like mad when their arms swooped toward me.

The light under the door shadowed, and then the shadow moved. Dani was standing on the other side. Moving back and forth.

Doing what?

A boy learns early that what happens when a woman is in the bathroom, either alone or with a cluster of others in some public ladies' facility, is absolutely no business of his. Living with Dani in our apartment, I'd learned something about her that would have shocked my younger self: A woman's bathroom activities are pretty much as mundane and moderately degrading as any male's.

Dani never shut the bathroom door—not when she showered, not when she urinated, not when she took a shit, not even when she changed her tampon. She might swing the door so she was obscured, but she never closed it. Often, if I was nearby, she'd engage in full conversation with me, sometimes swinging the door completely open so she could hear better.

Yet here she was, behind a closed door.

Her shadow slid back and forth. Should I knock? What if she didn't answer? What if I tried the knob and it was locked? What if I threw my shoulder against the door to pop the flimsy lock and the door crashed against an open drawer jutting from the vanity?

What was she doing in there?

I pictured Dani on the other side of the door, staring at herself in the mirror, inch-worming her feet forward and back, a nervous habit she did the night we first kissed, and one she did sometimes when on the phone or even in school, waiting in the hallway outside her classroom for her students to arrive. It was a nervous tic sort of thing, but I found it cute.

But what was she doing now? "Dani?"

Her shadow stopped.

"I'm sorry," I said. "I'm just stressed. Okay?"

No response.

But there was a sound behind the door, faint, almost a whisper but not quite. Soft like a whisper, and yet not any letter-sounds to decipher. I leaned close to the door, closer.

A faint moan? "Dani?"

She's hurting herself, I thought. I had no reason to suspect this was the case, of course, but the thought—the fear—was there just the same. As a teacher, I'd sat through numerous presentations about teenage suicide, and I knew the clues to look out for.

My fist was up to knock when the door swung open. I pulled my fist, but not before Dani stumbled backwards as if I had actually punched her.

I watched, too surprised to say anything or even move, and Dani would have been all right if the bathroom rug had stayed out of it.

It slipped beneath her planted heel, and that leg lifted up and her balance shifted, and she fell. Had she landed on her butt, it might have hurt, but she would have shaken it off. (Incidentally, she had a butt I absolutely loved: womanly, with the perfect curve and squishiness.) Instead, her left elbow hit the edge of the toilet and her open palm smacked into her jaw. Her teeth clacked together. Any harder, and tooth fragments would have pebbled the floor. Her butt hit the tile and she snapped back into the wall. Her head bounced off it, and a framed stock photo of a volcano tilted askew above her.

Her furious expression stopped me before I barely made it a foot toward her. She grabbed the toilet and yanked herself into a crouch and stood. She wobbled, caught the counter. "What the fuck?"

"Are you okay?"

"What the hell, Mike?"

"The door was closed. I was worried."

"Because the door was closed?"

She was angry, really angry, but she also sounded confused, and my explanation about her never closing the door when we lived in the apartment seemed terrifically childish. I said nothing.

"I wanted privacy, okay?"

"I'm . . . sorry."

She touched the back of her head and then her jaw. "Jesus."

"I'll get you some ice."

"I'll get it," she said. A drop of blood popped at the corner of her mouth.

"You're bleeding."

She touched the spot, smearing it, and examined her fingertip. I saw my father in this same bathroom, nose to the glass, grooming scissors pressed to his cheek, blood beginning to gush. "Great. Thanks, Mike."

"I said I was—"

"Sorry, I know."

I reached for her, but she batted my arm away. Her face flushed dark red spots, and a threatening glare cleared her eyes as if they were the only thing about her in focus.

She opened her mouth to say something and gagged. It was a hard, phlegmy sound, almost a choke. Her hands flapped out toward the sink and she seized the faucet handles, hip-checked me aside, and leaned over the sink, hair tumbling down her cheeks, and she hacked, strained, pained, mouth wide, throat bulging, and a clump of vile, blackish gunk slapped into the sink.

CHAPTER 7:
LOVE IS CRAZIER

DANI HAD ISSUES. I knew this. I could be flippant, I suppose, and dismiss her mood swings as typical hormone-related female behavior, but other than that idea being sexist and insulting, it was also wrong: I was no psychologist (hadn't even taken one course in psychology or human behavior), but if forced, I'd say Dani was somewhat of a manic-depressive.

We'd been living in the apartment just a month or so when I came back from the liquor store with two bottles of red and found Dani at the dining room table, head down on her arms, body heaving in deep, tear-clogged gasps.

I'd almost dropped the bottles. "Dani? Are you okay? What happened?"

I squatted beside her, rubbed her back.

Slowly, her crying eased, and she wiped at the tears and the snot and turned to me. She looked so sad, a discarded kitten in a rain-clotted gutter, and I took her in my arms and hugged her as tightly as I could. "What happened?"

She shook her head. "That's the thing, Mike. Nothing happened. It just came over me."

"What do you mean?"

"I'm sorry. I should've told you."

"Told me what?"

She took a deep breath. "I was doing so well. No anxiety, not really anyway, no anger. Not at all. Then I was driving back here, to our place, our home, and I couldn't breathe. I was hyperventilating by the time I made it inside."

"It's okay."

"I got sick."

"You mean . . . "

She forced a laugh, sad and self-derisive. "I puked in the garbage can."

I smiled.

"You think that's funny?"

"It's cute you're embarrassed."

"Thanks."

"You know what's embarrassing? Shitting yourself."

"I'll try to work up to that."

"No. I mean, I've shit myself."

"When you were a kid?"

"Senior in college. I'd been at a frat party all night and, stupidly, thought I'd go to class the next day, all hung over, try to tough it out. Halfway through a god-awful lecture about the socio-economic viability of twenty-first century Marxism, I had to run to the bathroom. I made it maybe ten feet from my chair before it just came out."

"You shit yourself in class?" she asked.

"See? I'm the one should be embarrassed."

"Was it diarrhea?"

"Are you asking me to relive such an embarrassing moment in my life so you can feel better about yourself?"

She leaned toward me. "Yes. That's exactly what I'm asking."

I moved closer, our lips very near. "It was a massive mustard-gas explosion that tore right through my underwear and speckled the floor with blackish-green feces."

She laughed. "You're so romantic."

We kissed and then, as often happened back then, the kiss got our hands moving, our clothes shedding off of us, and I followed her down the hall and into the bedroom.

We left the door open, and if anybody had lived with us, they would have had quite a view.

It was slow and sweet, punctuated with the softest moans of pleasure. After, we cuddled naked and talked for hours into the night.

"I'm sorry I'm a nutcase," she said.

"You're not a nutcase."

"A doctor might say different."

"I love you."

She stared at me, into me. "Now that's what's really crazy."

I was scared that time, for her. It was so unexpected, and I wasn't sure how I should react. There were other incidents, flare-ups of depression (crying fits; the time I found her sleeping in the bathtub) or mania (when she repainted the entire apartment over one weekend, moving all the furniture herself and working without sleep for forty-plus straight hours, her eyes in deep hollows, her skin pale), but I should stress that when I was worried or scared, it was always for her. I was never scared for myself. Never worried she might do something to me.

Not then.

CHAPTER 8:
A SKILLED PRETENDER

DANI WAS CURLED in bed to face the far wall, comforter bunched beneath her chin. I stood in the doorway.

"I feel you watching me," she said.

"Want me to get the air conditioner from my mom's room?"

"No."

"It's stifling in here."

"I'm fine."

"Can I get you anything?"

"No."

"Sure?"

"Some privacy," she said.

I started to say something, stopped, started again, then restarted one more time. "Love's the crazy thing."

"What?" she said.

"I was thinking about that time in the apartment when you slept in the bathtub."

"Dani's greatest hits of psychosis?"

"No." I went to the bed, sat on the edge. "I'm concerned." My arm wanted to reach out, touch the hump of her thighs.

She sighed, threw back the comforter, and sat up. Her hair dangled in sweaty tendrils. Shadow half-moons cupped her eyes. Her skin was the pale grey of a polluted haze hovering above a city. She looked awful. Blood had dried on her chin in the shape of a small question mark.

"Are you sick?" I asked.

"Mentally?"

"No. That's not what I'm saying."

"Then what, Mike?"

"You get stressed and sometimes have physical responses."

"Are you *Dr.* Mike now?"

"Dani."

She pursed her lips, a petulant child forced to listen to an adult.

"You want me to be honest, and I want you to be honest, too."

I braced against the expected retort, but the anger slid off her as easily as shrugging off a blanket. Her mood could change that easily, that suddenly and completely. It was always a relief, the real Dani stepping out from whatever dark cave she'd gotten lost in.

But it was also somewhat unnerving, the instant change from sad to happy, from angry to loving, and I'd wondered from time to time if Dani knew exactly what she was doing.

"I'm sorry. Really. I love you."

We kissed.

She's pretending, I thought.

Dani was a wonderful teacher, the sort of erudite, engaging educator that movies hold up as saviors of the disaffected and dejected. We taught down the hall from each other, and her voice sometimes boomed through the hall, with student laughter echoing after it. She'd jump on desks, wear goofy masks, and talk in exaggerated accents—foolishness in the name of literature, vocabulary, and grammar. After each class ended, she'd lean against her door in the hallway, face red, hair sweaty, and a small grin on her lips like she'd enjoyed vigorous sex.

"You're really great," I'd told her early on in our relationship. "Kids love you."

"It's helpful to be unpredictable," she said matter-of-factly. "But it's acting. I'm a skilled pretender."

She stared at me with those large, dark eyes, and I fought the urge to kiss her. A great moment in a romantic comedy, but in real life such things might be deemed sexual harassment. Still, though—those eyes, that stare. Man, oh, man.

"I got a bit overwhelmed," she said. "The hospital. Your mother. Moving here."

"It's temporary."

"I know. I want to be there for you."

"You are."

"Some help I am when I'm hiding in the bathroom or crying my eyes out."

"I love you. Truly."

The next kiss deepened, lingered, slipped along our chins and down our necks and under our clothes and we were naked and her legs hooked around my hips and she whispered into my ear, "Fuck me, baby. Please fuck me hard."

A skilled pretender, I thought. *She knows exactly what I want her to be.*

Even so, I gave her what she asked for.

CHAPTER 9:
INTO THE DARK

FALLING IN LOVE with someone and learning to live with that person are two different things. When Dani and I moved into my mom's house, we'd been living together for almost two years in an apartment. We loved each other, were compatible in conversation and in the bedroom. I loved her, and I'd coped with, and even grown fond of, her domestic habits that were so contrary to mine: always squeezing the toothpaste from the middle of the tube, never replacing the empty roll of toilet paper, never emptying a clean dishwasher, and never turning off lights in a room she was exiting.

Knowing those habits—tolerating them, anticipating them, and loving her for, not in spite, of them—was a testament to our mature love, one unhindered by suspicion, jealousy, or secrets.

I loved her, and I knew everything about her: her likes, her dislikes, her habits, her dreams.

That sounds so ridiculously juvenile and naive now, but I believed it, like millions of others before me who thought after a few years in a relationship that there were no more unopened doors, no stories left untold, no stashed secrets under the bed.

Besides, I knew she suffered depression and bursts of mania. I knew all of this, and I loved her completely. No matter what happened, we'd get through it together.

It's amazing how stupid we can be sometimes.

One moment we're lulled with contentment, because the days of bar-hopping and dating and awkward breakups are over and we've found the one to stick with for life, and the next we're on top of a cliff, the whole world spread out before us, and our feet are slipping toward the edge.

Closer . . .

Closer . . .

We're falling before we realize the ground has disappeared.

I woke in an empty bed.

"Dani?"

My voice echoed in the hallway. Brushstrokes of darkness sculpted into my future wife before bleeding into inky smears. It was almost three in the morning.

I called for her again. Nothing.

She wasn't in the bathroom, where I expected to find her in the bathtub, crying softly, perhaps. Not in the living room. Not in the kitchen, where moonlight glazed the glass door leading to the deck. The smell of chocolate lingered from Mom's baking, the cookies hardened to the pan, still on the stove where she placed them, and abandoned curls of sterilized plastic still strewn on the floor from the paramedics.

Something moved beyond the glass.

My bare feet slapped hard across the tile, and I was outside on the deck in the humid night. The June air was ripe with a swampy body-odor stench. Splintering wood poked at my soles. "Dani?"

The deck was empty.

Something brushed my leg, and I recoiled so quickly I stumbled sideways and scared Dusty into a sprinting hurtle across the deck and down the stairs, moving well for an old cat. He'd run out when the paramedics propped open the front door for the stretcher, and now he might not come back for hours. I'd forgotten all about him.

Way to go, Mike.

An owl hooted, deep-throated and loud, and branches slapped in hollow clacks. Mount Munacy hulked in the dark, as grand and menacing as it was in my nightmares where my father stretched his arms, tilted back his head, and dropped.

More branches clattered, and there was Dani stepping from the tree line, her blue nightshirt glowing so she appeared to float beneath a pale oval face.

"Dani!"

She spun around, black hair thwacking against her face, and froze, arms out, body rigid, head cocked toward the trees. I opened my mouth, but only a dry click came out. She hadn't stopped because of me—there was something in the woods.

I leaned over the deck railing. What if a coyote emerged growling, or a bear lumbered into the moonlight?

I moved quickly across the deck to the stairs and down onto the patio, and started up the hill along the far side, where the path was gradual and worn.

Dani approached the cliff edge, walking on her toes, body rigid, dancer-like. The cliff loomed over the house. A twenty-five-foot drop, maybe thirty, down to the yard.

"Dani!"

She stopped a foot from the edge. Weeds tangled around her calves. She tilted her face upward. Moonlight blanched her skin.

DEAD END

"Dani?"

She lowered her head, leaned forward, and peered over the cliff edge.

If she tilted forward even an inch more . . .

Fear wing-flapped in my chest. I took the hill fast as I could, dirt slipping and jagged stones stabbing.

Was she sleepwalking? I'd wondered the same about my mother, who'd gone into the woods as well.

Something in the air, perhaps.

My toes crunched against a rock, and I chomped down on a cry of pain. I limped to the cliff fast as I could.

"Hey," I said. It was the first thing I'd ever said to her three years ago, when we met in the copy room at Warrenville High School. Two months later, we were dating, and another two after, we had an apartment together.

She didn't respond. Her shoulders slumped, her back arched.

"Dani?"

My fingers paused in the space between us. The cliff edge was a single step away. "I think you're sleepwalking," I said.

She leaned farther.

I grabbed her waist, bony and fragile. She sagged, as if trying to pull me over the edge with her. The words SWEET DEVIL reflected silvery on her shirt. Her smile spread large. Her eyes were wide but unseeing, and there was something so awful about that smile. It was foreign, somehow. Not Dani.

Skin contracted along my spine. "Stop it." I pulled her back from the edge, shook her. "Dani. Stop it. *Wake up.*"

She giggled, young and girlish. Her arms toppled around my neck, flesh cold and damp, and she twitched her head to sweep hair from her face. Her tongue slicked her upper lip. It looked black. Was she flirting? Screwing around? Or was she really asleep?

Something in the woods.

I pulled her against me. Silence. What had I heard? A thing back there, in the darkness. An animal. Branches strained beneath weight and thwacked free in chaotic clatters.

Something back there. Something big.

She giggled again.

I was scared. Silly as that might be, it was late, I was tired, cold and exposed, and Dani was freaking me out—she'd come out here in the night and looked hypnotized, and her childish laugh, so completely unlike her, grated on my nerves, panic threatening to make me scream or run or lash out.

The owl hooted again, loud, and branches battered as it flew among the moonlight-dusted treetops, a wing cutting into the light like a shark fin slicing water.

Just an owl. That was all. No giant lumbering beast. No muscle-rippling predator.

"Come on, we have to go back inside."

Dani kissed me, but I didn't return it. I yanked her from me, nose to nose. "*Hey!*"

She recoiled, but I held tight. Recognition flickered, and she looked around, confused and afraid.

My heart thudded, and I was scared and embarrassed. I'd never shouted at Dani before. "I'm sorry. You were sleepwalking, I think."

She studied me, ss if I were something made up. Beyond her was the house where I grew up, and beyond that stretched a blackness of sleeping homes and all around us living woods. Night creatures unseen, hunting and killing. "How did I get out here?"

"You sleepwalked."

"I was dreaming."

"What was it?"

"I don't . . . Let's go inside."

"You were in the woods."

Oily pools gathered on her face. "I'm scared, Mike."

"It's okay. Let's go."

I hooked an arm around her, and she cried out in surprise pain.

"What?"

"My arm." She turned her left arm into the moonlight. A red spot swelled there. She touched it and flinched. "Ow. What the hell?"

"Something stung you," I said. "You were in the woods. Some night bug or something."

"Night bug?"

"A wasp, maybe?"

"They don't come out at night."

"Let's get some ice on it."

"Damn, it really hurts."

Something watched from the woods. I felt it there, hidden in the dark behind us. A creature. It was close. The moment I took a step, some big-bodied beast would crunch through the tree line. I'd wanted it to be that owl, but there was something else. Something much bigger. Something dangerous.

Even deadly.

It came back. It never left.

I moved Dani quickly down the hill and didn't look back.

CHAPTER 10:
REALITY CALLING

DANI TOOK A couple aspirin and fell asleep with a bag of frozen peas molded to her shoulder.

I watched her for a while, expecting her to sleepwalk again or whisper dream words, but she slept soundly and, eventually, I fell asleep too.

There were no nightmares, no sounds in the dark—only sleep.

It would be our last restful night for a long time.

～～

"Is this Michael Munacy?" a woman asked.

"Yes," I said into my cell.

"I'm Denise, one of your mother's nurses at Orange Regional. I've encouraged her to call you, but she won't do it."

Because I acted like a little boy when I learned Mommy kept secrets from me and I walked out on her. Instead of confessing that, I asked what was wrong.

"She's refusing dialysis."

I was in the hallway, and I peered back into the bedroom; Dani was still asleep.

"Mr. Munacy?" the nurse said in my ear.

"Sorry. She needs dialysis?"

"Her kidneys are failing."

"Failing?"

I walked down the hall, stepped into the bathroom. I felt pretty good, well rested, but my reflection was grayish and droopy, as if I'd aged ten years in one night.

My father's hand slapped against his ruined cheek and blood speckled the mirror.

"Sir?"

"Yes, sorry. I'm listening."

"Dr. Straub spoke with you yesterday."

"Was that his name?" God, yesterday seemed so long ago.

The nurse made an impatient noise, but one tinged with a touch of amusement too. "I'll try to reach the doctor on call."

29

"What about . . . Dr. Blatty?"

"He's a specialist."

"Nephrologist. Kidneys, right?"

"He's only here Tuesdays and Thursdays."

"How convenient."

"Dr. Blatty requested the dialysis."

"Without examining her?"

"I'm sure he saw her."

"Are you?" I asked.

Red spots on the mirror, counter, and floor.

"*You have to be careful,*" Dad said. "*It might be in the blood.*"

The nurse said something about trying to contact Dr. Blatty, and she crowded her promise with well-practiced apologies that sounded flat, but I cut her off and said something about dealing with this when I got there and ended the call.

My father peered back at me from the mirror, my face so much like his: the deep-set blue-grey eyes, the strong jaw. All I needed was a thick, dark beard.

"Hey, Dad," I said.

It could have been a touching moment, me talking to myself but really speaking to my dead father, and it could've been almost funny too, but instead I was a bit creeped out.

Scared of my own reflection. Afraid it might reveal something I didn't want to see.

CHAPTER 11:
MOUSETRAPS

DANI WAS STILL ASLEEP, and I didn't want to wake her. Instead of leaving a note, I told myself to text her in an hour or so. God knew how long I might be at the hospital.

I crammed an overnight bag with pairs of my mother's underwear, rolled socks, her nightgown, and her frayed blue slippers, along with several slacks and blouses and her toothbrush.

Her bedroom was stuffy and smelled of talcum powder. The walls were dirty in spots and speckled with water damage beneath the back window, where heaped a pile of binding-cracked paperbacks. Most were food-themed mysteries with bright cakes and pastries on the covers; a knife in a pool of raspberry jam on one cover looked almost too real.

Though cluttered with furniture, plastic hamper tilting full, both closets too stuffed for the doors to close, and the bed strewn with blankets and pillows, the room felt empty and forlorn, as if it knew my mom was not coming back.

Could that be true? She'd been fine a few days ago when we'd had Italian take-out together and discussed the move-in—would death be so swift?

I knew better than to wonder. I had only to ask my eleven-year-old self.

Old photos in silver frames cluttered my mother's dresser. Most were black and white, and taken in the forties or fifties of my parents in their separate childhoods: Mom in a dress with a ribbon in her hair; my father in a suit too big for him, his smile mischievous, his eyes staring past the photographer.

Their wedding photo was centered beneath the mirror. The colors were off, like they'd been developed incorrectly, so the white of my mother's dress was super bright and my father's face was a patchy blend of multiple pinks.

On either side of the picture were identical shots of me as a newborn, cradled in a blue blanket in my mother's arms. Then there was me at eight or nine with my father, both of us dressed in trench coats with matching red neckties and wide-brimmed fedoras.

In elementary school, a police officer had lectured us about Stranger Danger. He insisted we have a "safe word" to be used to identify non-kidnappers. I chose "trench coat." That safe word did nothing, however, to stop the parade of abductors who chased me through my nightmares.

When I set the picture down, my fingerprints stood out on the edges. I traced a finger down the dresser to leave a long, wobbly snake in the sheen of dust.

More memories gathered around me. They were everywhere. It was like walking barefoot across a room littered with armed mousetraps. No matter where I moved, a trap was ready to snag me back to some childhood event.

I felt her death then, saw it clearly: her make-up smeared corpse in a casket, my black suit wrinkling up my back, all my mother's friends staring at me, waiting for a son's parting words to his mom.

A flurry of heavy raps knocked on the front door.

✳

"Hi," a man said when I opened the door. A gleaming Jesus shimmered in reds and golds on his shirt.

He grinned. My face reflected in his aviator sunglasses. "Ned sent me," he said. He sounded jubilant, excited even. "I'm Logan. French."

I stared at him.

"I'm not French. That's my name. Logan French. Pleasure to meet you."

"Sure," I said.

"Mike, right?"

It took me a moment to introduce myself, shift the overnight bag, and offer my hand. His shake was a brief up-and-down squeeze.

"I'm sorry if I'm a little hyper," he said. "These retreats always invigorate me. I've been to several. There's a wonderful one upstate I've been to six times. This is my first time with Ned, and he's extraordinary. He knows God, if you get what I'm saying. There's preachers who know what God wants from us, but Ned knows God's brain. It's amazing."

I nodded, slowly. *God's brain.* What a weird, somehow unsettling combination of words.

"Heading out?" He pointed at the bag.

"My mother is—"

"The hospital," Logan said. "Oh, my, I'm sorry. Ned told me. My deepest hopes and prayers. I apologize. I get so . . . " He jittered in explanation.

"Rejuvenated?"

"Exactly. Yes, yes. I won't bother you any longer. Just know that God always has a plan. Always. Ned wanted me to give you this."

He handed me a pocket-sized book with an all-blue cover, on which puffy white letters proclaimed: *God's Waiting: How to Embrace His Will,* by Pastor Nedwin Loller. The back was a picture of Ned in a white shirt with his large cross around his neck. His stomach flowed off the edge.

"That book"—Logan tapped Ned's face with each word—"is a genuine blessing from God."

DEAD END

"Thanks."

"He inscribed it."

"God?"

Logan erupted in a chuffling laugh and even crossed his hands over his chest. "Oh, you are a delight." He leaned forward. "No, *Ned* inscribed it. Just for you."

I slow-nodded again.

He waited as I opened the book. On the inside cover, scrawled in black pen: *The sun shines for everyone! God Bless, Ned.*

"Sun-kissed believers," I said.

Logan watched me, smile plastered, and turned to face the sunlight. "Behold the power and the glory." He said it without a trace of sarcasm, of course, and walked down the steps and crossed over the lawn into the street.

God's brain, I thought.

A warm breeze rustled leaves. Trees had once swayed twenty feet from the house, but now they towered over the roof, close enough for branches to claw the white siding with skeletal fingers.

I thought of Dusty. He could be in those woods. He might be scared: frozen-scared, the way cats can get. He was old, could be lost. Could be hurt.

The sun was bright, but not among those trees where night never relented to day. I approached and stopped. In this spot on the front lawn where Del, next door, could see, I'd once screamed my face red when I was a little kid.

I was yelling at the trees to stay back, afraid they were creeping closer. It was an idea that took root from a nightmare and sprouted into a genuine fear of the woods. There I was, in my blue shorts and Ghostbusters t-shirt, with the uneven cut of my dirt-colored hair sagging over one ear more than the other, and my full-throated shouting whittling my words to hoarse screeches.

Mousetraps everywhere. Outside included.

"Dusty?" I made kissy sounds, but I was too far from the tree line. "Come on, Dusty."

The summer before he died, Dad found Dusty near the tree line. The cat was a dirt-cloaked, grey-and-white kitten who quickly became my best friend, following me everywhere and not letting me fall asleep at night until I rubbed under his chin for several minutes.

Something back there.

"Dusty?"

Something much bigger than a cat. *Heavy with life*, I thought, without any idea why. I didn't hear anything, didn't see anything, and yet I was sure *something* was in the woods.

Watching me.

Waiting.

It was so quiet—the eerie calm at the center of a hurricane, an expectant stillness of air—and whatever was among those trees held its breath too.

Then a bird chirped nearby, and a souped-up car motored past on Heintz Hill, and gnats buzzed in my ears.

I breathed out. A childhood fear. That was all.

"You better be waiting for me when I get back," I said.

A moment later in the car, I heard my words again, and hoped it was Dusty listening to me and not something else.

CHAPTER 12:
THE SUN SHINES FOR EVERYONE

FOR THE THIRD TIME in twenty-four hours, I was at the hospital. When my mother finally acknowledged my presence, she shook her head. "I'm not going to do it."

"Then you'll die," I said.

She glowered, a bad-tempered child in the body of a near-seventy-year-old woman.

I felt bad for being so blunt, and almost apologized, but what was the point of dancing around death? It was there. Coming for all of us. Some sooner than others.

"Ignoring it won't make it go away," I said.

Shrouded beneath multiple blankets, hands joined across her stomach, Mom stared out the window at the late afternoon. A commode was set up a few feet away, the smell of urine noticeable.

"You can't make it to the bathroom?"

She didn't even twitch.

"And you're not going to talk to me?"

No response.

I rocked from foot to foot. Since this was the ICU wing, the wall behind me was a set of giant glass doors, and I felt every passing nurse's stare. They no doubt remembered me. The guy who'd hassled a doctor into doing his job. Perhaps security had been called preemptively.

I felt fidgety. My heart beat too fast. I curled my hands in my pockets to stop them from twitching. Mom looked worse than she had yesterday. More tired. Burdened with it. Not moving only accentuated the impression. She wasn't resting—she was conserving what she had left. She was really dying. How could it happen so quickly? I was only twenty-five. Parents were supposed to live until their kids were in their thirties or forties, even fifties or sixties.

No one had told Dad—why should Mom be any different?

"Can I get you anything?" I asked.

She finally looked at me, a bit sheepishly, which felt so strange; it was a kid's look again, the expression a child might ham up to manipulate a parent.

"Chocolate," she said.

"Did Dr. Blatty see you?"

She offered the slightest of shrugs.

My mouth opened long before the words came out. "I'm sorry about how I reacted. I understand why you didn't tell me, but I need to know. I have a right."

"A right?" she asked. "I'm your mother."

We stared at each other.

"I'll get you chocolate."

I went in search. People glanced at me as I passed through the halls, before I realized I was talking to myself. Ranting, actually. Mom and her damn sweets.

She'd been a baker, could have had her own bakery, but she never took the risk. She worked for someone else for thirty-five years, until she couldn't stand on her feet or keep her hands steady enough to mix batter and shape frosting.

She enjoyed baking so much, she did it on and off the clock: our home was perpetually stocked with cakes, brownies, cookies, pastries, and chocolate candies, and I was quality control: it was my task to taste every treat while she stood near, apron smeared with chocolate and her hands clamped in anticipation.

"*De*-licious," I always said, but never took more than a few bites, and I certainly never enjoyed seconds. Like Dad, I didn't care for sweets. If I did, I might be over two hundred pounds instead of one-sixty.

Mom, however, loved baking *and* eating.

Excluding yesterday's cookies, she hadn't baked anything in at least three years. In the absence of original creations, my mother satisfied her cravings with store-bought pastries and ladyfingers and sugar-glazed donuts and apple fritters and all varieties of chocolate, from Nestle bars to Lindor truffles.

The gift shop sold bags of individually wrapped Ghirardelli chocolates for nine dollars.

Mom gobbled one and savored the next. She made wet, sloppy noises as she chewed. I sat down and tugged Ned's book from my back pocket.

The sun shines for everyone. God bless, Ned.

The first page read in huge letters: *GOD LOVES YOU.* The next page read: *Here's How You Can Love Him, Too!* On the opposite side was the publishing information. Published by JCE Press. JCE was spelled out beneath: *Jesus Christ the Empowered.*

An eyebrow creeped up my forehead as I found the first page with more than one sentence on it: "God loves you. Yes, indeed, He truly does. Too many people wander this world despaired in degrees of depression. God wants you to be happy. This humble little book will show you the way."

The pages flickered across my thumb. The last page was this:

DEAD END

GOD
WANTS
YOU
AT
JCE'S RELIGIOUS RETREAT
7-Day Faith Restorative!
Embrace
God's
Will!
Be
EMPOWERED!
FIND
SALVATION!
FINALLY!
ONLY
$999!

The package also included meals and shuttle service. Beneath the cross were instructions for reserving salvation: send check or money order payable to the First Church of Jesus Christ the Empowered, C/O Pastor Nedwin Loller, to mailing address . . .

I shut the book. "Doctors ever come in here?"

"After how you behaved earlier, they're staying away."

"I apologized."

"Not to the doctors."

"I want to know what's going on."

"You're so much like your father."

"How so?"

"He was impatient, too."

"I want someone to come in here and tell me what's going on. That's not unreasonable."

"I didn't say unreasonable. I said 'impatient.'"

She was opening a third chocolate. I glared at her, challenging, and her gaze slid off, but the chocolate stayed in the wrapper in her hand.

"Your lips are moving," she said.

"What?"

"Ward was always talking to himself."

"I remember." Even at the kitchen table, book beside him, Dad would whisper to himself. I'd strain to listen, hoping he might be saying things about me.

"What I remember," Mom said, "is how you used to yell at the trees." She was seeing me as the little kid in blue shorts and Ghostbusters t-shirt, veins bulging in my neck. "Standing on the lawn and shouting. Like a crazy person."

"I was a kid."

"Pediatrician said you'd grow out of it."

"You asked the doctor about me yelling at trees?"

She shifted on the bed, slow and slight, legs not even twitching. "Nowadays a doctor would prescribe Ritalin or Adderall."

"You're probably right. Half my students are on some behavior-altering drug."

"Ward should have been on something," she said. "After his second heart attack, he was on Xanax. Those were wonderful months. He was so . . . pleasant."

"I was too young to remember," I said.

"He went a long time before the third one. They call the third heart attack 'the widow maker.' Did you know that?"

Ned's book turned over and over in my hands, the pastor's pallid face a flashing moon.

We sat there in mutual silence for a while.

Daddy had a heart attack.

Red spots on the mirror. "It might be in the blood."

Yes, Mommy.

"The wedding's only three months away," I said.

She nodded.

Nurses walked past, as did one woman in a long white coat with an air of superiority who must have been a doctor, but no one came into the room, and I resisted the urge to stand in the hall and yell, *Does a guy have to die to get to see a doctor around here?*

I played with a question on my tongue. "Was Dad okay? I mean, mentally?"

"That *is* a question."

"Meaning?"

"What happened that day your father died?"

"He died. A heart attack. That's what you told me to believe, anyway."

"You enjoy punishing me?"

"You brought it up."

She thought for a moment. "It must've been so tough for you."

"It was a long time ago." I glanced at the time on my phone, not very subtly.

"You'd rather be somewhere else, I'm sure," Mom said.

"Dani's not feeling well, and . . . " *Watching you give up is too infuriating to tolerate,* I added in my head.

"I'll be fine."

"You need dialysis."

"An open window doesn't stop the rain," she said.

"That's what it's come to, fortune cookie witticisms?"

She laughed, and her smile was unexpected, a shooting star across the sky. Then it was gone. "You can open the window, stick your head out, and stare at the clouds, but that won't stop the rain. My kidneys aren't going to get better."

"Why treat anything ever, then?"

She didn't respond.

"How long have you known about your kidneys?"

I waited, and so did she, before responding, "You are so much like Ward."

"Is that supposed to be an insult?"

"Are you still afraid of those trees?"

"I was a kid." Inside my chest, however, my heart didn't know the difference and responded in rapid beats. Mom's dirty feet. Dani stepping from the tree line. Dusty lost in the dark woods. Something lurking. Watching. Waiting.

It came back. It never left.

"It was your father's fault."

"What?"

"He was afraid of the woods, too. A grown man afraid of trees. Called it an atavism. Fancy word for a childish fear. Your father loved fancy words."

"You're saying I inherited his fear?"

"He told you many times not to go into the woods, but he wanted to be absolutely sure you would stay away. He read some book about subliminal messages, and he would stand over you while you slept and whisper, 'Stay away from the woods. Stay away.'"

While she quoted my father, her voice dipped a few octaves and seemed to vibrate from her throat instead of out of her mouth. It was a bit freaky, and I felt gooseflesh creep along my back. I pictured my father whispering over me while I slept, his words weaving themselves into my dreaming mind and netting into a fear I didn't understand—a fear that would make me the weirdo kid everyone figured for troubled.

A kid who nowadays would be heavily medicated. "He really did that?"

"More than a few times," she said. "Something about things in the woods. 'Full with life,' he said. Or maybe, 'Heavy with life.'"

Heavy with life, my mind echoed. "Why didn't you stop him?"

"You were a child. I didn't want you getting lost in the woods, either."

"Why were *you* in the woods?"

She began to open a third chocolate. "Looking around."

"Were you sleepwalking?"

She was turning the chocolate over in her hand.

"You said something before you collapsed in the kitchen. You were looking out the door toward the woods and said something. You remember?"

She nodded. "You should go back there, into the woods. It's actually pleasant. Don't let your father's fear live on."

"You need dialysis."

So much like a child again, she eyed me while the third chocolate slipped between her lips.

"The rain's coming," I said.

CHAPTER 13:
REALLY DYING

TURNS OUT, the storm clouds had already gathered. Driving home, I pulled over to answer a call from Dr. Blatty, the one and only.

"How serious is it?" I asked.

"Very."

"Tell me."

"Without dialysis," the doctor said in formal, professional tones, "she has limited time remaining."

"You mean dying?"

"Two weeks. Probably less. It may also be very painful."

"She know this?"

"I spoke with her first thing this morning."

"How could this happen so quickly?"

"Are you her health proxy?"

"I . . . don't know what that is."

The doctor sighed, and static buzzed my ear. He launched into a rehearsed speech about health proxies and HIPAA forms and living wills and powers of attorney and DNRs.

I told him thanks, hung up, and didn't move. Cars passed, and one honked, but those were far-off sounds, as distant as a subliminal whisper.

Mom was really dying. Dr. Blatty—the nephrologist—insisted dialysis begin in the next seventy-two hours. If not, she might die within a week. Maybe sooner.

Her life might be down to its final few dozen hours, and she was in a hospital bed eating chocolate like nothing was wrong.

My hands grabbed the steering wheel and squeezed. I kept my jaw clenched against the scream trying to escape.

CHAPTER 14:
SOMETHING HEARD

ALL THE KITCHEN cabinets were open. Dishes were stacked, and glasses were crammed on shelves, so there was no more room for anything else. A cabinet under the counter contained dozens and dozens of Tupperware containers and twice as many lids. I recognized a yellow tub as the one Mom filled with her homemade cheesecake bites.

Dani stood, hands on hips, before all the open cabinets, several of our cardboard boxes open around her. Her hair was pulled back and her sweatshirt sleeves were tugged to her elbows. Blushed cheeks were almost comical against her pale skin.

And here I was, expecting to enter our apartment and find Dani sobbing at the dining room table, or to discover all the walls had been painted and Dani was passed out on the couch, smears of paint dried on her arms.

"Dani? You okay?"

"I needed to get something done," she said. Her voice started strong and thinned out. "I was trying to organize things, and I heard something."

"What?"

She shook her head. "It was faint. Like paper crinkling, but not. I don't know. I thought it was coming from the pantry. A mouse, maybe."

The pantry was open, completely stocked with canned foods, cereals, pasta sauces, and boxes and boxes of cake, cookie, and brownie mix. I wondered how much of it might be expired, perhaps long since.

Dani had cleared out the bottom two shelves, and Saran wrap and tinfoil and Ziploc boxes capped a mound made of bags of flour and chocolate and jars of Prego and boxes of angel hair pasta and God knew what else.

"I really thought I knew what I was doing," she said.

I went to her. "It's okay. I'll help you."

"Mike . . ."

"Yeah?"

"I might've been sleeping when I heard it, the sound." She looked back to the pantry and said to herself, "Maybe it was closer to a buzzing."

"Hey." I touched her chin.

"But then I was in here," she said, "doing this, and then . . . I don't know."

"It's stress," I said. "That's all it is. It's going to be okay."

"Why am I like this?"

"It's okay."

Her expression crumpled into tears. "I'm really scared, Mike."

I hugged her tight and told her it was going to be okay. "We'll get through this. We'll—"

"Ow," she said, and broke the hug. Her hand went to her left shoulder and cradled it gently.

"The sting still hurts?"

"Maybe I developed an allergy."

"Let me see."

"It's okay. I'm all right. I'm sorry, I'm . . ." More tears came, and she tried to laugh through them. "You really don't need this in your life right now."

"I love you."

She wiped her eyes with the cuff of her sweatshirt. "I love you, too."

We hugged again, and I was careful not to touch her shoulder. Maybe she *was* having an allergic reaction to the sting. It could've been a big wasp, or maybe some other poisonous insect. *Night bug*, I'd said.

"I'm sorry. I'm so selfish. How's your mom?"

"Not good. She needs dialysis."

"Will it help?"

"She's refusing it."

"I'll go talk to her. Sometimes it takes a woman."

"That sounds rather sexist."

"Is it still sexist if it's true?" Dani asked.

I mirrored her smile, and for a moment there, the world felt all right.

"I guess we should clean—" She turned to the cabinets, stepped forward, paused, and sneezed, loud and hard. Something wet slapped against the floor.

"Whoa," I said. "That was—"

Impressive, I was about to say, but the word didn't make it. What her sneeze expurgated was a splat of black, tar-like mucus. The clump missed a cardboard box labeled ASS STUFF to explode on the red tile. It might've been the gooey remains of a fat bug. One pregnant with baby bugs.

Diseased bugs.

"Back in middle school," I said, "this kid, Bobby Lyon, told me some girl he knew developed a nasty, bulging pimple on her face, and it got bigger and bigger, size of a golf ball, he claimed, and when it ruptured, hundreds of baby spiders scurried out all over her face."

"Huh?"

"What you sneezed is how I pictured— You're bleeding."

A thick, dark red stream of blood ran from one nostril over her lips, and onto her chin. She wiped at it, stared at her fingers a moment, and panic flickered through her eyes like something bright and sharp.

Dani hurried to the bathroom, shut the door, and turned on the ceiling fan.

I stood there among all the pots and pans and boxes of brownie mix.

On the floor, two stainless steel bowls waited on a rubber mat before the dishwasher. One held a puddle of water, the other a heap of dry food. The mat declared in green letters: DUSTY.

CHAPTER 15:
A BOOK BURNING

THE DAY WAS HOT, but easing toward evening. On the front lawn, I scanned the trees. They loomed, heavy with darkness.

"You hiding my cat?" I asked.

The trees did not respond.

"Come on, Dusty!" I whistled, made kissy sounds, and called for him several more times. "Where are you, buddy?"

I crossed the lawn toward the trees. Those trees were tall when I was young, and now they towered. The woods bordered the other two houses on Mullock and extended deep toward town. I'd never crossed through it.

Coward.

One created by you, Dad.

Staring at them now and knowing Dusty could be back there somewhere—and something could be hunting him—I *was* a coward. I walked the tree line and called for him, but I didn't cross the threshold. A squirrel scrambled across the ground and scaled a trunk. Birds fluttered. Beyond the first several feet, darkness shrouded what might be back there.

I called for him again, and movement caught my eye.

A slippery shadow rustling leaves. Was it Dusty? The squirrel again? Something else?

Watching me.

"Stay away from my cat," I said. My voice was small, almost scared.

Tomorrow, when the sun was high and bright, I would search back there. Doubt chipped away immediately (*Stay away from the woods. Stay away. It's heavy with life back there.*) at the promise, but I nodded at my vow and headed around back. Who knew, maybe I'd get lucky and Dusty would be waiting on the deck.

Someone stood on Mount Munacy. At the cliff's edge.

From my angle, with the dimming sunlight sweeping across overhead, the person was faceless and alone. One of Ned's religious retreat members, most likely, squeezing in some extra prayers.

Trying to find God.

I angled for a better view, my hand up to shield off the light, but then I said screw it and started up the path to the top. It was my property, after all.

So are the woods, my mind offered.

It was the kid in the suit and clunky sneakers. He was wearing those white sneakers, but red shorts replaced the pants, and the jacket and tie were gone; yet he was wearing a dress shirt again, flapping free like loose skin.

He held a small book, and I recognized that, too, of course. An identical copy was wedged in my pocket.

The kid tore a page from Ned's book, crumpled it, and dropped it. Then he tore another one. And another.

He didn't see me—completely focused on his task at hand—and it felt surreal watching him, like stumbling upon a wild animal before it senses your presence.

Several more crumpled pages joined the others at the kid's feet. He tore and tore, and then held the book held before him. *I rip these asunder*, I thought.

He dropped the book on the pile. Ned's face might be gleaming off the cover up at him.

I opened my mouth to ask if he wanted to rip up my copy, too, when he took something from his pocket. Sun spiked off it like he was holding a star.

Not a star. A Zippo lighter.

He flipped the lid, rolled the thumbwheel like he'd done it a hundred times, and lowered the lighter to the paper pile. A single flame grew large as it jumped to the paper.

The kid stowed the lighter and reached under his untucked shirt to pull something else from his back pocket. Sun glinted off this, too.

I don't know if my shouts—"Hey! *Hey!*"—came first, or if I was already running up the dirt path when the kid yanked the red cap off the bottle and tipped it to squeeze a stream of lighter fluid onto the fire.

"*HEY!*"

The fire bloomed several feet high as the kid turned to see who was yelling.

He might have come out unscathed, singed eyebrows perhaps, if he wasn't wearing that loose dress shirt. The dangling cuff caught fire, and flames licked up his forearm.

His blank expression morphed into a contorted, screaming rictus. He stumbled back several feet. Fire sprouted off the sleeve like some magic trick. I sprinted up the rest of the hill. My thighs hurt and my side was cramping and my pulse thudded in my temple, but I made it as the fire engulfed his arm and surged toward his shoulder.

I grabbed the kid by his other arm and he yanked out of my grip. I was so surprised, I watched his big sneakers tangle, and he stumbled sideways and fell. His head bounced off the ground, and his pain-wracked cries echoed into the sky. I told him to stay still, stop moving, but that may be wishful thinking, me trying to rewrite the past in my favor, because I heard my voice saying over and over again, "*ShitShitShitShit.*" My hands pounded on his arm, crunched flame against body and dirt. The fire plumed toward my face. I beat it back as the heat ushered out a wave of sweat on my cheeks. I could have been fighting the fire for ten minutes, but I'm sure it was only a few seconds. The fire was out, and the kid's arm smoldered with the stench of cooked fabric and charred meat.

"You're all right," I said. "You're all right, you're all right, you're all right." With enough breath, I might never have stopped repeating those words.

The small paper fire hooked with the wind, and the tuft of weeds at the cliff's brink caught fire in a blaze, and there was Dani on the deck, standing at the railing, watching silently, mesmerized, entranced, a supplicant before a burning altar.

CHAPTER 16:
BURNED BUT UNBOWED

THE KID SLOUCHED against me and sobbed, but he didn't seem in any immediate danger. Not of dying, anyway.

His arm was another story. I'd stopped the fire before it spread too far past his elbow, but the flames did considerable damage in only a few seconds. His sleeve was scorched and glued to his skin in bubbly patches. It looked like a really bad case of poison ivy rash, blistering and weeping, but it was a burn, a severe burn smoking of barbecue.

My hands were too warm. I was afraid to look at them.

"What's your name?"

He cut through his cries to tell me.

"Okay, Isaac, I'm Mike. It's going to be okay."

Dani watched from the deck, unmoving. Was she sleepwalking again? *"Call 9-1-1!"* I yelled, and she ran back inside.

I took a breath.

To Isaac, I said, "You're going to be fine. I'm going to carry you down the hill. Okay?"

He nodded and wiped at his tears with his good arm. The injured one lay across his lap, smoldering.

One arm under his knees and the other across his back, I hefted him and started down the hill. He was maybe sixty, sixty-five pounds, but I barely noticed. I felt strong, able to go for miles.

Halfway down Mount Munacy, I was breathing a bit faster and my thighs hurt with the effort to stay upright, but I kept going. I was in decent shape, mostly, though I couldn't tell you the last time I'd been to the gym, but the physical strain felt separate from me, a thing outside my body.

Fiery drips fell from the burning weeds at the cliff's edge, like flaming rain.

I didn't stop—kept going right across the lawn and into the street and down Mullock, toward the yellow house at the bottom of the road. The entire world consisted of me and Isaac, him slumped in my arms, my steps crunching pebbles and dirt.

The boy cried in jagged hiccups, and my breath huffed shallowly with each step.

A woman in a jean skirt shouted something that might have been "ohmygod" and ran toward me. Her skirt flapped against her thighs above bright red knees.

The door to Ned's house opened, and the self-proclaimed preacher stepped onto the porch. He filled the entire doorway.

Isaac stretched out his good arm and called to his mom.

Instead of handing him into her arms, I lowered to my knees and set Isaac against me, and the woman dropped before us. She was crying and fawning over him and touching his face and hugging and saying, "Your arm, your arm, your arm."

Another door opened from Ned's house. This one was where the garage used to be. It was bright white, with a gold cross painted on it. Ned had converted his garage into a tiny church. Tax deductible, I was sure, for his religious retreat.

From that space emerged the rest of his followers. Logan French jogged over. Jesus' face bounced on his chest. The others approached more slowly, and the teenage boy who'd been wearing vestments to match Ned's joined him on the front steps.

"This is terrible," Logan said in the same exuberant, excited voice. "Terrible, terrible."

"Your arm, your arm," the woman repeated.

Isaac cried hard and freely. He was in pain and shock, but I envied him a little, sick as that sounds. It wasn't his pain I coveted: it was the *way* he wept. Children do it so easily, without fear or self-ridicule, no self-consciousness at all.

I once fell off my bike, scored a bleeding knee, and Dad told me to stop crying. *You're weeping like your leg's on fire.*

A man in a flannel took out a cigarette and patted himself down for a lighter. He didn't find one, and stood there with the unlit cigarette jutting from his mouth.

Another guy, this one in a black suit with a pale, elongated face, leaned over us and peered down, a curious spectator. He looked like a mortician.

"Terrible, terrible," Logan said.

The gathering parted, and Ned was there. He was a monolith, enormous and imposing. He'd swapped his priest garb for baggy pants and a drape of a dress shirt, but the cross remained, a centerpiece above his bulging stomach.

Ned held up his wadded hands and bent over to see the injured arm. I feared he might topple onto us, but he was surprisingly balanced with all his weight, and he peered at the arm like a doctor. He asked if an ambulance had been called.

"On its way," Dani said. She'd run down the hill and now sucked air. She seemed dazed, but no longer hypnotized. She coughed a few times, but didn't hack up anything.

Ned's wide neck bunched and flopped. He wasn't quite as large as the people on *My Six- Hundred-Pound Life*, but he might get there in time.

"Let us pray," he said.

All heads bowed, except mine, Dani's, and Isaac's. While Ned offered a prayer about God's mercy and healing, Isaac silently wept, staring at his mother. Only, no, he wasn't looking at his mom, her head down, hands clutched together—the kid was staring at the other people.

Was it the suited mortician he kept staring at, or Mr. Flannel-and-unlit-cigarette? Perhaps it was Flannel's missing lighter Isaac had taken, or maybe the man had given it to the boy. I hadn't been raised in any formalized religious manner, and I had a healthy (or perhaps unhealthy, depending) skepticism of people who professed devout faith in the Man in the Clouds. These people were even more suspect: they believed Ned Loller was actually a holy man. I was sure he'd never attended seminary.

Ned knows God's brain.

Before the prayer ended, a police car turned onto Mullock. An ambulance arrived seconds later.

Dani and I stood back from the scene. I felt her next to me, but we didn't embrace, didn't even touch, both of us too dazed to seek comfort. Cold prickled along my arms, but my palms were hot. The skin was bright red and tender, speckled with pin-sized blisters. My head throbbed.

The woman went with her son in the ambulance and the others turned to Ned.

"We'll follow in the bus," he said, and turned to the teenage boy. "Get Wes."

The kid ran inside the converted garage.

Wes was a young guy, mid-thirties. He wore blue pants and a dress shirt, tucked but open at the collar. His hair was a dark, curly mess. Strands hooked across his forehead.

Ned spoke to the cop briefly, who nodded, and then Ned led his group to the yellow bus parked at the curb. Wes got behind the wheel and everyone loaded in. When Ned stepped aboard, the bus listed toward him.

It drove to the corner, paused—beneath the back window was stenciled: GOD IS LOVE—and turned onto Heintz.

Beneath the Mullock Road street sign was a large DEAD END sign. The side facing uphill was clouded metal, graffitied with spray paint, long-since faded and unreadable.

Dani and I stood in the street with the cop. My legs wobbled. On the opposite side of Heintz Hill, a man watched us from his front lawn. He was middle-aged, greying, with thick glasses, a beard, and body hair curling around an orange polo. He was almost familiar, though I often felt that way about older men with beards.

So much like your father.

Officer Koryta asked me questions, and I answered. He had a prominent eyebrow ridge, but the face beneath was friendly. He scribbled in a small Field Notes memo book, and I pointed to his chicken scratch and said it was amazing he still used paper and pen, didn't the department have iPads officers could use?

The cop paused, stared at me a beat long enough to make me think I was in trouble, and asked why I hadn't tried to stop Isaac from setting the fire.

"It happened so fast," I said.

"The child didn't say anything?"

Had Isaac's lips been moving as he crumpled paper and squeezed lighter fluid on flame? A prayer? A curse? "I don't know."

"He was burning a book, you said?"

"Yes." I took my copy from my back pocket and held it up like a piece of damning evidence.

The cop read the title aloud and flipped the notebook shut. "I'll be in touch."

"You don't want the book?"

"Keep it," he said. "You might need it."

He left, and Dani touched my hand. I recoiled and tried to laugh it off.

"Are you okay?"

I was crying, but didn't bother to wipe at the tears. "I don't know."

"Shhh," she said and hugged me. "It's over. You saved his life."

"Or I almost killed him. If I hadn't called out to him, he wouldn't have been distracted—"

"Hey," she said looking up at me. "You did more than most people. More than I did."

Her eyes flickered with unease for a moment, but then she was pushing her fingers through my hair and telling me it was going to be okay. Less than an hour ago I'd been the one telling *her* that, but here was the Dani I'd fallen in love with. Relief brought fresh tears.

Across the street, the bearded guy was gone.

CHAPTER 17:
NIGHT PASSION

THE NIGHT QUIET all around, I couldn't sleep. Fire leaped off Isaac's arm. It flamed toward my face. I beat it back. My palms throbbed.

Over and over.

I willed myself to sleep, but that's a bit like screaming at someone to calm down, except sleep took me, or I at least slipped into the foggy world between consciousness and darkness, and I felt Dani next to me, not in a dream but in bed, her body curled close, her breath on my ear.

She was whispering something. Dirty things. In the earliest days of our relationship, the routine of our intimacy was established in drunken sex and teenager-like make-out sessions in the car. The way I kissed her neck and cupped her breast. The way she teased her hand over my thighs, and the way she whispered into my ear.

Sometimes I heard the words, but whatever she said—*I want you, take me, do me*—didn't matter: it was the hot breath tickling my ear in an urgent pant that buzzed my nerves.

The warm wind of staticky words tunneled into my ear.

My hand curled around Dani's jutting hip bone. She mumbled something. I pushed my hand between her legs, and she groaned again and spread for me. I rubbed her in the way established long ago. My fingers tugged at the edge of her panties, and then I was in her wetness and she spread further. I kissed her neck. I cupped her breast.

It went slowly until I couldn't stop myself, and then she was on her knees and my thighs slapped against the backs of hers and she was grunting and I thrust faster and faster. Her hands curled bunches of the sheet and she bit the pillow. Her back arched and she shoved to smack every thrust. I lasted another few seconds before screaming in release.

A faint rubbing sound, as of coarse fabric, over and over. Something else, too— whispering.

I was too tired to wake fully, and my eyelids would only open a slitted view into the room.

The angle was crooked, which made what I saw seem weirder than it probably was: Dani paced slowly back and forth from one wall to the other. When she reached the wall, or the nightstand beside me, she bumped into it, paused, turned around, and walked to the other wall in small, shuffling steps. Her bare feet rubbed the rug with every step.

"Dani?"

She stopped, a few feet from the far wall.

"Come back to bed."

She giggled and continued forward, hitting the wall, turning, and heading back toward me. I caught her wrist, but her feet kept moving, and I had to tug her toward me, sliding out of bed to keep her from falling.

I turned her toward me. The room was dark, but her pale skin was almost glowing. She didn't look well.

"Hey," I said and kissed her gently, right on the lips. Her eyelids fluttered, and I smiled. "You were doing it again. Sleepwalking. You okay?"

"It's making me do it," she said, voice small and scared.

"What is?"

"You shouldn't have brought me here."

"Dani, it's okay, it's—"

"We're going to die here."

My breath caught, and my skin tightened around my knuckles, elbows, and knees. "Dani, wake up."

"I am awake." She sounded drugged. "I should cut my hair." Her hand curled into a fist full of her long, black hair.

"What?"

"It'll get caught in the branches."

"Dani," I said slowly, firmly. "Wake up."

She giggled again and I shook her, much harder than I intended, but I was scared. Dani had her manic-depressive episodes, but now she was also sleepwalking and saying strange, cryptic things. Maybe she needed to be medicated.

"Get the scissors, Mike. We can go together."

"Dani, stop this right—"

She yanked her hair hard, and her head snapped to the side with a loud crack.

"Jesus, Dani. *Stop!*"

I shook her again and her hand fell free and she hiccupped a sob, and then she was crying against me, and I held her. I saw her stepping from the woods, saw her standing in the middle of the cluttered kitchen, saw her on the deck watching me beat the flame out on a child's arm.

Something's controlling her, I thought, and immediately dismissed it. It was only sleepwalking. Stress-induced. Some form of catatonia or severe anxiety, most likely.

That sounded probable, but it also didn't help me in any way. What was I supposed to do?

"Why is this happening to me?"

I rubbed her back, caressed her long hair, and fought against my own tears. There was nothing I could say.

CHAPTER 18:
MAGIC CODE

THE NEXT MORNING at school, I called the hospital. The receptionist connected me to my mom's room, and the line rang and rang and rang.

I called back. "My mom didn't pick up."

"Perhaps she's been taken for testing. Hold on. I'll connect you to the nurse's station."

The line rang and rang. And rang.

"Hi," I said, hoping for three times being a charm, "but no one is picking up, so can you give me an update?"

"Her name?"

"I just told you."

"Sorry, sir, I—"

"Munacy. Beatrice."

"Thank you." A moment later she asked for the HIPAA code.

"The what?"

"It's the code your mother was given that she may share with anyone who she wants to know her medical information."

"I'm her son."

"So you have the code?"

"I do not have the magic code, no."

"Then I'm sorry, sir, I can't help you."

I was in the faculty room at a far table by myself, with a stack of essays long-past due for grading. I smacked my hand on the stack. "Can you connect me to her room again, please?"

"Her name again?"

I laughed, and my hand curled the top piece of loose-leaf into a crumbled ball.

"Dialing now," the woman said.

After twenty-five rings, a woman answered in an exasperated voice. "Yes?"

"I'm trying to reach Beatrice Munacy, my mother. Is she there?"

"No."

"Do you know if—"

Click.

I gaped at my cellphone. "Bitch."

Mrs. Tims, almost seventy and still teaching French, was coming into the faculty room right then, and she immediately swiveled on her flats and headed right back out.

You're a better son than you're pretending to be.

Maybe Mom was getting dialysis. I should call back, as many times as necessary, and demand the information, stupid code be damned. I should do that, but right then the task felt too heavy, too much burden and annoyance, and yet I also hated myself for not at least trying.

Coward.

CHAPTER 19:
WRONG, WRONG

A STRANGE WOMAN stood in my driveway. She was half naked in a skimpy nightgown.

Dani had offered to go to the hospital for me—"Let me talk to your mom"—so at least I didn't have to worry that this woman was Dani sleepwalking again.

I parked my Camry halfway up the driveway. The woman paced back and forth before the garage doors, peering through the windows over and over, and shaking her head and counting something off on her fingers.

"Hello?"

The woman froze. She didn't turn to see who had spoken, just stood there as if I might ignore her if she were perfectly still.

"Can I help you?"

Could this be one of my mother's friends—one who was maybe not altogether there, or losing it to Alzheimer's—and she'd come here to visit, found no one home, and was unsure what to do? But where was her car?

She's from the woods, I thought. It was her stare that I'd felt when calling for Dusty, or when Dani emerged from the woods. She was old and confused, had somehow gotten lost in the woods . . . Right, and what, no one went looking for her?

"Are you here for Beatrice? I'm her son."

The woman turned toward me. She was in her seventies, maybe eighties, frail and wrinkled. Her nightgown had been washed a million times, and her body showed through in places.

She was barefoot. Her poor feet were dirty and streaked with a little blood. Maybe she *had* come from the woods.

Wisps of hair floated across her brown-mottled scalp. Her eyes were wild with panic. She might burst into tears or scream or even attack me.

I raised a hand. "Hi."

She counted off her fingers rapidly, one hand and then the other and back again. She did this three times, counting to thirty in a mumbled rush of breath. Her hands curled into knotty fists. "The colors are wrong here," she said. "Wrong, wrong."

DEAD END

The word echoed in my head: *Wrong, wrong.*

My father leaning toward the bathroom mirror, those little scissors piercing his cheek, that word over and over in a mantra. *Wrong, wrong, wrong.*

It might be in the blood.

I stepped closer and knew who this was. "Mrs. Summer?"

Those wild eyes narrowed. "Wrong. *Wrong!*" She spat the words at me like an insult or a warning.

Del and Suzanne Summer lived in the house next door, between my mother's and Ned's. They didn't have kids, and so there was no reason for me to interact with them, but I knew who they were. "You're Suzanne, right?"

Those eyes grew huge again, and her hands trembled toward her face. I stepped closer, both hands up to say it was okay, which was the wrong move because a scream gathered in her chest and flexed her throat and croaked free in a deep, grating rasp, startlingly loud and powerful.

I stopped, backed up. "It's okay," I said. "It's okay." I was trying to be calm, but I sounded a bit panicked. I felt it, too.

The scream pushed wide her mouth. Red splotches bloomed across her cheeks and squiggly blue veins throbbed in her forehead. The sound barreled out of her as if from a bottomless reservoir.

If we were outside a house along Heintz Hill or most any other street in Warrenville, neighbors would be opening doors and running over to help, but here at the top of dead-end Mullock, it was only Mike Munacy and an old lady screaming for all she was worth.

Her shout invaded my head and ice-cracked my nerves. I wanted to scream at her to shut up, the way I sometimes did when my students were out of control, but like those unprofessional outbursts, screaming at this woman would only make matters worse.

I slipped my cell out and was about to dial 9-1-1 when I heard someone else yelling.

"Suzanne!"

Del Summer hurried, as best he could, up the sloping lawn from his property. His pants swished around his legs. Skinny like his wife, though not frail, he slipped only once on the way over. The sleeves of his button-down were rolled up to the elbows. Sinewy muscles tensed along his forearms.

Suzanne's scream ceased, and she gratefully accepted her husband's embrace with immense relief. They hugged, and Del kissed her cheek and hugged her again. He cupped her face and spoke to her, nose-to-nose. I couldn't hear what he said, but Suzanne calmed further, softened, nodding her head in slow agreement. I had been about to call the police, who would have frightened her even more, even stirred her into a full-on panicked escape, and she might have ended up in the backseat of a cop car, when maybe all I had to do was talk to her calmly and reassure her everything would be okay, the way I would if she'd been a hysterical child with an arm on fire. The way I was with Dani during what I was starting to think of as her fits.

Or the way I should be to a mother who was dying.

From his back pocket, Del tugged out a pair of flat slippers. He knelt before her and she leaned on him and stretched her feet for him the way a woman of royalty might for a servant, her toenails dark yellow and chipped. He carefully slid on each one.

He stood and turned to me. They were holding hands. Something tweaked in my chest.

"I'm very sorry," Del said. "Her aide was supposed to be here an hour ago, and sometimes, if no one's watching, she'll get it in her head to take off."

"No harm done," I said.

He appreciated me a moment. "Welcome home, Mike."

"Thanks."

He seemed about to say something more, but then turned back to his wife. Hand in hand, Del and Suzanne Summer walked down the driveway and followed the road back to their own home.

CHAPTER 20:
I'M NOT ME

DANI CAME HOME fifteen minutes later.

"Must've been a short conversation."

Dani stood in the kitchen doorway, hand rubbing her neck, gaze on the floor. She worked her feet back and forth in little steps, her cute habit that now seemed peculiar.

"Thanks for trying. How are you feeling?"

"Mike, I'm going to ask you something, and I want you to be honest."

"Okay."

"Did your father really die of a heart attack?"

"That's what it says on his death certificate: cardiac arrest."

Her eyes finally found mine. "You were alone with him when he died."

"Yes."

"That's awful."

"It was."

"Your mom said you've never talked about it."

"There's nothing much to say."

"Are you scared to tell me? Afraid I can't handle it?" Her voice trembled.

"I'll tell you, but not now. It's too much."

"For you or for me?"

I tried a chuckle, but it came out flat and lifeless. "I shouldn't have let you go see her."

"What's that supposed to mean?"

"You're upset."

"I'm not."

She didn't sound upset, either. She sounded nervous but calm, almost drugged-calm, and the tail end of each sentence wavered with the threat of tears. I was the one upset, annoyed my mother had gotten Dani on this train of thought; angry, in fact, that whatever my mom told her had worsened Dani's anxiety. The sleepwalking would continue. Her physical reactions to the stress— the coughing, the sneezing, the pale, sickly skin—would only get worse, too. She looked like she might vomit at any moment.

Her right hand went to her mouth, and I thought I was right about her puking, but she nibbled on her fingernails instead. I'd never seen her do that before.

"I can't sleep, Mike," she said around her fingers.

"You mean . . . at all?"

"Two hours a night. That's it. I can't take it. I really, really can't. And I don't know what I should do. I'm not myself. I'm not me. I tried Tylenol PM, but it didn't work. So what if I double the dose? Should I do that, Mike? Should I double the dose? Triple it? Take the whole bottle? Or what? What should I do? What should I do? What should I—"

She screamed. Veins pulsed in her forehead like jagged cracks threatening to rupture, and red swirls bloomed in her cheeks and along her neck. She stepped toward me and crumpled.

I caught her and eased her to the ground, as I had my mom in this very room only a few days ago.

"Please," she said. "I need to sleep."

I carried her down the hall, cradled like a child. She was surprisingly light. She hadn't been eating much. In fact, I couldn't remember seeing her eat more than a bite or two of anything since before we moved here. To *my* boyhood home.

"It's my fault," I said when I tucked the sheet across her.

"I'm the crazy one," she said.

It was hot in the room, so I said I'd get the air conditioner from my mom's room, but Dani said not to. "I'm cold."

I sat on the bed beside her and rubbed her back for a while.

Eventually she slept.

And I prayed she would stay that way. At least for a few hours.

CHAPTER 21:
BOX OF HORROR

I GRABBED A BEER and went downstairs, seeking distraction.

Ever see *Hoarders: Buried Alive*? It was a bit like that down there. Always had been. Both Mom and Dad were pack rats (and everything I created was added to the accumulation—be it scribbled, nonsensical crayon drawings or construction-paper turkeys and Valentines or the lopsided, felt-bearded, googly-eyed mug I'd made for Father's Day that had a hole in the bottom), and after Dad died, Mom doubled down on the behavior. After retirement from baking, she tripled down. It was lucky the whole house wasn't filled with bags and boxes and other people's discarded furniture and knickknacks. Only Mom's poor health stymied the accumulation.

There were boxes and plastic bags and books and yellowing newspapers and stacks of old *Time* and *Newsweek* and half-broken toys (including a rocking horse yanked from someone's curbside trash pile, whose paint-peeling face time had mauled into a nightmare) and Christmas decorations and plastic storage container after container packed with baking pans and molds, spatulas of all varieties, hundreds of little plastic decorative cake toppers, and rolling pins and cooling racks and cookie cutters and bags for icing and God knew what else.

My father often sat down here at an ancient typewriter set against the far wall. It was on a rickety green metal table. Sometimes there was a rapid *clack-clack-clack* and sometimes it was slower, and there was one time I recall distinctly there was no clacking. I'd peeked around the railing and there he was at the typewriter: not typing, not even moving, sitting still, hunched, hands in his lap, a solitary lamp haloing his body and darkness shrouding the mounds around him.

Where was that typewriter? All his accumulated paraphernalia was down here somewhere. Most of the books cramming the shelves on the walls and lining the baseboard and stacked in the far corner were his, along with the stacks of newspapers, and there had to be even more stuff buried here, including that typewriter.

I'd tried a few times to clean out, or at least somewhat organize, the mess down here, but each effort ended in surrender. There was too much, and now there were also boxes of our stuff from the apartment. The times I tried to make some headway, Mom refused to let me throw anything out. *Things have value*, she said. I held up a stack of dry, crinkled newspapers. *Just because you can't see it, doesn't mean there isn't value.*

I picked up a stack of papers, perhaps the same one my mom had objected to jettisoning, and the twine binding broke with a dusty snap. Papers slid over my feet. They crunched and crackled underfoot. I tossed them onto a heap of tangled bungee cords.

Sure, the papers had value—as kindling.

Part of me hoped to find something interesting, and another part hoped it was all easily discarded junk. I didn't want to find, for example, some of those drawings I did in sixth grade of my father on Mount Munacy, his uneven stick arms jutting from his stick body. Those drawings had earned me a trip to the school psychologist, so afterward I never drew another.

Working slowly, I made a narrow path toward the far wall where the typewriter always was, and I was sweating and getting tired when I found the coffin.

That sounds odder than it is. It was a coffin-shaped bookcase my father hired a carpenter to build for him, and the six-foot tall, colonial-style coffin stood down here with five removable shelves crammed with books and writing pads and magazines and newspapers, of course. My mother was not approving of the coffin, but she tolerated it. At least until his death, when she began burying it under all her accumulated junk.

Maybe I should uncover (*exhume*) it and stand it back up. I grabbed a few garbage bags full of who-knew-what and tossed them aside and opened the coffin lid—and found the box.

It was a large cardboard box labeled "Ward" in my mother's hectic, almost unreadable script. Cluttered inside were dozens of paperbacks, VHS tapes, several clipped stacks of typing paper, and a couple of well-worn, orange-covered Rhodia notebooks.

The paperbacks had bright comic-bookish covers and featured monster claws tearing through the cover or fog-choked graveyards with creepy churches in the background or gleaming, blood-streaked knives or ghoulish children with unnerving grins or skulls blanketed in multi-legged insects. They had titles like *The Exorcist* and *The Parasite* and *Song of Kali* and *Off Season* and *Books of Blood* and *Pet Sematary* and *Ghost Story* and *The House Next Door* and *Misery* and *By Reason of Insanity*. Horror novels, mostly, though I also found *Letters on Demonology and Witchcraft* and *Popular Delusions and Madness*. This last one was a coverless paperback with the word "EVIL" in large block text on the exposed page. Directly above it, someone had penciled *25¢*. A yard sale purchase. I flipped through it and a six-inch skinny metal ruler fell out. It was stainless steel, made in the U.S.A. with one rounded edge and a flat sharp-cornered lip opposite. Where it fell out, several sentences were underlined in pencil: *It was thought that the earth swarmed with millions of demons of both sexes, many of whom, like the human race, traced their lineage up to Adam, who after the fall was led astray by devils, assuming the forms of beautiful women to deceive him. These demons "increased and multiplied" among themselves with the most extraordinary rapidity. Their bodies were of the thin air, and they could pass through the hardest substances with the greatest ease and many unfortunate men and women drew them by thousands into their mouths and nostrils at every inspiration; and the demons, lodging in their bowels or other parts of their bodies, tormented them with pains and diseases of every kind, and sent them frightful dreams. The number of these demons amounted to no more than seven millions four hundred and five thousand nine hundred and twenty-six.*

The penciled lines were so perfectly straight they could be part of the published page.

I saw my father hunched over, perhaps at the kitchen table during dinner, reading intently, this straightedge in one hand, a sharpened Blackwing pencil (his favorite) in the other. Heard the scratch of graphite along paper.

Something sharp cut my thumb. I'd been squeezing the straightedge, and my thumb was pressed into one of the corners.

A single drop of blood bloomed on my thumb. I smeared it across the GENERAL brand symbol on the ruler, appreciated it a moment, and then sucked the wound until it stopped.

There were also two small, slender books with almost matching black covers: one was a copy of the New Testament in tiny print, and the other was *A Manual For the Use of the Lodges Under the Jurisdiction of the Grand Lodge of the Most Ancient and Honorable Society of Free and Accepted Masons.*

I hefted the box back toward the stairs and set it down in a safer location, where I wouldn't be buried alive (perhaps in the coffin) if a pile shifted and collapsed. I inhaled the sweet mustiness of old books.

The Masons book was full of prayers and dedications and ceremonies and oaths. The book was old (April 18, 1912), the cover stressed, the corners raw. The Bible-thin pages flickered across my non-injured thumb.

A small piece of paper fell out. This was to be expected. Along with Dad's habit of meticulous underlining, he was always scissoring out book reviews and movie blurbs and other articles in some way relevant to books and movies he owned and carefully folding them between the pages of those books or inside those VHS-tape cases. This was not an article. Folded once and about the size of a standard Post-It, the paper was tissue-thin and waxy like butcher's paper. On it, rigid blue-penciled letters read: COWAN.

I tested the word on my lips. It sounded like an old word, foreign, perhaps Gaelic. But it also sounded familiar.

Weren't the Masons a secret organization shrouded in mystery? Was it true most presidents had been Masons? Or that the Masons were responsible for everything from the founding of our country to the killing of JFK? Or was all that bullshit? Inside the front cover, in my father's distinct, punctilious penmanship, it read: *Ward Munacy, Century #100.*

Another quick flip through the book revealed no additional notes or single-word messages. Trying to imagine what the word meant or why my father might have written it and set it inside this book was, of course, a futile effort, in some ways a pathetic endeavor for a son who never had a chance to understand his father.

I set the book aside, along with several paperbacks out of which old articles and perhaps more single-worded notes threatened to spill, and flipped through one of the notebooks. Most of it was budget notations and notes related to articles my father edited for *Encyclopedia Americana*. Two full sets of encyclopedias anchored the bottom shelves on the far wall. Some of them bulged with Dad's personally-selected addenda of newspaper and magazine clippings. How much was also written among the entries on those encyclopedia pages?

The marginalia of his life, I thought. Except these books and movies and the accompanying supplemental articles and handwritten notes (his intellectual paraphernalia) might have actually been the center of his life, and it was his wife and son who were penciled on the outer edges, small notations carefully scribed, but no more meaningful than a footnote.

I sifted through the VHS tapes as if the box were a bargain bin at a flea market. The collection included classics like *Psycho* and *Dracula*, but there were also films I'd never heard of, like *Dementia 13* and *The Vampire Lovers* and *Monkey Shines*, which featured a maniacal grinning monkey on the cover with a bloody straight razor gripped in clawed paws.

Then there was a cover of a man staring at his own reflection in some dingy bathroom mirror. He looked haunted and was clearly insane. The movie was *Henry: Portrait of a Serial Killer.*

It was Halloween and I'd come home from school (I was in third or fourth grade) and found my father watching this movie. In the scene I saw from my angle in the stairwell, two men attacked a woman in her home, ripped off her clothes, raped her, and killed her. The woman's screams were so loud. I almost ran upstairs—I shouldn't be watching this—but something else caught my eye. Something weird about Dad sitting in a folding chair facing the TV only a few feet in front of him. Something about his head. It was bald. Dad had full, bushy, dark grayish hair, but this scalp was hairless, pale, with squirmy red and blue veins scribbled through it. As I tried to make sense of it, the head turned. Unlike Dad's, this face was beardless—but worse, monstrously worse, you could say—there was a smaller blood-red face bulging from the side of his head, an inner twin birthing itself from my father's cheek. A low moan quickly grew louder and louder, and I wasn't sure if it was from the TV or from the thing that was my father. Dad slowly stood and turned toward me. His arms lifted. His hands shook. His face was a fat, ugly lump—two grinning mouths, two noses, and three eyes, the twin head bright red like a fresh wound quivering with life. That quavering, throat-rattling moan filled the room and behind it, still playing on the TV, a woman screamed and screamed. The TV light strobed around my father. His shirt was streaked with blood. Only a costume, but I ran, and by the time I shut my bedroom door and pushed in the flimsy lock, the scary moan was Dad's laughter.

Talk about memories.

Later that Halloween night (I did not go trick-or-treating, and even ate a bowl of chili in my room because I was too afraid to come out), I watched from my bedroom window as a cadre of teenage boys in hockey masks with candy-weighted pillowcases sprayed shaving cream all over my father when he emerged from the coffin, standing on the front porch and draped in spiderwebs, wearing that two-headed costume with a bloody sickle in one hand. The cream crisscrossed his shirt and clogged the mouth, nostrils, and eye holes. Dad tore off the mask with an enraged howl and chased the boys down the road. The sickle was held high in the moonlight, and Dad's scream echoed through the night.

You're so much like your father, Mom said.

CHAPTER 22:
DELUSIONS AND MADNESS

LIFE HAS ECHOES. These are unexpected connections hinting at some greater design at work. Ned would credit God. Others might mention karma, or dismiss it with a shrug and say *déjà vu*.

It doesn't matter. But the universe *is* interconnected, through space *and* time. The echoes are real.

Sometimes you recognize it when they happen, but mostly it isn't until later when you realize how close you were to the thin boundary between reality and something bigger. Something dangerous.

In the box were several clipped-together typed pages. There were six packets, and they were all copies of the same thing: a short story.

The Ritual of Taurobolium
by Ward Munacy

The story was dedicated to H.P. Lovecraft.

Clipped to the last page were three rejection notes from different magazines and an acceptance letter from *Rune*, an Ohio State University literary magazine, dated May 1973. My father was twenty-one and a published author. I never knew.

I read the story.

A woman is haunted by dreams of naked people assembling around a blasphemous, ambiguous gravesite. These dreams grow more and more vivid, and in them she sees her grandfather who recently died, his body scaly in decay, yet possessed with life. Then her son finds a wooden toy bird buried near a dead oak, and the woman becomes convinced the bird comes to life at night while she dreams. One night she wakes to the sounds of chewing from her son's bedroom. She discovers the bird, as alive as she feared, feasting on her child. Eating his eyes. Unable to stop herself, as if under "some demonic spell," the woman soaks her hands in her child's spilled blood and slathers it all over her face, breasts, and crotch. This is, apparently, the Ritual of Taurobolium, a blood bathing. She walks naked into the night, chewing on something that might be her son's cheek, and falls into an open grave by the oak. Naked people circle the grave, hand in hand,

and the reanimated corpse of her grandfather steps from the circle. He is naked, and she—"as if no more than a puppet on a string"—spreads her legs.

She tries to scream, "Oh, my God, no, please, no," but she cannot.

The story's last line was particularly vile: *Something slimy entered me.*

In the immediate wake after finishing the story, I marveled that Dad never told me he wrote a story and, better yet, got it published. Considering what was in this story, it wasn't unreasonable for him not to tell his eleven-year-old son, but I felt a pang of regret for never having shared in my father's literary success, such as it was. It made me proud, and also hopeful. I'd always loved to write. I taught English. Maybe I could get published too.

I reread the story.

Life has echoes.

It wasn't the necrophiliac, incestuous finale that echoed for me (though that part did turn my stomach a little—nice work, Dad), but the line about the woman feeling like a puppet whose strings were controlled by some sinister, otherworldly power.

Mom: *Like something took over me. Everything fell away.*

Dani: *I'm not myself. I'm not me.*

Something controlling them.

I sat there a while, trying to entertain an idea I didn't want to articulate, then finally chose a paperback I read years ago, and headed up to bed.

The stairs creaked with every step.

CHAPTER 23:
WHEN SHE WAKES

IT WAS LATE by the time I went up to the room.

I'd been downstairs a long time, but I guess time flies when you're sorting clutter and reliving old memories.

I stopped outside the bedroom doorway, hearing something. Was it Dani? Was she talking in her sleep? A whisper of words so faint I couldn't be sure if I was hearing it or not. Then it was quiet again.

She was asleep, a small shape beneath the comforter. In the dim light from the moon and stars glazing the window, the shape kept shifting, a silent, morphing trick of the eye.

God, it was hot in here. Sweat pimpled along my sides and back.

Dani had said she was cold, so maybe she was sick. Feverish. That would help explain her behavior. Obviously, she suffered some form of manic depression and anxiety, and the move-in and my mother's subsequent failing health exacerbated her behavior, but heap a flu and its brain-baking fever on top of those things and maybe that explained the sleepwalking and the whispering and—

The sting.

I set the paperback on the nightstand and slid out my iPhone.

The flashlight was so surprisingly bright I squinted against it, then peeled back the comforter (Dani shifted but didn't wake, curling toward me in a fetal position) and slid the light onto her while trying to keep her face in shadow.

Her nightshirt was pulled crooked, her left arm completely exposed.

The site of the sting was deep crimson, completely enflamed and swollen almost her full shoulder width and pruned like a soaked fingertip, and in the middle of the fleshy bulge a jagged hole leaked yellowy-green pus. Some had dried in crusty, cracked rivulets, a volcano surrounded by fractured lava. This was no typical allergic reaction to wasp (*night bug*) venom.

Black tattoo-like veins slithered down from the infection to her forearm. It almost looked like she'd Sharpied her arm, a bored kid in study hall writing on her skin. A vine-like design weaved and overlapped all around her arm.

Blood infection, I thought. *This is very, very serious.*

DEAD END

I had to wake her and take her to the hospital *right now*.

Her name was on my tongue. She was finally sleeping. She needed to go to the hospital, no question, but would a few more hours make a difference? It wasn't as if the sting infection would lead to amputation.

Right. As if I had any reason to know what I was talking about. People suffered snake bites and even spider bites and their flesh rotted, blackened—tissue necrosis—and that definitely led to amputation.

"Dani?" I said, almost too quietly for even me to hear.

She didn't stir. Sleep was good for her (*Good for the infection, too*, my mind added. *Give it time to spread those black marker lines all the way down her arm and across her shoulder, up her neck and—*), and I didn't want to wake her.

I was worried, even scared, she would be different. It was an ambiguous fear, one I couldn't articulate or even properly picture, but unclear fears have a way of quickly spreading (so like an infection) in a fog that plumes inside the brain, obscuring and concealing, which only makes the fear worse.

Anything could emerge from that fog.

That worry might be childish, but in the middle of the night such fears gather strength easily. The adult, and thus hopefully more rational, part of my mind insisted I wake her now, get her dressed and to an emergency room, but that same logical dictate was pushed aside by the selfish certainty that once awake, Dani would be a mess, crying that she didn't know what was wrong with her and simultaneously refusing to go to the hospital.

I felt bad for her, but I also wanted to delay the inevitable.

Coward.

A true man, a true adult man, wouldn't hesitate like this: He would wake his future wife, insist she get medical help, and then drag her to the hospital, if necessary. He wouldn't stand here indecisive and afraid of ensuing conflict; he would *act*, he would be *brave*, he would be *responsible*.

Instead, I stood there, helpless. I've learned the word for that condition: damnation.

I straightened, and the iPhone flashlight splashed over more of her body. With the nightshirt tangled tight around her, it was easy to see that the problem was even worse than an enflamed, infected sting.

Dani had always been skinny, but now she was on her way to anorexic. Her hips protruded and her knees were clunky, and the flesh beneath her breasts hooked over her lowest ribs like her guts were scooped out.

Numerous splotches smudged her thighs and stomach: a dozen and maybe more, most the size of nickels, and varied in color from dark purple to light brown. Small bruises.

How could she be bruising so easily?

It might be in the blood.

Among the numerous pills my mother swallowed every morning with a glass of sugary orange juice was one called warfarin, which sounded like something Vikings practiced but which was actually a blood thinner (best way to prevent strokes and heart attacks, other than adopting a healthy lifestyle, of course) and along with the warning not to eat green vegetables or consume fish oil for fear of the blood thinning too much, the long list of possible side effects included deep, excessive bruising.

Dani wasn't on any medicine (she had a natural aversion to it, or at least a skeptical suspicion; wouldn't even take aspirin for a headache), so maybe she had an iron deficiency. Or the bruises were a byproduct of the infected sting. Or—

The closed bathroom door. The soft whisper of sounds I couldn't place.

—she did it to herself.

I pictured her in the hallway bathroom before the mirror, fingers pinching her flesh. Pinching hard enough and long enough to burst capillaries, tissue blushing blood, small wounds that darkened to purple and brown smudges. The thought had been there originally, perfectly clear—*she's hurting herself*—but I'd refused to accept it. Dani wasn't some troubled teenage girl. She was an adult. She wasn't the type to give herself bruises, or slice scissors across her thigh or arm the way many girls did, finding the pain to be a release of stress that also provided a needed sense of control.

That wasn't her, couldn't be.

I leaned closer to her legs. But were those scratches among the bruises? Cuts?

"No," Dani said, as if in protest to my unspoken thought.

The word startled me frozen, leaned over her, iPhone flashlight blanching her legs. My breath caught and, for a second at least, my heart stopped.

More trickled out between her lips, not words (not recognizable, anyway), but meaningless whispers, a susurrus of nonsense that slithered out of her and slipped along her body.

I strained to discern meaning, but the cracking consonants and hollow vowel sounds refused to coalesce into words or anything even remotely recognizable. The string of vocal noise continued without her pausing for breath.

Speaking in tongues. This thought came from nowhere or, more precisely, from the dank basement of my mind where macabre ideas sprouted in ugly mushrooms. I had very little idea what the practice of speaking in tongues actually entailed (though for some reason I knew it was technically called *glossolalia*), but that didn't stop the thought, because it had been planted at some point, seeded and fertilized, no doubt, from some horror novel I read years ago. *She's speaking an ancient language, the tongue of the gods.*

Silliness, of course.

Even so, I had to wake her. If I didn't, I'd suffer a seriously bad case of gooseflesh; but what if she wouldn't wake? What if she kept speaking (*in tongues*) like this and I couldn't break her out of it?

"Dani?"

I'm not myself. I'm not me.

My hand touched her hip, smooth as polished stone, and I shook her gently. "Dani, you need to—"

Her eyelids sprang wide open. Black eyes peered out.

Trick of the light, I thought quickly. "Dani, we need—"

She screamed. It thundered out of her, not one of frustration or rage or even fear—it was a scream of predatory warning.

"*No!*" she yelled. "No, no, no! *Get out!*"

I backed away and hit the dresser. My phone clattered on the floor, the flashlight shining directly up into my face.

Dani sat up in one smooth movement. "Stay away from me! No! *Get out!*"

She was screaming toward me, but not at me. Her eyes were open (not black but shadowed), but she wasn't awake. This was her sleepwalking again; only instead of soft steps and quiet whispers, she was enraged at something, screaming at some dream creature to stay back, to keep away from her.

"Dani!" I shouted. "Wake up!"

She growled, full-throated.

I braced myself, imagining she'd launch from the bed, arms stretched before her, hands curled into claws, but all at once she deflated, anger slipping off her as her body went slack, back slumping, head dropping toward her chest. She leaned forward, and if I hadn't gone to her, she would've toppled onto the floor.

Holding her, I was scared. She was dead weight against me, and when more breathy sounds came from her, my whole body tensed.

Not a whisper this time, though—merely a gentle, throaty snore.

CHAPTER 24:
WORSHIP

THE JUNGLE TREES peeled back and a giant Easter Island head birthed through. Carved smooth with a heavy brow, a pointed nose, and pursed lips, it rose into a dirt-colored sky. It was Dani's face, blown up huge and made of ebony. The goddess.

I heard chanting.

Nonsense sounds, primitive clicks and glottal clucks, but there was a word in there, a single word, and it scared me in a way only such things can in a dream.

Louder and louder.

The stone idol was a towering monolith, filling the sky, but there was something else—something even bigger—looming behind it, a leviathan, an enormous thing that radiated limitless power, and it saw me, reached toward me with a hand as large as the world—

I woke with a huff of air trapped in my throat, and forced it into a silent chuckle. Sweat slicked my body.

I wasn't in my bed, not in my room. My head was plump with the jungle dreamworld, the distant chanting thumping with my racing heartbeat.

My mother's room. The dusty dresser and mirror, with the identical pictures of me as a newborn. The pile of baking-themed cozy mysteries. An ancient teddy bear with one thread-sagging button eye.

The door was closed, locked, a rocking chair wedged against it.

Was I really that scared of Dani that I not only wouldn't sleep with her, but I felt the need to securely lock myself in an adjacent room?

The answer was clear and cold and terrible: yes.

My father's dying word wasn't needed to remind me what I was. Dani had exploded in a fit of rage, screaming at something (*Get out!*), and I should've woken her, by any means necessary, and taken her immediately to the hospital. At the very least, her arm needed medical attention.

But no, she'd passed out against me and I'd laid her back on the bed and tucked the comforter around her, and then had locked myself in my mother's room. I'd needed sleep, too, and it had taken me as if by force, my body an accomplice to my mind's cowardice.

DEAD END

A bar of light glowed under the door.

Had I turned on the hallway light? Had I left it on?

A shadow cut through that bar of light—passed through it in a dark, shuffling splotch. Dani was up and pacing.

Her shadow reappeared. It stopped on the other side of the door.

My breath caught.

Time stretched. Stretched.

A hard, fleshy slap severed the quiet. Another. And another.

Hurting herself. Worse, now, than pinching. What came after slapping?

"Dani?"

Again, quiet stretched and stretched.

"I'm sorry," she said in a terribly small, weak voice.

She headed down the hall.

The goddess walks. I rushed to the door, yanked the rocking chair aside, and stepped into the hall in time to see her enter the bathroom. The door closed and the little lock clicked.

By the time I reached the door, I'd picked up speed, moving fast, and I lowered my shoulder and the weak lock popped, the door smacked open and banged against the wall, and I had to catch the sink to keep from tumbling forward into the tub where Dani stood.

"Dani, stop!"

She wasn't doing anything, just standing in the tub, looking hypnotized, had probably been about to curl up and try to sleep.

"*Dani!*" I said far too loudly, worsening my own fear, but it had the desired effect: she woke from her sleepwalking hold, slipping from it in a jittering, spastic convulsion of limbs and head, a bug fighting free from a cocoon.

"Dani?"

"I need to sleep," she said in that tiny voice. She looked around, confused.

"I know."

"I don't know what to do." Tears choked off her words, and she sobbed freely.

The goddess weeps.

I went to her.

All must genuflect before the Weeping Goddess.

From the jungle dream, the chanted word that had scared me awake echoed with the frantic, erratic, staccato beat of my pulse, as if the dream's audio track was now part of my bloodstream: *worship worship worship worship worshipworshipworshipworshipworship*

"I can't take it anymore," she said, and sobbed against me. "I don't know what's happening to me."

"It's going to be okay," I said, sounding far more calm and confident than I dared feel.

Glassy with tears, Dani's eyes looked up at me with a child's desperate hope.

CHAPTER 25:
HOSPITAL INTERLUDE

A SHORT DOCTOR with facial hair so manicured it looked painted on assured me Dani's condition wasn't life-threatening. "Even so," he said, "we are going to keep her overnight for observation."

"The infection . . . "

A nurse passed us in the hallway. She was familiar, perhaps a nurse on my mother's floor. I felt her judging me.

We'd been at the hospital almost three hours already, and we were still in one of the ER examination rooms, and this was only our second conversation with a doctor.

He nodded and there was something childlike about it, and I wondered if his facial hair really was painted on, a little boy playing dress-up. "It's from a . . . creature?"

"A wasp, I think."

"You saw the wasp?"

"No."

He turned to Dani, lying there on the gurney, a sheet pulled across her though she still had on the sweatpants and sweatshirt she'd tugged on before we left home. "I didn't see it either," she said.

He caressed his chin, and I expected his hands to blacken. "We'll treat it with a heavy dose of antibiotics and some general antivenin and see what happens. If the infection spreads, we'll have to get a bit more aggressive."

Amputated stumps waved somewhere in my mind. "But she'll be okay, right?"

"Oh, certainly. We'll see to it."

"Great. Thanks."

"Are there any other symptoms we should know about?"

I started to speak, and Dani touched my wrist. "No," she said. "Just the arm."

The doc nodded, said he'd be back, and left.

"We're here to get the help you need," I said.

"And I will."

"It's more than an infected sting."

"Once that's healed, I'll be able to sleep. I know it."

I'm not myself. I'm not me.

"The sleepwalking, Dani. It's more than just taking a pill. There's other . . . issues."

Get out!

She stared at me, not angry (not completely, anyway), a bit sad (her eyes getting slippery again), and more than a little worried (her fingers teased between her lips, and she chewed tentatively on the nails). "You think I'm crazy."

"No. I'm concerned. I saw the bruises."

"It's nothing."

"Did you do it to yourself?"

"Mike . . . "

Sobs choked any following words, and I hugged her. She cried for a while, but I didn't let go. I held her tight, promised her I always would, and that together we would make it through this.

"Hey," I said.

"Hey," she said.

When the tears ebbed enough for her to speak more than one word, she said I should visit my mom. Something heavy weighted my stomach, but I nodded, kissed her on the lips and on her forehead, and said I'd be back.

"I might be in an actual room," she said.

"Don't worry—I'll find you."

CHAPTER 26:
LOVING THY NEIGHBOR

ONE FLOOR UP, my mother had visitors.

Ned Loller and three of his "sun-kissed believers" stood around my mother's hospital bed with her propped up in a sitting position, multiple pillows wedged around her. She smiled inside the oxygen mask and stretched doughy arms toward me. Purplish lesions stood out on her flesh. Her veins seldom cooperated with phlebotomists.

I hugged her, careful of the tubes and her oxygen mask. The skinny black guy was there, chin sprouting grey whiskers, and the man in the same red-and-black flannel who looked desperate for a smoke, and the tall man with the elongated, sallow face who'd been in a suit the other day. Today he wore a plain button-up, and bright jeans so blue it appeared the dye might slick off on his hands if he touched them.

Had they visited yesterday and stayed late, or was this a crack-of-dawn pilgrimage?

"Wonderful to see you, Mike," Ned said. He was across from me, my mother between us. "We've discussed you quite a lot, in fact."

"Have you?"

Nods all around. "Oh, yes indeed."

My smile failed to keep. "Thanks for visiting. It's very considerate."

"Love thy neighbor."

"Of course."

My mother's hands cradled one of mine. She stared up at me, wide-eyed and hopeful. "I'm so happy you're here."

Ned offered introductions, pointing as he named the three men: Edgar, Steven, and Warren.

"Named after the town, are you, Warren?" I asked.

The tall man with the vibrant jeans didn't smile. "No," he said in a deep crackle.

I told them I taught at the high school. "Go Wildcats."

No laughs that time, either. "Go Wildcats, indeed," Ned said. His face was so wide, and his cheeks so heavy, it was like a medical dissection when he spoke, his lips the gaping incision.

76

DEAD END

The skinny guy—Edgar—shook my hand and Mr. Flannel, to be known now as Steven, did likewise. "My mother died of lung cancer," he said. There was a fidgetiness about him; his fingers twitched and scratched at his stubble as if he couldn't control them.

"I'm sure there were others in your . . . group," I said, thinking of loquacious Logan French, he of the Jesus t-shirt-wearing ilk.

"My son Theo was here," Ned said.

"Didn't know you had a son."

"He is a blessing like no other. Smartest person I know, and a true man of God."

"Your wife?" I asked.

My mother's hands squeezed mine.

"We are divorced," Ned said. "Sad thing when a marriage does not work. I could not help her the way she needed."

"Sorry."

"Not at all," Ned said. "The Lord shows the way. And where is your wife?"

"Here, actually. But we're not married yet." *Yet* echoed in my mind, a word shouted into the mouth of a cave.

"What happened?" Mom asked.

I mentioned the sting (though not the black Sharpie lines of infection), her sleeplessness (but not her sleepwalking, or sleep*speaking,* or sleep*screaming*), but stopped there. "Some antibiotics and she'll be fine," I said.

"Maybe we'll visit her next," Ned said.

"She's not yet admitted."

Mom tugged my hands. "We need to talk."

A copy of *God's Waiting* was on the bed. Was it Isaac's copy, resurrected and reborn to once more haunt the world and seduce the unbelievers into sun-kissed disciples?

"How is Isaac?" I asked.

"Doing wonderfully," Ned said. "Some scarring, but no skin grafts necessary."

"He's here?"

"Being discharged this morning. Wes and Theo are driving them back to Mullock, while we visit here with your lovely mother."

"Well, thank you for . . . being here with my mom." Inside my mother's hands, my own hand throbbed like an injured muscle.

Edgar didn't extend his hand this time, though he bowed slightly. "Your mother is a remarkable woman. We should all be so lucky."

"Thanks."

Steven gave me a nod and headed out. His hands spider-crawled along his throat. Warren came closer—looming—and I actually stepped back a little, as if afraid he might reach for me with those long-fingered mortician's hands. Then

Ned was hugging my mother, and the absence of her hands around mine felt the way my foot does when the shoe and sock are stripped off after a long day's work.

"I shall see you again soon," Ned said to me, fat hand on my shoulder. "God bless you—both." He had to sidle slightly to get to the door. "God can heal. God will show us the way."

"Right," I said. "Thanks."

He lingered a moment, that salesman's smile hanging there, steady, as if his cheeks were sculpted plaster.

"Are you one of the converted now?" I asked my mom once he finally left. The hope in her face shrank behind an almost childish hurt. Like I'd called her *fatty*. "It was nice of him to visit," I said, trying to redeem myself.

"Yes, it was." She grabbed my hand again. I fought the urge to swing it from her reach. "It's wonderful."

"His visit?"

"I have hope now."

"The doctor say something?" Hope stumbled into my own voice. When the doctor spoke to me, he was grim, but maybe doctors didn't know half of what they thought they knew.

The oxygen mask distorted her grin into something reptilian. "I'm ready now."

"For dialysis?"

"No," she said, and held my stare unblinking. "To die."

She said Ned had assured her God was with her, He was waiting, and her fate was in His almighty hands. Ned acknowledged how scared my mother must feel, and held her hand while he told her of all the bedsides where he did the same thing for people near the end, and "they always go when they are ready and God is waiting." By the time she'd relayed those lines, my mom was crying. "I'm ready," she said again, her voice a tinny rasp. "And God *is* waiting." I handed her a tissue and told her that was great, I was happy for her, and my head swelled with blood-pumping heat. She was dying, and now she *wanted* to die. I wasn't happy—I wasn't sure what I was. Confused? Angry?—but should I be happy? Shouldn't I be pissed some self-proclaimed preacher cajoled my mother into surrender? She shouldn't be rejoicing in death. She should be manning up for dialysis. My eyes felt tight, like they might pop from their sockets.

"What are you thinking?" she asked.

"I don't know."

"Your father would get the same expression. Said the same thing, too, when I asked what he was thinking. He could've been a good poker player. Maybe you can."

"Right."

"I'm okay," she said. "Really."

A few tears managed to slip free. She patted my arm. I apologized, which seemed the right thing, since she wasn't crying.

"No reason to be sad," she said. "It isn't going to get me."

"What isn't?"

"The monster. The one that got Ward."

My skin pebbled. Had she really said . . . "Monster"?

"It came back," she said, almost to herself. "It never left."

"Stop."

"What?"

"What monster are you talking about?" My chest was tight, my heart a clutched, panicked bird. She was delusional. Perhaps the meds were screwing with her head.

She patted my hand. "What happened the morning your father died?"

"He had a heart attack, remember?"

She didn't take the bait. "I'm sorry for what you saw that day," she said. "I'm sorry I wasn't there. I knew he wasn't doing well. I just didn't realize how bad it had gotten. He was always a bottler. Like you. Try letting it out. You'll feel so much better."

"Ned give you that advice, too?"

"God's waiting."

"What. Monster."

"There's monsters everywhere, Mike. They lurk in shadows. They peer out from dark corners. From trees. They're always hungry. But the light of God pushes them away. In the light, God forgives. I see that now."

"That's what you meant, monsters are a goddamn metaphor?"

Her smile was pitying.

"So, God wants you to die?"

"God wants whatever He wants. If you accept that, you'll be so much happier. Thanks for visiting, Mike."

My mouth wouldn't close. Her stare, eyes red-rimmed, cheeks pale and sagged in wrinkles, challenged me to question her, but I couldn't. I wanted to scream, and I wanted her to scream. She shouldn't be so happily obsequious. So content to capitulate. "Mom . . . "

"I'm going to be okay," she said.

I was in an anger-fueled daze, which at least helped quell my uneasy fear as I walked out and return to the ER, but Dani had been moved to a room several floors up and by the time I found her, she was asleep.

Outside, the sun was pushing upward, and its heat pushed down.

CHAPTER 27:
DEAD IS BETTER

A **SCOTCH-TAPED PAPER** fluttered on the front door.
The handwritten note was simple:

> Mike—
> I have your cat.
> Your neighbor on Heintz Hill,
> Rom Fort, house #51

Rom Fort's house was the one directly across from the opening to Mullock. He answered on the first knock. "It's good to see you, Mike."

I recognized him immediately: the man in the orange polo with the thick glasses, whom I'd seen when Isaac was in my arms. But I also sensed a deeper familiarity. "We know each other?"

Rom scratched his beard: a thinking gesture, not the OCD-frenzied one of Steven, the flannel-wearing smoker. "I was friends with your father," he said. "I had a veterinary business in town. He would come by. Sometimes you tagged along."

I kind of remembered the pet shop, a sharp smell of animal, the cacophonous chorus of barking dogs, but the memory slipped from my grip, a muddy something falling back into the moist ground from which I'd scooped it free. "We only had one cat," I said.

Rom appreciated me a moment and was more genuinely mortician-like than pale-faced Warren had been, could have been actually welcoming me into a funeral home. Funny how part of us knows what's happening before the full mind comes on board. Some people might call that precognition or intuition or dumb luck. I think instead it's a warning system that offers one final opportunity for us to flee.

"Come on," he said.

We headed up his driveway to the garage. He asked about my mom and I gave him the update, though not her sudden enthusiasm for death.

80

"I'm sorry to hear that."

"Thanks."

A sinking feeling weighted every step. Dusty was dead. Of course he was. I'd known that much—the warning system was flashing red—but I'd also been hoping and gladly fooling myself. Maybe Rom had lured Dusty with a can of wet food and grabbed him. Maybe he'd even used one of those cages designed for catching strays. It made perfect, fitting sense even now, as Rom led me into the one-car garage and gestured to the sheet-covered lump on a workbench: he was a veterinarian, after all, and he knew how to rescue a runaway kitty.

But Dusty was dead.

I reached toward the shape. My hand hovered.

"It's not that bad," Rom said. "I've seen worse."

So I lifted the sheet and folded it back from Dusty's body. He lay flat, stiff, eyes and mouth open, pink tongue bulging free.

"He was in the road," Rom said. "You passed the blood stain."

"It's my fault," I said. "He got out when my mother went to the hospital. I thought he would come back. I should've searched the woods. I'm sorry, Dusty." My fingers traced the curve of his head. "A car hit him?"

"Not a car."

I petted Dusty's head and under the chin where he liked it best, scratching with my fingertips. His fur was smooth, but beginning to take on a staticky stiffness. I stopped.

"It was a bus." Rom pointed across the road. A short yellow bus was parked at the curb outside Ned's house.

"Ned's bus hit the cat?"

"Happened just this morning. Cat ran out of the woods like something was chasing him, right into the road. Bus could've stopped, too, but kept going. The driver was a young guy. Messy hair, curly. He shrugged, walked away. But that kid—the one you were holding—he cut across the street toward it."

"Isaac," I said.

"Wasn't sure what he was going to do, you can never be sure with kids, as with animals, and it's a good thing, too. I thought he wanted to get a closer look. Curiosity. But he made to pick it up—"

"My cat?"

"Yes. His arm is in a cast, but it didn't stop him from reaching. What happened to him, anyway?"

"Set himself on fire."

"Really?"

"An accident. Of sorts. You think he wanted . . . what with my cat?"

"Don't know. I stopped him. Brought the cat back here. I knew it was Beatrice's."

"Thank you." I could see Rom was thinking. "What is it?"

"The kid said something as I was picking Dusty up. I didn't quite catch it, and when I asked what he meant, he ran back to Ned's. A little young to be one of the pastor's disciples."

"Sun-kissed, to be exact," I said.

Rom ignored my comment, still thinking. "I can't be sure, but it sounded like he asked about the blood."

"On the street, you mean?"

"Probably . . . "

"But?"

"Nothing. Doesn't matter." He looked directly at me, a soft expression. "I'm sorry."

My hand trembled on Dusty's body. "You think the driver did it on purpose?"

"Unless he really didn't see, but I saw the whole thing. He could've stopped."

I should cross the street directly to Ned's house, pound my fist on the door, and demand to see Wes the bus driver. I wouldn't even give him a moment to ask who I was or what the hell I wanted—I'd cold-cock him right in the nose. Asshole.

"Then again, I'm the wrong one to ask."

"You said you saw it," I said.

"I'm not a fan of the Holy Church of Nedwin Loller."

"Jesus Christ the Empowered," I said. "He gave me his book."

"Vanity press," Rom said. "Fitting."

I traced my palm from Dusty's head to his tail, his spine tiny bumps. Poor Dusty. He was solid, as if he'd been stuffed by a taxidermist. Death gave him more girth and that felt significant, meaningful, like death meant something, even a cat's death, but it was only decomposing tissues swelling with gas.

My nose twitched at the smell, a milk-sour odor carrying a certain sweetness, and the stench was tolerable if you didn't know where it was coming from. He looked almost completely normal, save for the speck of blood on his chin and the fat tongue. Tiny lightbulb arcs reflected in his eyes.

"I'm sorry," I said to Dusty.

I wiped at my tears and rubbed the mess on my shirt, one hand on Dusty. He was old, but cats could sometimes live for twenty years or more. He'd had more time left. When he was a kitten he would sleep curled on my pillow, and I would fall asleep to the gentle rhythm of his breathing against my neck.

Rom was right behind me. I stopped crying, covering my face and pinching my temples to do it, but that pushed out more, as if the tears were twisted from a sopping sponge. Adults do not weep over dead cats. Men, especially, do not cry over dead animals.

Rom's hand on my shoulder was strong and grounding. "It's okay," he said. "Sometimes dead is better."

What was I supposed to say to that? How could such a thought be appropriate? How was dead ever better?

DEAD END

I'm ready, Mom said. *God is waiting.*

"I've seen a few animals survive a car-hit and never be the same. Changes in personality. Physical impairment. Terrible and heartbreaking. Trust me."

I kept crying, shoulders heaving a bit now, lips trembling too, the way a little boy cries. There was no point disagreeing with him. No point in even discussing death. It comes, it takes, that's it. Death doesn't care if we think it's unfair, or cruel, or if we welcome it. Life guarantees death. You're born. You're sentenced to die. This damn cat that I loved was dead not because of what I did, but because it was ever born in the first place. And whose fault was that? The Big Guy's, the Upstairs Man, Mr. I'll Show You the Way.

No reason to show me, God, I thought, *I'll just follow the trail of corpses.*

"I'll help you bury him," Rom said.

I turned around, the tears ebbing, and couldn't say anything. He hugged me. After a moment, I hugged back, this man I barely knew, whom I couldn't quite remember. It was a fierce embrace, muscles tensed, bodies pressed together, my hands bunched in heavy fists, and I squeezed him as hard as I dared, as if I could overpower the grief inside me.

CHAPTER 28:
EVERY DEATH IS MEANINGLESS

"I CAN HAVE Dusty cremated," Rom said, "if you'd rather do that."

The table wasn't a typical workbench—it was metal, cold and clinical, a veterinarian's table—but then, this was no typical garage. Tucked in among rusty tools, cracked snow shovels, water-stained boxes, and shelves of half-empty paint cans and bug spray were glass canisters and stainless-steel boxes and small medical bottles and what might have been a bag of syringes, and a medical rolling cart with multiple drawers, and even an IV stand on wheels.

"You could open a practice in here."

"I don't know why I kept so much. Sits in here getting dusty."

I laughed. It quavered, sounding a bit crazy.

"Shit. I'm sorry."

"It's okay. Just a cat."

"No. It's never 'just a cat.'"

I slid the sheet under Dusty and carefully scooped him into my arms. "I want to bury him."

That felt right. The way it should be. My muscles flexed at the prospect of digging. The exertion would feel good. I wanted the soil to be tough, and the endeavor to leave me too weak to do anything but pass out.

"You have a spot in mind?"

"Yes."

"Let's bury him and have a beer in his honor. Always my custom after putting an animal down."

"Beer at work?"

"Or a shot of bourbon. Or two."

I carried Dusty. His body was heavy, though that was really emotional weight, and his head lolled in an awful wobbly, loose way. The sheet flapped against my legs.

Rom carried a pointed shovel and a hoe. There was a shovel or two in my mother's garage, along with a rusted pickaxe. My father had used the pickaxe to dig a hole once when he was concerned about the ground being "water-logged." I might have been seven or eight, and when I'd asked him what he meant he stared at me, face red and sweaty. "That we'll drown."

DEAD END

Did anyone in Ned's house watch us walk past up the hill? Were they in Ned's private church? Who were they, really? Societal rejects? Mental defectives? What was Ned doing with them?

They all ride the short bus, I thought without any sense of humor.

I decided I would come back out here, late tonight, a small knife in hand, and stab the bus's tires. All of them.

"Where we headed?" Rom asked.

"Behind the house," I said. "To Mount Munacy."

Draped in ancient spiderwebs, the pickaxe leaned against a far wall in the garage. Beside it on metal shelving, old WD-40 cans mingled with rusting cans of spray paint and wasp spray.

The sheet was wrapped tightly around Dusty, who waited several feet from where Rom started to dig. For a moment, the sheet moved—gently rising and falling. Breathing. Trick of the imagination, of course. Same thing had happened during my father's wake. Dead and in his coffin, Dad still managed to breathe. Then he was cremated, which solved that problem.

It was hard, gravelly soil. "Sure there isn't a different spot?" Rom asked. "This could take a while."

I hefted the pickaxe onto my shoulder. "This is the spot. Precisely."

The axe swung fast and pierced several inches into the ground. *Thunk*. The next swing went deeper, and the following deeper still.

It took a while, but that was okay. Sweat slicked my back and along my temples and neck, and my arms and legs throbbed, but it felt good. An act of penance. Rom took a few turns with the axe. His greying hair flapped wildly as he swung, and his glasses tilted crooked. We shared the shoveling and dug the hole a good three feet. He worked hard, too, grunting and sweating. Perhaps he needed his own penance.

"Should be deep enough," Rom said.

He meant deep enough to keep any wild animals from sniffing out the corpse. I shoveled deeper.

Dusty was quite stiff now, and had to be curled more tightly to fit into the hole. I did it as gently as I could. I imagined his spine snapping, his bloated body rupturing, and now the smell worsened as if it had burst, but the stink was still sweet somehow, like rotting apples.

"I want this to matter," I said. I was kneeling at the grave. "I want it to mean something."

"Every death is meaningless," Rom said.

"You think so?"

Red streaks scarred the sky, and the sun was a mushed, radiant orange. I knew it took a while, but the digging had eaten up most of the day. "Yes," he said. His eyes hid in shadowy caves.

Did Dusty have a favorite toy somewhere in the house? The sheeted shape was so alone at the bottom of the hole. "Maybe you're right."

We filled in the grave by hand and smoothed over the dirt. I hefted a large rock from the edge of the woods (pausing a moment at the trees and peering into the dark—was something back there, watching me, a thing heavy with life?), grunted with the weight, back muscles and arms straining, and set the rock directly on the grave.

Come get me, I thought, looking back into the dark woods. *I'm not scared.*

The dirt filled the spaces between my spread fingers. I patted it. The ground pushed upward. Breathing. Last breaths.

Sleep well, Dusty.

As a child, I screamed make-believe war cries from high above on Mount Munacy, and I threw plastic army men over the cliff to plummet to their demise on this spot. Later, my father stared up at me from where he'd fallen. His eyes were white, his lips bloody.

Coward.

Rom's face was shadowed. I was too tired to even thank him.

"Let's drink," he said.

CHAPTER 29:
GARAGE TALK

I **GRABBED TWO** cans of beer from the small fridge wedged between shelves in Rom's garage. The fridge offered two choices: lime seltzer and Saranac beer.

"Seltzer by day, beer by night," Rom said.

The first sip was glorious—the beer hurt my teeth, made my whole mouth spasm, and lacerated my throat. I finished half the can in two gulps.

"I'm sorry about your mother. Beatrice is a wonderful lady. A tough woman. Strong."

"Not sure how tough it is to refuse dialysis."

"Choices, I guess. But I'll tell you: she's exactly the sort of woman your father needed. He died way too young."

My second beer opened with a pleasing fizz, and I swallowed enough to start a good buzz. "I feel strange admitting this, considering what you've done for me already, but I really don't remember you. I'm sorry."

Rom didn't miss a beat: "I first met Ward when he brought an injured bird to my clinic. He found it in the woods. Guy had a broken wing. Your father came in cradling him, paid for the bird's care. The bird recovered, in case you're interested. I remember it flying off. Wing good as new. Toasted to it.

"That was a good thing your father did. After, he would stop by occasionally, and sometimes you were with him. You must've been eight or nine. I had a beagle named Thurman back then, and you used to squat in front of him and stare at him, like you didn't know what he was. Or you were trying to read his mind."

"Weird kid."

"All kids are weird." He smiled to himself and finished his beer. "You're the spitting image of him."

"The beagle?"

He chuckled. "Maybe. You got that same look in your eyes Ward had."

"My mother would concur."

He was staring at me, but before I could ask "What?" he got up from his folding chair and fetched two more beers. I had barely started my second, but he set a third at my feet.

"You remember when you attacked me?" Rom asked.

"Attacked? You're joking, right?"

The sun was gone now, a whole day lost to the digging of a grave, and mosquitoes and moths swarmed the outside light pooling on the driveway. The only streetlamp on Mullock lit part of Ned's lawn and that ugly yellow bus. I thought of its tires again. I could hear the powerful pop and releasing air.

"This was a week or so after Ward passed. You were on your bike and trying to gain enough speed to pedal uphill to your house. You tried again and again. You'd make it almost halfway before turning back.

"I came outside, and you were straddling your bike and staring up at the hill. I told you to really give it your all. I said something about pushing through the pain. You stared at me, not saying anything, not moving.

"I walked closer, a few feet away, and you flinched. I reached out, because I thought you were going to fall. I grabbed your wrist and, *whoa*, you unleashed a scream something awful. High-pitched and ungodly."

"Trench coat," I said.

"What?"

"Stupid thing from childhood. Sorry if I hurt you."

"You kicked me a good one right in the shin and growled at me. I see that perfectly, can still hear it, growled like you were a dog. You might've bitten me if I didn't let go."

"That's awful." I could almost recall the moment. After kicking him, I took off and pedaled up the damn hill and right onto my driveway. Amazing how my mind hid the incident, stowed in a box of bad memories stashed at the far corner of a cluttered mental closet.

"You're definitely your father's son."

After his second heart attack, he was on Xanax. Those were a wonderful few months. He was so . . . pleasant. "Did my father have a temper?"

"He had his moments."

"Was he aggressive?"

Rom thought for a moment. He was debating whether to tell me the truth or obfuscate it, perhaps with clever euphemistic phrasing, like doctors did. Mom wasn't dying, she simply "had limited time remaining." Dad didn't have an anger problem—he was "prone to moments of pique" or maybe he was "calmness impaired" or perhaps "overcome with passions," though that made him sound like he had a masturbation problem or, to be even more euphemistic, a "propensity to self-gratify."

"Ward Munacy could get very focused."

"You mean obsessed?"

"A bit manic at times, I guess. He was a passionate man."

"Was he overcome by his passions?" I laughed at my joke and waved it off. "So he *did* have a temper, right?"

"One summer, he went on a killing spree."

"What?"

"Wasps. Bought a dozen or more cans of wasp spray, walked around with one all the time. There was a nest under your deck, big one, or so he claimed, and he was worried there were more nests somewhere. Feared they were in the attic or in the walls. Killing every damn wasp he could find was his focus for a good three months. You could say he was pretty intent on that."

I pictured my father on a wasp-killing rampage, a can of spray in each hand like an exterminator gunslinger. Had he dared venture into the woods? Had he been stung? Did black lines darken his skin? Was it even worth wondering? "I was thinking of things my mom said."

"Ah. Mothers. My mom could heap the guilt like no other. Such is their talent."

"You have kids?"

"No. Lee, my wife, and I decided not to. Wasn't our thing." He was staring at me again as he had earlier, as if he could see inside my mind and read my thoughts. I certainly hoped not.

"What's on your mind?"

"An old man's thoughts."

"You're not old."

"I'm sixty-five, Mike. You don't tell a sixty-five-year-old he's not old. Old is old."

"Okay."

We sat in silence for a while and drank our beer. My mouth swelled and tasted somewhat metallic.

"The kid—Isaac?—you saw him set himself on fire?"

"Front row center."

"How did he do it?"

"He was burning a book Ned wrote."

Rom raised his beer in a silent toast and sipped.

I told him what happened—the torn pages, the lighter fluid, the Zippo, the burning flesh and charring weeds—and showed him my still-red and pimply palms, and asked him what he thought made a kid do something like that.

"Ned's probably molesting him."

I smirked, but Rom wasn't joking. "You think so?"

"Religious types."

I wasn't sure what he meant, exactly, but maybe he was right. Why else would the kid go to such a visible place to burn Ned's book? It was a cry for help. I'd been there to help him with the fire part, but who was helping him with the Ned part?

"But I'm biased," Rom said. "Some people are just fucked in the head."

"You mean about his religious retreats?"

"Never attended."

We drank, and the night settled more deeply outside the garage. My biceps were twitching, and my right foot kept cramping, but it was a good sort of hurt—the kind that came from real labor, the sort of strong-fisted exertion that made you feel like a man. Now *there* was a euphemism for masturbation.

"You're smiling again."

"A young man's thought."

"You're not that young anymore," Rom said.

"I certainly don't feel young."

"Adulthood is about coping with our deteriorating physical self."

"You read that in a fortune cookie?"

"Off a motivational poster, actually."

We laughed and drank and for a few moments there I felt really good, like all the bad shit was separate from me, shoveled up and heaped on a barge floating out to sea while I sunned on the sand.

"You know your father had a story published? Creepy thing about some toy bird that comes alive."

"Yeah. It ends with necrophiliac incest."

A pause, and Rom burst out laughing. "That's the one."

"I found it. He never told me about it."

"Not exactly a kid's bedtime story."

"Didn't know he wanted to write."

"He was a book guy. All book guys want to be writers. You must have considered it."

In my past, there was a dog-eared black-and-white composition book in which a detective tracked a serial killer who lived only in shadow. He might have been magical somehow, though I wasn't sure. I wrote it in fourth or fifth grade, penning it during recess. I sat in the shade and wrote while my peers chased each other and rode down slides and threw pebbles at one another and the monitors watched me curiously, like I was the real danger. I'd called the story "The Dark Man."

"We had that in common," Rom said.

"You wanted to be a writer?"

"No. The horror stuff. He brought in the bird, and I made a comment about some old movie—one where animals go crazy, attack people—and he cracked up."

"What was the comment?"

He opened his mouth and stopped. "Doesn't matter. Point is: he got the reference and it became our thing."

"Old movies?"

"*Nosferatu, Village of the Damned, Night of the Living Dead*. Things like that." Did the list include *Henry: Portrait of a Serial Killer*?

DEAD END

In a warbling voice, Rom said, "They're coming to get you, *Baaarbaraaa!*" His arms reached for me in classic zombie style, and I saw my father's outstretched arms, his fingers poking at the sky.

"Sorry," he said. "I'll blame the beer."

"No, no," I said. "I'm tired."

"After all the digging, I'm surprised you can even walk."

"Downhill's easy. The trip back up is going to be a bitch."

He pointed at my aching hands. "I don't see a ring. Not married?"

"Not yet." Those two words were almost mocking me. "Name's Dani. Short for Dantilla. Her mother's a hippie type."

"She move here with you?"

I told him about her being in the hospital, too. "Antibiotics should fix her up."

"Shit, I'm sorry. Crappy luck."

"You think women are crazy?"

There was a pause, and Rom burst out with a hearty, full-chested laugh. "Oh, definitely," he said. "You're only making that conclusion now?"

"No, but I thought I'd found a sane one."

"Every man thinks he has, then he gets married."

"So I should just accept it?"

"Depends. Crazy how?"

I didn't know where to start, or if I should. It wasn't that Dani was crazy, after all; she was manic depressive, or bipolar, or whatever it was called, and that was a chemical imbalance or something in the brain. Then again, even if psychotic behavior was caused by chemicals, did that make the behavior any less psychotic?

"That bad, huh? Looked like you fell back inside your own head."

"Sorry. I was—"

"Do you love her?"

"Yes. Absolutely. I just . . ."

"Nope. Don't go headed in that direction. You love her? Really love her? That's what matters. I'm not going to feed you BS from a Hallmark card—love, marriage, ain't easy, it's damn hard actually—but if you really love her, the hard times won't matter. Not in the long run."

I did love Dani, no question, and if I were to be completely honest with myself, I'd admit that I'd sort of sensed something off about Dani when we started dating—a strange comment, a sly glance, a fidgety finger. There was something hidden in the soil of her personality, and it began to sprout when we lived together, but it was growing big, shooting out vines, spreading. Rom was right, though: if I truly loved her, it didn't matter what might be in that earth or what grew from it.

"The gears are turning in your head," Rom said. "Maybe there's another way to look at it, too."

"What's that?"

"Even if your woman is fucked mentally, maybe you are too."

Now I burst out laughing. "Gee, thanks."

"Fucked-up people find each other," he said, and my laughter quieted, because his words sounded truthful and more correct maybe than anyone would care to admit. "You got a lot going on. Explains how hard you were digging. You were practically screaming, swinging that pickaxe."

"Was I?"

"Makes sense. You're under a shitload of stress and you aren't even thirty."

"Twenty-five," I said.

"I guess you are a young man, but—"

A clattering, jangling cowbell cut him off.

Rom heaved himself to his feet with a deep breath, said he'd be right back, and went inside. When the door opened, the sound of the ringing bellowed into the garage.

He was gone five minutes.

I sat there sipping beer and trying not to think, not about real life, anyway. Thoughts did form, however, as they do, but instead of more cryptic, depressing, "dead is better" aphorisms, it was an idea for a story beginning to take root. I hadn't written anything other than lesson plans and college recommendations for years, but maybe I could now. Might distract me, at least. It wouldn't be some cop thriller with a magical serial killer, but a domestic drama crossed with a ghost story, perhaps a haunted house tale. A house surrounded by creepy woods, of course.

When Rom came back, he forced a smile and slumped onto the folding chair. "That was Lee. She's got stage four ovarian cancer."

I felt awful. Here I was asking questions about my father, who had been dead for fourteen years, not to mention all my juvenile talk about women being crazy, and meanwhile Rom's wife was only a few feet away suffering cancer. All women might be crazy (to a certain degree), but that didn't mean the men who loved them wanted them to die.

My apology sounded so weak and stupid.

He grabbed two more beers, and we silently toasted. Rom's wedding ring was tarnished gold.

"The meds usually keep her knocked out for a while. Sometimes, though, she fights her way through them."

"You don't have any other help?"

"It's not going to be long."

"Oh."

"I read one of those 'survive cancer' books. It advised that cancer was a crucible. A true test of character and commitment. It could help you discover what you were really made of. Your real timbre."

"Sounds distinctly unhelpful," I said.

"It sounds like total bullshit. You know what's funny? People have been dying of cancer, all sorts of cancers, since man first walked this planet, but people used to die quickly. Now we have 'treatments' and 'therapies' and all sorts of 'methods' to 'postpone the inevitable.' It's such a damn waste. There's no dignity in it."

"Only euphemisms," I said, and drank.

"Your father and I enjoyed horror movies for the same reason. There's ghosts and monsters and disorder, but you're safe in your chair. It's about chaos and irrationality, but it's *your* anarchy. You can stop the movie or put down the book any time you want. You have control. Somebody wants to make a real horror movie? Film an oncology ward."

"Yeah."

Rom drank.

Every death is meaningless, I thought. *But maybe, sometimes, dead is better.*

I stood. "Thanks for everything."

"Hey, Mike."

I turned back. Mosquitoes hummed near my ears.

"The joke your father made, it was a quote . . . "

I waited.

"All these people are trapped in a rundown house because animals are attacking everyone who's outside, cats are clawing at people's faces, dogs mauling legs, birds pecking out eyes, and this one woman freaks. She wants to know why this is happening, and she turns to the main character and says in a frantic, hysterical voice, 'You caused this. You! *You're evil!*'"

Rom said it with pitchy fanaticism and contorted his face into a crazed grimace, his eyes magnified huge behind his glasses. "Well, anyway, it's what your father said to me when he brought that bird in."

I didn't say anything.

CHAPTER 30:
DEAD END

I FOUND IT under a mud-speckled window and buried beneath garbage bags stuffed full of outdoor cushions. The cracking black cover crumbled as I unveiled it.

Made in the USA, the Underwood typewriter was a foot-tall hunk of metal weighing easily thirty pounds, maybe as much as fifty. Aside from a few cosmetic cracks, and a fading logo, the green keys were all there, and a ribbon of ink stretched between two spools. I tested a key. It clacked pleasingly against the cylindrical roller. Underwood was the same typewriter Ray Bradbury had used. I was pretty sure, anyway. At the very least, it was the same one my father used.

The box of my father's stuff (what I was now thinking of as my *Father's Remains*) was beside me where several books and VHS tapes were stacked at my feet. *Pet Sematary* by Stephen King was on top. I'd started reading it yesterday. An old guy in the book named Jud tells Louis, the young, doomed father, no matter what he wants to believe, that dead is sometimes better.

Instead of Jud, I had Rom.

An angry cat hissed off the cover, with a graveyard in the distance where a solitary figure carried a child's body, small legs dangling. Dusty was in my arms. I smelled that sour-sweet decay. I turned the book over. There was a small stack of blank, yellowing paper in the box. I grabbed a sheet and rolled it into the typewriter and tabbed the black spacebar until the carriage was centered.

I sat there among all the hoarded boxes of knickknacks and bags of cushions and baking supplies and whatever else was down here, and there was my father at this typewriter, its distinct clacking sound, or its silence that time he'd stared at it without moving. He'd been thinking of something, as I was now, a story, something big with possibility. Not my tale of the shadow serial killer, and not Dad's horror pastiche.

I typed quickly. Each clack was a hard, heavy smack. Like a metallic punch.

DEAD END
A NOVEL
BY MICHAEL MUNACY

I sat back. The folding chair creaked.

Was I actually writing a novel? It was late, I was exhausted and still buzzed, and there were more important things I should be doing. Much more. Like calling the hospital to check on my mom and my bride-to-be.

How many hours of dull class time did I pass in high school by escaping into my imagination? How often did I do it now? Papers needed grading, lessons designing, handouts copying, but instead I drifted into the make-believe galaxy between my ears. It was an escape hatch, and also a survival mechanism. Reality is too awful to confront head on, and a little imagination changes focus, rejuvenates the mind like a dip in cool water on a hot day.

But could I write a novel?

"What do you say, Dad?"

I searched what remained in the box, and at the bottom was a copy of *Rune*, the magazine that published his story. The page was marked with a faded movie stub. *The Exorcist*. A pencil drawing of a big-beaked bird filled the page and pecked at the title, "The Ritual of Taurobolium," only that last word was crossed out with a single, perfectly straight pencil line and another word written beside it in Dad's rigid letters.

The Ritual of ~~Taurobolium~~ COWAN
by Ward Munacy

Cowan. It was the same word written on the butcher paper in the Masons book. Some echoes are so loud they're practically screams. What the hell was Cowan?

"How about an answer, Dad?"

He didn't speak up.

For a bio, it read: "Ward Munacy favors horror and dark fantasy, likes football and intelligent women, and believes John Dryden was right about dreams."

Dryden was an English poet from the sixteen hundreds. I'd been required to memorize a list of poets for a course in college, but I didn't remember any of Dryden's poems. Still, something teased the corners of my mind. A connection. Another echo, this one more of a whisper.

I set the magazine on the green metal typist desk beside the Underwood. The magazine's cover was a desolate moonscape.

I typed:

The day my wife and I moved into our home on Heintz Hill, I met the man who could have been my father.

The ink was a bit faded. You might be able to smear it away, but so what? I had started. I felt even bigger with possibility. I only had one sentence so far, true, but there was more. A lot more. I sensed it there, like a buried dinosaur skeleton only I could exhume.

I hunched over the typewriter and got clacking.

Pages piled up on top of *Rune*, and I began to feel what I was writing was not a story pouring out of me, but one trapped in this typewriter. It all seemed to be there—the young newlyweds full of foolish hope, the zealot neighbor, the pyro kid, and the curse that doomed the young marrieds from the moment they unpacked their U-Haul. The story was all there. I had only to punch the right keys.

I've thought since that the story wasn't trapped in the typewriter or buried in the soil of my subconscious—it was coming from somewhere else, and I typed it without realizing I wasn't the creator. I was in the magical flow of creation, where everything concrete fell away as did time, but there's also a better word for that state: possession.

I wrote until three in the morning. The first chapter was done, one neighbor dead from suicide, and the second chapter halfway finished, the main character desperate to convince his wife that his father's death wasn't such a big deal, but she wasn't buying it. Women can be so headstrong.

By the time I staggered upstairs to bed, I'd forgotten all about knifing the stupid bus tires.

CHAPTER 31:
RATHER URGENT NOW

DUSTY'S GRAVE WAS open, his white shape a big eye in a muddy skull socket. He was sheet-shrouded but alive. He meowed. Muffled, panicked, desperate to live. An enormous pile of dirt towered over me. Wads of cold wet earth weighted my hands. I threw them. The clumps pelted the cat and dirt exploded against the sheet. Dusty shrieked, sounding hurt and almost human in his pain. Dirt refilled my hands.

My arms swung forward.

I woke with the next explosion of dirt. For several seconds, I couldn't move. My muscles were too sore, my body too tired. My hands were cramped into fists.

Worship, I thought.

Foggy sunlight filled the windows, and my head felt fog-filled, too.

After making coffee (careful to navigate around all the crap still piled all over the kitchen) and forcing myself to down a few bitter sips (the only coffee in the house: a can of Folgers my mother kept in the freezer), I had to call Dani, find out when she was getting discharged.

My phone was missing.

It wasn't on the nightstand in the bedroom or hiding under the pillow or wedged between headboard and wall, not waiting on the bathroom counter, not downstairs by the typewriter and the dozen or so typed pages (I marveled at those pages a moment, thinking how crazy it was I'd actually written the words on them), and it wasn't on the floor somewhere or accidentally added to any of the nearby piles of hoarded crap.

My phone might be at Rom's, but if it wasn't, that left only one place.

Outside, the hill loomed before me, the cliff like a giant, curled tongue. Charred weeds sagged off the edge where Isaac had burned pages of Ned's book and almost torched himself. Was Ned abusing him, as Rom believed? Was it any of my business?

Directly below those burned weeds was the rock that marked Dusty's grave, and right beside it, my iPhone.

Miraculously, it turned on.

There were three voicemails from the hospital. I squatted at Dusty's grave while I listened.

The rock had been moved. Not much; an inch or two, maybe. The dirt left a smooth trail, and in the middle of the trail a scoop of dirt was clawed out. I touched it as if expecting a vision to come to me. Not that I needed one to know what happened: an animal had sniffed the corpse and made a half-hearted effort to dig it up.

My fingers traced indented claw marks.

In the woods, an owl hooted.

A nurse was saying, " . . . we wanted you to know it's rather urgent now."

Urgent? What was—

I replayed the second message. It was a nurse on my mother's floor, urging me to come in because "Mom's condition is worsening." The third message was more to the point: "She could go any minute."

CHAPTER 32:
TOO LATE

MY **HEART BEAT** so frantically as I crossed through the hospital entrance that I thought it might rupture and I'd collapse flat onto my face, dead before I hit the tile.

As Dad went, so might I. Just a heart attack, right, Mom?

The elderly woman at the welcome desk handed me a pass and asked if I knew where I was going. I must have looked panicked, because she moved quickly and didn't say anything about those damn HIPAA rules or any magic code. "Yes," I called back as I was halfway to the elevators.

A man slumped inside the elevator, hand on the metal bar. In his other hand, he held a helium *It's a Boy!* balloon, and a blue teddy bear head jutted from his armpit.

He caught my stare and immediately looked down. Damn right. Bully for you, you brought a new person into this mess we call life. Congratulations. Here's hoping your child is the first one to discover immortality.

An old guy blinked at me from the bed where my mother had been. A blood-stained bandage sagged off the side of his head.

"Sir?"

I spun around, and the nurse who spoke stepped back. "Where is she?"

"Beatrice Munacy was moved one floor down. Room 451."

As in Fahrenheit 451, I thought. *The novel about burning books Ray Bradbury typed on an Underwood.*

I took the stairs, tripped, almost fell. The nurses on my mother's floor watched me run past. A skinny black nurse with dreadlocks mouthed something as I passed. I thought it was, *He's too late.*

The door to 451 was closed.

My mother lay completely still on the bed. She was so small, a shrunken version of herself, the sheet taut around her belly, her arms weighting it tight on either side. Her fingers were swollen and curled as if she'd been making a fist. All tubes and wires were gone. All machines were dark, turned off.

It took me a moment to look at her face.

The bed was raised up in a slant, and she was slouched to one side, almost touching the plastic rail. Her eyes were closed, her thin hair a wispy mess, and her mouth was sagged wide open, drawn and slack.

Like she'd unleashed a terrible scream before dying.

Too much. It's all I was thinking. *Too much death. Too much stress. Too much emotion. Too much trouble. Too much everything.*

I grabbed the bed rail.

It came back. It never left. It isn't going to get me. The monster. The one that got Ward.

She'd been ready to go, and now she was gone. I hadn't been there. Maybe a nurse was there for her, or maybe she'd died alone.

Every death is meaningless.

There was a gentle knock on the door, and the dreadlocked nurse came in. Her expression was pure sympathy. "She passed just before dawn. It was quiet, peaceful."

The blood specks dotting Mom's chin suggested otherwise.

"Kidneys?" I asked.

"I can get the doctor."

"It's okay."

"We tried dialysis," the nurse said. "The strain was too great."

Too great. Too much. Too late.

"So, she died of . . . "

"Cardiopulmonary failure." Mom's wide-open mouth was a final, desperate gasp for air. "Is there anything you need?"

I shook my head and said, "I don't know what to do."

She approached and appraised my mother. "It's okay. Take as much time as you need."

Crazily, I felt like she was talking *to* my mother. Communicating with her. Reassuring Mom that she could leave me here with the body and ascend to the next world. Who knows, maybe that's exactly what the nurse was doing.

A Ghirardelli wrapper poked from one of my mother's curled hands. A last chocolate before she went; only the wrapper was unopened.

CHAPTER 33:
IT FEELS SO OLD A PAIN

I CALLED THE only funeral home I knew of in Warrenville, made the arrangements, and spoke briefly to a doctor who offered condolences and a limp-wristed handshake, and I was escorted to a cubicle where another stranger expressed her sympathies and pointed where to sign for the hospital to release the body.

I sat in the lobby for a while. I didn't cry. I didn't scream. I unwrapped the chocolate that was in my mother's hand and placed it on my tongue. It slowly melted. My muscles were sore, my back pinched in burning spasms, and my neck was tight, but that was all secondary to the throbbing, strained flex of pain deeper inside. It was an old pain, but as present as the fingers I felt tapping my face in a secret but meaningless message.

In some ways, the pain was an old friend.

Welcome back.

CHAPTER 34:
DAY TROUBLES

DANI COULD TELL immediately what had happened.

She was dressed in sweatshirt and sweatpants and looked okay, still tired but not as frazzled or distressed, and she came to me and we embraced. She said she was sorry, that my mom knew I loved her, and Dani promised to help in any way she could.

I didn't cry, but I did weep, and I was thankful beyond words for not having to tell Dani what happened. If I actually said the words *My mom is dead* I would cry, and it would hurt even worse than the pain returning to take up residence inside me.

Even though Dani was cleared to leave, we still waited another hour for a nurse to come in with the discharge papers and prescriptions for antibiotics, a low dose of steroids, and a sleep aid, and another twenty minutes for someone else to arrive with a wheelchair to bring Dani downstairs, as per hospital rules.

We were quiet during the car ride back, and quiet at CVS while we waited in plastic chairs for the scripts to be filled, though my mind bloated with enough random thoughts for a roomful of talking people.

It came back. It never left. You're just like your father. She died alone. All women are crazy. Do you love her? Stage four ovarian cancer. Every death is meaningless. The kid said something about blood. Ned's probably molesting him. Dead End. Dusty dead in my arms. Dead and in the ground. My mother open-mouthed, straining for one more breath, just one more. Sometimes dead is better.

Dani touched my hand. "Hey."

"Hey," I said.

***

It wasn't until we were back on Mullock that we said more than those single-syllable words to each other. I asked her if the doctors had said anything about her trouble sleeping or the bruises on her legs.

"The infection is already healing," Dani said. "The black lines are all faded. I think I'll sleep fine."

"That's good." I meant it, but the way Dani was speaking struck me as odd—

too measured, too deliberate, as if she was weighing every word she allowed to exit her mouth.

As if she were trying to hide something.

A skilled pretender.

"There's something else," I said. She waited. "I found the cat."

"Oh, good."

"He's dead."

Dani took a shower, and I sat in the kitchen, surrounded by ivy wallpaper that appeared to move a little in the fluorescent light if I didn't stare at it directly. As a boy I'd imagined a little man lived in that ivy, like the Jolly Green Giant, only this Ivy Man was much smaller and a bit insane perhaps, jumping among the tangles, imprisoned, forever searching for a way free.

I read a short story in college about a woman trapped in a room where she goes insane, believing living things are trapped in the room's yellow wallpaper. The professor claimed it was a story about feminism, but I'd disagreed then, and even more strongly now.

It was a horror story.

Dani had closed the bathroom door, but not locked it. That was a good sign, I hoped. I would give her ten, maybe twelve minutes, and I'd listen carefully for any sign she might be . . . doing stuff to herself in there.

In the shower, Dani hummed some tune. It wasn't anything familiar, and the longer I listened, the less familiar it sounded, as if it were something I once knew but could no longer recall. She interspersed words as she hummed, but the water drowned them out. I resisted the urge to sneak down the hall, press my ear to the door.

When the door opened, not quite ten minutes later, I peeked around the edge of the doorway and caught a glimpse of Dani's naked flesh before she shut the door to the bedroom.

Wet spots splotched the carpet. She hadn't dried. Hadn't even wrapped a towel around herself. But at least she'd bathed.

I couldn't resist the urge to check on her, and I avoided the dark spots as I tiptoed to the door. My life with Dani had become a series of closed doors, her on one side, me now eavesdropping on the other. "Dani?"

No response.

I nestled my ear against the door. There was a rustling, maybe sheets, maybe clothes, and a fragment of indistinguishable whispered words, and then nothing.

"Dani?"

Seconds dragged, half a minute, longer, and no sound. Had she disappeared? I strained to hear even the tiniest sound. Nothing.

Quiet as I could, I got down onto the floor and peered under the door. The space wasn't even an inch high and the carpet obstructed the view, but I saw the dresser and part of the bed, saw all the way to the opposite wall.

She wasn't there. Even angling from the far edge of the door, I still didn't see her. Of course, the one place I couldn't see was on the bed. And here I was on the floor, staring under the door, a wet spot near my cheek.

I should've opened the door and walked right in—it was my old bedroom, after all—but I was nervous, even scared. What if she was sleepwalking again? What if she unleashed another scream and tried to attack me?

Two bare feet stepped directly into view, so close I could poke them with a finger. They squished into the carpet. The way Dani's second toe hooked over the adjacent one was something I'd joked about when we first started dating. I said it was like crossing your fingers behind your back when you were pretending to tell the truth.

Water bled down her ankles, followed the greenish veins in her feet, and wet the carpet. She'd been standing to the right, pressed against the wall, out of view.

Above, the doorknob turned.

I didn't move. If I scrambled away, she'd hear and open the door as fast as she could. If I stayed like this, maybe I could pretend I was trying to blot up the water trail. Oh yeah, was I soaking it up with my hands?

The knob turned with a faint metallic jiggle, and stopped. The feet squelched away from the door, out of view.

She was back against the wall. Standing there, perhaps still naked. Waiting.

Odd, certainly, but also unnerving.

Was she waiting for me to open the door so she could startle me? That seemed unlikely, considering all that had happened in the last day or so. Which meant what, exactly? She was standing, perhaps still naked, pressed up against the wall because . . .

She's going to attack me, I thought, and waited for a dissenting comment. There was none.

I stood quietly as I could. "You okay, Dani?"

"I'm going to try to sleep, I think." Her voice quavered, just a little. And it was coming not from mere inches away on the opposite side of the door, but from the other end of the room. I heard the flap of sheets, the squeak of bedsprings.

Some part of me, one I didn't want to trust, felt her still standing there against the wall. Waiting for me to open the door.

Waiting . . .

CHAPTER 35:
NIGHT TROUBLES

WHILE **DANI SLEPT** (hopefully), I worked on my novel—tried to, anyway. My young newlyweds visited with one of their neighbors, witnessed a domestic squabble between husband and wife, and vowed to never let their love disintegrate into petty hatreds.

"What about into fear?" I asked.

The mauled rocking horse stared at me with what remained of its decaying, peeling mess of a face. I thought of my father's story, of the flesh-eating bird in it.

I drank a beer to get the creative juices flowing (and to calm my nerves a bit), toasting Mom with every sip. Then I drank another one, clacked out a few horrendous sentences, and looked through my Father's Remains.

But my mind, for once, was not absorbed into my father's macabre interests. I was too worried about Dani. She'd gotten medical help, but what she needed now was psychological help. She'd never agree to go on meds, but if she suffered another bout or two like the other night, what choice would she have?

She'd always had tendencies toward depression and mania, so maybe the infection in her arm had screwed with her brain a little, and now that the injury was healing, so too would her extreme emotional reactions.

That might sound possible, but it didn't seem probable. Could I actually force her to seek help?

I'm scared for you, I'd say. "Yeah, and myself," I added aloud.

The rocking horse didn't respond, and I drank more beer.

Even slouched in an uncomfortable folding chair, I felt sleep numb my limbs and cloud my thoughts, quieting them, smothering.

Somewhere distant, a familiar sound: the creak of the floor above, the gentle steps of someone pacing.

Or maybe that was a trick of my imagination.

I woke with a wet crotch and a sore neck.

Jesus, I pissed myself, I thought. But I hadn't; I'd fallen asleep with a nearly empty beer in hand, and the bottle had tipped to spill its dregs onto my pants.

The day's sunlight had faded toward sunset. Days were slipping past me almost too rapidly to believe. Was this what old people meant when they said life goes by in a blink?

I heard something. It sounded like whispering. "Shit," I said.

Halfway up the stairs, I paused. The whispering was louder, and there was another sound, too. Slight scraping sounds. It sounded so familiar, yet also foreign. Something I should know, something I'd heard often.

I took the next few steps slowly, trying to hear what was going on upstairs, the sounds small and vaguely threatening.

I crossed the landing, started up the second set of stairs, and stopped. I'd been in this same spot, a box unloaded from the U-Haul truck in my arms, when I saw my mom standing at the glass door staring out toward Mount Munacy.

The kitchen was dark. Beyond it, through those glass doors, reddish light cleaved the cliff into a piebald hulk of red sunlight and black shadow.

Dani was in the kitchen, dressed in her purple-and-gold Albany sweatshirt and matching pants. She'd been (or still was) sleepwalking again, and now she was on her knees in the kitchen among all the pots and plates and glasses and boxes of expired food from the pantry.

Her words, if they actually were real words, were spoken rapidly; the deep tones fell away and the higher-pitched sibilant sounds hissed like tiny snakes that slithered from my grasp. Her whispers slipped through the house, the soundtrack of some dream, or nightmare.

Speaking in tongues, I thought as I had the other night.

Was it true people could speak in weird languages, dead languages, forgotten languages (*ancient tongues*) without even realizing they were doing it? I thought there were religious fanatics somewhere in the Deep South who handled snakes and spoke in weird, creepy ways. Glossolalia. *The tongue of the gods.* That sounded like a sci-fi paperback from the sixties, but was it true? If so, was it something close to possession? Did Ned believe in it? Perhaps he practiced it. Maybe he could translate.

Dani wasn't speaking in tongues. She was speaking nonsense, sure, but only because she was sleepwalking. In her head, in whatever dreamworld that now held her, she was engaged in a perfectly lucid conversation. Her vocal cords couldn't keep up with the events unfolding behind her eyes. Now that sounded not only possible, but very probable.

Yet here I stayed, standing on the stairs, unsure of what to do, afraid of how she might react if I shouted to wake her or—and this was the really troubling part—dared to enter the kitchen and even touch her.

That familiar-yet-foreign sound again: metal on metal.

Scrape. Scrape.

Her head was down, long hair dangling before her as a veil. Her shoulders slumped. Her arms were moving, hands doing something in her lap.

DEAD END

Scrape. Scrape.

I continued up the stairs, crossed into the kitchen doorway.

The crimson and shadowed hill was so bright, for a moment I couldn't see Dani right there on the floor before me. Just like the other day, there was still the redolent smell of my mom's last batch of cookies.

Dani, on her knees, hair obscuring her face, was whispering a successive series of accentuated sibilants. Not a language. Not even close to a language. *A curse*, some panicked voice spoke up in my mind. *She sounds like a witch reciting the words to a spell or a curse.* But that was silly, irrational. These were meaningless utterances, the product of some nightmare world. I imagined millions of snakes pursuing her through some bleak landscape that fell away into a terrible abyss. And all the while, the hissing *siss* and *shh* growing louder and louder until her whole world was one screaming cry of static.

"Dani?"

The whispering stopped as if her throat had been cut, and she twitched like something had bitten her. A snake, perhaps.

"Dani?" I asked again. "Are you awake?"

In a small voice that was almost lost, she asked, "Do you hear it, too?"

I knew I should go to her, take her in my arms, but I didn't want to step any closer. Coward or not, I sensed I should stay right where I was. "You were sleepwalking again," I said.

"The buzzing. It was so loud. Gone now."

She said she'd heard something the other day when I found her "organizing" the kitchen. She'd thought it was a mouse.

"It's okay," I said. "Let's get you back to bed."

She raised her head and shook it slowly. Her nose protruded through her drape of hair. She rattled off a sentence of s-noises that could have been a prayer. Or a curse.

"Dani," I said more sternly. "*Wake up.*"

Scrape. Scrape.

Then I saw it: she held a large pair of metal scissors loosely in her right hand, resting on one thigh. The blades were easily seven inches long, maybe even nine. Those were in the drawer under the microwave, where they'd been my whole life. Dad had used those scissors to cut articles from the newspaper, and I'd grabbed those scissors when I was seven or eight and run back to my room, intent on cutting something, and halfway there, my feet tangled, I fell, and the pointed end, facing up in my hands, stabbed me in the cheek, a half-inch below my eye. It could have ended quite badly. Mom had screamed at me, and my father actually spanked me while I was still bleeding. *Don't run with scissors*, he said and slapped my butt hard. *You want to lose an eye?* SLAP.

You're so much like your father.

Scrape. Scrape.

The sound was slow and slight, not at all the distinct *snip-snip* of scissors, but a thing more menacing and dangerous. Dani's hands were opening and closing the scissors in a sluggish, absent-minded way, and the sibilant whispering continued, lips bumping up against each other.

Scrape.

I heard her asking me the other night to get the scissors. *I should cut my hair,* she said. *It'll get caught in the branches.*

The scissors closed with an immediate, sudden, metallic snap. The pointed end that had almost stabbed me in the eye was very sharp, perhaps sharper than a carving knife.

"Why do people die?" she asked in that quiet voice again.

"Put down the scissors, Dani." My voice was steady, almost.

"The sound is everywhere," she said. "Buzz, buzz, *buzzzzzz—*"

"*Dani!*"

"It won't stop, Mike," she said in a stronger, deeper voice, a tone I'd never heard her use. "It keeps buzzing, *burning* my brain. Why won't it stop? Why? *WHY?*"

Her fingers tightened in the holes, scissors stiff.

"Dani, put—"

"*Leave me alone!*" she screamed.

And swung the scissors directly upward toward her throat.

CHAPTER 36:
UP ON MOUNT MUNACY

I THREW MYSELF at her, and caught her arm in a tangle of both of mine. Her skin was cold and moist. *Terror sweat*, I thought quickly, and then she was screaming, high-pitched and frantic, and fighting against me, pushing and pulling, the scissors still in her grip and slicing through the air between our faces.

"Stop!" I shouted. *"StopStopStop!"*

Her black hair swished back from her face and two completely white eyes (*thick, milky, plump like maggots*) peered through at me, and in my surprise, she found the leverage to fling her arm across her body and toward my face.

The scissors opened and a blade sliced across my forearm. Had I been a half-second slower, the blade would have gouged right through my face, cheek, nose, and perhaps even my eye. The cut was plenty deep enough, pursing open my skin right down to the ulna. I didn't know that in the moment, of course, would only find out about it after yet another visit back to the hospital, but the pain was immense, scattering black dots across my vision, and I swear I heard the metal blade scrape along bone. Why the hell were they so sharp?

If she'd wanted to, Dani could have brought the blade back toward me, stabbed me in the chest, or tried once more to pierce it through her own throat or sever her carotid artery, which would have sprayed blood all around the kitchen, splattering on the ivy wallpaper.

Those images crowded my brain in a single overlaying image, but I'd fallen back, something hard poking me in the side, and I was too shocked to do anything.

That's what scares me the most when I think about it—how close we were to everything ending in a splash of blood.

The scissors clattered to the tile.

"Dani . . . "

She crossed the kitchen, slid open the glass door, and paused. "I'm sorry. It's the only way."

"Dani, it's going to be okay."

"No," she said, calm, measured. "I have to go."

"Dani, stop—"

She ran.

Her bare feet smacked rapidly down the deck steps and slapped across the patio and onto the grass before I even made it to the stairs.

She was running up Mount Munacy. Her hair streamed back over her shoulders, and in the dimming light it almost looked like she was flying upward, a plane taking flight.

I ran after her as fast as I could.

It might be in the blood.

My father's bleeding face. His crucified arms. His head tilted back to the morning sky. His fall. Over and over, these images in my head as I ran after the woman I loved. I tried to scream for her to stop, but only a single-syllable "*NO!*" came out between thin, ragged breaths.

Dani crested the top of the hill. Dying sunlight so richly red it was almost as purple as the colors on her sweats plastered her in a tableau of sharp-edged shadows, her hair flying behind her, her arms and legs stretched in a running sprint.

I couldn't get there in time.

But Dani didn't run for the cliff's edge—she ran for the woods.

Because the tree line was farther from her than the cliff edge, I reached her with only a foot to spare before she would've been in the dark of the woods. Even being right behind her, I might have lost her then. She was running fast, and I have no reason to think she would've slowed down.

That scares me, too, of course, the possibility of her slipping from my grip and vanishing among the trees.

She didn't slip, though.

My hand caught her elbow and yanked her back. She twirled toward me as if this were some well-practiced dance move, and thunked into me. We stumbled back and she batted at my hands, shouting for me to let her go.

Something in the woods. Very close. Big. This wasn't a childhood fear, some abstract notion my father had planted in my subconscious while I slept—this was real, tangible. Something *was* back there.

"Dani, stop. Please. *Stop! Stop*—"

"*It won't let me sleep!*" she shouted.

"*Stop!*" I yelled back as best I could, almost wheezing for air.

Dani wasn't wheezing, not gasping, hardly breathing heavily at all. "*I must go to it!*"

Beyond the tree line loomed an enormous creature. The last of the crimson sunlight carved it from the darkness. It was watching us, though I couldn't see its eyes. Something buzzed nearby, and I smelled rot, thick and putrescent.

Dani punched me in the face.

DEAD END

I saw her fist coming and tried to dodge it, and managed to save myself a direct nose-crunch, but she scored a glancing blow along my cheekbone. I did not, however, let go, pulling her down to the hard ground with me.

Her knee found my crotch, on purpose or just lucky, and she was loose once again.

My hand caught her heel, a momentary grab, but it was enough to throw her off balance. She kept running, but her direction was changed back toward the trail she'd run up, and her next steps staggered worse and worse, and then she fell forward into an awkward momentum-propelled tumble that bounced her body as she rolled down the hill, her limbs flopping, head bouncing.

She stopped almost halfway down the trail with a heavy, awful *thwack*.

I staggered to the top of the path. Dani lay sprawled, unmoving. Her head was twisted awkwardly, and I thought she'd broken her neck, like Dusty.

To my left, the woods were too dark to see anything, but I felt the creature there, watching. Waiting.

Dani's chest rose and fell, rose and fell, and I couldn't tell if I was relieved or horrified.

PART TWO:
THE GOSPEL ACCORDING TO NED (THE DIRT GOSPEL)

———◆◆◆———

"Many priests encouraged the superstition of their parishioners by resorting frequently to exorcisms whenever any foolish persons took it into their heads that a spell had been thrown over them."
—*Memoirs of Extraordinary Popular Delusions and the Madness of Crowds*, Charles Mackay, 1852

———◆◆◆———

"I'm not myself. I'm not me."

———◆◆◆———

CHAPTER 37:
ESCAPE HATCH

IF **NOT FOR** writer's block, I wouldn't have found the body. At least, not so soon. Ned told me later, and with great confidence, why I was the one who found the corpse.

God had willed it so.

God, after all, has a plan.

I was stuck in the middle of chapter four. My main character—Nick—woke in the night to strange whispering sounds and was ever so slowly walking down the dark hallway toward the kitchen where Kelli, his wife, was . . . Well, there was the problem. I didn't know what, exactly, she was up to. It would have been too easy for Kelli to be the Dani stand-in and have the imaginary kitchen be a ransacked mess, Kelli in some possessed state kneeling among glasses and dishes and slowly sharpening a large carving knife (swapping scissors for a knife), but it felt wrong to steal so directly from my life—like plagiarizing, in a way. This was supposed to be a novel. Fictional. And, unlike real life, it had to make sense.

Dani was at a psychiatric facility in Rockland County. The doctor at Orange Regional had explained she needed a five-day psych eval, and he'd recommended where. "It's the ideal place for such situations," he'd said.

Such situations. There was something foreign-sounding about those two words, or maybe it was the clinical way the doctor spoke them that made them mysterious and ominous.

It was also another euphemism, and it bothered me so much because it was indicative of adulthood. Getting older, getting married, living as a responsible citizen—*such situations* are their own sort of courtroom convictions and prison sentences.

Since we were not yet married, I wasn't listed on any of Dani's medical records, and there were no HIPAA (maybe I could title my novel *Haunted by HIPAA*) forms or any other form where our names appeared together, so Dani's mother had to agree to the doctor's decision. If not, the doctor would have her "temporarily committed," requiring a thirty-day minimum stay.

"I'm sure Dani doesn't want the wedding cancelled," I said on the phone. It had taken several back-and-forth calls to reach Dani's mother.

"Dearie," Helen Tremblay said, "there may be no other choice." Helen lived in Santa Barbara, California, where she'd moved when Dani entered college. She worked at some hippie hemp shop and occasionally sent Dani pamphlets for healing retreats along the West Coast. The last one promised refreshing ocean breezes and aura-enhancing chakra crystals.

Dani's parents had divorced when Dani was five, and Christian Tremblay had loaded his Ford pickup and headed somewhere south. His whereabouts were unknown. Absent fathers were something we had in common, though mine had a pretty solid excuse.

"It's stress," I said. The more I said it, the more I could almost believe it. *Coward.*

"Honey," Helen said, "I can tell you aren't telling me everything, so I can only guess it's maybe a little worse than even you know."

"The doctor seemed optimistic," I said. I didn't mention how Dani had tried to kill herself. Or how she'd attacked me. Or my fear that she might be schizophrenic.

"I know my daughter, sweetie, and she isn't simply going to bounce back. This is going to linger."

I didn't like that phrase—*going to linger*. Was that another goddamn euphemism? "I think *you're* not telling me everything."

"I'll write you a letter."

"What? Why?"

"It helps me get everything right. Isn't it tragic how no one writes letters anymore? You'd think physical paper vanished. A lost art. Such a shame."

"You're not too worried, right?"

"Honey, I raised Dani alone for twelve years. I know all about worry. You have no idea what it's like to be a single mother."

"My father died when I was eleven. It was just me and my mother."

I expected her to ask how my mother was, and then I could drop the truth on her and see if it pushed something more substantial from her than a condescending *honey*, *dearie*, or *sweetie*. Instead, she went on as if I hadn't said anything.

"There were trying times, oh yes, but I did my best. She seems to love you, so this is your responsibility now. I'll call the hospital and let them know."

"You aren't coming to see her?"

Somewhere behind her, people were laughing. "I know this is tough for you, darling, but I can't simply step away from the obligations and responsibilities I have here. I was the best mother I could be, and now is my time. We each make our own way in this world."

"Did anything happen when Dani was younger?"

Helen didn't respond for a moment. It sounded like she was speaking to someone else, her hand muffling the receiver. "I'll sit down and write you that letter, love."

DEAD END

Love? I chuckled. "I know she's manic depressive."

"Sweetie, it's called bipolar disorder these days."

"But she has it, right?"

"Whatever helps you sleep." She hung up.

I sat in the kitchen, where I'd crammed things haphazardly back into the cabinets and pantry, and wondered what the hell I was supposed to do.

This is going to linger.

She isn't simply going to bounce back.

There had to be a history of mental illness, right? Helen didn't explain it over the phone because there were other people around. Sure, okay, but write me a letter? Did she mean the issue was so insignificant it could wait a few days? Or was Dani's mother that inconsiderate? That oblivious?

A white-bearded doctor at the psychiatric hospital told me I shouldn't visit Dani for forty-eight hours—"It is necessary, undisturbed observation time."

"And what happens after the evaluation?" I asked.

"We will make the decision."

"You mean, keep her longer?"

He touched my arm. White hairs curled around his knuckles. "We'll do our best," he said.

So there I was, trying not to think about what might happen if the doctors kept Dani longer or, and more troubling, if they released her in a day or two and she wasn't really better, and I sat downstairs at the Underwood, three or four beers sloshing in my belly, and tried to write an escape hatch for myself.

An hour and only a half-page later, unable to decide what Kelli was doing in the kitchen, I made another cup of coffee and went out on the deck. The June morning was cool, the sun gradually warming toward a hot afternoon. The school year was over, Dani and I missing the last several days, but since there hadn't been any students and all Regents exams were done, administration hadn't made a thing out of it, and here I was alone in my boyhood home, my mother off to be cremated (a choice I'd made without knowledge of her wishes—whenever the topic would come up, Mom said it was bad luck to discuss *such situations*) and my future wife in some white-walled headshrinker's lab.

I felt like screaming. It would feel good, let loose with a full-throated, primal holler of rage and frustration. It gathered in my chest, but I didn't let it free. The scream would sound too much like Dani's when she launched off the bed or fled for the woods. *It won't let me sleep*, she'd said. *I must go to it!*

One of us needed to stay sane.

And that's when I saw it: on the clifftop slumped a heap of rags, or maybe a lumpy garbage bag, but it wasn't either.

A child's arm dangled over the edge, the little fingers tangled in the burned weeds.

CHAPTER 38:
THE DEAD WILL SPEAK

BLACKENED SKIN STRETCHED in striations like hardened lava, a wrinkled, blistered destruction. His eyes were black holes, his nose melted into what remained of his cheek. A few white teeth shone starkly. His scalp was charred, all but a few wisps of hair seared away, and in places ashy bone flaked free. One arm curled into his ribs. The other stretched out to hang over the cliff's edge. I thought of Loller lifting his arms to the sky. Of my father, reaching, of Dani . . .

If I'd eaten anything, it would have come right back up.

Only shards and fragments of clothes remained, except for the clunky white sneakers. They were charcoal-dirty but unburned, like they'd been placed on his feet after the fact.

Isaac.

I pictured him out here ripping pages from Loller's book. He'd lit the pile with a Zippo and uncapped the bottle of lighter fluid. Flames erupted off his arm. *Foomp.*

Accident or suicide?

"Shit, kid," I said. "What the hell were you thinking?" My voice wavered.

The first cop to arrive was Officer Koryta. Walking him up the hill to the body, I felt his stare boring into me. The novelist part of my mind cast him as a hitman in a book not yet imagined.

"This is your property?" he asked.

"My mother's," I said. "She just died. So I guess now it is mine."

"I see."

"So," I said, sounding like a total idiot trying to make small talk, "I'm not sure what to do."

I pointed and stepped aside. Koryta stopped and told me to back up even more. I went back almost fifteen feet, to the edge of the woods. The forest was thick behind me and alive with birds and squirrels. An owl hooted far back, and my skin prickled. But there was nothing enormous looming back there, not anywhere close, anyway. Nothing I could sense.

There's nothing back there, I told myself. *Childhood fears.*

Dad whispering to me in my sleep: *Stay away. It's heavy with life back there. It came back. It never left.*

The cop's boots crunched dirt and twigs. He stopped again within four feet and fished out his cellphone. He clicked off several pictures. "Did you touch the body?"

"No."

"You didn't move it?"

"No."

"You didn't touch it at all?"

"No."

He took several more shots from a few angles, leaning over for some and squatting down for others. He contacted dispatch on his walkie, relayed codes, took more pictures.

"Tell me again what happened."

I told him.

"You didn't see anything last night? Hear anything?"

"I was . . . " He waited. "My wife, er, fiancée, had to go to the hospital."

"Why?"

I swallowed. "Nervous breakdown."

The cop took a breath and slowly let it out through his nose. He touched the sooty ground a few inches from the body, and smudges blackened his fingertips. He smelled them, like someone tracking animals in the wild. "You didn't touch the body?"

"No."

"You ever set fires up here?"

"He did," I said, "the other day. When you were last here."

"This boy? Up here?"

"Yes."

"He's the same one?"

"Yes."

"Burning a book?"

"Yes."

"Your book?"

"No. The one I showed you that you didn't take. It's by—"

"You didn't move the body?"

"No."

"Think hard," he said. "You want to get this right."

"What's that supposed to mean?"

"What do you think it means?"

"Officer, I didn't do this."

"I didn't ask if you did. Are you telling me *someone else* did this?"

I started to respond and stopped. The question sounded like a trap, like *When did you stop beating your wife?* "I think he came back up here to burn the book again, maybe, and it got out of control. He had lighter fluid on him the other day. And a Zippo."

"You smoke?"

"No."

"Own a Zippo?"

"No."

"Your wife?"

"She's not my—no."

"But she had a nervous breakdown unrelated to this boy's death?"

"Yes. She's manic—uh, bipolar, I think."

"I see."

"Well, it's more complicated, but—"

"You didn't touch the body?"

"*No!* Jesus, what is with—"

Officer Koryta spun on his toes and made as if to charge. It startled me, and I backed hard into a tree. In the woods a branch cracked. The cop stepped toward me, hand on his belt near his holstered gun.

"Sir," he said, "you need to remain calm. Whatever I ask you, you need to answer truthfully. Do not try to understand what I'm doing or why I ask certain questions. If I ask you the same question a dozen times, I have my reasons. Got it?"

I nodded.

"You're sure this is the same kid?"

"Yes. The sneakers." He stared at me, and I looked past him at the body. Tufts of green grass curled around the soles of those sneakers. "Who else would it be?" I asked.

"I'll ask the questions."

I thought of every book and movie I'd read and seen in which cops interrogated people, and all those people eventually refused to answer any further questions until legal representation arrived. Should I do that? Even if I dared, I'd look like an idiot. I didn't know any lawyers.

"I need you to come with me."

"You're arresting me?"

He smirked. "I need you to exit this area, go inside your house, and wait."

"Okay." He didn't move, and so I remained against the tree.

"The dead will speak," he said. Those eyes pierced me. "In the end, they always speak."

CHAPTER 39:
DEAD KIDS LIVE FOREVER

THEY ARRIVED EN MASSE.

I was trying to read (Louis Creed was grieving over his own dead son and thinking terrible thoughts about the creepy woods and the burial ground beyond that had an unpleasant way of bringing back the dead) when there was a knock on the door. From my angle on the living room couch before the bay window, I saw the group clustered on the front porch.

Not cops this time. The police had been in and out of my house and all around the property for most of the day, and again I thought of fictional characters who would have demanded a lawyer and a search warrant. They took more pictures of Isaac and a pair of paramedics loaded him on a stretcher, white sheet finally covering the burned body, and took him away.

Officer Kortya brought two other officers, and a man in a beige suit who identified himself as Detective King. The detective questioned me at length, including asking the favorite question of the day about whether I'd touched Isaac's corpse or not. He asked about Dani, and I told the whole truth. To King's credit, he didn't smirk when I described how Dani was whispering creepy things, how she ran for the woods, how she cut my arm, and how she punched me in the face.

"Have you questioned Ned Loller?" I asked.

The detective pursed his lips and clucked his tongue. "You know him well?"

I thought of Rom. *Some people are fucked in the head.* Rom had also said Ned was probably molesting Isaac. "He's a neighbor," I said. "My mother knew him."

"She around?"

"She died."

"Recently?"

"Yesterday," I said, and wondered if it wasn't the day before yesterday. It was disturbing how whole days could vanish, an ice shelf cracking free and splashing into the ocean.

"My condolences. Cause of death?"

"Natural." My tongue felt fat.

"I assume you have an opinion of Nedwin Loller?"

"He's religious," I said.

"Meaning . . . you don't trust him?"

"Maybe not."

"Maybe?"

"I don't know."

"They implied the hill behind your house is a sort of holy dais," King said. He shifted his weight, and appeared to straighten an inch taller. "Know anything about that?"

"A dais, huh?" He watched me, unblinking. "My mother let them use it."

He eyed me a moment. "This investigation is ongoing, so you'll be nearby if I need to ask a few follow-ups?"

I managed to squeeze out a "Yes," tongue fat and now, throat narrow. They left and I thought to read for a while, try to push away reality, but that wasn't successful, and panic gripped me, a hard fist squeezing my lungs and heart.

Detective King had asked about the last time I saw Isaac, and I told him the story of the book burning, but that wasn't the last time I saw him. Dani and I were in the back of an ambulance, she strapped on a gurney, me squatting near her, a towel wrapped around my lacerated forearm. The blue and red lights flickered off the houses on Mullock and there was Isaac, standing at the bottom of Ned's driveway. He was alone, and he watched us pass. I caught his gaze, but his stare was empty, not curious, not scared—empty.

There I was, a little boy close in age to Isaac, riding in an ambulance just like that one, the paramedics trying desperately to revive my dead father, and I stared out at my street with no feeling at all. I was hollowed, empty.

Isaac had set himself on fire, and perhaps he did it moments after the ambulance turned onto Heintz and drove away.

There was nothing I could have done. I have to believe that.

Have to.

I was almost grateful for the distraction of Ned Loller and his sun-kissed disciples. "Hello," I said, the way I might to a mortician leading me to the viewing room.

Ned's lips, like two slugs, stretched into a wide grin. "God bless you, Mike."

His arms spread wide and took me in a hug before I could get away. For a moment, he was the whole world, enveloping me against his massive body, the fat heavy (*with life*) and thick, yet also soft and moist with sweat. His gold cross wedged under my chin, hard and sharp.

He broke the hug and gripped my shoulders. His face was a moon looming above me. "Nina extends her deepest gratitude."

"I'm not sure for what. I didn't do anything."

"There is nothing hidden that will not be disclosed. God will bring all things into the open."

How vaguely accusatory, something Officer Koryta or Detective King might have said—minus the ecclesiastical bend, of course. "Meaning what?"

"How does God bring the hidden into the open?"

"He just does it?"

"Angels, Mike. God sends His angels to bring the truth into the light. You are one of God's angels."

It should have been quite complimentary and even endearing, if not obviously overblown, but the way Ned's smile hung on through his words morphed his face into a mask. He had another mouth behind the one he showed the world. The salesman's mouth, and it was always making a pitch. Even so, did the salesman believe in what he was selling?

"An angel would've saved Isaac."

"An angel," Ned said slowly, "does whatever God wills. As we all do."

Ned stepped around me with a bit more adroitness than I expected, and started up the stairs. No invitation necessary.

Logan was next, shaking my hand in both of his, up and down rapidly, and effusing about how "terrible, terrible" events sometime befall even the most devout. His shirt today featured a floating, dignified Jesus, arms spread, glowing crown on his head.

Edgar's skinny black hand felt brittle, and for a moment I felt somewhat strong. Then he was ascending to the kitchen with the others.

The last two—Warren and Steven—didn't offer hands. Warren scaled the stairs in only three steps, moving ghost-like, quick and fast. Steven nodded and tugged up the rolled sleeves of a blue-and-green flannel.

They waited for me in the kitchen. Four of them sat around the table where I'd scarfed so many bowls of Kellogg's Corn Flakes and downed a million cups of OJ and ate God knew how much spaghetti, and let's not forget all those chocolate treats I taste-tested. Ned leaned against the sink. His body completely obscured the wall behind him. A few stray pots were stacked near his feet.

The place almost looked organized. If anyone opened a cabinet, however . . .

A hidden world, I thought cryptically. *Right beneath what we see.* "Is this an intervention?"

"We were terribly sorry to learn of Beatrice's passing," Ned said. "You should have told us. We found out at the hospital, and boy, did we have egg on our faces."

Egg on their faces? Were these people for real? A kid was dead. "Where's your son?"

"Theo is helping our poor Nina through this challenging time."

Challenging time? Ah, the power of euphemisms. "And your driver?"

Ned didn't seem to understand, and then he laughed. It sounded both deep and light, and I thought of someone speaking underwater. "You mean Wes? He's a lot more than a driver."

"Where is he?"

Ned's thick brow bunched in rolls.

"He ran over my cat."

Ned didn't say anything. The four at the table watched me, curious and expectant, as if waiting for me to have some sort of freak out. I spoke slowly in short, succinct sentences: "My mother's cat, actually. He got out, and Rom down the street found him. Said your bus hit him. Saw it happen. I buried the cat. Dug the hole. His name was Dusty." I might have sounded like a little kid, but the rage was real. And now a child was dead, and I wanted there to be a connection, a link between Dusty's death and Isaac's.

"Roman, you mean? A good man with an ailing wife. We have had our disagreements over the years. Your father tended to side with Rom."

"You mean, thinking of you as a charlatan?"

"Faith can be scary to some people."

"Not faith," I said, "fanaticism."

"Is that how you think of us? As fanatics? God is real, Mike. So are His angels. His love is pure and endless, vast as all the galaxy and everything beyond it—all that He created. So, too, is the Devil real. He does not have horns or cloven feet, does not gallop around wreaking mischief. He is evil through and through, having fallen from Heaven by his own volition. He delights in misery and pain because that is all he has left. His was the sin of hubris. How often such is our sin as well."

"Are you here to give me a Bible lesson?"

"How is the state of your soul, Mike? You must be hurting."

I wanted to curse him out, demand he leave, declare all his beliefs idiotic and dangerous, but the words wouldn't come and that angered me more, as if something inside me believed what Ned was saying. "Why are you here?" I asked through clenched teeth.

Ned held up one puffy hand. The grooves on his palm were narrow crevasses in broad rock. "Please, Mike, let's remain civil. I'm not here to offer a Bible lesson. I am sorry about your mother and the cat. However, I can assure you we were not responsible for either."

"Rom saw the bus hit my cat."

"Do you believe in God, Mike?"

"That's it. You can leave. *Now.*"

His mask-grin hung there. *Another mouth behind that one. A world beneath.* I wanted to sink my fingers into his mushy cheeks and rip his mask off. I imagined the way it would stretch and stretch until it finally split along the temples and jaw with a rubbery, elastic tear, and then the real smile would be revealed: a slimy, serrated-tooth-filled mouth. An alien mouth.

Steven stood and gestured to the sliding glass door. "Okay if I smoke out there?"

I couldn't quite form words. I'd told these people to get out and they'd ignored me. Now what, start throwing things? Perhaps a carving knife? Or maybe scissors?

He moved toward the door, and seemed to push through the green ivy stretching across the wall behind him. It was a bizarre optical illusion. For a moment there, he was actually cutting through a veil of real vegetation. Then he was at the door and out on the deck before the word "No" made it to my lips. He lit a cigarette and strolled to the far end, where a coffee cup still remained from the other morning.

Was that from the morning after my mom collapsed? That felt so long ago already.

"Mike." Ned's hand sank onto my shoulder. "We aren't here to upset you. That is the last thing any of us want." The remaining three at the table nodded, well-practiced; Logan especially, a child eager to please. "We aren't bad people. I'm sure Rom has told you a few unfavorable things, but we are not the narrow-minded inculcated you may think. I am certainly not some grand proselytizer. I'm only a man. My life has had its struggles and challenges, more than some other people's and certainly fewer than most, but I know a thing or two. I know God is real and wondrous and He works through us in the most astounding, divine ways. We are each vital components of His glorious design. There is a plan, Mike. For me. For you. For everyone. If you can be open to that, you can discover the truth. The world is not what it seems. We are God's dream. And He loves each and every one of us."

God's dream.

God's brain.

A hidden world.

Listening to him was like seeing Steven walk through the wallpaper—I was somewhat entranced, even hypnotized, though it was only a trick. Perhaps Ned *was* a hypnotist and it was how he gathered his flock. That sounded *almost* possible. I'd ask Rom what he thought.

Even aware that he might be doing something to me, I felt calmer, almost relaxed.

"Tomorrow night we will offer Isaac into God's arms. We would very much like you to join us. Will you, for Nina, for Isaac?"

"You want me to go to his funeral?"

"Tomorrow at seven. God bless."

He led the way out of the kitchen. The others stood, pushed in their chairs, and followed him out, down the stairs and back outside. Edgar wished me a good day, and Logan grinned and nodded as he passed, as if confirming some secret negotiation between us.

Steven Rush was still on the deck.

"Your friends left," I said.

He didn't turn from the railing. He flicked ash into my coffee mug. There was something off about all of these people, but maybe Ned was right. Maybe they weren't simple-minded fools, but genuine believers, and as a skeptic I found that peculiar. Though even if they were true believers, that didn't automatically make them innocent. True believers, after all, never considered other perspectives. God was all-powerful, had a plan for everyone, and that was that.

Steven dragged on what remained of his cigarette and dropped it into the cup. It fizzed.

On the cliff, yellow police tape caged off the peak, and numerous little numbered flags on sticks crammed the area. The flags rippled in the breeze.

"This must be tough for you," Steven said. Uneven stubble stretched up his cheeks and down his throat. He lit another cigarette.

"I was thinking the same for you," I said.

He blinked into the sun. "Can you imagine how awful it must have been?"

"I don't want to think about it. Why do you?"

"Happening right here on your property. Under your nose. You were home, too, weren't you?"

"No . . . There was an emergency."

"Another ambulance. It's funny. He might have been back here when paramedics were tending to your . . . wife, is it? Who knows, maybe they could've saved him, too."

Isaac standing on the driveway, watching us pass.

I felt hot and nervous. It had been a long day—felt, in fact, like one never-ending day that started with Mom's collapse—and something inside me was trying to push outward, to peel back my skin and escape. Something hidden. I was afraid what that might be.

"It's not me," I said.

A stronger breeze flapped the flags.

"Can you even fathom such pain? Burned to death. That's pretty awful." Steven's tone was sincere, but tinged with an un-flavorful curiosity.

The flame burst high off his arm. His skin rippled and charred. "Why would a young boy do that?"

"Why would anyone?"

"People don't," I said. "There must have been something awful he wanted to escape."

"Or somewhere truly wonderful he wanted to go."

He meant Heaven, of course, or whatever similarly glorious afterlife Ned and his sun-kissed disciples believed in, but it sounded flippant. A young boy was dead, and dead in a terribly awful manner, yet this guy was content to smoke his cigarettes and muse over the kid's physical pain and everlasting glory.

That was the problem with these religious types, these believers who saw all things in black and white, good and bad, God and Satan: their beliefs shielded them from the complexity of genuine, confusing emotions.

126

DEAD END

How did these people fall into this? I wondered. *Ned the hypnotist.* "I'd like you to leave," I said.

"Of course you would," he said. "I won't be far away, in case you want to get something off your chest. We're not Catholics, but confession is good for the soul."

"I don't know who you think you are, but you have no right to accuse me of anything. You want to pretend you're holy or blessed or whatever, but from where I stand, you and your fellow Followers of Ned, or whatever you call yourselves, are deluded morons. Whatever your reason is for believing in a false priest, it's your problem, but you don't get to come here, to my house, and pretend you know the truth." My hands were shaking.

"Nice speech." The second butt joined the first. Another dying sizzle.

"You know what concerns me?" I said, and stuffed my hands in my pockets. "None of you is upset a child is dead."

He plucked out another cigarette from the pack in his chest pocket and lit it. "Dead kids live forever," he said, as if that pithy remark held universal acceptance. The plastic lighter slipped into his jeans pocket.

"You should get a good lighter," I said. "You know, like a Zippo."

He made a *hmmpf* sound and walked to the deck stairs, descended, and disappeared around the side of the house.

CHAPTER 40:
MEDICAL EXPLANATION

I CALLED CASTLE Hill Psychiatric Hospital. After passing through the receptionist's gauntlet of questions and HIPAA-related numbers, Dr. Marshall came on the line. He spoke in something close to a British accent, soft, voice floating alone in a vacuum. "You're calling about your wife?"

"We're not married yet. Three months away, actually."

"I see. Are you listed on her medical release forms?"

"Yes."

"You're her approved contact?"

I laughed. If I didn't, I'd start screaming. Adulthood, I was quickly discovering, was a trial of absurdities. Standing among the stacked boxes and piled bags downstairs, I considered hurling myself headfirst into the mess. The rocking horse could bear witness.

I assured Dr. Marshall I had all the proper clearance and secret codes, and the universe was not going to explode if he told me about Dani.

"She's doing well."

"What about her arm? Her bruises?"

"High-test antibiotics and steroids have cleared up the infection. Allergic reaction to a bite or sting."

"Allergic reaction?" I asked.

"I understand she took quite a fall, but no bones are broken, and the bruising and cuts will heal in time."

"And mentally . . . " I wasn't sure how to phrase it.

"She will be discharged the day after tomorrow."

I'm not me. It won't let me sleep. I must go to it. Get out! "Really?"

"There was quite an . . . incident between you two, yes?"

Incident. Now there was a euphemism. "You could say that."

"She's been diagnosed previously with bipolar disorder?"

"She told you about it?"

"She's been very open."

"Really?" And in my head, her matter-of-fact tone: *I'm a skilled pretender.*

"At first we suspected schizophrenia, or similar psychosis, perhaps even pregnancy-related, but—"

"Pregnant?" The Underwood was before me. If I tripped forward and hit the metal hulk head-on, it would crack my skull wide, and I might be dead before my body thumped to the floor. My head throbbed with the prospect. "Is she . . . "

Dr. Marshall chuckled, professorial and derisive. "No, no. Blood test came back negative. She's not pregnant. You know, it's not exactly politically correct these days to say a woman's behavior is because of hormones, but the medical science can't be disputed. A woman's body, after all, is far more complex than a man's, and pregnancy can induce certain psychological disorders."

"But she's not pregnant?"

"No."

"You're sure?"

Another chuckle. "No. Disappointed?"

"But it *is* hormones?"

"In a manner of speaking. Bipolar disorder is extremely serious, and can include dramatic mood swings and even lead to rather violent behavior. It can be managed successfully, however, through medication. It's less of a hormone issue than a chemical one in the brain."

"But she'll be okay?"

"With treatment, yes. It has to be carefully managed. You must be vigilant."

"Did she tell you about sleepwalking?"

The doctor made a thinking sound, a musing noise. "She's slept quite soundly here, according to the staff. You've witnessed her sleepwalking?"

"Yes. It's like she's in a trance, and she says weird stuff and I'm afraid she'll hurt herself."

The doctor breathed into the phone and static crinkled in my ear. "We'll give her something to help her sleep. Perhaps there's a trigger of some kind that provokes these sleepwalking episodes."

"We moved into my mother's house, and that's when she really got bad. My mother collapsed, had to go to the hospital. She died yesterday."

"Ugh, I'm terribly sorry. Those events can certainly serve as catalysts for the extreme bipolar responses you witnessed, and are no doubt the cause of her sleepwalking."

"What do I do?"

"This is a moment of relief. She's going to be okay. There will be a few bumps along the way, but she has responded well indeed to our treatments. You'll want to keep a close eye, of course, and bring her for regular checkups. It's all about diligent management. But this is a happy moment. We don't always get those."

In the box beside the typewriter, horror novels with bright bloody covers mixed with equally morbid VHS tapes, whose cardboard cases were as dog-eared and raw as many of the books. My Father's Remains. His actual, corporal remains—his ashes—were long gone, of course.

"Mr. Munacy?"

"Sorry. Yes?"

"Do you have any questions?"

Am I marrying a crazy person? "No. Thank you."

"Don't hesitate to call if anything creeps up. We'll see you the day after tomorrow. Cheers."

He hung up, and I fell into the chair. The thirty-four pages of *Dead End* waited in a stack beside the typewriter, a red Swingline stapler holding them down.

My fingers touched the keys and trailed off into my lap.

If anything creeps up.

I must go to it.

It came back.

It never left.

I'm not me.

I'm a skilled pretender.

I cursed and punched my knees. The pain helped steady my thoughts, though offered no clarity, no explanation.

I had a future wife in the nuthouse and a mother in the funeral home. It sounded like the punchline to a really shitty joke.

CHAPTER 41:
TRIAL OF ABSURDITIES

THEN THERE WAS ISAAC.

I had managed to avoid thinking about him—and avoided looking outside at Mount Munacy, where all those yellow evidence flags made little plasticky flapping sounds in even the slightest breeze—but now my mind was on him again, as if I'd been walking along, staring at the clouds, and had fallen into a hole.

And when I blinked, I saw him up there, crumpled in against himself, skin and clothes charred in a black, crumbling hide, and his one unscathed hand reaching out over the cliff's edge, fingers curled through burned weeds.

The small hand was the worst. It was possible, though not easy, of course, to tell myself the whole thing was a put-on. A fake. The body was so ruined it was practically someone's failed sculpture of a corpse, perhaps mummified, the hair seared off, the nose and ears collapsed and brittle, but that one hand—so small and sickly white—and those clunky sneakers wouldn't let me entertain such thoughts. A kid was dead, and in a horrendous manner.

I should be relieved Dani was't pregnant.

It was one thing to worry that a child we might have would become one of the open-mouthed, cellphone-gazing cows who populated our classes, and maybe he or she would do stupid things or fall into drugs or get in trouble with the law or be an unlikable asshole; yet now it was also possible to condemn the kid to a cruel, fiery finale.

It wasn't suicide.

Maybe Isaac had ventured up the hill to burn more copies of Ned's book, and his Zippo-and-lighter-fluid combo got the better of him again. Or maybe he'd doused himself and touched the flame to his skin. Or maybe someone did it *to him*.

There was Isaac in my arms as I carried him down Mullock. He sobbed and his head rested against my shoulder and my arms were straining, my thighs burning, but I could have walked all the way to the hospital, if needed.

Was that the curse of fatherhood? I didn't know Isaac, and yet my heart broke for him. So young and small and helpless. I tried to help—didn't I? In the end the kid was dead, right there in my backyard, and maybe that was a metaphor for parenthood: No matter what you did, no matter the hopes you had, no matter how much or how deeply you cared, bad shit—even life-ending, horrendous shit, be it cancer or violence—was going to get your kid somewhere along the line, and there wasn't a damn thing you could do to stop it, and your heart wouldn't simply break—it would shrivel and rot.

All part of God's plan.

Ned knows God's brain.

Someone killed him.

Mr. Flannel had come on a bit strong, hadn't he? The acne-scarred smoking man was motivated to place blame for Isaac's death as far from himself and Ned's disciples as believable. I was Suspect #1, and Steven had probably told as much to Officer Koryta and Detective King, and soon Warrenville's finest would come knocking with a few follow-up questions, and maybe the interrogation would end with my hands behind my back and a cop magnanimously advising me of my rights and telling me to watch my head as he guided me into the back of a cruiser. Then I really would need a lawyer.

The dead will speak. In the end, they always speak.

But the voice of the dead can say whatever anyone wants it to. Truth was relative, especially when a child was dead. Could Steve be responsible? Or Logan, he of the ridiculously upbeat attitude and garish Jesus-themed t-shirts? Why not Warren, who appeared creepy and somber in his black suit? Or Ned himself? Maybe his little church was only a crooked branch on the Christian tree, or maybe it was another thing entirely, something diseased and dangerous. A cult.

Bring forth all young babes so that ye Lord might pour forth His glory upon them in His Heavenly Kingdom, and let the child be purified in the hottest immolation of fire and wood.

Thus saith the Fire Gospel, Amen.

I needed to find out what really happened—accident, suicide, or murder.

Okay, Sherlock, what's first? Question the neighbors? Scan for DNA evidence? Get a gun?

My chest felt tight, the downstairs cramped and getting smaller. I couldn't take a full breath, only a blade of air.

Heart attack.

Though it would be funny in a macabre way, I wasn't having a cardiac event. The onset of a heart attack wasn't chest pain, but chest *pressure*. I had acquainted myself with the warning signs. But it made me wonder: how much pressure could one body tolerate? How much strain until arms snapped, backs broke, hearts quit? How long before a stable mind tottered, tumbled, and plummeted?

Dani wasn't pregnant, but what would happen if she did get pregnant? What if she tried to hurt our baby while it was inside her? What if, after nine months, or a year or two, when she was holding our child, she got it in her head to draw a bath and hold the poor thing beneath the water until chubby limbs floated instead of squirmed?

Pregnant and crazy.

What a really awful reality show, I thought, and startled myself with a laugh. It echoed around me. I sighed heavily—loudly—because it helped soothe away the creepiness of my worries, and the pimples along my arms.

Fingers massaging my temples, I wanted calm, a cranium of gentle, peaceful waters. I could almost hear the soft slap of water against my small boat, or against the side of a bathtub.

Calm, calm, calm . . .

My mother's gaping mouth.

Dusty's protruding tongue.

Dani's hands clutching the scissors.

Isaac's curled hand in the charred weeds. The crinkle of a chocolate's wrapper. The smack of shovel into earth. The *FOOMP* of flames. The sizzle of flesh blistering and blackening. Mom's face contorting into a monstrous grimace to scare me down the hall. Rom as an old, hysterical woman: *You're evil!*

Again and again, these images flashing brighter and brighter, the sounds louder and louder, over and over.

And over.

Until—

CHAPTER 42:
FAMILY HISTORY

I KICKED MY Father's Remains. The box shook, contents jostling and tumbling over each other. A catalog envelope, the sort that holds a small stack of typing paper, peeled from along the inside of the box like a rind of dead skin.

More of my father's writing, perhaps.

The envelope was faded, the seal long dry and the metal clasp broken. There were no identifying marks.

I slid out two stapled packets. They were typed, but it wasn't another creepy, incestuous story from dear old Dad.

The top packet cover sheet was letterhead from County of Orange, Department of Mental Health. The letter was addressed to Mrs. Munacy: "Enclosed please find the documents you requested regarding the Intake Evaluation initiated by Dr. David Benson."

Stamped in black ink on the next page, a warning:

CONFIDENTIAL AND PRIVILEGED
FOR PROFESSIONAL USE ONLY
NOT TO BE USED AGAINST
PATIENT'S INTERESTS

With a slippery feeling inside my stomach, I read through the packet, and then the next. Even if I wanted to stop, once I started I had to know all of it.

My parents had sought therapy in 1994. The opening description summed it up this way:

PROBLEMS (Precipitants): The Munacys are an intelligent, articulate family who turned to therapy to treat depression, couples' issues, and anger problems. Beatrice Munacy, 47, suffered severe depression in the years following the birth of her children. Ward Munacy, 46, is a mild-mannered, "bookwormish" man, but is described by Mrs. Munacy as "having a bad temper." Their son Michael, 6, suffers nightmares, violent tantrum outbursts, and an overactive imagination.

Both my parents were dead, and yet it felt wrong to read this. If Mom had wanted me to know any of this, she would have shared it. Then again, maybe that's why it was here in this box, because she knew one day I'd find it.

My father "put some holes in the walls at home," and my "emotional outbursts (anger and fear)" were directly blamed on my father for "fostering an acrimonious, hostile home environment."

Of that, I had no memory.

You're suppressing it, a voice said in my head. *You buried the truth like you buried Dusty. Dug the hole deep, covered it up, and dropped a heavy rock on it.*

My mother's voice, very much still alive in my head: *He would stand over you while you slept and whisper, 'Stay away from the woods. Stay away. It's heavy with life back there.'*

I read on:

There is immediate concern for ~~the safety of~~ this family. Ward is the product of a rigid, educated family in which learning was emphasized and criticism deemed necessary to encourage achievement. He appears unable to reconcile this background with the love and gentleness needed to be a good husband and father. He exhibits irrational behavior at times and may be functionally erratic.

"Functionally erratic"? Another euphemism. Did the doc mean functionally psychotic?

I pictured a doctor clad in a brown sweater vest, a smoldering pipe nearby, typewriter (an Underwood, perhaps) clacking this report, saw him type "the safety of" and then go back to strike through it. Did he doubt his first instinct? Why not white-out over it? Leaving it there was like hiding something beneath a sheet you knew someone would uncover.

The last page of the first packet was an INITIAL TREATMENT PLAN advising ongoing counseling—couples' and individual—and a "15-day observation stay under the care of professional medical neurological experts."

A handwritten note scrawled in cursive at the bottom: *Patient refuses medical stay.* It was dated May 2, 1999.

The next packet was from Dr. Benson. It was five pages, typed, single-spaced. The same confidential and privileged warning stamped each page. The first pages were summaries of my mother, father, and me, and the rest comprised a detailed plan for treatment.

CHRIS DILEO

Ward Munacy is an editor of high school science textbooks, who has three master's degrees — ScEd, Zoology, and Physical Anthropology. He taught high school science for two years but was asked to leave because of temper-related concerns. He has heart disease from an untreated bacterial infection and this has resulted in hospitalizations over the past decade. His condition requires medication and reduced activity. He is at high risk for heart attack.

I was five and repeatedly falling behind my mother's snapping flats, and the parking lot stretched into the horizon where a castle-like building towered. Inside, Dad was on a hospital bed recovering from heart attack #2, the sheets so incredibly white I squinted. His hand was steady as it reached toward me.

An untreated bacterial infection? Was that before or after Ward slaughtered wasps for three months? Maybe he was stung, and if wasp venom had weakened his heart, it might have also poisoned his mind, too.

Though slight of build, Ward has a temper rivaling even the most aggressive of larger men. I have witnessed Mr. Munacy terrify a room full of muscled men with his startlingly dramatic rage. Ward tends to be quiet and reserved, an introvert, but I wonder if this is a disguise he wears to conceal his true, bellicose nature. He may have learned to hide his real self at a very early age.

I read that twice. *Did my father have a temper?* I'd asked Rom.
He had his moments.
Yeah—I guess so.

Beatrice Munacy is a baker who worked briefly as a high school Home Economics teacher. She is the product of a prideful, working class upbringing. Much like her husband, she values her intelligence and is well read and scholarly. There was no history of depression or erratic behavior until following the birth of her children.

That birth was complicated by placenta previa (placenta blocking birth canal), and Mrs. Munacy hemorrhaged severely on the bedroom floor before going to the hospital. She was hospitalized for two months. The twin boys were delivered by Caesarean section and were both healthy.

136

DEAD END

Twins?

I reread everything again. There were two references to Beatrice's "children." Was it an error?

Following the rough birth and long hospital stay, Beatrice suffered depression, sometimes quite severe. She states that one night she locked herself in the bathroom and put Ward's straight razor to her arm. She did not cut herself, but stared at herself for almost an hour before her husband broke the door open. She says she was "not in the right mind" and "felt like someone else was controlling [her]."

Like something took over me. Everything fell away.

A cold chill slicked my spine. Mom had never told me any of this, of course—not about my twin (assuming that wasn't an egregious typo) or her contemplating hurting herself, even killing herself—and it felt unreal (and unnatural) to learn these truths while sitting among accumulated crap in my parents' house with both of them dead.

I read on.

Mrs. Munacy sought counseling with a neighbor who is also a minister. This seemed to help, she says. However, she grew increasingly concerned about her husband's "uneven, discordant" behavior.

Following the death of one of the eighteen-month-old twin boys, Mrs. Munacy once more collapsed into depression, this time tinged with paranoia. She does not accept that Caleb Munacy could have died from Sudden Infant Death Syndrome. There is no reason to believe anything else was the cause, but Mrs. Munacy's theories include suspicions against her husband and her surviving child, Michael

Nothing was around me. I was floating somewhere out and beyond. I felt only emptiness, like the entire universe was airless, vast darkness, and cold.

A brother who died? I didn't know how to begin to process this. In a way it changed everything about how I understood my life, and in another way it changed nothing. My entire childhood was sibling-less. No brother. No mention of one. But did it matter? Why the secret?

Suspicions against her husband and her surviving child.

She'd really thought her husband or her year-and-a-half-old child was responsible for a baby's death? Why would she think such a thing?

Depression, of course. I saw a younger version of my mom, a version existing as a compilation of pictures as opposed to actual memories: imaginary snapshots in the bathroom, face pale, eyes slack, razor dimpling flesh.

She wasn't in her right mind. Postpartum depression. Untreated, it could last for years. She might have gotten good at concealing her depression from my father, who had his own health concerns, and her unchecked fears and paranoia had burrowed deeper into her mind. No rational woman would reasonably suspect her husband or her young son had, even in some small way, been responsible for another child's death.

Would she? Or was I really that naive?

Steven Rush's cigarette butt dropped into my coffee. Sizzled.

Michael Munacy is a young, healthy, shy six-year-old boy. He has few friends and plays mostly by himself. He is typical as a young, slightly underdeveloped child, but he suffers occasional tantrums that are described as "startling" and "disconcerting." During these tantrums, Michael screams and screams and flails about. He is very difficult to control in such moments, though the outbursts are typically short-lived and leave Michael even more reticent than normal.

He admits to having nightmares in which "monsters chase me." He often wakes from these terrors bathed in sweat and screams himself hoarse for his parents. Mrs. Munacy believes these nightmares are caused by her husband's anger and "trauma he may have witnessed." There is nothing to support this idea, and a one-on-one conversation with Michael revealed nothing unusual about the young boy's life.

There were a few tantrums, screaming fits in which I would anchor wherever I stood—in the kitchen, my room, the driveway, the classroom, the grocery store—screaming high-pitched and indecipherable words, my face bulging redder and redder and tears popping down my cheeks. People would stare, afraid to touch me, as if I were a live wire.

I saw my fourth-grade self standing on a pile of kids' books beside a white bookcase and screaming the F-word in heedless succession so it sounded like I was mimicking spinning helicopter blades. My classmates stood back. The teacher gawked. A recess monitor approached and paused, and brought the whistle hanging around her neck to her lips and blew it as hard as she could. Little hands slapped over ears throughout the classroom. I kept on screaming until I fell down, out of breath and sobbing.

ADDITIONAL COMMENTS: This family is fairly tough on itself. They want to live up to the Rockwellian ideal. There is concern, but this therapist sees no immediate reasons for drastic treatments. Mr. Munacy must work to keep his temper in check, Mrs. Munacy must be open about her depressive tendencies, and Michael Munacy should be watched for warning signs. Other than tantrums, he appears well-adjusted. However, he should be observed carefully. His frequent nightmares may be proof he's unconsciously harboring hidden animosities toward his parents. He is not dangerous, but he admitted to playing with a lighter he found in the street. He may be likely to engage in risky behavior as he gets older.

My tiny fingers rolling the thumbwheel, as Isaac's had . . .

A strip of paper was stapled to the bottom. The note on it was typed like the rest of the document: dated December 6, 2001.

Following Ward Munacy's untimely, natural death, Mrs. Munacy and Michael visited together once more and refused further counseling. They were cautious, yet amiable enough. It is unknown how witnessing his father's death will shape Michael's psyche.

That was it.

There was a canyon-sized gap between those initial reports and the final stapled post-Ward's death note. Where were all those other files? Did they exist?

Stacked boxes and amorphous bags crowded around me. Those files could be here somewhere, hiding like mice. Or, better yet, mousetraps. Or they were locked safely in some filing cabinet at a medical center or maybe in Dr. Benson's office, if he was still around.

Suppose I contacted him, gained access to those files. What more could they tell me? I sort of remembered the office: dark-leather couch, wood-paneled walls, dim lamplight.

May be harboring hidden animosities.

Even as my mom lay dying in a hospital bed, she clung to her long-concealed suspicion. Did she die thinking Dad murdered my twin, or that I helped in some way or at least witnessed it?

Watch for warning signs.

Like what, exactly?

CHAPTER 43:
WOMAN IN THE NIGHT

SOMETHING MOVED PAST the window.

There were four windows down here—two facing Del's house and two looking out under the deck. It was complete darkness out there. The only light came from the dusty-shaded lamp close to the typewriter that cast a dim yellowy haze around me.

Nothing out there. Trick of the imagination, or maybe a deer strolled past. What else could it have been? The Dark Man come to life, to demand I finish writing his story I started in elementary school?

I chuckled uneasily, and immediately stopped. It sounded choppy, uneven, and it made me more nervous.

Nothing there.

I dropped the stapled packets into my father's box (*Remains*) and set my hand on the pages of *Dead End*, a witness swearing on the Bible to tell the whole truth.

My fingers drummed.

How should I react to what I read? Did it make any difference? A twin who died. My father's furious temper. My mother's suicidal ideations. All of which added up to what?

Nothing. They were dead, and I was what was left. It would have been better to never have read those reports. Some secrets, especially family secrets, should stay hidden, because all such things can ever do is corrupt memory, infect thought with doubt, and breed resentment.

I heard something.

A woman's face peered in through the far window. She was so close, her nose almost smushed against the glass—wide, black eyes; wrinkled, ghostly skin.

I might've screamed.

Through the window, Suzanne Summer shouted, "Wrong! *Wrong!*"

She pushed her face completely against the glass, and her nose melted into her lips and she was some fat, squished bug. Her words shook the glass in muffled distortions. "*Wrong! Wrong!*"

I was a contestant on a game show in Hell and she was the deranged host, damning my silence as an incorrect response. I stumbled out of my chair and tripped over the box. For once, I could be thankful for all the stacked boxes and heaped bags, because they caught me before I could smash my face on the floor.

Suzanne turned from the window. Her white nightgown, the same over-washed one she'd worn the other day, swept around her, a wispy wraith that slapped the glass and vanished into the dark.

Outside, the night was warm and humid. It slicked my skin like grease. Inside, it was somewhat cool, and my breath caught for a moment as I went down the front porch and headed around the side of the house. Like stepping into a sauna.

The woods stood tall and thick and completely black, shadows layered upon shadows. An owl hooted somewhere close, and mosquitoes buzzed.

"Suzanne?"

She wasn't at the window, or anywhere nearby. Had she run into the forest? Should I go after her? Would I?

I passed the windows. Yellow light glowed across the tops of boxes stacked up against the walls. One of them was labeled TOYS. Were my Matchbox cars and G.I. Joes stashed in there? What other childhood memories waited for me to unearth them, Jacks-in-the-box eager to startle me with their forgotten truths? The rocking horse watched me with its blinded eye.

The sound of pebbles crunching pulled me along the house, toward the deck that ran the house's full length.

Although the night was completely dark, I felt Mount Munacy looming. The cliff at night was huge. It towered over the house, reached into the sky. It hulked there, a living thing, a breathing thing, a terrible, monstrous, hungry thing that once consumed my father.

I stopped at the edge of the deck. Pebbles and grey stones covered the ground under here. Metal poles stood every six feet, but they were painted black, so I held my hands out to find the closest one and avoid a forehead-thunk. Gravel crunched beneath my shoes.

"Suz—"

A cold, damp hand grabbed my arm. The fingers clenched. Short, rounded fingernails dug with surprising strength.

Suzanne launched herself off the side of the house where she was hiding—like Dani pressing herself against the bedroom wall—and her mouth opened wide, and for a terrible, disbelieving moment, I thought she meant to bite my face.

"*All wrong!*" she shouted. The words scraped in a grating rasp.

I stumbled back and smacked into one of the metal poles. I brought my head forward in time to save my skull.

"*She's lost!*" Suzanne cried. Moonlight cut through clouds and shone upon half her face, bright white and ghostly.

I almost pushed her back and ran, as if Suzanne were a predator from the woods seeking victims in the night, but my hands found her bony shoulders, and I steadied my own feet.

"Suzanne," I said, calmly yet loudly enough to stop her jittering. "It's okay. I'm going to help you. Will you let me help you?"

She shook her head back and forth, but her grip eased on my arm. Her lips quivered into a gruesome grin. "She's lost." This time, her voice was soft, the words desperately sad.

"Who is lost?"

She leaned closer. Baby powder and body odor. *L'eau du elderly*. "Mable," she said. "In the woods."

"Mable?"

Her tongue, blackish-blue in the broken light, slicked her skinny lips. "The trees took her. They hide her. They're evil." Unlike Rom's mock-hysterical quoting of a similar phrase, Suzanne spoke with complete sincerity, an emphatic whisper, and that made it much scarier.

"Who is Mable?"

"It won't let her leave. I have to find her."

I shook her, just enough. "Who are you talking about?"

"My daughter."

She let go of me, pulled from my grip, and darted out into the yard. Had she run the other way, she might have scaled Mount Munacy. Would I have let her? What if she ran to the cliff? What if she fell—or jumped?

"*Suzanne!*" I shouted.

She stopped, one leg stretched behind her, and her gown fluttered as if she was a ballerina striking a pose. Shadows rippled across the trees.

"I'll help you," I said.

The moonlight blanched away her wrinkles and livened her eyes into youthful sparkles. Even her bare feet in the grass made her look younger. I might have said she was beautiful.

I reached toward her. My hand was steady.

Slowly, gradually, she took it.

CHAPTER 44:
A CRUEL JOKE

HER SKIN WAS tissue-paper soft and just as delicate. We walked across the lawn to Del's house. The thick air pushed against us, and darkness hovered close.

Del's front door opened, and he came out. His heavy sigh was a small breeze.

I waited in the kitchen while Del settled his wife in their bedroom. The kitchen was patterned in tan wallpaper, and barely big enough for a two-person table. There was not, however, a curl of ivy anywhere.

A small window over the sink looked out on the backyard, where the trees were a wall of night. From down the hall I heard whispering, the creaking of bedsprings, the flapping of sheets.

I debated simply leaving, and debated long enough that Del appeared in the doorway. "Come on," he said, and exhaled through his nose. "Let's have a drink."

Del's downstairs was spacious, hoarding-free, decorated in a brick facade with a gleaming wooden bar at the far end. A wood-carved plaque on the wall read "Del's Drinks."

He opened a bottle of Wild Turkey Rare Breed, cutting the plastic wrapping off with a small, curved blade that he folded and slipped into his pocket, and poured two bourbons neat, and we sat on black-leather stools. Mine made a thick crinkly sound.

"Thank you," he said.

We clinked glasses and sipped. The liquid burn was close to glorious, slicing my throat and cleaving my stomach.

"She moves slow, usually," Del said, "but when she wants, she can take off. Sometimes when she's hobbling along, hand on my arm, I wonder if she's playing possum. I think she's being coy, the way she used to be. Only instead of acting like she isn't interested in me, all schoolgirl cute—boy, was she ever good at that— she's faking that she's frail and the moment my guard is down, she's gone."

I'm a skilled pretender, Dani had said.

I sipped bourbon. "Is it Alzheimer's?"

"Doctors can call it whatever they want," Del said. He shifted on the bar stool, and his short-sleeve button-down pulled tight along his arms where liver spots blotched a faded three-word tattoo: SQUARE LEVEL PLUMB. "It's old age and it's madness and it's a cruel goddamn joke. That's what it is."

"I'm sorry."

I felt small and stupid sitting at Del's private bar discussing his wife while I was wearing a sweaty *Moby Dick* shirt Dani had bought me last Christmas. *Is this an erotic come-on?* I'd asked her. *I don't have any idea what you could mean,* she'd said and sauntered from me, hips swaying.

"Not your fault. I should thank you."

"It's nothing," I said like I understood.

Del slowly turned his glass of bourbon. The minute sound of the glass's bottom sliding on the wooden bar top was the distant scratch of a mouse behind wallboards.

"This is going to sound terrible," he said, "but I'm way too old to give a damn about what anyone else thinks anymore. Especially not some kid like you."

"Maybe I should go."

"You can't until you finish your drink, and, as my father used to say, you can't walk away on one leg."

"I'm not sure I—"

"You have to have two drinks, minimum. It's how a man drinks."

"Sure." I was turning my own glass now.

"I come across a bit rough," Del said, "but I'm not an idiot. You probably think I'm some curmudgeon, maybe an all-out asshole, but let me tell you something, okay? You think at whatever age you are—twenty-something, right?—that you know how things are. You don't. You don't know anything. Your father died when you were a little kid. Must've been hard, but it didn't teach you anything. It didn't teach you bad shit goes on. It *continues.* On and on. That's what life is, Mike: an endless string of bad shit. Maybe punctuated with a few laughs,if you're lucky."

"My mother just died and my future wife is suffering a nervous breakdown," I said. "I think I know about bad shit."

He raised his glass and downed the rest of his drink. I did likewise. The burn now left a metallic slick on my tongue. He poured fresh drinks and stood behind the bar. His hands gripped the lip. I smelled wood polish and something else—an unpleasant garbage-rot.

"Sometimes," he said, "I *want* her to get out."

"Your wife?"

"We have an aide during the day, weekdays, for six hours at a time, but at night it's just me. Insurance won't cover more than thirty hours a week. Cheapest rate I could find for additional help was eighteen bucks an hour. Maybe it's reasonable, I don't know, but you add that up and ask yourself if you could afford a few thousand dollars a week."

I hadn't thought about money at all. I wouldn't get another paycheck until school resumed in September, but the final check was a balloon payment, so I was flush at the moment. Even so, that amount wouldn't cover such an aide for longer than a few weeks at most. If Mom had been released from the hospital and needed an aide . . . But she was dead, and that alternate reality, for better or for worse, could never exist.

"We had a dog, years ago. Dasher. Chocolate Lab. Great dog, very affectionate. One day he was acting crazier than usual, jumping and snapping at me. He got out, ran off. I searched for days, weeks. Put up flyers. Walked these damn woods. Nothing. Never found him. Just *poof!*—gone."

"That's terrible."

"Well, maybe somebody found him and took him as their own. Maybe he lived the rest of his days with a loving family. Some nights, though, I hear a dog barking somewhere, and I wonder. I can pretend, can't I?"

"Sure."

Del grunted a single laugh. "Another one of my father's phrases comes to mind: wish in one hand, shit in the other, and see which fills up first."

"I've heard that one."

"It's truthful." He finished his second bourbon and set the glass down gently. I started to lift mine and stopped. My stomach wasn't quite ready.

"For a moment earlier," Del said, "the house was quiet and calm, and I could almost know contentment. Not happiness, but contentment. You don't understand the difference, but you will someday. You know why I was content?" He didn't wait for me to answer. "Because Suzanne slipped out the door into the night. She was gone, like Dasher. My dog was never found, but you brought my darling bride back straightaway, didn't you?"

I forced another sip. It took effort to swallow.

"You think I'm ungrateful," he said. "Maybe I am. Doesn't matter. I don't care. Life is a long parade of suffering—death will be a great relief."

"Hers or yours?" I asked.

"I'd quote my father again, but I get you don't listen well. Aren't you supposed to be a teacher?"

"Do you have a daughter?" I asked.

A crooked smile creased his old face. It reminded me of the jack-o'-lanterns I used to carve when my hands were small and unsteady.

"She was looking for Mable," he said. "Her ongoing obsession. She thinks the poor girl is hiding somewhere. Lost, maybe. I'm surprised she didn't run into the woods. Hell, maybe she'll find Dasher. What's left of him, anyway."

My question was rude, but it was late, I was tired, and Del was something of a bastard. All things considered, maybe it was okay to be impolite. He was ungrateful, and I didn't care if he believed his life was some long, torturous trek; he was a bitter fool who reveled in death fantasies. He might well think differently when Suzanne actually died. Unless he cared for his damn dog more, which seemed very possible.

"I know a few sayings of my own," I said. "Like you don't know what you have until it's gone."

Del studied his glass for a while, and I should have gotten up and left, but I stayed on the bar stool, drink in hand. Challenging him. It felt good. Like I had power.

"Having a kid is like throwing darts in the dark," Del said. "We missed the board." He chuckled, dry and sad. "She was what used to be called a mongoloid child. Trisomy 21. We couldn't take care of her, not when she was five and behaving like an infant. We did what was right. She's been a ward of the state for thirty-six years. I haven't seen her in ten."

"That's awful."

"You don't understand, and maybe you never will."

"Why don't you discard your wife, too?" My head throbbed, warm and bloated.

"Not so easy," he said as if my question were serious. "When we had Mable, times were different. Kids with those problems were never seen. They were stowed in basements or sent off to special facilities. It wasn't a money issue. It was a societal thing. The malformed. The disabled. The senile. They were dealt with. Nowadays, you can't go into a nursing home on the state's dime unless you have less than a thousand bucks to your name, and those places are shit holes. Want something better? Pay up. Can't do? Well, here's an aide for a few hours a day, you figure out the rest."

"How can you be so callous?"

"No, you're lucky. Your mother died. Imagine if she'd lived. Imagine if she was bedridden. You think you'd become some selfless hero? What if she endured, day after day, year after year? What then? You'd want her to die. You'd pray for it. Is that selfish? Callous?"

I took a breath, held it, and swallowed the rest of the bourbon. I slammed the glass on the table and stood, feeling strong, powerful, hero-like. "I don't care what you think," I said. "I know what pain is, and hurt, and I sure as hell know life can be cruel. What I don't need is a lesson from some jaded sad sack like you."

"You're still here."

Something close to a grunting cough erupted from my throat, and I flung my hand forward into the glass. It shot off the bar, and Del sidestepped fast enough for it to smack the back wall instead of his chest. The glass knocked askew a picture of an L-shaped square ruler and a compass. It hit the "Del's Drinks" plaque, and the glass fell to the floor with a solid, dull *thwunk*.

CHAPTER 45:
ADULTHOOD

I COULDN'T SLEEP.
The house quiet all around me, I saw Isaac's burned face, the skin wrinkled, black-charred and peeling. The empty eyeholes. And there was Dusty, laid out on a metal table, pink tongue fat in his small mouth, blood droplets speckling his pink nose and my mom's sagging, unhinged mouth. The dead trying to breathe.

My heart beat faster and faster until I finally threw back the sheets and sat up. Mom's face levitated before me—unmoving, slack-jawed, and dead.

I was cold, shaking, but I did nothing to stop the tremors. My heart thumped harder and harder, and my mouth tasted of sour metal, and my stomach knotted in a familiar, soon-to-be-sick way.

Watch for warning signs.

A twin. A brother who died from SIDS when he was eighteen months. Was that common? Wasn't eighteen months pretty old? Could it be a heart defect? Might I have a similar condition, a time bomb in my chest?

My brother rolled over in his crib and suffocated against his pillow or a bunched-up blanket or—

Someone suffocated him.

Ward has a temper that rivals even the most aggressive of larger men.

Dad's hand pressing the kid's face against the pillow, Dad turning away while the baby's cries were muffled and his breathing constricted until it finally ceased. Ward Munacy staring in horror.

It could have been me.

Calm down, Ward. Someone talking to my father. Someone I couldn't see, but in the memory, my father was shaking his head, his suit sleeves bunched around his elbows and shoulders. *I'm a coward*, he said. *A goddamn coward.*

Was that an actual memory? Of what?

I was six or seven. Crammed into a black suit, I wobbled my feet and watched the ceiling lights reflect on the gleamy surface of my shiny shoes.

Dad was in the other room. *Coward. A goddamn coward.*

Before me, a coffin. But whose?

I went to Mom's bedroom. The room felt bigger than before, as if my mother's permanent absence allowed it to expand.

The identical pictures of me as a newborn cradled in a blue blanket were not, it seemed, identical.

Now I saw how different they actually were. Mom wore the same blue-and-white hospital gown, perched up in the same hospital bed, her hair in the same sweaty mess, and even the angle of the shot—Dad staying in the same place while the nurse changed one baby for the next—was the same; but in one picture, Mom held the baby at a steeper angle, her elbow above her ear, so the infant's face was less hidden. Almost unnoticeable, unless you knew they were different babies.

The blanket-wrapped newborns looked so similar. Which one was me?

No way to know.

I'm the twin who lived, I thought.

A dust-free line marked where I traced my finger along the dresser. I thought of a cowboy drawing a line in the dirt. Time to choose your side, partner.

Bullshit. I shouldn't have to deal with this. It didn't make a difference if I'd once had a twin but the kid died. I was alive. Screw that kid. Screw my parents, too, for keeping the damn secret.

Was there a grave somewhere for my twin? Were his ashes in some nondescript container in a box downstairs? Maybe they were right under my nose, in any of the dozens of knickknacks cluttering this dresser.

I snatched up both pictures. The frames clacked together, and my fingers slid through their dusty sheens.

I wasn't going to deal with this. It was over, long over. What was dead should stay dead. There was far too much to worry about. Too much shit, as Del might say, and I felt it all stacking up around me.

There was my mother's funeral, and her bills, and her life insurance, and town and village and school taxes, and medical bills, and all the stuff in all those boxes downstairs, and God knew what else, and there was Dani, my beautiful bride-to-be whom I loved with all my heart, who'd gotten very sick but was apparently going to be okay because, oh yes, she was bipolar, perhaps functionally erratic, and what would it be like when she came back, how many sleepless nights ahead and endless crying fits, and sleepwalking episodes, whispering nonsense, and would I have to hide the knives and the scissors and the razorblades and any other damn thing with a sharp, metallic edge, or should I be like Del and give her off to the state, and then there was school, too, with all those needy, lazy students, their irritating parents, and the willfully ignorant administrators, and all the papers to grade for the next thirty years, and all my own damn bills and inane responsibilities and this was called **ADULTHOOD**, in tall, giant caps and bolded because, *holy shit*, if you could survive this you could survive anything, but in the end it didn't matter because it was ashes to ashes we all fall down and none of it meant a *goddamn thing*.

DEAD END

I hurled the pictures across the room.

They hit the wall above the bed and glass shattered and tiny pieces of the frames snapped off in every direction. A deep dent scored the wall.

I screamed a curse and walked out.

In the hallway, my fist punched a much better hole.

CHAPTER 46:
GARAGE TALK, PART II

I SWALLOWED THREE Tylenol in the morning. "Worship," I said to my sallow-faced reflection: bloodshot eyes sagged above puffy skin.

A shower helped, but then I was alone at the kitchen table eating cereal so slowly the milk turned to grayish mush before I realized I'd been there for almost an hour.

Outside, the day was warm but not too humid. On the cliff, all those little flags rippled behind the police tape. The cops would be back soon, no doubt, and they might bring more investigators, even top-ranked detectives. A child was dead, after all.

Suicide, accident, or murder?

Isaac standing alone on the driveway, watching us pass. Was it in his mind at that moment to ascend Mount Munacy and set himself on fire?

That sounded so insane, I refused to believe it. Had to be an accident.

A fat crow cawed at me from a white birch tree set back from the cliff. As a kid, I pretended that tree was magical—The Keeper of the Dark, I called it. So long as that tree stood, the woodsy darkness wouldn't spread beyond the tree line boundary. There was comfort in such thoughts, but of course I was an adult and could no longer entertain those silly ideas.

I thought of going downstairs to the Underwood and the manuscript waiting beside it, but I grabbed my keys and drove into town instead.

An aimless walk through the grocery store (wasn't hungry) found purpose in the beer aisle. The teenage girl working the checkout stared at me like I was some terminal cancer patient who'd wandered off the ward. "Aren't you a teacher?" she asked.

Rom was home, and when I raised the twelve-pack of Sam Adams, his smile was genuine. "Thought I'd thank you for the help with Dusty."

Bottle caps popped off and hopped across the garage floor. He gestured to the two twelve-packs. "Early for beer, no?"

"Seltzer's not going to cut it," I said.

It wasn't yet three in the afternoon and there we were, drinking beers on folding chairs in his garage on a summer day. It was something to be grateful for.

DEAD END

Mullock Road rose before us, my house perched at the top of the dead-end street. Mount Munacy loomed behind it, unseen, but I couldn't pretend it wasn't there.

"I've been thinking about your father," Rom said.

I'd updated him about almost everything: Mom, Isaac, Dani, Del. He nodded and we made casual comments about the "bitch of it all," but Rom felt it safer, I guess, to go back to familiar ground. My father had been dead a long time. It wasn't as if talking about him could make the situation worse.

"He did have a temper," Rom said. "When he was laid off from Prentice Hall, you were nine or ten, he stopped here before going home. Back of his Pontiac was crammed with boxes. All his office stuff, and all the damn books he could carry out."

"Yeah," I said, "now they're somewhere in the basement with a whole bunch of other shit."

"Your parents were never much for the feng shui life."

"I was cleaning out my room once, probably in middle school, and I threw out all these stupid pictures I drew when I was like four. Stick figure stuff. My mom went through the garbage, pulled out all those construction-paper drawings, and scolded me for throwing them away. I'm sure they're in the basement, too."

"Might find some interesting stuff."

"Already did."

He waited, but when I didn't elaborate, Rom went on with the story of my father's layoff. The last several years of his life, my father was unemployed, which no doubt exacerbated his heart condition, and the night he came home with those boxes, his car's headlights cut slashes across my bedroom ceiling, and I sneaked to the bedroom door to peer through the crack as he slumped up the steps. His trench coat sagged off him like wrinkled skin.

"Ward cursed about the ungrateful bastards for a good hour or so, and at one point grabbed a shovel and was out on my lawn swinging it around like a baseball bat. He bashed it against the ground a few times until the damn thing broke. Handle fractured in a splintery mess."

I thought of Dusty, of digging, of how cruel life could be.

You're so much like your father. "You think he might've been bipolar?" I asked.

"Ward was a good man," Rom said. "You want to know more, that's natural, but you should hold on to the memories you have. Don't try to reshape your vision of him. Let it be what it is. Whatever I say is just going to warp it."

"Little late for that advice," I said and sipped my beer. "Did you know I was a twin?"

His reaction was something of a cross between surprise and amusement. I hoped he might spit out his beer and utter some macabre warning about not digging up the past, because what's buried is meant to stay that way, and maybe he'd even warn me not to look in the crawlspace under the stairs because I might find something unpleasant.

"Sure," Rom said. "Ward mentioned it. I didn't know him at the time, remember. We weren't friends until you were several years old."

"What did he tell you?"

"SIDS."

We sat in silence, and then Rom tilted his beer toward me. "This is a terrible segue, but you and your bride-to-be planning on having children?"

My chuckle was perfectly cryptic. "Maybe. Hadn't really thought about it."

He let that obvious lie pass. "You'll make a great dad."

"Why's that?" *Watch for warning signs.* I finished my beer and opened another.

"I can tell. Ward was a good dad. He was."

I took a long slurp. "Trying to get a shine on before the funeral?"

Ned's house was quiet, perhaps empty, the yellow bus missing in action.

"Someone is responsible," I said.

"You're going to play detective?"

"You should come. We can talk to his disciples or followers or believers or whatever they are and compare notes."

"I'd rather not attend a child's funeral, but he wouldn't let me in anyway."

"Oh, right. Bad blood. Why is that?"

Rom downed a healthy gulp. "I told you Lee and I decided not to have children, but that's not the whole truth. We had a child. Baby boy. Named him David Anthony Fort. He was stillborn."

"Shit. I'm sorry."

"Lee used to go to church every Sunday. I never bothered. Didn't see the point. Her priest—Episcopal guy, friendly enough, I guess—came to the hospital. He read a few prayers, did his thing, holding my hand and Lee's, and then he looked at us and said with complete certainty: 'It is God's will.'"

It is part of God's plan, Ned said in my head.

Ned knows God's brain.

We're all in God's dream.

"I opened my mouth to tell him to screw, and Lee beat me to it. 'Fuck off,' she said." Rom laughed loud and hard and I chuckled along with him, but I couldn't laugh as hard. Did that many people really believe God had a plan, that all the bad shit in the world was His will? Every dead pet? Every dead child? Every cruel act? Every chemically unbalanced brain? Every natural disaster? Every lone gunman in a high rise? Really? Or was that belief comforting because it was too hard otherwise to reconcile with life's chaotic savageness?

"Ned and his wife would hold services on their front lawn," Rom said. "I had front row seats. It was mostly harmless, I guess, but they had a baptismal in the yard, this big bulky metal thing, and Ned would baptize people. Actually dunk their heads right in it. All ages. I saw him baptize his own kid."

"Theo," I said.

"Kid was young, not an infant, maybe two, and crying like crazy. Something about kids—they can scream and cry pretty damn loud. Must be a built-in survival mechanism. Anyway, Ned dragged the kid to the baptismal and got one of his congregants to hold the boy's legs while Ned pinioned his arms and dunked him in the water."

"You saw this?"

"Right from my front porch. I can't say he tried to drown his kid, but I can say he held the boy, face first into that water, for a lot longer than a traditional baptism requires. Ned was shouting out some prayer to God. Said something about driving out Satan. I can still hear that. His voice echoing. When they finally stopped, the kid was choking and coughing out water, but the screaming fit was over."

I saw my fourth-grade self screaming a barrage of curses while standing on a pile of books as students and teachers gawked and a monitor blew her whistle until she was red-faced, too.

"So," Rom said, and sighed. "I filed a complaint with the town and tried to have him kicked out."

"Really?"

"Oh, yeah. I claimed his behavior was 'improper and depraved.' I said he was putting people at risk, including his son. I wanted him gone."

"I can't believe you did that."

"My favorite part of the phrasing was 'Nedwin Loller's unauthorized ecclesiastical enterprises promote a prurient, immoral lifestyle.' Great, right? I'm no writer, but I'm still proud of that."

"The art of euphemistic expression," I said. "What happened?"

"A few town board meetings. Ned gave a good speech, even got a few board members to pray with him. Heads bowed and hands raised. Asking God for guidance, of course. They found no evidence of improper behavior, and that was that. Actually, a few months later, Ned's was officially granted status as a place of worship, so he doesn't pay property taxes."

"You think he promotes an immoral lifestyle?"

"His wife divorced him less than a year later." Rom shrugged and tipped down the rest of his beer. "Now a kid is dead. You're the one playing detective."

"She didn't get custody of Theo, though."

"But now you're thinking, wondering."

"You should get the Neighbor of the Year Award."

A car passed, and another. The second one pulled into the next-door driveway. Tall bushes surrounded Rom's yard to offer a sense of privacy, but there were lots of people in the area. Houses dotted either side of Heintz Hill in both directions. Even so, it was almost too easy to pretend those people didn't exist. The whole world might well be this house and the three straight ahead on Mullock.

"Your father tolerated Ned better than I ever could."

"You mean they hung out?" I asked.

Rom made an indeterminate gesture. "Maybe he thought his soul needed saving."

My father and Ned? Ward Munacy was never religious. I don't remember ever going to church save the occasional Christmas Eve; we certainly never went regularly, and God and Jesus were never mentioned unless my father was cursing.

"I want to thank you for everything," I said.

"Isn't that what the beer's for?"

"You really helped with Dusty, and all this shit I'm going through. There isn't anybody else to turn to. It's funny, you know? My parents are dead. My fiancée is in the hospital. I don't have anyone. I mean, there's a few friends from college, but they're friends you call up to hit the bar, not to wallow with in pity."

"You don't need to thank me. I'm happy to help in any way I can. We can wallow in pity all night long."

"Thanks."

"I told you not to thank me."

"Right."

It was on the edge of my tongue right then to say something about Rom being sort of like a father to me, practically a replacement, but I couldn't quite arrange the words. I thought of telling him about my just-begun manuscript, about the opening line that so clearly was referring to him: *met the man who could have been my father.* Another thought, however, tumbled right out of my mouth, as if it'd been waiting for my guard to be down.

"You actually believe every death is meaningless?" I asked.

"Was that a bit harsh? Sorry."

"Don't apologize. I've been thinking about it, and maybe you're right. In the end, no matter what sort of life you've lived or anything good or bad you've done, you end up in the same place. What's the point?"

Rom adjusted his glasses and smoothed the hair around an ear. "Well, if life were a greeting card, I'd tell you it's the memories you leave behind, and the love you give that matters. It's about little moments of joy."

"And if life's *not* a Hallmark card?"

"Then it's all one big shit show."

Lee's bell clanged from inside the house.

"I should go," I said. "Enjoy the beer. I have a funeral to attend, after all."

"Before you go," Rom said, "I could use your help."

CHAPTER 47:
HOME IS A PLACE OF DEATH

THE ROOM SMELLED strongly of antiseptic, but that was preferable to the oily body-stink gathered beneath it. The bedroom was dark, the blinds drawn against the summer sun, and a small lamp on the nightstand provided the only light.

I'd expected a hospital bed, even IV lines and a beeping heart monitor, but there was only a regular bed, a box of tissues, a commode, a collection of medicine bottles, and a silver-framed picture of Rom, Lee, and a brown-and-white beagle posing on an expanse of lush sun-blanched grass.

There was also the dying woman wilting beneath the sheets, of course.

"Honey," Rom said. He bent toward her. "I heard your bell. What is it?"

The small copper cowbell was clutched in her hand across her chest atop the comforter.

Lee was in her sixties, but she could have passed for eighty-five. Her face was sunken into her skull, her cheekbones two protruding wings. Her body was a bunch of whittled sticks beneath the sheet. Grey hair fluffed around her head in thin patches. Glazed eyes rolled across the ceiling toward Rom.

"Hi," she said, whispering it. The word crackled.

"How are you?"

A black cat peered up where it was curled beside Lee's legs.

Yellow teeth pushed from Lee's skinny, chapped lips. "Pain," she said.

"I can't give you any more meds for another two hours."

"*Hurts,*" she said.

"You remember Ward Munacy? Lived up on Mullock. His son Mike is here."

"Hi," I said, voice tight.

Her eyes were slippery, but not from tears. They looked like they were gradually melting. She was slumped sideways, head barely on the pillow, and now stretched toward Rom. He leaned closer. "Hurts," she said again.

"I know, honey."

Rom gestured for me to go around to the other side of the bed. "Help me pull her back into place."

I stood there with both hands dangling, unsure. Then he held up the end of a sheet laid between her and the one on the mattress. He told me to grab the other end and we slid the sheet up, and with it, Lee's body jilted into position: body center, head on pillow.

He caressed her face. His thumb dried a wet spot on her cheekbone. "Better?"

"Hurts," she said and sighed, exhausted.

"I'll be back, okay?"

In the hallway, the bedroom door closed but not shut, Rom turned to me. "I have things I could give her. Medicine left over from my vet days. Could speed things along. She's already on morphine, and it will do the trick, of course. I could simply double the dose. Her breathing will get shallow, she won't be able to take enough oxygen, and . . . "

I said nothing.

Outside, I could breathe again, though the medicinal odor persisted, clinging to me.

"Funny isn't the right word," Rom said, "but you get what I mean: It's funny how your home can be a place of love and hope for so many years, and then it can be a place of death, and death can be welcome."

"I get what you mean."

"Sorry," Rom said. "I shouldn't have brought you in there. I could have moved her myself. It was selfish of me."

"It's okay."

"No," he said, and touched my shoulder. "It was selfish. After what you've been through, I heap this upon you, too. I'm an asshole."

"It's fine. Really. Cool cat. Always wanted a black one."

"Nightshade, we call her. She stays in there all the time. Keeping vigil."

"I'll see you around, Rom."

I started to go, but he stopped me.

"You wondered if there's some purpose to all this, some reason why we go through one bad thing after another. I don't know, Mike. I don't. But the cat, she's twelve. Getting up there. We used to have a lot of animals—cats and dogs and bunnies and a couple of turtles, even a ferret for a little while—but as they gradually passed, I couldn't bring myself to adopt new ones. I think about all the love invested in each of those animals. I think of all the animals I ever treated. All the ones I put down. I think about your mother's cat. All that love, and what do you get for it? A hole in the ground? A bunch of memories? I'm not sure it's worth it."

I didn't know what to say, or if I should try to leave again. Rom was thinking of something, considering. "I'm sorry."

"Forget it."

"No, I'm sorry I joked how you moving back home made all this shit happen."

"It was a joke, I know."

"You didn't cause it. Life did."

"Maybe I am evil," I said, "and I don't know it yet."

"Your father believed in curses."

I couldn't stop my eyebrow creeping up my forehead.

"Mullock Road." He pointed at the sign. "Google it. The spelling is different, but Ward thought there was something to it." Rom looked around, and it was so desperately sad—a lonely man with nothing to do but wait for his wife to die, and no one to talk to about it. He sighed. "Don't bother Googling it."

"Okay."

"Your father thought the name was a misspelling of a demon's name."

"Really?"

"It's not. It's named after an Indian tribe, part of the Lenapes, who lived in the Hudson Valley. The tribe broke into smaller groups when the white man tried to push them away. One group was the Mul Lok, see?"

"My father didn't know?"

"He knew."

"But you said—"

"I've read some town history—retired people will do most anything to stave off reality, and daytime TV is enough to make you consider suicide—and there isn't much about the Indians, but apparently the Mul Lok lived in the woods around here. What made them unique, the reason they broke off from the bigger Lenape tribe, was their belief that death was temporary."

"Like reincarnation?"

"Meaning they believed the dead could rise again. The body would be imbued with a new soul and live again. Like zombies coming to eat your brains."

"Your reading offer any tips on performing such a ritual?"

He smiled, sad and wan-faced. "Sadly, no." He stared past me up the hill. "If there was something to it, Ward believed that hill behind your house was the perfect place for a ritual like that."

"Reverend Ned would agree," I said.

"The name, though—Mul Lok, not Mullock—was what the Lenapes called the creature living in the woods. They worshipped it. They named themselves after it."

Was he putting me on? Making this up as he went along? "A creature? Like a coyote?"

"Like supernatural. Probably big, scary. Most Native American cultures believed in similar things. The Navajo believed in skinwalkers, shapeshifters who disguised themselves as deformed animals. Others feared the Wendigo, an ancient monster that if you even looked at it, would drive you insane. Turn you into a cannibal."

"A cannibal, huh? Okay. So, what's *this* supernatural creature doing?"

"Waiting. Lurking."

"For what?"

"To eat dead souls."

"Eat dead souls?"

"When a body takes on a new soul, the old one is sacrificed. It dies and cannot rise, because the body still lives. I can believe that. Or, at least, that the Lenapes believed it."

"Sure," I said, "and the creature must exist, because otherwise all these dead souls would be polluting the environment. Puts global warming to shame."

Rom was appraising his hands as if reading a secret message. "The real problem is, where are these new souls coming from? I didn't find any answers, though I have a theory."

"Angels dropping from Heaven?"

"Try the other direction." He pointed between his feet. "Suppose the Lenapes perform their life ritual and it summons many spirits fighting to return to physical form. Only one can get into the corpse, presumably. Then the Mul Lok hunts down the stray souls."

"And eats them?"

"Right. So, I wonder: what if some souls escape?"

"One could be watching us right now," I said.

"Could be. Searching for a new body to inhabit. Circling like a vulture."

"You should've taken up golf instead," I said. Though he sounded sincere, almost maudlin, I wondered if this was an elaborate joke. Rom enjoyed horror, after all, *Night of the Living Dead*-type stuff, and if that love for the macabre was as deep as my father's, it wouldn't be unlikely for Rom to try to spook me. Dad had done it with a two-headed mask and a movie about a serial killer. Maybe Rom was reading *Pet Sematary* as well. We could have a book club.

Or maybe he wasn't lying; it was just that some myths really were horror stories.

Rom raised a hand in a silent toast. "You believe souls exist?"

"Should I?"

"Personally, I'm thinking death should be the end and we should be grateful."

CHAPTER 48:
GOOGLING A DEMON

I GOOGLED. The Lenapes had once populated this area of the East Coast, but there was no mention of a faction called the Mul Lok.

That word, as well as Mullock, brought up nothing, but Google suggested I try "MOLOCH," and my screen filled with the picture of a demon.

It was a drawing of a giant bronze statue in the shape of a man with the head of a bull, horns curving up toward the sky. Seven chambers were carved into the creature's chest, stacked one-three-two-one, and a large hole at the base of the statue resembled a tunnel underpass.

It wasn't.

Fire raged inside the bottom opening, and inside those seven chambers people's faces were contorted in anguished screams. Desperate and agonized, those people stretched their arms around prison bars and howled for help or mercy or a quick death.

I couldn't make sense of the liturgical terms on Wikipedia, but the gist was simple: Moloch was a demon that demanded human sacrifice.

Another drawing showed hundreds of people bowing before a Moloch statue while a robed priest offered a squirming infant to the demon's fire. In the background, a dozen trumpeters played their instruments toward the darkened sky, and tucked into the foreground near the statue's base, a young boy was on his knees, his hands slapped over his horrified, weeping face.

Wrong, wrong.

My father's face angled toward me in the bathroom mirror, blood squeezing from scissor wounds: *You have to be careful. It might be in the blood. The bad things come back.*

I was in the office across from Mom's bedroom, and I'd cut a path through the clutter of Amazon boxes and shopping bags to get to the computer. This room hadn't always been the office, however. It was the nursery at one time, and my brother and I had slept in here.

Was I sleeping as my twin's heart stopped?

Was it my father's hand clutched over an infant's mouth?

Moloch demands a sacrifice.

CHAPTER 49:
DENIED IN HEAVEN

THE YELLOW BUS was back, and a hearse now joined it, the driveway blocked.

My dress shoes clacked against the concrete. In the woods, a squirrel chittered in its huffing, unnerving way and scurried through the underbrush. Crows cawed from the woods. I adjusted my tie. The collar was already wet with sweat.

The day quieted to silence.

I was alone. Mullock (*Moloch? Mul Lok?*) Road was deserted. If it were dark out, I might have gotten the creeps a little. Sounds childish, but I did have the creeps a bit, even with the overcast yet completely lit day. In my defense, I had a lot of macabre shit on my mind, not to mention I was headed to a child's funeral.

If the day comes when the unnaturally quiet street or the mysterious creak of stairs don't make your skin prickle and tighten, that's the moment you've forgotten that bad things exist. There *is* evil in the world. Good people go crazy. Children die. Monsters are real.

The hearse's windows distorted my face into an oblong blob. I might have stood beside it and simply rocked from one foot to the next and watched my reflection warp and re-warp. It was preferable to what waited for me only a few feet away.

Coward. Goddamn coward.

I glanced across to Rom's house, expecting to see him standing there, beer in hand, giving me a "go get 'em" wave, but no one was around. He was tending to his wife, his house now a way station for death.

It could have been the same with my mom—regardless of what an asshole Del was, he was right about that much. I should be thankful she'd succumbed so rapidly. Death can be welcome, and waiting for the inevitable is a particular sort of hell, so I hoped Rom would find peace soon, knowing that what I was really hoping for was Lee Fort's death.

I was looking for any reason to delay my arrival, so it was no surprise the back of the DEAD END sign caught my eye. The faded graffiti formed into words, and it was like an optical illusion revealing its double nature.

DEAD END

ONLY COWARDS HERE

Life has echoes.

I stood there a minute, expecting the words to reform into something else: an answer from beyond the grave, perhaps. I sensed possibility, a thing pushing inside my mind, an answer, an explanation, a reason, but nothing happened. You cannot force an epiphany.

I walked up Ned's driveway to the white door with the painted gold cross.

The door was centered in the middle of what was once a single-car garage. Above the door, in black letters, it read: **Whoever Denies Me Before Others Is Also Denied In Heaven**.

Did the "me" mean God or Ned?

My hand floated above the gold knob. I wanted music beyond the door: a loud organ, or a rollicking choir in the midst of full-throated lamentations, anything to conceal the noise of my entrance. I turned the knob and attended church for the first time in years.

CHAPTER 50:
THE GOSPEL ACCORDING TO NED

HANGING LANTERN LIGHTS cast fragmented polygons on pictures of Jesus carrying His cross closer and closer to the site of crucifixion—these pictures hung on the walls leading to the altar, where a nearly life-sized Jesus dangled on His cross from the ceiling. If you looked quickly, you'd think it was someone's hanging suicide.

Ned stood before the altar, beneath that Jesus, and behind the small white coffin. A bouquet of white roses was set on top, the green stems incredibly vivid. As green as the grass surrounding my father's shaking fingers.

Bulging extra-large in a draped orange cassock, Ned stretched out his arms and each of his chubby fingers. I expected him to make a grand statement about life and death and God or, at the very least, reassure us mourners that while we might not understand God's will, He has a plan, oh yes indeed, and this time it happens to involve a child's death by immolation, but please don't let such a little detail waver your faith, because the man upstairs knows what He's doing.

Ned sighed heavily: his arms fell, his head bowed, and he stood there staring down at Isaac's coffin. A white sheet concealed the metal bier beneath.

The mortician stood to my right. His suit was crisp and grey, his face powdered like he was about to go on TV. He was young, too, maybe thirty, or even closer to my age, and that seemed wrong. A mortician should be old, tall, and gangly, and free of powdery makeup.

Warren Barlow, who actually looked as a mortician should, was seated to the right in one of the six cherrywood pews. Logan French had swapped, or at least covered, his Jesus t-shirt for a traditional suit, though Steven Rush kept his flannel and simply added a clashing black tie.

Nina Calla sat in the front right pew, with Ned's son beside her. He wore the same long white robe he wore the morning I watched these sun-kissed disciples ascend Mount Munacy. It draped him, a little boy in a bed sheet.

Opposite them was Edgar Press, the skinny black man whose presence felt even more odd, probably because of his blackness, and behind him was Wes, the curly-haired bus driver who'd killed Dusty. He shifted, and his weathered blue chambray shirt pulled tight across his shoulders.

Ned kept staring, and the awkwardness mounted. Did he not know what to say? Was this going to be me in a few days, standing speechless before my mother's casket? Well, no, because there wasn't going to be a coffin, just a simple box urn containing her ashes. Me stupefied to silence, though? Yeah, I could see that.

No music, no speaking. The sounds of breathing gathered into a collective inhale/exhale, like the room itself was alive. I smelled cologne and mustiness and sulfur.

I looked around, anywhere but at Ned or Nina, who sat back-stiff, mannequin-solid. The space was no bigger than my mom's garage, but the white walls and bright blue-painted ceiling expanded the room, except Ned's enormity shrank it back down and the child-sized coffin condensed it even more.

Ned placed his hand on the coffin beside the white roses. For a terrible moment, I thought the weight of his hand would tip the casket. The coffin would hit the floor with a hard crack and the lid would burst open and out would tumble Isaac's burned corpse, or maybe, and somehow worse, a suit-sleeved arm would hop into the space between lid and base, the blackened hand—or if we were lucky, the unscathed one—jamming it open. Nina would faint. Ned's jaw would drop in a taffy-stretch of shock.

Worship.

That Grand Guignol spectacle didn't happen, but it existed in my mind (*heavy with life*) just the same. That's the way it is with all horrible thoughts: they're real, even if they're not.

"In the Bible," Ned said, slowly, softly, "there is the story of Abraham and his son Isaac. They were good, devout followers of God's way. Chosen people. God spoke to Abraham, telling him to take his son Isaac up the Mountain of Moriah and offer him for a sacrifice."

I sat in the pew all the way in the back, nearest the door, but even so, Ned and the coffin were only a few feet away. I shouldn't have come here. Being here felt like an admission of guilt, or like I was some sicko who got off watching people grieve.

"Abraham did not beg God to rescind this request. He knew the Lord's power and might. So he and Isaac ventured up Mount Moriah. As they ascended, Isaac asked his father where the lamb was they would sacrifice. Abraham smiled at his son, placed a gentle hand on the boy's head, and said, 'God will provide.'"

The room felt hot. Sweat ringed my collar and dampened my armpits. The pew creaked, and I forced myself to be still.

"But when they reached the top, there was still no lamb to sacrifice, and after Isaac gathered dried sticks, Abraham built an altar, and Isaac asked again what they were meant to offer God."

Ned's hand caressed the coffin. "Abraham touched his son's head. 'You,' he said. 'God demands it.' And before the boy could resist or run, Abraham grabbed him and bound him with thick ropes to the altar. He lifted his knife, and from the sky boomed the voice of God. *'Here I am,'* God declared. 'Do not lay a hand on your son, for now I know you fear God. You did not withhold your son, your *only* son, from me, and so I will show you mercy.' Abraham spotted a ram caught in the brush. He promptly sacrificed the animal in thanksgiving for God's mercy."

Ned's hand slid off the coffin. No one moved, not a shift in the seat or an arm scratch or a raised hand to catch a gentle cough.

"God is bigger than everything. God is the world. He is the Word. He is the way. He is the answer to all."

Another dramatic pause, and Ned's tone softened. "Imagine the horror," he said, and finally looked at the congregation. "The terror. For father and son. They must have been so frightened, yet Abraham did not turn from God's command. The Bible does not tell us how Isaac reacted to his father binding him to the altar and raising a knife above him, but it is not much to imagine that while Isaac might have been so dreadfully scared, he might have known God's reassuring presence while his father's hand trembled and the blade shook. With the sky so close above, Isaac glimpsed the face of God and knew, regardless of outcome, he would be saved."

Ned sidled around the coffin toward the first pew, where Nina sat.

"Now," he said, his voice rising along a vocal scale from baritone toward alto. "Imagine the relief when God's voice boomed from above. The gratitude. God's mercy. We cannot possibly fathom such a thing, if we have not yet experienced it. *Salvation.*

"To be saved by God. Glorious, yes? Now, I could stand here beside this coffin and remind you how lucky each of you is. God has saved you, yes? He has shone His holy light into each of your hearts. This is true—but to stand here and say such a thing is not only insulting, it is degrading."

He paused.

"I do not mean to us." He raised a hand and curled his fingers, so only the pointer remained. "I do not mean our lovely Nina, either. Hers is a terrible pain, and I cannot pretend to offer balm for her injury. It may never heal.

"No, when I say 'degrading,' I mean toward God. We may hate Him right now, oh yes indeed, but it is His will."

A burble of laughter threatened in my throat. I bit down hard on my tongue. Ned stared at me, and the mortician behind me cleared his throat.

He'd caught me off guard. I'd imagined before this started that Ned would say something of God's plan, but when he spoke he was far more sensitive and insightful. My prejudiced expectations crumbled around me, and I nodded when he mentioned how Nina's pain might never heal. Then he fell back on the whole "it's God's will" bullshit believers use when earthquakes kill thousands or a gunman slaughters dozens of school children or the doctor's scan for cancer comes back positive.

Or a father dies.

It is part of God's plan, Ned told me only a day after my father died. *I can promise Ward entrance into Heaven if I baptize you into my church.*

Now, Ned smiled in a terribly sad and uncomfortable way, all that fat folded in wrinkles and bloomed rouge smudges.

Keep yourself in check, I told myself. *You're here to find out who killed that boy.*

Officer Koryta might be quite surprised to learn I'd jumped into freelance private investigation, but I knew this much was true: if Isaac hadn't killed himself (on purpose or accidentally), then someone in this room *must* be the killer.

And if it was suicide?

"GOD," Ned said in a booming voice, "advises He is the resurrection and the life. He who believes in Him, though he die, yet shall he live, and whoever lives and believes in God shall never die!"

Ned took a breath and, beneath his cassock, his weight drooped. He'd screamed those words, shouting them in fanatical confidence, but no one flinched. They were too numbed by Isaac's death, or too used to Ned's deafening proclamations.

Or too brainwashed.

"We must take comfort in this," he said in almost a whisper. "Impossible though it seems."

Light fractured off the large cross on his chest. I squinted against the glare.

"Isaac was a wonderful boy. He was truly one of God's gifts. We each of us benefited from that gift. In his absence now, we are left to question God's will. Why would He do this? Why be so cruel?

"Abraham did not question when God told him to take his son up the mountain and offer him as sacrifice. He would have done anything God demanded. Such is the essence of faith. It isn't simple belief—it is unwavering acquiescence."

Or complete stupidity, I thought.

Ned stopped. He was staring at me. "The Church of Jesus Christ the Empowered is a humble church. We are few, but we are adamant, zealous even, in our faith. Let us now pledge our un-flailing devotion."

Everyone rose. I awkwardly joined them. Had he said *un-flailing*? He was one step away from Jonathan Edwards and some good old-fashioned Puritan fire-and-brimstone preaching.

Ned began to recite a prayer and the others picked it up immediately, so everyone spoke in the same steady-paced monotone. Less Jonathan Edwards and more creepy cult: "We are the church. We are the lovers of Christ, He who is empowered and empowers us. We believe in one god, *THE* God, and never question His right, power, or will."

It went on like that.

I stared at the white coffin. It blurred, floated. There was a dead kid inside that thing, an actual child, burned to death. Or maybe he'd been lucky enough to die before the fire. Perhaps murder and then fire was a preferable truth. I hoped his death was quick. Painless.

Mullock Road was cursed.

This idea was not startling or ridiculous, not surprising or dismissible. With Ned standing huge before a child's white coffin, I knew it to be true—the road where I grew up was cursed.

This didn't mean there were evil supernatural powers orchestrating each private misery. There wasn't some grand (*Guignol*) scheme that put Isaac on Mount (*Moriah*) Munacy with lighter fluid in one hand and a silver Zippo in the other. There was no ghost that infected my mom's heart with congestive failure or crippled her kidneys, no spectre clouding Suzanne's addled mind, no sadistic wraith coaxing Lee's cancer to spread—and there was no demonic presence working the strings when Dani attacked me with scissors or tried to run into the woods.

Yet Mullock *was* cursed.

In the end, did it matter?

Every death is meaningless.

"Michael," Ned said, startling me from my thoughts. Perhaps saving me. "Would you be kind enough to join me up here?"

I opened my mouth and produced only a dry crack of sound.

He gestured. "Please."

When I still did not move, the others turned to look—faces one after the other like dominos falling, and the last pair of accusing eyes belonged to Nina Calla.

How dare you sit there, she seemed to be thinking, *while my son is dead in that box.* I got up.

The walk was only twenty feet or so, if that, but I took it slowly, and all those faces lengthened the distance, so I might've walked for hours.

Ned's hand engulfed my shoulder. His palm was hot and sweaty. Behind him, a white cloth covering the altar made it a magician's table. A gold chalice sat in the middle. Above and almost touching, the hanging Jesus' feet swayed ever so slightly. I felt the coffin there, a heavy thing, a terrible thing, and eventually could no longer ignore it.

Beside Nina, Theo Loller watched me with fascination and something close to envy. Or jealousy. If he wanted to come up here in my place, he was more than welcome.

Coward.

"Are you a man of faith?" Ned asked.

"Faith?"

His small white teeth gleamed inside his bulbous smile.

"I believe in God," I said.

"Well, yes. You are not a heathen. But I'm asking about faith. We are all people of faith here. Deep, deep faith. It scars our souls."

I waited for him to correct himself, but he didn't. He'd meant to say faith *scars* people's souls.

"Yes," I said, because I had no idea what to say.

The room closed around me. The air thickened. Heat flushed through my chest. "So you are a man of faith?"

"Yes."

"Excellent." His sweaty hand gripped harder. "Your mother spoke highly of you. A mother's love for her son is nothing short of God's love for His son. Steadfast, bottomless, and fierce."

"Yes." The word barely sounded. My mother's dead face, her jaw hanging slack.

"We would very much like you to join us."

"Join you?" I swallowed. My throat felt tight.

"Can I tell you a story, Mike?"

I didn't respond. The room closed in, the other people now only inches from me. They stared, unblinking, mouths closed, lips perfectly rigid. They were lock-step followers, the Kool-Aid drinkers in Jonestown, the black-sneakered Heaven's Gaters.

"Isaac was a lovely boy," Ned said. "Beautiful, in fact. He loved God with a ferociousness I envy. He did not suffer doubts. He believed. He was faith itself. He loved that hill behind your mother's house. When we prayed up there, his was the most contented face. His death is a painful, terrible loss for us, but it is a grand, glorious event for God. And for Isaac. He now revels in the glory of Heaven.

"The cliff is sacred now. Whatever the reason, God chose that place for Isaac's ascension. We cannot guess at God's will. We must simply acknowledge it, and obey."

Fire *FFFooomped!* along Isaac's arm, and his face stretched into a horrified howl.

"Will you join us in declaration?"

The salty taste of blood filled my mouth. Had I bitten my cheek? What was he asking, exactly? Did I want to be one of Ned's sun-kissed believers? "I'm not much of a . . . congregant."

Ned's laughter burst out so powerfully I stumbled backwards. I bumped into the coffin and in my head, the casket tipped, fell, cracked open with a wooden snap, and Isaac rolled across the floor to smack into the first pew, where Nina stared down in blank shock.

"Will you pledge your faith with us?" Ned asked. His other hand came up and clapped my other shoulder.

What choice did I have?

CHRIS DILEO

"I will," I said.
"May God bless you."
Then Reverend Ned kissed my forehead.

CHAPTER 51:
ONLY COWARDS HERE

THE MUSHY FEEL of Ned's wet lips was still on my skin twenty minutes later when the service ended, and Ned led the recessional outside.

The coffin was loaded into the hearse.

Down on Heintz, Rom was watching from his open garage door, beer in hand as I imagined earlier. Ned's service featured redundant prayers but no Communion, so alas, no wine.

It ended with Ned wishing, "The peace of the Lord be with you," and everyone responding, "And also with you." With resigned practice, people hugged one another. They even hugged me, and I was too polite (or too coward) to refuse. Steven Rush stank of cigarettes. Edgar smelled like wood polish, and Nina was stick-thin and fragile in my loose grip. I couldn't even find the words to tell her I was sorry for her loss.

We watched from the driveway while the small white coffin disappeared into the back of the black hearse. The rear door clanked shut with metallic finality.

Nina choked a sob, turned, and Ned cushioned her in his arms. She cried freely, and none of us moved. Somewhere far off in the woods, birds tweeted and cawed, and farther off, maybe well down Heintz Hill, children were laughing. It sounded so joyful and completely awful.

The hearse rolled slowly to the DEAD END sign—*Only Cowards Here*—and turned right on Heintz and drove away. Its waxy sheen reflected distorted smears of the three houses on Mullock.

I wanted to run up the hill to my home, but I stayed where I was. If none of it mattered, it should be easy to leave, and though inside the tiny church I was sure every death was meaningless, I now felt otherwise. Something about the hearse door closing and the wobbly reflection of the houses across the door reminded me why I was here: life was blurry, a distorted mess of what we wanted it to be, and somehow we had to navigate our way through it.

Had to find truth and meaning.

A child was dead, and I needed to somehow make things better.

The tableau on the driveway confirmed my basic suspicions: everyone was congregated near Ned and Nina, except Steven Rush, who tucked a cigarette into his mouth and stepped onto the side lawn. He lit it too quickly for me to see if he used a Zippo.

I approached and a strange, amused grin tweaked the corner of his mouth. "You can't resist, can you?"

"What?" I asked.

"Playing detective. It's why you agreed to come here. You don't care about Isaac."

"I know why I was invited," I said, staring him dead-on. "You think I'm responsible. You're the one playing detective. Did you hope I'd break down during the funeral and confess?"

He dragged on his cigarette. His face was pock-marked from long-ago acne. "You called us deluded morons. And here you are."

Behind us, Ned said, "Let us go inside and break bread." He held Nina's hand and led her up the front walkway toward the door. Edgar, Logan, and Warren followed.

Wes and Theo stood talking near the church door. The bus driver saw me and nodded. I hadn't hugged him, but he hadn't tried to hug me either. He knew. Knew Dusty was my cat. Rage seized me, and I fought the urge to charge him, knock him to the concrete, and smash his skull against it. That might make me feel better.

You're so much like your father.

"How's your wife?" Steven asked.

"Tell me why."

"Why I asked about your wife?"

"Why you're here. Why are you part of Ned's little church? There's only a half dozen of you, so what's the point? He spent money to build a church in his garage, he doesn't pay property taxes, yet it's only the few of you. Why?"

"This is a retreat. I believe Ned told you that, didn't he? You think because we're a small group, we're a cult, right? Ned isn't a pastor in the traditional sense, but he isn't a cult leader, either. He isn't out to peddle falsehoods in exchange for donations. He isn't a proselytizing crook. He's after something bigger."

"What?"

"Truth."

"Cute," I said. "What makes you certain I'm to blame for what happened?"

"I'm not certain. Why are you?"

"I don't trust any of you," I said. "I'm not certain about any of this, but I am certain something *unseemly* is happening here. I want to know why a child is dead."

"Unseemly, huh? I had a teacher like you back in school. Smart guy, and a smartass, too. Pompous. Thought he was so much better than the rest of us. Used big words to make us feel stupid. Got his rocks off making us feel small."

"'Unseemly' isn't exactly a big word."

170

"See? You're that teacher."

"You said 'dead kids live forever.' You were talking about Heaven."

"Isaac," he said, musing, "is at peace now. It must have been so awful for him, so scary, but he's free now—and safe."

"In a better place," I added.

"I get it," Steven said, "you're trying to be proactive. You're here because if you can help figure out what happened to Isaac then, in some way, you've made a difference and brought a little order to the chaos of life. Right?"

It pissed me off that my motivations were so nakedly obvious.

"It's all Ned's trying to do, too. You might not want to believe it, but his church, this retreat, it's all an act of defiance against a chaotic world."

"Religion only confuses the facts."

Another long drag. He squinted against the exhale of smoke. "You're so confident, aren't you?"

"I'm not the pompous one," I said. "I'm searching for meaning and you're picking a fight."

I turned and headed up the walkway to Ned's front door. Wes and Theo had already gone inside. I went right in.

My hands balled into fists.

CHAPTER 52:
GOD'S DREAM

THE INSIDE OF Ned's home was strikingly similar to my own, except everything was reversed. The stairs led to the left instead of the right, the kitchen was opposite the bathroom instead of up against it, and the glass door to the deck opened from the dining room, not the kitchen. It was like being in an alternate reality version of my house where everything was slightly off, yet recognizable.

Logan French accosted me so quickly I thought he was going to tackle me, and I raised my hands as if to punch him. He didn't flinch, just grabbed my arm and pulled me toward a china cabinet, where crucifixes of all different styles lined glass shelves. His tie sagged loose from his collar and swayed as words spilled from him in a faucet torrent.

"What did Steven say to you? Steven. What did he say to you? I saw you two talking." While he spoke, Logan glanced around me toward the stairs and the front door beyond, again and again. "Well?"

"I'm not sure what you're—"

He leaned close. He smelled of baby powder. "Steven doesn't trust you. Doesn't like you." Logan's accompanying smile was out of place, another mask-smile. "He thinks you're responsible. That's the only reason you're here. He convinced Ned to invite you."

"I didn't do anything," I said.

"Ned has a saying. 'In God's dream, we all gleam.'"

A line from my father's story returned to me: *Dreams, they say, are true.* Dryden, the old poet. Another life echo. "What?" I said.

He started to say something, and the front door opened with a suction-pop. Steven entered.

"A heads up, that's all," Logan said. He crossed the kitchen so fast he might have been wearing skates. He joined the others gathered around a table, where a six-foot sub sat uncut.

"It's funny," someone next to me said.

Theo Loller, now in typical-teen t-shirt and jeans, had come down the hall from his bedroom without making a sound. His lanky arms dangled at his sides. The white v-neck pulled tight across a muscle-less chest.

DEAD END

"What's that?" I asked.

"Everyone is starving and afraid to eat."

"Being polite, I guess."

"So, what did you think?"

"Of?"

"The service. My dad's church."

"Interesting."

"I'm sorry he made you get up in front of everyone. He can be overbearing."

Rom's voice in my head: *Ned's probably molesting him.* "It's okay," I said.

"It's awful, is what it is."

"No, it's fine."

"I mean," he said, "Isaac. *Awful.*"

"Oh. Right."

Theo was fifteen—attractive, if a bit scrawny (though probably preferable to taking after Daddy's gigantism)—but he spoke with an assuredness and ease beyond his years. I dealt with teenagers every day during the school year, and some were more mature than others (previously home-schooled kids were the most mature), but Theo, who must be home-schooled, surpassed even those kids. Here was a well-adjusted, intelligent young man who happened to have a father who'd consecrated his garage into a church. Was it success against all odds, or were my prejudiced expectations slapping me in the face yet again?

"I'm sorry you got dragged into this," Theo said. "Considering what you've been through with your mother and now your wife. She's sick, isn't she?"

"Doing better, actually."

"Good."

"Yes, it is."

Steven, standing at the top of the stairs, nodded at me, or maybe at Theo, and joined the sandwich crowd, where Edgar took up the knife and dared to make the first cut.

"He doesn't like you, in case you haven't noticed."

"I've noticed. Been warned about it, too."

"Logan, right?"

"Right."

"When these groups come through, they always start out as blanks, you know, and then they quickly take on personalities, and after a few days, I know them quite well."

I smiled. The kid had said "quite." Whoever said that word, except highfalutin professors at cocktail parties? Home-schooled children of self-anointed preachers, it seemed.

"Should I leave you alone?" Theo asked.

"No, no. Sorry. I was thinking."

"Confessing?"

I stared at him.

"Joking," he said.

"Right."

"You don't have to stay. You don't have to let us use that hill, either. My dad wants this street to be one big church. A commune. He'll probably ask if you want to sell your mother's house."

"Mount Munacy."

"Excuse me?"

"The hill behind my house. It's what I used to call it when I was a little kid. You only just met these people?"

"Steven has been here before. This might be his fourth retreat. The others are new, though."

"Including Nina and Isaac?" I asked.

"She was in a shelter."

"Homeless?"

Theo lowered his voice. "Abused. Her husband is an alcoholic. She and Isaac have been staying with us a while."

"Shouldn't he know about Isaac?"

"We invited him." Theo tilted his head and shrugged in a "we tried" gesture.

"What about your bus driver?"

"Wes. He picks everyone up. We've had as many as twenty people at a retreat."

"Did you see Wes hit a cat in the street?"

Theo studied me. A red zit flamed on his right temple. "It was yours, wasn't it?"

"Yes."

"I'm very sorry." He touched my arm. His maturity startled me again. Most adults wouldn't act this compassionately. Was it faith that matured him or—I couldn't help thinking—was this his schtick, a well-oiled routine? Learned and honed from watching Daddy. A skilled pretender. "It was a complete accident."

"He could have stopped."

"The cat darted across the road. Terrible."

"For who—Wes or my cat?"

"I know you're upset. I'm sorry. If you want, I'll get Wes and he can tell you about it."

My fingers crimped into my palms. "Better not."

"I am sorry."

"Rom Fort saw it happen."

"His wife is dying."

My mouth opened and closed. I didn't need this fifteen-year-old kid to clarify his meaning. Rom's wife was dying (*it hurts*), and that must be screwing with Rom's head. A thing like that could corrupt how someone viewed everyday events. My mother had just died, and Dani was undergoing psychological treatment, and my own mind felt like a gelatinous mass floating in cerebrospinal fluid, which of course was exactly what it was.

I wanted answers because I needed permanence. I needed things to be nailed down, or at least tethered to something solid. Blame would work. Wes had killed Dusty. It was all his fault. He was the enemy. That would help keep things grounded. It would help even more if his guilt were the product of cruelty.

"I don't believe the cat had to die," I said.

"And I don't believe Isaac had to die," Theo said.

"You think it was suicide?"

"Or his father. They lived in Poughkeepsie, not far. Might have been easy to find her, track her down. Alcoholic rage."

"Kill his own kid?"

"Suicide by fire is just as extreme."

"Do the police know about this man?"

"Of course." He shook his head and reached into his jeans pocket and removed a folded piece of paper. It was a picture printed off the Internet of three men standing shoulder to shoulder. Black Sharpie circled the man in the middle. He was smiling, but his eyes weren't in on it—he had a cold, steely expression, the look of a man who never shows vulnerability. "Isaac's father, Bud Calla."

"Bud?"

"Nickname. William Calla. Goes by Billy or Bud."

"You think he killed his own son?"

"I think he might be creeping in the woods right now, watching us. He's unstable."

"Who're the other guys?"

In the picture, the three men sagged together in rumbled jeans and stained Carhartt sweatshirts. Isaac's father was smirking with the arrogance of indifference.

"AA buddies."

"So, because he's an alcoholic, you think . . . "

"Because he was abusive, dangerous, and unstable."

"Seems like a reach," I said.

"Because no father has ever committed prolicide before?"

"Prolicide?"

"Instead you suspect us?"

"I didn't say—"

"Be skeptical," Theo said. "Even the Bible encourages healthy skepticism, but it's frustrating how people like you always think people like us are hiding terrible secrets. Think we're up to devious, awful things. We want to find out what happened to Isaac as much as you do. More, actually. You didn't know him. We did."

I felt chastised, and fresh anger surged through me, but it tamped down quickly. He was right. Simple as that. A young boy was dead. Maybe suicide. Maybe murder. These people were not followers of Moloch the Demon, who demanded a fire sacrifice. These people might be a bit deluded, a tad inculcated, but they weren't doing anything suspicious. Not unless praying to an invisible spirit in the sky was questionable. "I'm sorry, I . . . "

"Maybe you should go," Theo said.

CHAPTER 53:
THE GOSPEL ACCORDING TO NED, AGAIN

NED STOPPED ME before I reached the driveway.

"We didn't scare you away, I hope," he said. He loomed huge above me on the porch. He blocked the entire doorway, a moon eclipsing the sun. "It meant a great deal you were here."

I was sweaty and uncomfortable, and my head hurt. I wasn't going to say anything, just nod, even wave, and walk away, but there was too much inside me, and like heavy waters rising against a weakening levee, I was helpless to stop the flood.

"I'm going to give you one chance," I said. "A lot of bad shit has happened recently. It can't be coincidence, right? There has to be something else going on. *Has* to be. Do you believe God is responsible? Because if you do, if you genuinely believe it is *God's fault*, then I'll accept that, and at least I can target my anger. I need somewhere to put it. Something to throw it at. So tell me. Do I get to throw it at God?"

He considered, perhaps even thought of turning around and going back inside where no one was going to try to eviscerate belief with a blunt scalpel.

He thumped down the steps.

"Do you know what an apostate is?" he asked.

"No."

"It is someone who acknowledges God is real, and then willfully, knowingly, turns his back on God, religion, and faith. It is far worse than an agnostic or even an atheist, both of whom may be forgiven. The apostate, however, openly, even pridefully, chooses to ignore truth."

"Assuming there is a truth," I said.

Ned grabbed the railing to help him down the last step. One day he'd need a cane, or even a wheelchair—assuming he lived that long.

"Why do bad things happen?" he asked. "Why do people die? You've experienced a fair amount of death in your life, haven't you, Mike? A man's first symbol of God's might is his father. His first symbol of God's love is his mother. What does a man do when those symbols are gone?"

"*People*," I said. "Not symbols."

"Do you hate us?"

"I don't trust you."

"I'm sure Steven spoke to you. He seeded some thoughts in my mind. How much do I actually know about my neighbor? How could I be so blindly trusting? What if he—meaning you, Mike—is somehow responsible for what happened to Isaac? What if? *What if?* Steven can be very persuasive."

"Maybe Steven is trying so hard because *he's* responsible. You thought about that?"

"I've prayed about it. Prayed more fiercely than I ever have before."

"God answer?"

"I don't expect answers," Ned said in a teacher voice, "but I am open to them."

"How delightfully noncommittal."

"I don't believe you had anything to do with Isaac's death. I think Isaac did it himself, which is what I told the police."

"Your son thinks it was the boy's father."

"Theo is a wonderful young man, but like many teenagers he is susceptible to the gossipy grand, the cinematic, the hidden mystery that twists reality toward convenient absurdism."

I smirked, but I liked the phrase—*convenient absurdism.*

"No man would do that to his son," Ned said.

"You might be surprised." I was thinking of those books in my father's Box of Remains. Books about the bad things we do to each other—all those killers had done unimaginably horrible things to others, even to loved ones. One father tied his ten-year-old son to the boy's bed, doused him with gasoline, and lit him on fire because he wanted to teach his son the dangers of playing with matches. So reads the Gospel According to Moloch. The kid had somehow survived and lived, severely disfigured, at a state facility. His father went to a maximum security mental hospital, where he died from multiple stab wounds to the throat and groin. When God failed to intervene, it was the people's job to dole out justice.

"And Isaac?" he asked.

"What about him?"

"You were there when he first attempted to take his life. What did you see in that moment?"

The boy's dull, blank expression. Someone completely numbed to his own awful actions. Hypnotized. A puppet. *FOOOMP!* The leap of flame. So much screaming. "Your point?"

"It's my fault," Ned said. "I should have seen. Should have been more attentive. I hesitated, you see. I knew what to do, but I didn't want to believe it."

"You're saying . . . What're you saying?"

"God has a plan, and part of that plan is to push us into action. We must not be passive. We must act. We must be brave. We must learn and be better people. God is *the* teacher. The world is our school. I failed. Again."

"Meaning?"

He stared, half-lidded. "I've seen something like it before."

"What?"

He looked at me clinically, a scientist looking at a mouse shot full of experimental drugs. "You don't know much, do you?"

"About what?"

"They tried to protect you, your parents. You were young, of course, when your father passed, but your mother, all these years, she never wanted to burden you."

My twin. Dad's books. My mother's words: *It came back. It never left.*

Sweaty as I was in the day's thickening humidity, I felt a momentary chill. "This better be leading somewhere."

"It was Ward's idea. *That* you should understand. He believed, you see, and belief brought me in, and it led to everything else."

"What are you talking about?"

"It was a sad situation," Ned said. "A boy. That's why, of course. Ward saw the boy and thought of you. Something had to be done, and, like I said, Ward *believed.*"

"*Believed what?*" I nearly shouted. The trees and the darkness beyond echoed my words.

"They tried therapy. They tried medicine. They prayed. Nothing worked. Please don't think reality is anything like in the movies. It might be if the victim were older, his psyche shaped by popular representations, but this was a boy, a child. We tried our best. We really did."

"With *what?*"

"An exorcism." Ned breathed out slowly. His body settled toward the ground, as if anchoring.

I smirked and forced a chuckle, and it cracked into a grating bark of laughter. "An exorcism? Seriously? I have no idea what you're talking about."

Ned pointed next door at Del's brown house. The faded wood-paneled siding and the dying tree in the yard made the place forlorn, a forgotten thing. "Del was there. He and your father were Masons."

A Manual for the Use of the Lodges Under the Jurisdiction of the Grand Lodge of the Most Ancient and Honorable Society of Free and Accepted Masons.

"So?"

"Talk to him. I was brought in to help, but I wasn't ready for my lesson. Not then. We each face judgment. God gave me a second chance with Isaac. It pains me to admit I failed yet again. I will fail no longer."

"Tell me," I said.

"Ask Del."

"*You* tell me."

"I know my path. You must find yours."

From inside my suit jacket, I yanked out Ned's book. *God's Waiting: How to Embrace His Will.* The slim book flapped in my hand.

"I saw Isaac tearing up a copy of this book. That's what he was doing on the hill, tearing up your words and setting them on fire. He wasn't suicidal. He was trying to hurt *you*. Believe what you want, but you're peddling heaps of bullshit and hurting people."

We stared at each other.

"There is a type of person worse even than an apostate," Ned said. "A Cowan. It is someone too cowardly to believe. He is too chickenshit to accept the truth."

I threw the book on the ground. It hit with a weak *flap*. I resisted the urge to stomp on it.

"Worship," I said. "Fucking worship all you want."

CHAPTER 54:
SQUARE LEVEL PLUMB

I FELT HIM watching me, expecting me to cut across the lawn right to Del's door.

I went home. Following Ned's directive would be like donning a white robe, praying with him, and being one of the sun-kissed.

Only Cowards Here.

I felt the echo again, louder and clearer: not "coward"—*Cowan.*

Only Cowans Here.

The word sounded like *coward*, which was exactly how I felt, but it wasn't. What the hell was *Cowan*? Was it a real thing? Had he said "exorcism"? Was Ned serious or screwing with me? Or was he so far gone into his own bullshit he couldn't appreciate how ridiculous he sounded?

Downstairs, I found the slim black book. The butcher paper-thin sheet with that word written in blue pencil was where I'd left it, tucked between pages. *Cowan.*

I flipped through the book. Strangely, CONTENTS was the last page in the book. It was a list of ceremonies. Most involved the granting of degrees or the installation of officers and foundation stones, whatever those were. No exorcism rites. Perhaps one was cleverly disguised euphemistically.

It was Ward's idea, Ned said.

"What the hell were you up to, Dad?"

The book had been with my Father's Remains, appropriately stashed in his custom-made coffin bookcase, which included horror and true crime novels and my father's story about a woman who fell victim to a demonic spirit that possessed a toy bird and took control of her, too.

So much like your father.

I threw the book down. It bounced and slid into a half-crumpled box. Then I picked it back up and walked right out the front door.

Del answered the door without surprise. He palmed a glass of bourbon, and looked at me with sad, red-swelled eyes. "You have some follow-up questions, I take it."

Once more, we sat at his bar. The dark wood gleamed. The "Del's Drinks" plaque was still crooked. He poured me a drink, and I set the Masons book beside it.

"You feel you're on the cusp of some great mystery," he said. "Like there's a whole canyon of unknown just beyond your toes. You want me to tell you what's down there. Or maybe you want me to give a push."

"Tell me about the exorcism."

I slid free the small piece of waxy paper. My father's handwriting was almost a voice itself, and Del was silent a moment, hearing it too.

He sipped his bourbon. "Ward kept everything," he said. "Your mother was the same way. Hoarders. You know, when you don't throw things away, those things sometimes turn on you."

Mousetraps.

"This was after Mable," he said. "We all have our reasons for what we do, and she was mine. That and the brotherhood."

"The Masons?"

"That's what you want to know about, isn't it?" His fingers drummed on the bar, inches from the book and from that age-old scrap of paper.

"The exorcism," I said. The more I said it, the easier the word came out, and the less (*conveniently*) absurd it sounded. I said it again and again, but only in my head. I had to stop myself. It sounded too much like a mantra. *Exorcism, Exorcism, Exorcism*. As if I were under a spell.

"It wasn't what you think," Del said. "Not like the movies. Demons babbling in ancient tongues is for the Catholics and the liberals in Hollywood. Not what we were doing. Although Martin would have tried the Catholics, but he was one of us first, before he was anything else."

"Martin?"

Above, the floor creaked.

"Suzanne," he said, and pointed up. "Sometimes she paces. Back and forth. Hours at a time." He sipped his drink again, and leveled his old-man gaze at me, bloodshot and hazy. "What is it you're after?"

"I want to know."

"Not good enough. Tell me why. Then I'll tell you."

"*What* happened?"

"I've got all night, and a lot more liquor to drink," Del said. "How fast I drink it is up to you."

"My wife," I said, without realizing the words were there behind my lips. "Well, my fiancée. We're getting married soon. She's been in a psychiatric hospital the past few days. The doctors tell me she's okay. Chemical imbalance, bipolar disorder, treatable, but . . . I don't know. She was really out of it. I don't want to say *crazy*, but—"

"Say it," Del said. "Crazy. All women have their moments. Part of what it means to be a female. They all go a little mad sometimes."

"This was different. Scary."

"When Suzanne was younger, she went scary once a month."

"I'm not talking about PMS. I thought maybe she was schizophrenic." I started to take a drink and stopped. "She's getting out tomorrow."

"She try to hurt you?"

I opened my mouth, but didn't say the words.

"You don't need to explain. The problems between a man and a woman are private matters. Family problems are private. It's how I was taught, and it's how it should be. Nowadays, every damn person shares every stupid little thing about himself. You've got reality TV and the damn internet—a culture feeding off misery. Germans have a word for it: *schadenfreude*."

"Tell me what happened."

"This isn't only about your future wife, is it?"

"What about privacy?"

"You came here. Knocked on *my* door. Shoved that stupid old book in *my* face and demanded to know about something that happened years and years ago. I got a right to ask what I want. You don't like it, you can go."

"Fine."

Del was looking at me with amused suspicion, and also delight. In the space it took me to take a breath and admit what was also gnawing at my mind, I realized Rom was the father I wished I had, and Del was the father I was afraid I'd really had. My conception of Ward Munacy was a few shared moments and some vague notions about what he stood for and what he might have tried to impart to me. I thought of his Box of Remains, of his short story, of his arms raised at the end of the hallway, face contorted into a goofy monster, of him rising in the flicker of TV homicide, his head a rubbery, three-eyed, two-mouthed nightmare, of him on Mount Munacy, arms crucified, the sky so vast and blue behind him, of him dying on the ground—*Coward*, he'd said.

But that was wrong. *Cowan*.

"I'm afraid my father was unstable. I'm afraid he might have done something terrible. And I'm afraid I'm like him."

Del's gaze softened. Some.

"Okay," he said. "I'll tell you. First, it starts with this." He slid his sleeve up to his shoulder. The faded tattoo sagged on ropy muscle. It was three words stacked in block letters:

SQUARE
LEVEL
PLUMB

"It was our motto at Century One Hundred, our Lodge, and we held fast to it. A Mason must take pride in his work. Craftsmanship is a lost art. Everything is faster and shittier these days. No one takes the time to build. I'm not only talking about construction. Everyone is in a rush, and willing to settle for good enough or barely even good. A true Mason never settles. Everything you do must be square, level, and plumb."

He tapped knuckles on the bar with each word.

Above us, the floor creaked.

CHAPTER 55:
ALL SCARY STORIES ARE TRUE

"**MARTIN HAD A** son named Randall," Del said. "Cute kid. Good child. Liked trains and playing cowboys and Indians. He always wore a red-and-white bandanna around his neck. He'd pull it up over his mouth and nose, stick out his hands like guns, and I'd put up my arms and say, 'No, don't shoot. Please.' He was a good American boy. The sort to make any father proud.

"He had a red bicycle. I don't know anything about the model, but its handlebars were those curved, high ones, the kid's arms practically up over his head. You remember that rush of being a kid on a bike, pedaling hard down a hill, wind beating against you, feels like you're flying?"

"Sure," I said, "though I usually rode the brakes."

Del paused, a smile lingering. "You ever walk the woods?"

"The woods? Not really, no."

"Yeah, didn't figure you for the courageous type."

"Rather not get Lyme disease."

He dismissed me with a little wave. The truth was that at the mention of the woods, my heart kicked up a gear. "They lived on Blackford Court. If you walk behind this house, directly into the woods, and keep going, eventually you'll reach Blackford Court. Cute little cul-de-sac, little bushes in the median, extra-wide road. Houses with picket fences out front. Tree on each front lawn. Kids playing in the driveway. You get what I'm saying?"

"It was safe?" I asked.

"Safe as you can get. Neighbors know each other. Care for each other's kids. Good ol' American suburbia."

"What happened to him?" I asked.

"A teenager in a Ford pickup hit him. Teen was going forty in a twenty zone, right at the bottom of Blackford. Randall was thrown off his bike and bounced across the road more than thirty feet. His blood stained the concrete in hard splats."

"Jesus," I said. My drink waited, but I didn't lift it.

"Driver said Randall swooped right in front of him, said the kid had one arm out like he was pretending to shoot him. Both legs were broken. Right elbow shattered. Skin stripped raw along his spine, and several vertebrae chipped. Broken nose, skinned chin, but his face was otherwise fine. Luck of the roll, I guess. Maybe the bandanna protected him. Stranger things have happened, believe me. The kid's face was okay—his head was not.

"He was wearing a helmet, too, if you're wondering. Bulky silver thing, maybe it was loose. Came off when he hit the ground, scored a dent in the side. His skull took the rest of the abuse. Didn't crack, though. Might have been better if it had. His brain swelled. If the ambulance was even one minute later, or the helicopter couldn't pick him up so quickly down on the soccer field, Randall would have died. Too much pressure on the brain. Like a balloon popping."

I saw bloody gray matter ooze from small ears, and tried in vain to shake the image away.

"Traumatic brain injury, TBI is what they call it, can be quite severe. Long time to recover and, most likely, you never fully return to who you were. Of course, Martin was happy his boy survived. He was going to live. We're always happy in those moments. We tell ourselves we want our child or our wife or whoever to live. Life alone will be enough. Later, though, when reality settles in, we think differently. At least, we do if we're honest with ourselves.

"Martin was a Brother Architect, same as your father. Means they were higher up than some, but not as high as others. I wasn't yet installed as Master Mason, just a Marshal then, but I was on my way."

"What does any of that mean?" I asked.

"How the lodges were organized."

"What was the purpose of the organization?"

Del looked down, smiled. "Betterment of the community. Like the Rotary Club or the Chamber of Commerce. Like those, only better."

"Better?"

"It was a brotherhood. Call it a fraternity, if you want. Doesn't matter. We had high standards. For work. For life. For the Brotherhood. We held each other to those standards, and we were there for each other no matter what happened. We were family. United in our cause and our collective belief. We were loyal. Another word that doesn't mean what it used to—loyalty."

"Sounds like a cult," I said.

"You call it what you want. Sure, we had our ceremonies. That book is full of them, but the ceremonies weren't sick or cultish. They were like traditions. They wove an unbreakable thread through each of us. United us. Made us stronger. You're worried you're like your father, but it's your mother you sound like. She never approved of it, of us. I know that. Thought it was an excuse for men to hang out and drink." He raised his bourbon. "Beatrice wouldn't let us hold funeral rites. She had your father cremated. Sacrilegious for a Brother Mason. At least back then, don't know about now. I haven't associated in many years. Probably a bunch of fruitcakes defending transgendered weirdos."

He downed his drink and exhaled for several seconds.

"Something you need to accept if I'm going to tell you the rest. This is a scary story. A good one for a campfire but, like such tales, you might be tempted to dismiss it. Don't. The thing about scary stories is, all of them are true. One way or the other. They are all true."

"I think I know what you mean," I said.

"Sure," he said. "Sure you do."

CHAPTER 56:
WITH EYES LIKE THOSE

"**SIX MONTHS AFTER** the accident, Martin asked for help. I don't mean help with the medical care or Randall's day-to-day needs or even monetary help. This was something else entirely."

I downed my drink and managed to keep it down, for now. It burned my throat and roiled my stomach, but it also steadied my shaking hands. While he spoke, Del poured me another, but I didn't touch it.

"Keep in mind what we're talking about. The boy was young, a kid, and he suffered a traumatic brain injury. Kids are resilient. Almost pliant. They bounce back much faster than adults. Power of youth.

"Randall had been in a coma for two weeks. Physical therapy for three months, but three months later he was almost normal. Hair grew back to almost cover the scar where part of his skull had been removed to allow the brain to swell and recede. He no longer had any of the physical tics, or even the speech impediments the injury caused. His destroyed elbow was even functional again. All his bodily functions worked normally. It's important you understand, because you'll want to say the boy was still suffering aftereffects. You'll want to blame the accident and the trauma. I certainly wanted to."

I waited.

"Martin hadn't been to any meetings in a while, understandably. We kept in touch, of course. What's a brotherhood for, after all, if not to be there for one another during rough patches? Well, when I finally saw him, I saw it wasn't simply a rough patch.

"He came here, and we sat in this very room. His hair was a mess, greasy and tangled, his shirt half tucked in. I see it so perfectly—the flap of his button-down hanging loose over one thigh. Martin was always a neaty-neat type of guy. Punctilious, to use a word an English teacher might appreciate, so seeing him like that bothered me. It wasn't scary—not then, not yet—but it worried me. He reminded me of a ball of string gradually unraveling.

"'I need your help,' he said. Sat right where you're sitting and looked at me and asked for help in a voice like splintering ice. 'Of course I'll help you,' I said. 'Anything you need.'

188

"And he measured me with his gaze, like a guy who isn't sure he should say the next words on his tongue. But he did, of course he did, and it changed everything. 'Something has my boy,' he said. I asked what he meant, thinking he'd left out a word or two—*something is wrong* with my boy, not *something has* my boy. 'It's not the TBI,' he said. 'It's something worse. Something sinister.' He leaned toward me and whispered, 'Something evil.'"

Above us, the floor creaked. The basement felt hot. I thought of Rom reciting the line from some horror film: *You're evil!* In my head, Rom's voice was high, fluttery, abuzz with mania, the humor long gone.

"I thought he was overreacting, of course," Del said. "Well, there's overreacting and there's simply reacting. I asked him what he meant. What was bothering him. Not even blinking, he said, 'A demon has my son.' Time dragged out then, sort of stretched and stretched. 'I'm not sure I get you,' I said. So he told me."

Del had told this tale a few times. He had the dramatic pauses, the pacing, the building sense of dread. Half-drunk in some VFW hall, he probably regaled his fellow brother Masons, young men with amused grins, humoring the old guy and maybe getting a bit creeped out too.

"'Randall talks to himself,' Martin said. 'Not like little kids sometimes do, imaginations spinning in their heads. Conversations with stuffed animals. No, he lectures himself. Scolds himself. "Mean boy," he was saying yesterday. Over and over. "Mean boy."' I asked Martin if it was the TBI, and he snapped at me: 'You don't understand. Talking to himself is only one thing. There's more. Much more.'

"'He doesn't sleep,' Martin said. 'Not at all. We put him down, tuck him in, and he closes his eyes, but he's pretending. We can tell. He used to do it sometimes when he was a toddler. He'd pretend and then actually fall asleep. Not anymore. I sat in his room for three hours the other night. Three hours. Randall was in bed, perfectly still, eyes closed, breathing steadily. He wasn't sleeping. I could tell. Just pretending.'"

Dani screamed in my head: *It won't let me sleep!*

Del cleared his throat and continued.

"Martin paused for a good minute or two. He told me he must've fallen asleep in Randall's room, because one moment his boy was in bed and the next he was right in front of Martin, inches away. Martin was so surprised he screamed and slammed his own head back into the wall.

"Only light in the room was from a Batman nightlight, so Randall's face was crisscrossing shadows. 'But I saw his eyes,' Martin told me. 'Glowing like a cat's. Studying me.'

"I tried to tell Martin he was tired, exhausted, and his mind had gotten tangled with grief and fear. 'It's all in your head,' I said. 'No,' he said. 'It's in Randall's head. *Something* is in there. It's bad. Very bad.'

"Martin lifted his right arm, curled his hand into a pistol and pointed his forefinger to his temple, thumb up, and made shooting sounds over and over. 'That's what my boy did,' Martin said. 'He might've done it for hours if I didn't grab his hand.'"

Del made a soft puffing sound, as if the imaginary gun shot nothing worse than air. I saw the kid in superhero pajamas standing in the dark, unmoving save for the imaginary gun to his head, and saw the boy's lips pursing to make gentle push-of-air sounds over and over, perpetual suicide in whisper.

"'We lock his door at night,'" Del said in the tired-sounding voice he was using for Martin. "'But last night I woke with a start and there he was, standing in our bedroom doorway. The moonlight silhouetted him, turned him into something ghostly, and I thought I was having a nightmare. *Hoped* it was a nightmare. My son pissed himself. Standing right there in the doorway. Urine soaked his pajamas. *Stank*. Acidic and awful. Never smelled anything so awful.'"

I swallowed, but something was stuck in my throat, and I kept swallowing, and finally pushed it down with bourbon.

"'He smells all the time now,' Martin told me. 'Like he hasn't bathed in months. But he has. We wash him every day and he still stinks. Body odor, and something worse, too. A sour-milk stench, and putrid rot.'

"He said Randall only ate raw food. Nothing cooked. Not chicken fingers or French fries. His preference? Cold ground beef right out of the package. Scoop his hands and slurp it off his fingers."

Should I believe any of this? Wasn't Del screwing with me, getting what fun he could from trying to scare me with this nonsense?

"He said his kid was losing his teeth, too. 'Dropping right out of his head.' I didn't know what to say to him." Del picked at a crack in the bar wood. "Martin had been through something beyond comprehension, except maybe to parents who actually see their child blue-lipped and cold on a morgue table. You think about what I said, about how we always want our loved ones to live. Just survive. Make it through this. If they live, it's all that matters. Yeah, right."

A small white coffin. The clack of the hearse's door. The blurry reflection.

"He said there were times they couldn't find Randall."

"He was hiding?"

"They'd search the whole house. Even down the street. Nowhere. Like he vanished. Then he was there, in the house, standing there as if he'd been the whole time. Hiding in plain sight."

"What does that mean?" I asked.

"Don't know, though I did know what he wanted, and I tried to talk him out of it. 'I'm not saying he has special powers,' Martin said. 'I'm not saying he's turned into some malevolent beast, but I'm also not saying he isn't headed that way. We're scared. My wife won't go near him. When I'm with him, I feel how *off* he is, how wrong. I'm afraid he might do something to us.' Martin paused then, wiped his tears. 'I'm afraid I might do something to him. Please. You have to help me.'

"I didn't want to," Del said, "but when Ward found out, he insisted. He was adamant. He *believed*. We had to at least try. So, God help us, we did it."

I was leaning over the bar, listening intently, falling into Del's story despite my skepticism. The story was well practiced, but it was spoken with the confidence of unquestioned memory, of something haunting him still.

The floor above creaked, and I started.

"Told you it was scary."

I was rubbing my arms, and forced myself to stop.

"We needed a priest," Del said. "Your father asked Ned. The perfect choice, really. He was unaffiliated with any church, yet he was a practicing Christian. I made him a temporary Warden of our lodge.

"When we did it, I saw the truth. Up until that moment, I'd doubted. I went along with Ward and Martin, because that's what it means to be in a brotherhood, but I doubted it—until I saw."

"Saw what?" I asked.

"Something behind the boy's eyes. Creeping there. Something lived there that was not Randall. I can't explain it better than that, but if you'd seen it, you would agree. Ward saw it, said the same thing. Something there, *living*, inside him."

"What did you do?"

"We carried out the ceremony. Maybe we shouldn't have done anything. Just let it alone. Maybe he was just a little kid with severe brain damage, and all we did was torture him so badly he died."

"*What?* He died?"

"Randall died," Del said. "Maybe the ropes were too tight. Or he choked. Suffocated. Dehydration. I don't know. Actually, though, I think Randall died in the street beside his red bike and his dented silver helmet and something else— *something terrible*—took his place."

"How'd he die?"

"I'm telling you, Michael, the boy was already dead."

"*What did you people do?*"

Del lifted his glass, tilted it and appreciated how the light played across the liquor, and waited for me to calm. "We drove out the Cowan," he said. "Tried to, anyway."

I stood. My legs wobbled, rubbery. The bar's gleam slipped back and forth. "No," I said. "Tell me what happened to the boy."

"What we did," Del said calmly, "what happened, stained us. Followed us. Stuck to us like slime you can't wash off. Ward felt it worst. He thought people were following him. Said his skin was always crawling. Thought something was coming for him. Coming right out of the woods. You know why he did it?"

"Because he was mentally unstable?"

Del grinned around the rim of his glass. "He did it because of your dead twin." He paused, watching me. "Did you know you had a twin who died?"

"What do you know about it?"

He shook his head slowly. "That loss took a lot from your father. Life's a losing battle, and in the end everyone loses everything, but some people lose more than others along the way. Your father was like that. After your brother died, he was never quite the same. When Martin came to me and asked for help, I knew what Ward would say. Maybe I didn't want to do it, but I went to Ward knowing full well what he'd say. He thought if we saved Randall it could balance the scale a bit. Maybe tilt it in his favor. Maybe life wouldn't be one long losing parade for him. Instead, we really screwed up."

"No," I said, "you didn't 'really screw up'—you killed a child."

"When your father died, I was grateful. It was an end for him. He'd spent so much time fearing what might happen next. When his brother, your uncle, was killed in a highway crash, Ward was sure it was the curse or the demon or the Cowan or Satan. Punishment, he believed. You were young, six or seven maybe, but I remember you at the funeral. Sitting there and staring at your feet, kicking them back and forth."

That stray memory returned: a young me trying to distract himself at a funeral.

Calm down, Ward.

I'm a coward, my father said. *A goddamn coward.*

Or had he said *Cowan*? Was there a difference?

"He was so afraid something would happen to you. Expected you to get cancer or get hit by a car or fall on the sidewalk and snap your neck. He drove himself crazy, thinking and thinking. Worrying. Scared to death for you. He believed he was cursed, but our minds are the real curse. Can't say I blame him or his suspicions. We know what we did, and we have to own up to it. Your father owned up first. When Suzanne was diagnosed with Alzheimer's, I knew it was part of my punishment. My owning up will be soon."

"But what was it?" I slammed my fist on the bar. My drink bounced. "*What the hell was it?*"

"You have your father's face, and you're scared, so the resemblance goes deeper, but it's not only skin and hair. It's not just your eyes, either. You're Ward all over again. Getting obsessed. Getting angry. Righteous anger, you might say. What happened took a toll on him, and I see this is taking a toll on you. Ward couldn't focus. Lost his job. He was already consumed with the macabre, horror movies and Stephen King novels, but it got worse. He bought creepy masks and films about serial killers. Had that stupid coffin bookcase made. The tendency was already there, I suppose. You know he wrote a horror story, an ugly thing about incest?"

I stumbled, buzzed and heavy with anger. I stabbed a finger at him: "*You killed that boy.*" The words cut between my teeth.

"Officially, it was pneumonia. The boy had a weakened immune system."

"What *really* happened?"

"I'll say one thing," Del said, calm as ever. "Martin and his wife were grateful. They had a funeral and a burial, and they found peace in their grief. They moved away, got on with their lives. They'd wanted Randall to live, just survive and be alive, and they thought it would be enough, but in the end they were so thankful for his death. So happy for it."

My breathing was hard and fast. I wanted to slam my fist on the bar again, leap across it, pin Del to the wall and punch him until he told me the complete truth. Punch and punch and punch.

I turned from him and started out.

"You asked about Mable," Del said. "What I saw in Randall's eyes, I saw again in my own daughter's. You think that's bullshit, but I'll tell you: with eyes like those, how could I keep her?"

Above us, something fell with a hard, dull thump.

CHAPTER 57:
GOD OF DIRT AND STONE

I WENT TO Dusty's grave.

My cat wasn't the only one buried there. A few days after my father was roasted into a heap of grey ashes, Mom had handed me a small plastic container. It was in the shape of Mickey Mouse's head. The round ears were comically large. Inside was a handful of ash. "It's your father," she said. I took it in my hands as if it were a newborn kitten. Mom nodded and turned away. I brought the Disney urn outside.

At the top of Mount Munacy, on the edge of the cliff, I'd set down Mickey's head and arranged my G.I. Joes around it. This would be the apocalyptic battle for the Holy Mickey idol. An all-out war for the Mouse Head of Ashes.

Many soldiers were lost during battle. The action figures tumbled off the cliff and screamed all the way down. The fighting was fierce and chaotic, and somewhere amid the madness of war, my arm flew out and smacked the Holy Idol.

It tumbled off the cliff.

The mouse skull split in midair and my father's ashes clouded a streak down to the ground. The two halves of Mickey's head cracked against the ground and more ash plopped out.

I raced down the hill. I tried to scoop the ash back into the base of the head, but it slipped between my fingers and spilled loose, and I scooped again and again and it mixed with dirt and little pebbles. I dusted it off G.I. Joes and traced my fingers along the plastic edge of the container to peel off every little bit I could. More ash silted through the air, dusting my hair and my shirt, sprinkling my cheeks and settling on my eyelashes—a sheen of human remains.

"NO!" I screamed. I was crying and I felt so helpless and angry. "*NO! NO! NO!*"

I'd punched the ground, hard. My middle finger snapped. The pain was immense, liquid fire. I screamed and punched the ground again. And again. Army men cracked against my fingers. Tiny jagged stones cut my flesh. Blood spotted the ashy dirt, which in turn stuck to my skinned knuckles.

My father's ashes mixed with my blood.

DEAD END

It might be in the blood, Dad said.

"*NO!*" I'd screamed and punched until my hand was swollen, pulsing, numb and burning. I grabbed the bottom of the makeshift urn with what ashes I managed to dump back in it, and I stood tall before Mount Munacy. Scattered fragments of plastic Mickey's head lay all around my feet. I'd been screaming and punching the ground and stomping my feet, mushing plastic and ashes and dirt.

My father stood on the cliff, blue sky behind him. The air thickened with his presence, and he raised his arms to his sides—crucified against the heavens.

"Worship," I said fourteen years later, standing in the same spot where I'd punched the ground so many times it took a month for my hand to heal. I'd told Mom it was an accident.

When I buried Dusty, there were no plastic pieces, no ash—just dirt, like the ground long ago digested what I'd lost there.

"What did you do, Dad?" I said. "What did you and Del and Ned do to that little boy? And my brother? What happened? *What was wrong with you?*"

Like the young boy smeared with his dead father's ashes, I knocked back my head, puffed out my chest, and screamed and screamed until my throat screeched into silence and the entire world vibrated with my primal cry.

CHAPTER 58:
UNBURIED

DUSTY'S GRAVE WAS several feet to my left. I glanced at it before heading back inside—and stopped.

The stone had been moved, lying off to the side, and where it had been the ground was dug up. I'd noticed a claw mark the other day when I retrieved my phone, and now it seemed that whatever animal had tested the ground before had come back and taken all it could unearth.

From where I stood, I couldn't see the bottom of the hole. I did not want to go closer, did not want to look and see Dusty's torn, rotting corpse.

I looked.

The sheet was there; the body was not.

Not believing, fully expecting the cat's corpse to appear, as if its absence were a trick of my eyes, I tugged out the sheet by one corner. Loose dirt speckled free.

The hole was empty.

No torn remains on the ground. No tuffs of hair. No skin or bones.

The animal had come out of the woods, dug up my cat, and carried him off into the woods, perhaps back to its underground lair where it and its young feasted on feline carrion.

I felt sick.

Sheet dangling from my hand, I stared up at Mount Munacy and at the woods beyond. "Are you watching now?" I called. "Are you? How dare you take my cat. You've no right."

The (*convenient*) absurdity of what I was doing didn't stop the words from coming. Whatever animal had dug up and stolen away with Dusty was long gone, but this wasn't about some night creature or my poor, dead cat—this was about my father, his madness, and what he helped do years ago to a young boy.

"There is no monster," I said. "No demons. Just madness and cruelty. I've had enough. I'm done with this." I paused, started to turn away, and squared my shoulders toward the woods again. "If you don't like it, go ahead and come for me. I dare you."

The woods were silent.

CHAPTER 59:
COWAN IN THE NIGHT

THE WHISPERS WOKE ME.

I didn't want to wake. My muscles were sore, the bed comfortable. No nightmares, and what dreams came were innocuous and forgotten the moment each gave way to the next.

The soft push of air on my ear stirred me, and I moved closer to Dani. The sheets were cold. My hand draped her waist, slid along her hip bone, and curved over her butt. It felt fuller, the way it was when we first met, plump and so lovely to caress.

I pulled her close, pushed my arousal against her, and smelled the tinge of her night sweat—but she wasn't in bed with me, *couldn't* be in bed with me, because she was in a psychiatric institute under observation, locked in, maybe even straitjacketed in place.

A startled cry crackled in my throat, and my whole body palsied. A dream. Must be because—

"Cowan," Dani whispered.

I didn't move, wasn't sure if I *could* move. My body was sunken in the bed, weighted with sleep. This was a nightmare (*worship*), and I had either to ride it out or somehow startle myself out of it.

"We must go to it," Dani said. "*Now.*"

Something touched my face—cold and slippery.

I flung myself backwards and was too late kicking my feet under me before the bed ended, and I fell to the floor, knees and elbow taking the abuse.

My heart only now kicked into high gear, and electric energy charged through me. A dream. It seemed so real at the time because dreams were like that, they could seem completely real even down to the minutest detail, but that's all it was— a fabrication produced from a stressed-out subconscious. No big deal.

Someone stood in the doorway.

It was Steven Rush. He'd broken in, or maybe dear old Mom had given Ned a set of house keys, and now Steven was here to kill me, make it look like a suicide, and then Isaac's death could be blamed on me without any further questions asked. Officer Koryta and Detective King would love that.

"What do you want?" I asked.

It wasn't Steven; it was a human form, and the right size and shape for Dani, the long hair veiling past her shoulders to make it appear she wore a hood. The Shadow Dani in the doorway might be staring at me, or turned away from me.

"Cowan," Dani said again, a soft whisper.

The scream filled my throat again, but I clamped down on it. I was still dreaming. *Lucid dreaming*, it was called. I pinched my forearm hard enough to scatter white spots across my vision. I dared open my mouth to speak, but clacked my teeth back down. I didn't want to speak to whatever this was because if it replied, I would scream, and if I screamed and *didn't* wake up, well, that was a risk not worth taking.

"Cowan," Dani said again.

The figure moved into the hallway. Smoothly. As if floating.

I caught my breath, listened. No sounds of feet on the floor. No creaking of floorboards. Nothing.

"A dream," I said to myself. "A dream a dream a dream."

Slowly, I stood.

Was I still asleep in the bed beside me? For a blink, I saw myself hooked beneath the sheet, asleep and alone. But it wasn't true. I was standing here, completely awake.

I approached the hall, each step slow, deliberate.

An empty, dark hallway. Except it wasn't empty: the figure was there at the end of the hall. It stood out, a silhouette darker than night.

I could tell myself it was my imagination, or my mind was trying to be helpful offering up a hallucination to assure me I wasn't crazy, but there was something there. I felt the weight of its presence.

The hallway stretched.

"Cowan," Dani said again.

The figure moved into the kitchen. Soundlessly.

I was halfway down the hall before I realized I'd taken one step. *It is a dream*, I thought. *I'm sleepwalking*. Relief like I've never enjoyed swept through me. I was sleepwalking, still asleep. So what if I'd never sleepwalked before? I was stressed. Very stressed. Yes. This made perfect sense.

Nothing to fear.

I stopped in the kitchen doorway. My toes curled over the cold metal saddle separating carpet from tile. I reached for the walls, but stopped. If I touched the wallpaper, the ivy might slither over my fingers.

Shadow Dani stood at the glass door. Her outline glowed. Were I religious, it might have struck me as holy.

I opened my mouth to speak and couldn't say anything. What if this imaginary Dani responded? What if she wasn't fake, not a hallucination, not the conjuration of a lucid dream, but real? Actually, truly, genuinely real?

DEAD END

A ghost, I thought. *Dani's dead.*

Somehow she'd found a way to kill herself. A broken mirror, a shoelace, a pen—she found something and used it before the nurses or doctors could stop her. Maybe she did it in secret in her room and she was yet to be discovered, or maybe she'd made a grand stand in some common room filled with gown-clad patients and pronounced she was done suffering and jammed a pair of scissors in her neck.

The phone would ring and wake me and Dr. Marshall would say he had terrible news.

The Shadow Dani stepped through the glass and onto the deck.

The compulsion to follow was strong. I wanted to. Wanted to follow her through the kitchen and outside. But what then? I would descend the steps, cross the patio and Dusty's unearthed burial spot, and ascend the hill, again in bare feet. Rocks would poke and stab. Dirt would crumble between my toes. I would scale the hill and the black woods would grow larger. Every tree looming. Hidden faces and jagged, gnarled limbs. Stretching for me . . .

My father's arms reaching out, a throaty moan rattling through his teeth, his eyes slicking to cream white—and the sky pulls back and the trees creep closer and closer, their claws carve the blue morning, and Dad steps off the cliff and falls and falls and falls, crumpled, broken, dying.

Cowan.

I entered the kitchen, the cold floor beneath my feet.

Compelled by some greater force.

No. I did not want to do this. No. It might be a dream and I was still in bed, but the floor chilled my skin, and my toes pressed into the grouted grooves between two tiles, and that was far too real for any dream.

Sleepwalking. Yet I couldn't snap out of it. Couldn't wake.

Something had slithered its way inside me, some sinister presence, a dark thing with sentience but not rationality. It was hungry, this thing, knew only hunger, and it wanted Dani and it wanted me, too. She wasn't here—couldn't be; she was safely trapped, perhaps in a white-walled room—but it could have me, feed upon me, but no matter how much it consumed, it would never be satiated.

Dozens of small, desperate hands pushed against the inside of my ribs: pure fright, as sharp and unbridled as any I suffered as a child.

Let this be a dream, a lucid nightmare, and let me wake in bed wrapped in sweaty sheets and discard this horror into a subconscious trash can and wedge the lid down tight.

Shadow Dani crossed the deck toward Mount Munacy and the night swallowed her. Was she crossing the deck still or floating through air to the cliff, sliding between trees into the unknown beyond?

Moonlight vanished and the glass door iced black. Mount Munacy was shrouded, but there. Always. It loomed. Grew larger.

Another step. I clenched my jaw, willed my legs to stop, and yet that thing inside me urged me forward, and if it had a voice it would have been soothing, seductive: *a few more steps, love, and you'll see things you've never known. Come to me. Be with me. Let me hold you.*

I fought against that compulsion the way one does against any terrible, sweetly inviting promise—an intangible, slippery battle, one easily lost.

"No," I said. "*No.*"

I stopped. Grabbed the wall. Flat and papery. I was breathing hard, sweating, but in control.

Something stood next to me, almost touching me.

"Mike," Dani whispered.

This time, the scream escaped.

CHAPTER 60:
HEARING IT, TOO

IT **TOOK SEVERAL** minutes to gain some control. With the kitchen light on, I could catch my breath and begin to push the (*ghost*) hallucination away. It would linger long into the bright sunshine the way the worst nightmares do, and it might be waiting for me again at dusk, but Dani was being released later today (*or sent to the morgue*), and once she was home that would stop the bad dreams.

You'd like to think that, wouldn't you?

The fluorescent light was humming and I squinted at it, happy for the light yet irritated by that sound. It rode along my nerves and vibrated around my teeth. It seemed much louder than usual, but that was only because I was focusing on it.

At some point, squinting up at that light, I heard the sound coming from somewhere else. Another trick of the mind—just add it to the list—but the more I concentrated, the more sure I became that there was another sound coming from somewhere.

The pantry.

The sound was louder now, angrier, as if it knew I could hear it. I turned the knob slowly and creaked open the pantry door.

I'd jammed everything back into the cabinets and drawers and pantry. It had' not been organized at all to begin with, but now the pantry was a real mess. Bags and boxes crushed onto every shelf. Spaghetti sauce jars and soup cans and bags of different-colored baking chocolate and Nilla wafers and Triscuits and olive oil and dozens of dusty boxes of brownie mix—almost everything expired—wedged on top of and crammed against each other.

My hands reached toward the shelves, a blind man trying to find his way. The sound was coming from in here . . . somewhere.

I listened.

The sound is everywhere. Buzz, buzz, buzzzzzz . . . .

Had Dani actually heard something? Was I hearing something? Was I dreaming?

My hands spider-crawled up to the top shelf, which Dani had not disturbed and neither had I, where a faded box featured a picture of a red carafe. Perhaps it was used one Christmas gathering decades ago. I took it down. The box crumpled in my hand, and the carafe almost fell out the bottom, but I caught it.

On the shelf was a Mason jar.

I stared at it. Stared.

The wasps in it were alive.

They quivered and bounced their fat yellow-and-black bodies against the glass, over and over, angry to escape. Long, papery wings flapped, but that sound was lost beneath the buzzing. *It keeps buzzing*, Dani said, *burning my brain*. I stepped closer, went up on my toes—only five or six wasps in there, but they were each easily two inches long, and one of them had a black stinger another inch or two long; it slid on the glass, slicking through a trail of grayish liquid. Poison.

Untreated bacterial infection.

I reached for the jar. If Dani hadn't put it there, that meant . . .

To reach this shelf, my five-foot mom would've had to drag the step stool from the hallway closet, where it was wedged way back behind half a dozen old winter coats and at least one busted vacuum, and managed to keep her balance while she moved the carafe box and positioned the jar—

I touched the glass, my middle finger on the raised ridge of the cursive B in "Ball Mason," and the wasps went for it. Two of them went for my middle finger, one investigating with its black eyes and probing antennae, and the other simply stabbing its stinger at the glass. *Plink. Plink. Plink.*

—but the real problem was this: how did Mom collect them? I saw her walking barefoot into the woods, entranced, sleepwalking, saw her crossing the dark woodsy threshold into whatever waited beyond, but then my imagination could follow no further.

The wasp with the long stinger didn't bother with my fingertips on the glass; it kept circling the jar as if it knew better. As if it knew it were being taunted. As if it were planning its escape.

A reddish yellowy muck beginning to mold was clumped at the bottom of the jar, and that brought back my mom in the woods, squatting down to set the open jar on the dirt and stepping back, silver jar lid clutched in her hand; she waited for the smell of the sweet jam to entice a few wasps, and once they flew in she slapped the lid on, screwed it tight, and walked back.

But why?

The Cowan commands it, I thought.

I took the jar off the shelf and stepped back. The wasps buzzed louder. The stabbing wasp tried more desperately to sting my finger. *PlinkPlinkPlink.*

My other hand cupped the lid. It was vibrating.

The power of the wasps. Worship. Worship. We are the First Order of the Wasp Worshippers. Release the Queen. Know the power. Behold the greatness. The Cowan commands it. Cowan, Cowan, Cowan . . .

The lid slowly unscrewed.

"Cowan, Cowan," I repeated.

The wasps approached the lid. Their wings flapped crazily, eagerly. Desperate for freedom, one of them torpedoed at the lid, hit with a hard *thwack*, and dropped into the graying jelly at the bottom. It squirmed, wings sticking and tugging free again and again.

The lid was loose. One more turn and it'd be completely off.

"Cowan, Cowan, Cowan."

The lid trembled in my hand. The wasps gathered at the jar lip, save for the one stuck in the jam and Big Stinger, who stayed at the bottom but no longer circled.

As if from down a long corridor, a voice hollered for me to stop what I was doing to snap out of it to not let them free to please stop stop *STOP STOP STOP STOP!*

The lid lifted and a wasp head poked over the jar's mouth.

STOP!

The wasp turned its head, and its ink-black eyes reflected my dull-faced stare. Its wings flopped free. Another wasp crawled over the edge. The one in the jam shook its body frantically. Big Stinger launched off the glass.

STOP!

A desperate, scared cry escaped my mouth, but it was as if another part of me were screaming, horrified at my actions—and I squeezed the lid back down and screwed it tight fast as I could.

Big Stinger hit the underside of the lid hard and kept pushing, vibrating strength that was so startling I almost dropped the jar. The wasps on the verge of escape squealed in a buzzing horrified screech that couldn't possibly be real, and oily guts bled down the glass.

I wanted to throw the Mason jar across the kitchen. My arm tensed with the urge, but I grabbed the jar with both hands and forced myself to carefully set it on the counter.

A severed piece of wasp squished between my bare toes.

Take it to the woods.

The thought was clear and calm, reassuring. Yes, I could take the wasps into the woods, pick the jar up and head right out onto the deck, march up Mount Munacy, walk among the trees where the night thickened to an even blacker cloak, and open the jar and let the wasps fly back to their nest.

You have to kill them. This thought was just as clear, but almost hysterical in its frantic insistence. *Kill them all. Destroy the nest. It's the only way.*

Should I check the garage for wasp spray? Go on a killing spree?

I grabbed up the jar and turned toward the sliding door. The wasps hummed, like I was holding a jar of electricity.

CHAPTER 61:
DANI RETURNS

"I DON'T WANT to be here," Dani said.

We were riding up Heintz Hill, a minute from Mullock. It was the first thing she'd said since I'd picked her up, other than a quick "Hey" and an "I love you," followed by a peck on the lips. She sat stiffly in the passenger seat, body tense. A purplish-brown bruise pulsed along her jaw where she'd taken a good hit tumbling down Mount Munacy. Other bruises and scrapes marred her face, neck, and hands, but none was as deep as the one on her jaw.

"What?"

"Your mother's house. Where *you* grew up. I want to go back to our apartment. Our place. There's too much of you in that house. I'm crowded out. You've already lived a whole life there."

"It's our house now. My mother's funeral is the day after tomorrow."

"I'm not trying to be difficult, Mike. I was just in the hospital, you know."

Picking Dani up from the hospital that morning, I'd expected to be led down white, fluorescent-lit halls where metal gates sectioned off corridors—dividing patient rooms by severity of illness: the manic, the suicidal, the disturbed—but instead there was a generic waiting room with uncomfortable chairs and framed pictures on the walls of serene landscapes (a wheat field at sunset, an old red barn centered against distant mountains), and Dani had been escorted out, asked to sign her discharge papers, given a slew of scripts, and wished a pleasant day. No doctor had asked to speak with me, and no nurse pulled me aside to offer any cryptic warnings.

Careful, someone should have said. *These treatments don't come with guarantees.*

Or maybe, *Watch for warning signs.*

"I know, but we can't pack up and move. Not yet. There's too much to do, and we don't even know if you're . . . "

"If I'm *what?*" Her tone was sharp, threatening. I thought of the scissors, stashed back in the same drawer where she'd found them during her sleepwalking episode. There were also knives in the kitchen. Lots of them.

"You seem stressed," I said, sounding like the anxious one.

She barked a laugh. "Stressed? Well, shit, Mike, no fooling you."

"What's wrong?"

"You didn't call me. I know you weren't allowed to visit, but you could've called. I asked. Calls were allowed."

"I'm sorry. Things have been chaotic here."

"Chaotic?"

"Were you able to get any sleep?"

"I was too busy staying up, waiting for your call."

I pulled to the curb, stopped. Dani jolted against the seatbelt. We'd had our share of lovers' spats, and even one full-blown argument that had something to do with the wedding, and now we were on the cusp of another fight, a potentially really bad one. I needed to be the calm, levelheaded one. I needed to show some understanding, some empathy, some consideration.

"Look," I said with way too much aggression, "you don't know half of what's been going on."

She stared at me, her eyes watery and red-tinted, but bulging with accusatory rage. She probably hadn't been sleeping. Why didn't the doctors give her anything to knock her out? At her feet, a plastic CVS bag crinkled with the paper bags containing her prescriptions. Each one featured different-colored warning labels. I hoped at least one was a sleep aid.

"Why don't you go right ahead and blame me? Obviously I'm too much of a burden for you."

"Jesus, you're not a burden."

"Take me to a motel," she said. "I'll figure it out."

"You're not going to a motel."

"You going to stop me?"

I almost slammed on the accelerator, thinking I would race up Heintz and over it and take her out to the main drag and find the closest motel, and tell her, *Here. This what you really want? Go ahead. Get out.*

So much like your father.

Slowly, my hands loosened on the steering wheel. I loved her—very much—but still, I was the one dealing with all the shit happening while she was attended to around the clock. I took a breath. This wasn't her fault. She was the one suffering, the one who'd been in the hospital for a psych eval. I was being the asshole.

"Okay," I said, soft, contrite, "something happened you need to know about."

"What is it?" She'd softened immediately. Here was the Dani I could trust. The Dani I didn't need to fear.

I told her about Isaac.

"This happened behind your mother's house?"

"On the cliff. The night you went into the hospital. Calling to tell you didn't seem like the right move."

"We can't go back there."

"Dani, we can't move yet. We will, though. I promise."

She leaned toward me, the belt tightening between her breasts. "Mike, it's not safe there. I can tell. I heard things. I can't sleep there. There's something wrong."

For a moment, nothing.

"You were sleepwalking," I said.

"I don't think so."

"What does that mean?"

She shook her head slowly. One hand rose to her mouth, and the tips of her fingers slipped between her lips. She looked like a frightened child.

"Dani, it's okay. You're anxious, nervous, I get it. You're going to be okay."

"No," she said, her fingers at her lips. "No, I'm not."

I started to speak, and cursed instead. I punched the wheel and the horn blatted. Dani recoiled, and I started to apologize and the tears came, fast and hard, surprising both of us.

They pushed from me more furiously than they had in Rom's garage with Dusty's body laid out before me. Those tears were for the poor, innocent cat I loved, but these were for more than me and my stress: I cried for my mother, dead in a hospital bed with her mouth hanging unhinged; for Isaac, whom I'd saved but who burned anyway; for Rom, whose wife was dying slowly in his own house; for my father, who died in front of me, hands shaking, eyes rolling back to white; and for Dani, especially Dani, my bride-to-be, the woman I fell for when she told me I dressed like a GQ model with my shirts and ties and added, "except those models are a bit more attractive"; the woman who smiled at me and touched my shoulder and looked into me in a way no one ever had before; the woman with whom I was supposed to spend the rest of my life, maybe as many as fifty or sixty years; the woman I turned to now and who, thankfully, embraced me.

"Hey," she said.

"Hey."

My tears stained her sweatshirt. "I'm sorry I'm an asshole."

"You're not an asshole," she said. "Just a bastard." She kissed my nose.

I shifted back behind the wheel, and she stopped me. Her fingers were back at her lips. "I know you think I'm crazy—"

"I don't think—"

"But we can't go back to that house."

Looking at her, I knew what had to be done. It was obvious from the redness in her eyes, from the way she chewed at her fingernails, from the fear crouching in her. "Should I take you back to the hospital?"

In the space of a held breath, the entire universe can hang. Had she said yes, or even offered a slight, apprehensive nod, I would have turned the car around and taken her back, and I have no doubt the hospital would've admitted her. But she didn't, and I was too much of a coward to do what I knew I should have.

We continued up Heintz Hill and onto Mullock and all that waited for us there.

CHAPTER 62:
BAD THINGS COME BACK

THE COP CAR was parked along the shoulder where the road ended. Nowhere to go from there—dead end—except into the woods.

Officer Koryta was coming around the side of the house as I pulled into the driveway. Yellow CAUTION tape and little plastic flags tangled in his arms.

"Case closed?" I asked, and immediately wished to take it back.

He appraised me up and down, and I thought of Clint Eastwood in *Dirty Harry*. He turned to Dani as she got out of the car, hugging herself, head bowed, hand at her lips. "You must be Dani."

She managed to lower her hand before answering. "Yes."

"How are you feeling?"

"Much better, thanks."

I didn't like how he was looking at her, studying her, scanning for clues. "Officer Koryta has been thorough," I said. "This hasn't been easy."

The strange-sounding comment brought the Detective Callahan gaze back.

"Have you made any conclusions?" I asked, sounding completely nervous and totally guilty.

He considered. "I understand you've been discharged from Castle Hill Psychiatric Center."

"Yes. Why does that matter?" Dani asked.

"Gathering information. A child is dead, you know."

Dani seemed ready to say something, but her hand went to her lips again. Had to be a tic from childhood. At least she wasn't sucking her thumb.

"It was suicide," I said.

"The night it happened, the two of you were home?"

"We were at the hospital."

"So you don't recall seeing or hearing anything?"

"No."

"It happened right there behind your house—"

"It's not mine."

"Pardon?"

"The house. I mean, it is, but it was my mother's. She just died."

"I'm sorry to hear that. What happened?"

"I believe I told you: poor health."

Koryta smiled in a small, mischievous way, one that wondered how lucky I felt, punk. "There's no reason to be defensive, Mr. Munacy. I hope we're all on the same team here."

"Kidney failure," I said.

A head nod. "If I have any further questions . . . "

"We're not going anywhere."

That little smile again, and Koryta walked down to his vehicle.

"That was odd," Dani said.

"Thorough, like I said."

Dani went inside, and I walked around back.

My father stood on the cliff. Then the light shifted and it was another police officer. Yellow tape curled off his arm. He was smoothing the dirt with his foot, sweeping it back and forth.

Wrong, wrong.

The cop crept to the edge and peered down. Did he wonder about the rock directly below, about the dug-up grave beside it?

He leaned farther. If he slipped . . .

Sometimes the bad things come back, my father said.

"Excuse me?"

I turned around fast, and was face-to-face with Officer Koryta. His hands, empty, settled on his waist near his gun.

"What?"

"You said something."

"Did I?"

"What were you saying?"

You think they're gone, but they're not.

They never left.

"I didn't."

He waved at the cop on the cliff, who started down safely along the gradual slope. "Are *you* all right?"

Wrong, wrong.

"Fine. It's been a stressful few days." *And maybe I'm going crazy,* I could've added.

"I can tell."

"Did you talk to Isaac's father?"

"We're pursuing all leads."

"He's abusive. Jealous. Maybe dangerous. Are you considering he could have done this?"

Sunlight swished around Koryta's head. "We'll do the investigating."

"I thought we were on the same team."

The other cop had joined. He was shorter and leaner. His name tag read: Merrin. He picked at his teeth with a fingernail, as though he'd picnicked on the cliff.

"We'll be in touch," Koryta said.

I followed them back to the front and watched them walk to the cop car and drive off.

CHAPTER 63:
POSSESSED BY MEMORIES

DANI WAS RIGHT, of course. No matter where I went in this house or on the property around it, those memory mousetraps were everywhere.

In a way, they possessed me, those memories, and wherever I went, particular moments snapped onto me. There I was screaming at the trees to stay away from me. And there were my tiny feet thumping up and down the hall from one parent growling like a monster to the other who cackled and hissed, arms raised. And there I fell, scissors in hand, and almost blinded one eye. And, older but just as stupid, there I stuck a straightened paperclip into the hallway electrical outlet. And there I sneaked up behind my father sitting motionless at the typewriter. And there he was again, before the TV, the screen a chaos of screams and blood. And the house filled with the warm smell of baking chocolate. And Dusty rubbing against my legs until I relented and petted under his chin. And there I was, over and over, entering the house to check on my widowed mother, to do her shopping, to take out her garbage, to change her light bulbs, to carry her laundry, again and again. And there I was only last week talking to my mother at the living room window and considering how strange it was going to be to move back home where all these memories waited for me. And then she was sprawled on the kitchen floor. And now she was dead.

Sometimes dead is better.

I watched Dani carefully, without trying to make it obvious. When she set out her numerous prescription bottles on the bathroom counter, however, my observation could no longer be ignored. "What?"

"Nothing."

Her smile was the condescending, "go fuck yourself" type I used to love, even find sexy. She would do it to get me going. Now, it sort of scared me.

"Can I get you anything?" I asked.

"A moment alone?"

The door shut with a metallic click. Were we so soon back to closed doors? The real question: who was going to come out of the bathroom—sane Dani, or Dani with an uneven glint in her eye and a pair of scissors in hand?

What if she overdoses in there?

DEAD END

I knocked on the door.

She opened it, exhausted and exasperated. "What?"

I mumbled some sort of response of little sense. Her annoyance softened, and she told me to stop worrying. "I'm okay, really."

A skilled pretender, I thought. "You know what meds you're supposed to take?"

"I didn't have a stroke, Mike. I can read."

"Right. I'm . . . "

She waited, but I didn't know what to say. "Give me a minute. Okay?"

The door closed again.

When she emerged some minutes later, she seemed good, relaxed, refreshed, her hair pulled back, her eyes a bit clearer.

I imagined cooking dinner together the way we did every night when we first moved into our apartment, but there wasn't any food in the house (at least, any not expired and/or freezer-burned), so we dined on take-out chicken parm at the kitchen table. The ivy wallpaper crowded in around us.

Chewing sounds punctuated the silence.

Various conversation starters played in my head, but none of them made it to my lips. What was it like at the hospital? Did the doctors treat you well? How much do you remember of what happened? Did you really mean to hurt me, to cut my arm? Were you hurting yourself? Do you really not remember sleepwalking? Are you actually okay? Why did you run for the woods? What's back there? What is it that keeps you awake? Have you really not slept? Are you insane?

Dani paused mid-chewing; she'd barely eaten anything: "You're studying me."

"I'm not."

Red sauce slipped off her lip and speckled her chin. Or maybe she bit the inside of her mouth. "I know it's been hard for you, but I was the one in the hospital. Okay?"

"Okay."

I kept watching her, of course, in fact studying her. She gave off a sort of electrical (*buzz*) energy, and it radiated in an almost tangible jitter that filled the air like static electricity, but it was also contained, suppressed, fighting to erupt— a thunderstorm gathering strength.

Dani stabbed a piece of chicken, brought it toward her mouth, and then dropped the fork into the tinfoil container. Sauce splashed.

"What?" I said. I couldn't look away. If I did, I might miss some telling detail, a hint she was faking normalcy.

She gave me that "fuck off" face again, and was down the hallway and in the bedroom in a matter of seconds. The door shut.

My life of closed doors.

I went out on the deck and watched the sun bleed to reddish orange and slip down into the trees where shadows pulsed and spread, consuming the world.

CHAPTER 64:
MIDNIGHT WORSHIP

I SLEPT FOR only an hour or so, my mind alive with the curve of Dani's breasts, the silk of her leg. Some intimacy could help us heal. I wanted to feel connected again. Wanted to know she loved me. Wanted not to be scared of her.

My hand slid (*creeped*) between her legs. I massaged her, slowly, delicately, and waited for the faintest moan of pleasure to slip free from her sleep.

She grabbed my wrist with surprising strength and pushed my hand away. Then she turned from me. I moved closer and draped my arm around her, a hug, nothing sexual. It was, of course, obnoxious to put moves on her, considering what she'd been through.

"No," she said. It came out in a hard hammer hit.

"I want—"

She grunted, suddenly furious, and shoved my arm off her. She got out of bed. Her sweats sagged like loose skin. She crossed her arms and stared down at me like I was a vile bug crawling in her bed.

"I'm sorry," I said.

"I can't sleep."

Of course she couldn't—she hadn't been sleeping, at least not well, in a long time. Even back at the apartment, there were nights when I swear she stayed up all night, lying still beside me, pretending.

"Didn't they give you some medicine?"

"Yes."

"Should I leave you alone?"

Pale light slipped off the window and scarred her chin. "No," she said. "I can't sleep."

"Close your eyes and—"

"I *can't* sleep. At all."

"Dani, I—"

She sighed, said, "Forget it," and walked out. Her steps vanished down the hall, night swallowing sound.

I got up, pulled on gym shorts, and went after her. She wasn't in the kitchen, not in the bathroom, not in the living or dining room, not out on the deck.

DEAD END

I stopped, listened. Nothing.

Where the hell did she go? Was she running up Mount Munacy, headed once more for the dark woods beyond? Maybe she was downstairs, or—

"Mike?"

I spun around. Dani stood in the kitchen doorway. She hadn't been there a moment ago, I was positive. She hadn't been on the deck, either. Could she have slipped outside and out of view and then back inside so quickly and silently? Why would she?

"Where were you?" I sounded pissed, because anger was the best way to not be scared.

"I'm sorry," she said. "I don't know what's wrong with me." Her voice broke on the last words, and I took her in my arms. We hugged and she rested her head on my shoulder. "I just want to sleep."

"You took your pills?"

"Yes."

"One of them is a sedative."

"I know." She was crying now.

"It's okay. Let's go back to bed."

"I can't sleep."

"I'll stay up with you."

She resisted, but quickly gave in and let me lead her back down the hall. I wanted to ask if she'd gone outside, but I also didn't want to ask. Was it possible she'd been right in front of me and I didn't see her? Was I losing it or . . .

Del's voice: *There were times they couldn't find Randall.*

Back in bed, she curled against me. Her hand on my chest was cold, even through my t-shirt. She *must* have been outside. It made the most sense—or at least the most plausible sense. She'd gone outside long enough to cool her skin with some night cold.

Except the night wasn't cold. It was humid and very warm. The A/C unit was still in my mom's room, so my (our) bedroom was sweltering, the air thick.

"Tell me what you did while I was in the hospital," she said.

I told her about Rom, implied but couldn't quite say he was sort of like a father to me, talked about his wife, and somewhere in the telling, I fell asleep.

Dani was whispering. She was sitting up next to me, back stiff against the headboard, hands tangled together in her lap.

I lay there, still, listening. The words slipped and slithered, and it might have been a quiet chant or a prayer or—

Worship.

"What're you saying?"

She stopped. "What?"

"You were whispering."

"I'm tired."

"You were speaking."

"Go back to sleep," she said. "One of us should."

"You didn't get any sleep?"

"I took NyQuil. That'll work."

"You shouldn't mix meds."

"I'm so tired. Why can't I sleep?"

The best I could do was rub her leg. After a moment, she brushed my hand away.

"What can I do?" I asked.

"Sometimes," she said, "I think I can fly. Maybe I'll float and rise right through the ceiling and into the sky."

"Everyone wants to fly."

"No," she said. "I think I really can."

"You're just tired. What can I do to help?"

"Nothing, Mike. Nothing."

My hand crept toward her leg. "Are you sure?"

She snatched up my hand and twisted it so fast I couldn't make a noise before she let go and uttered, "Sorry."

"I'll leave you alone." My wrist throbbed.

"You can't help me. No one can. I'm just *fucked*." Her voice broke and she sobbed into her hands.

There I was: a young child who tried and tried not to sleep but eventually did and who soon threw himself from a nightmare and screamed through tears into the dark, and my father rushed into the room, shirtless, pajama pants pulling crookedly across his thighs, his hair a mess and his eyes wild with concern—and I sobbed not with relief at his presence but in fear nothing could keep away the bad things, not the ones stalking me in dreams or the ones haunting this house.

CHAPTER 65:
BAD MEMORIES AND PAIN

SUMMER SUN MAKES everything better.

The morning brought clear skies and gleaming light. Even the humidity eased its full-clenched grip.

Dani was downstairs. She'd managed to push all the boxes and bags toward their nearest walls, which opened a two-person-wide path from one end to the windows at the other.

"Spring cleaning?" I asked.

She made a *humpf* sound as she set a lopsided box on top of smaller boxes. Their corners crinkled. The blue plastic handle of a toy vacuum stuck out from the larger one. "Sure," she said.

In the corner, the desiccated rocking horse watched with its one remaining eye. Its opposite side reflected in the gray screen of a dust-cloaked TV.

The Underwood was up against the wall now, my manuscript beside it. Had she seen it, read a few pages? A vague admonishment that the pages were rough, first-draft stuff, immediately sprang up in my mind. Those pages weren't to be read, not by anyone, not yet.

"These books and movies," she said, and lightly kicked my Father's Remains. "A box of horror."

"Exactly," I said. "Belonged to my father."

The same sweats from yesterday drooped in wrinkled, greasy folds. Her long hair was tangled in sweaty loops, and lack of sleep sank her face onto her skull like a wet paper towel. She looked pretty awful, and I felt so bad for her. I should take her back to the hospital.

She picked up the battered paperback of Stephen King's *It*. Green-clawed fingers stretched from a sewer grate. "Why keep these?"

"They're books."

"Creepy books. You want to give yourself the creeps?"

"They were my father's, so I thought . . . " What, exactly, *did* I think? Honestly: reading the books he enjoyed was a way of connecting with him. Was that so bad? At least she hadn't noticed the coffin bookcase. It was buried under random bags again.

The book fell back into the box, and she pulled out the magazine featuring my father's published story. "And this gem."

"My father wrote that."

"It's pretty sick."

I reached for it.

She raised the open magazine to face me. Cowan in written like before

The Ritual of ~~Taurobolium~~ COWAN
by Ward Munacy

"I get it, Mike, I do. You've almost got his penmanship mastered."

"What're you—"

"Look." She pushed the pages toward me.

At the bottom of the page, written with my hand but deliberately penciled in neat, block-letter print to imitate my father's handwriting:

COWAN COWAN COWAN
COWAN COWAN COWAN

She waited.

"So?"

"It's weird. Trying to copy your dad's handwriting."

I thought copying my father's letters as exactly as I could was a way to commune with him, and if I could get the letters just right maybe I would discover some answers. It was childish and weird, she was right about that, but wasn't it also sort of endearing?

"What's it mean?"

"What?"

"That word."

"Cowan?"

Dani twitched when I said it, as if someone had poked a finger in her side.

"I don't know. He made it up." The lie had come so quickly, so easily.

She stared, challenging.

"I tried to copy his writing. So what?"

"It's how you spent your time while I was in the hospital, Mike."

"What was I supposed to do? They told me you were under 'restricted observation.' That's the exact phrase they used. I'm sorry I didn't call, but—"

"Forget it."

The magazine dropped into the box. The stapled psychology reports (**CONFIDENTIAL AND PRIVILEGED**) curled off the edge over the story. I grabbed them up and they flapped wildly, as if I'd seized a bird.

"What's that, something else you wrote about me?"

DEAD END

My gaze flitted back to the typewriter and the manuscript. "It's not about you, it's—"

Dani sighed. "Whatever. I need to keep busy."

She grabbed a box and started to turn with it, and the bottom gave out. Old magazines, faded kitchen towels, and small liqueur glasses tumbled out. One of them cracked. Dani stood there, staring down at it, and began to cry.

"Hey."

She didn't repeat the word. *She isn't simply going to bounce back.*

"Dani, let's go upstairs and . . . "

Her expression hardened. "I don't know what's wrong with me. The doctors said I was stressed—anxiety-induced bipolar disorder. Dissociative disorder. It's all bullshit. I can't sleep. It's this place. We have to leave. *Please.* I have all these bruises and scratches, and I don't know how I got them. *I don't know what's wrong with me.*"

She stood there crying. She let me hug her. "I'm so scared," she said.

"Me too."

"Let's get out of here. A motel. Anything."

"My mother's funeral is—"

"Who gives a shit? Grab your suit and throw it in the car."

"It's going to be okay."

"Wishing doesn't make it so."

All the stuff piled around us, the accumulation of decades and decades, so much to sift through, so much to discover, to learn. Who were my parents, really? Was my father mentally unstable, or was there something else gnawing at his mind? Had he actually participated in an exorcism? Did that young boy die because of something my father did? What about my twin? How much did my mother know? *Suspicions against her husband and her surviving child.*

"I don't want to go alone," she said. "Please."

"Okay," I said. "We'll go. Tomorrow. After the funeral."

Her fingers were at her lips again. "Mike . . . What're you hoping to find here?"

"The truth."

"There is no truth—just bad memories and pain."

CHAPTER 66:
A BAD PATCH

WE SAT OUTSIDE on the front porch. I sipped a beer, and Dani gulped water from a glass bleeding condensation. Mullock Road was quiet; the other two houses might've been abandoned. Was Del drinking bourbon at his bar while Suzanne paced aimlessly back and forth upstairs? What were Ned and his sun-kissed believers doing? Praying in the garage-church? Worshipping Moloch the Demon, perhaps?

It almost seemed possible.

"Do you really think it's this place that's, what, haunted? Cursed?"

"You think I'm being irrational?" she asked.

"I didn't say that."

"But you think it's all in my head."

"No," I said, but had nothing else to add.

"Your father died here."

"I know."

"You never discussed it with anyone, not even your mother."

The future, like the past, can also loom darkly, like the woods crowded around us, a shadowland harboring all sorts of beasts. If I dared to tell her what really happened, I would be risking all sorts of danger. Something might awake and begin to hunt. My father's trembling fingers tapping on my cheek. His dying word daring me to spill the whole truth. "It's complicated."

"Everything is, Mike."

"I'll tell you what happened, if you tell me something."

"We're making deals now?"

"I spoke to your mother. I had to call her. Otherwise you would have been committed. HIPAA rules or something."

"What did she say?"

"You're my problem now."

"Ah, Helen. Selfless to the bitter end. I really must get her a Mother's Day card next year."

"She said something happened."

"Did she?" Dani gestured at me with her glass, almost empty.

"Said she was going to write me a letter."

"Her fucking letters. She wrote me one when I went off to college. 'Now you're an adult, so don't call me crying for help. You have to make your own way. *C'est la vie.*"

"She wrote that?"

"Only with a lot more 'dearies,' 'sweeties,' and 'sugarbunches.'"

"What'd you do with it, the letter?"

"Used my boyfriend's lighter on it."

"What was it that happened?"

"It was a 'bad patch,' as Helen called it. 'Just a bad patch, sweetie love.'"

She isn't simply going to bounce back. This is going to linger.

"I was on the varsity soccer team," Dani said, and turned toward the woods. Crows cawed back and forth. "I wasn't even good. I did it because I needed to do something, and the other sports seemed stupid for whatever reason. I only made it on the team because there weren't enough girls to cut. Anyway, the other girls were real bitches. Took it all seriously. There was this one girl, Erin, she always said stuff about me. 'Stupid,' 'loser,' things like that. I started dating this boy and suddenly I was a 'slut' and a 'ho' and all sorts of dumb names. The other girls sometimes said them too. Usually whispers, but not always. The coach heard it, I know she did, but she never did anything about it. She *wanted* us to play nasty. 'The weak always lose,' was her motto. Turns out, of course, Erin had dated the same boy the previous summer. I didn't know. He didn't tell me. A summer fling. So there we are during a practice, running drills up and down the field, and Erin cuts right next to me, trips me. Big deal, right? I fall. I told you I was a crappy player—I fell a lot. The other girls circled me like wild animals, feet stomping, cleats kicking up dirt, and Erin gets right in my face and says, 'Eat the grass, whore.' She kicked me in the head."

Dani spoke barely louder than a whisper, and when she repeated what the girl said, her words slicked with unforgotten viciousness.

"Shit," I said. "What happened?"

"She hit me pretty good. Had a black eye for a while, but I jumped up and tackled her. I was screaming and crying and my head hurt so bad, but I punched the little bitch with all I was worth. Over and over. Other girls tried to stop me, and I *growled* at them. It was surprising to even me, that sound coming out. Now who was the wild animal?"

In my mind, Dani's lips curled back and she snarled—and launched at me.

"The coach wrestled me off her, but by then I'd done serious damage. Erin was in the hospital for ten days. Broke her clavicle, her elbow, dislocated her jaw, and knocked out three teeth."

"Whoa."

"I kicked her ass. I was suspended. They had a superintendent hearing about whether to expel me. They didn't." Recounting this part of the story, Dani's voice flexed with distant, reminiscent pride.

"I bet nobody called you names anymore."

"Oh, they did. Once they knew what I could turn into, they wanted to see it again. The bullying was even worse. The boy dumped me, actually went back with Erin, all bruised and wearing a cast like she was. I was kicked off the team, of course, but the girls stalked me at school, followed me in little packs, taunted me. I didn't fight again, though. I was warned: if I so much as pushed someone, I was gone for good. So I put up with it. Two years of it."

"I'm sorry," I said.

She set down her glass and hooked her arms around her chest, fingers in her armpits, and finished her story.

"Every day, I walked around pissed off. I wanted to fight those girls, and everyone else, but I kept myself restrained. And I got more and more pissed. I needed an outlet. I hit myself. Started with little pinches. Did it hard as I could on my thighs. Soon I was slapping my face, hard as I dared. Sounds neurotic, but it felt good. A release. Helen knew I was doing it. 'Just a bad patch, sweetie,' she said. I'd go in my room and pinch my skin and slap my face until I was scarlet-red and completely numb. That went on for a while, and I even cut myself sometimes, but I got better. Slowly. College helped. A chance to start over. Thank God it was back then. Nowadays, the fight would be on YouTube, and follow me everywhere."

"Did you tell the doctors about this?"

"They didn't need to know."

"Dani . . . "

"What did Helen say, I was 'out of my sweet mind'? She was worried at the time, but not about me, like a normal mother. She worried about her own life. Was my behavior going to affect her day-to-day routine? Get in the way of her pottery classes or calligraphy lessons? She would have been happy to shuffle me off to some mental hospital. She tried to. I spoke to doctors back then, and you know what they concluded? I was a stressed-out teen—like millions of others."

"I'm sorry that happened to you."

Sunlight paled her face. "Being here brought it all back. It's like something here pried all that terrible stuff loose."

"Stress."

"I don't think so, Mike. I think it's something a lot worse than stress."

The phone rang. Sometimes it happens that way.

"Hey, Mike, it's Rom."

"Hey, sorry I haven't—"

"Lee's about to die."

CHAPTER 67:
BACK OF THE BEYOND

ROM MET US at the front door.

He looked awful: hair a mess, eyes sunken behind bruised smudges, magnified in his glasses to horrible clarity, and even his yellow polo sagged against his chest like a dewy rag.

Home can be a place of death, I thought, *and death can be welcome.*

I made the introductions quickly. I'd tried, briefly, to convince Dani to stay home, but she didn't want to be in the house alone. "I wasn't there for you with your mom," she said. "My head was somewhere else. I want to be here for you now."

She might want to believe that was the reason, but I sensed something else: she was searching for her own truth.

The house was quiet. We followed Rom down the hall. The bedroom door stood ajar, and in the gap lamplight glowed with a strange slipperiness.

Lee groaned. The noise crackled toward words but crumpled into a garbled croak.

"It's not pretty," Rom said.

"Nothing ever is," I said.

"I would have given her morphine, but she refused it. I could have forced her, but . . . "

He pushed the door open. Everything was as it had been the other day: the nightstand with the solitary lamp, the tissue box, the orange-and-white bottles of pills, the framed picture of Rom and Lee with a dog, the red cowbell clutched in Lee's curled hand on top of the comforter, the black cat, Nightshade, nestled in the crook of Lee's knee.

The only difference: Ned Loller, in a long purple robe, stood over her on the opposite side of the bed. The large gold cross rested on his curved belly. His hands hovered over her. Eyes closed, lips moving, he was bestowing some sort of prayer.

Or a curse.

Lee's head had fallen askew off the pillow, and her body—no more than a skin-wrapped skeleton—lay crooked beneath the sheet. Sweat pimpled her pale forehead.

The blinds were drawn against the day, and the summer light glowed along the window-frame edges as if the outside world were afire.

Rom leaned toward me to whisper. "She hasn't said much for a few hours, but when she still could, she told me to bring Ned. She wanted me to make amends. Can't do any harm, right?"

Ned's hands flexed above her, and he slowly raised his arms. His fingers played the strings of an invisible marionette. There was another one of those echoes: my father's story of the doomed woman who walked naked into the night as if controlled by an otherworldly power. Or Dani on Mount Munacy, running for the woods.

Lee groaned again, but she was too weak to do anything other than rock her head slowly, side to side.

Dani approached the bed.

The smells started to register: body odor and human waste and the chemical sharpness of cleaning fluid.

Ned saw Dani across from him, and grinned as if he'd expected her. Shadows filled his mouth. "You are Dani, Mike's betrothed."

"Yes," she said. She reached toward Lee, but her hand couldn't quite touch the sheet. The cat stirred and readjusted into a comfortable curl.

"I'm sorry," Dani said.

I went to her, cupped her shoulder. She stiffened beneath my grip.

"Let us pray," Ned said.

Worship.

Rom stood at the foot of the bed, and I thought of moving but didn't. He should be next to her, not us. Standing at the end of the bed, Rom was more supervising witness than soon-to-be widower, yet maybe he was right where he wanted to be.

"Dear God," Ned said, "look on your servant Lee, lying in great pain and weakness, and comfort her with the promise of everlasting life beyond this earthly turmoil. Amen."

"Amen," Dani said, and I whispered the same. How smoothly we fall into religious routine in the face of death.

Lee's skinny, dry lips peeled back from yellowing teeth and wormed as if forming words she could no longer enunciate. She moaned, a quavering, choppy gargle of broken glass ground underfoot, and the sound vibrated along my skin. The room's stink thickened, and every breath I inhaled stuffed my throat more and more with the pungent taste of decay.

"Almighty Lord," Ned said, "you sent your only son to save us, and when your servant Lazarus died of sickness, Jesus proclaimed he would rise again. Lazarus did, summoned forth days after death to once more walk the earth. His resurrection was the symbol and truth of God's glory. Oh, Lord, your son Jesus knew of Lazarus's sickness and chose not to heal his dying friend, for he knew there would be greater glory in bringing him forth from the grave alive. Here at the edge of life and death we stand, and we beseech you to grant special life everlasting upon your servant, Lee. Amen."

Dani echoed the Amen again, as did Rom, but I was too caught up in what Ned was saying. My knowledge of the Bible was pretty much limited to the religious cartoons I'd watched on TV as a kid when there wasn't anything better on. I knew Adam and Eve and Noah and Jesus and the crucifixion, but that was about it. I'd probably heard the story of Lazarus before, but I didn't know Jesus let him die so he could raise him up again. It seemed wrong, unnecessarily cruel. It was like the other story Ned mentioned at the funeral: Abraham and Isaac. God made Abraham think he must kill his own son. What sort of god did that?

Lee groaned again, only this time it pitched toward a scream, growing louder and louder. It tore her throat in a chalk-on-board screech. Veins squirmed along her temples beneath a cloud of thinned hair, and her hand lifted and shook violently. The cowbell cupped in her hand made a hollow clacking sound, and her head fell one way and then the other.

"*Huuurrrts*," she said. "*HUUURRRTS!*"

Nightshade jumped up and leaped off the bed and scurried out the door down the hall. Rom rushed to the opposite side of the bed, one arm out to push Ned, but he stepped aside and Rom was there beside his screaming wife.

He cradled her face, and she kept groaning that single word over and over, the guttural quake dragging out longer and longer so it filled the room and the air pulsed with it.

"Honey," Rom said, "I'm here. It's me. I'm here."

Dani grabbed my arm. Her mouth quivered like a child's about to burst into frightened sobs. I hugged her against me, her face pushed into the crook of neck and shoulder.

"*HUUURRRTS!*" Lee screamed.

"*It's okay!*" Rom shouted back, and there was something so horrible about the moment—dying wife and tormented husband yelling at each other as death tore one from the other.

Lee screamed the word again and her arm flung sideways. Hand grasped tightly around the bell, her fist slammed into the side of Rom's face. The smack must've hurt, but it was mostly surprise stumbling Rom from the bed. He might've fallen if not for Ned's body.

I broke Dani's hug and went to Lee. Her wrist snapped into my open palm; I grasped it. She tried to resist, but gave up. Her mouth opened for another scream and closed again. I lowered her arm back to the bed. Her fingers blanched around the bell. She squeezed it against the pain, or maybe it was the only thing keeping her here, in this world, grounded and alive, her existence reduced to a single sensation. Keep squeezing, keep living.

Her head trembled.

I let go of her wrist and touched her cheeks, as Rom had a moment ago. Her skin was soft and cold. She stilled.

"We're here." I sounded normal, like comforting the dying were second nature for me.

Rom was back at the bed, and I lifted Lee's head, the sheet oil-stained, and Rom slid the pillow back into place. She barely dented it.

Her eyes opened. They were grey and slippery, a foggy morning over a rainy harbor.

"It's . . . beautiful," she said, voice small.

"It's okay," I said. I'd missed my mother's final moments, but I could be here for Lee's. I didn't know her at all, but maybe this was a form of penitence, a way to heal guilt I hadn't realized I had. "It's okay."

My voice cracked, and Rom touched my arm. I let go, stepped back, and Rom was at her side like the other day, one hand caressing through her wispy hair and down the side of her face.

She was still staring at me. *Through* me.

"She knows," Lee said. "Wrong. *Wrong.*"

"Who knows?" I asked, and felt everyone watching me.

Lee strained, muscles tensing through her neck, eyes trying to focus on me but still seeming to look through me. "Something there. Behind. *Beyond.*"

I glanced behind me, half-expecting to see something—a wraith-like specter, perhaps, or even the ghost of my mother or father—but there was only Dani, her hands over her face, her own eyes wide and wet between splayed fingers.

Lee's head lifted an inch off the pillow. Her lips pulled back. "*Cowan,*" she said.

"It's okay," Rom said. "I'm here. You're safe." Her head settled back down.

"Something," Lee said, quieter, hardly a whisper. "Back of the beyond."

Those slippery eyes expanded. Fear swelled within them. Her lips trembled. Breath chopped, fast, short and quick. Her fear unbalanced something inside me, and I stepped back and Dani grabbed a handful of my shirt.

"It's okay," Rom said.

"No," Lee said. The word echoed in a shaky breath.

Rom struggled to find something else, something more. "I love you."

Her eyes bulged harder, any more and they might pop from their sockets, and a solid cord flexed taut inside her. Her arm snapped rigidly straight, fingers long and tensed at her sides. The bell rolled free along her skinny leg.

Breath trickled from her throat, the hollow exhale of a freshly unclogged drain. Thinner and thinner . . .

"Lee," Rom said. "I love you."

Her chest hitched, her breath caught. My own lungs caught. Was that it? Was she dead?

Her whole body rocked to the side as she sucked in a breath. Still here. Still alive.

DEAD END

"*Lee*," Rom said, almost crying the word. One hand on her face, he reached the other across her body to take hers.

Their fingers curled together.

She breathed out again, shallow, not even as substantial as a yawn, and her head tilted into Rom's palm, her mouth drooped. A dry-straw sound cracked in her throat.

And she was—still.

The grey, foggy harbor faded.

Rom tried to say his wife's name again, then dropped his head against the bed and wept.

Behind him, Ned backed toward the far wall. His chubby hand came up and rested on the gold cross hanging from his neck.

He looked frightened. Perhaps he was reminded of something. A young boy named Randall, maybe, a boy who'd gotten hit while riding his bike, who might've died in the street but who also died months later after a cruel and misguided attempt to help him.

CHAPTER 68:
LIKE FATHER . . .

I FOUND MYSELF in the hallway bathroom, grooming scissors in hand, leaning close to the mirror.

My father had stood exactly this way fourteen years ago.

I leaned closer.

"Wrong," Ward Munacy said to himself. "Wrong, wrong, wrong." He sounded excessively calm, focused. "Wrong, wrong, wrong."

He snipped hairs along his chin to his cheek. He petted the beard hair over and over, rubbing it down over and over. "Wrong, wrong, wrong."

My face was stubbly, but I'd never tried to grow a beard. Part of me was afraid I couldn't, but maybe I ought to try.

Dad tugged a cluster of hair. The skin stretched. The scissors snipped.

On the counter: an open bottle of Clubman—a tuxedoed top-hatted man on the green label, the baby-powder smell filling the bathroom—Dad's glasses balancing on the sink lip, and his wood-handled straight razor open and sharp.

"Dad?" It was a warm May morning, but my skin crawled with cold. I opened my mouth to speak again and—

Dad angled the sharp points of the scissors at his cheek, where fresh blood swelled, and pressed into his skin. Flesh pierced. His jaw tightened and his eyes flashed bright blue. Blood bulged in a teardrop and rolled into his beard.

He wedged the scissors deeper and twisted them while pulling up, as if trying to pry something out.

"Wrong, wrong, wrong," he repeated in fading breath.

Dusty rubbed against my leg, purring.

The scissors yanked up, the cheek hole opened wide, and thick blood blistered and spurted. Spots speckled the mirror. My father groaned—a deep, electric quaver growing louder and louder as the scissors widened the hole bigger and bigger.

The sound throbbed in the bathroom and echoed down the hall and clenched onto my bones.

"DAD!"

He dropped the scissors. They landed in the sink. Blood spotted the bowl and the counter. Blood flowed freely from the jagged tear in his face. Blood soaked his beard, ran down his neck, and wet the collar of his undershirt.

He breathed heavily, a man startled from a nightmare.

Dusty scurried down the hall into my room and right under the bed.

"Dad!" I said. "Your face!"

His hand slapped against the wound and more blood splashed over his nose and lips and plopped onto the mirror.

He turned to me. The red stain was spreading down his white shirt. Blood slipped between his fingers and dribbled on the tile floor. It flecked his toes.

We stared at each other.

And stared.

"Sometimes," he said, voice calm and distant, "the bad things come back. You think they're gone, but they're not. You can't see them, but they're sneaking, creeping, skulking right back. And then—they're back."

"Dad?"

"You have to be careful," he said. "It might be in the blood."

Red spots on the mirror, counter, and floor.

He stepped toward me and I backed into the wall.

"It followed me," he said. "That's what I think. It followed me, and it lives in the blood. There's too much. Can't possibly get rid of it all."

My throat constricted and my hands chilled limp.

"Stay here," he said in that same distant voice. "I have something to do."

He walked past me, hand pressed to his cheek and blood slipping free, and then he was in the kitchen and opening the door and stepping outside onto the deck.

Sharp pain fractured the memory, and there I was, twenty-five years old in the same bathroom, leaning toward the same mirror, little scissors piercing a hole in my cheek. Thick red blood bubbled.

I watched it roll down to my chin and drop off to splat the counter.

Do it again, a voice suggested. It sounded like my own, only colder. *Stab yourself real good this time—make your father proud and gouge the hell out of your face. Tear the skin. Maul your cheeks into serrated flaps. Let the blood flow. It's the only way to get the disease out. You must exsanguinate.*

The sharp ends of the scissors neared my cheek and moved toward my left eye. My hand was steady.

Go on. Do it.

Muscles tensed, throbbed.

"Coward," I murmured. But that wasn't quite right. "Cowan."

I said it again. And again. And again.

The word filled my mouth and I had to say it or I would choke, and once I said it, it bulged inside me once more and I had to say it again. It kept tumbling off my lips, splashing onto the counter, spilling onto my feet, stacking up around my legs.

"*Stop!*"

I threw the scissors in the sink. They clattered among a spray of blood drops. I heaved for air, gagged, choked. Slowly, I felt calmer, more myself.

That steely cold version of my own voice spoke up again: *You have to be careful, Mike. Very careful. If Dani finds out about this, you're going to be in serious trouble. She's the one with the problems, not you—this was a little hiccup, no big deal—and you have to keep it quiet.*

"Yes," I said. I turned on the sink and cleaned off the blood.

CHAPTER 69:
HAUNTED OR NOT

I OPENED THE door and caught my scream before it could escape. Dani was standing right there.

"What were you doing?"

"Nothing."

"You're bleeding."

"It's nothing."

She grabbed my wrist. "Something's happening to you, too, isn't it?"

"No," I said, but she saw through my lie.

The hallway was bright, but it felt late. My eyes hurt with exhaustion, and my cheek throbbed, and I was confused. How had I gotten here?

"You were sleepwalking," Dani said.

"No, I . . ." But she must be right. I'd never sleepwalked before, but neither had Dani. Maybe it *was* this house. Maybe there was something trying to control us. Haunting us. Something in the woods.

"We need to leave," she said. "Now."

"I'm okay. I was just . . ." What? Reliving the most traumatic event of my life?

"Tell me," she said. "What was it?"

It was right there, as it had been dozens of times before, the true story of what happened the day my father mauled his face and dropped off Mount Munacy to die of a heart attack, or perhaps from something else, but I pushed it back. I was afraid to tell her. Afraid that in the telling, I might collapse into a memory I couldn't escape. Not a mousetrap this time, but an open grave.

"Tomorrow," I said. "We'll leave tomorrow."

"Mike, either this place is haunted, or we are."

"One more night won't kill us."

CHAPTER 70:
WORSHIP THE COWAN

DANI'S CRYING WOKE me sometime later. Sleep almost took me back, but Dani's tears croaked into a guttural sob.

Hallway light cut across our bodies. She lay on the bed a few feet away, on her side, facing me. Her hands were tucked under her head the way a child might sleep. Her tears blotted the sheet.

We need to leave, I thought. *We need to get out of here and never, ever come back.* But another thought cut that one off: *It's not this house; it's her. She's always had mental issues, and stress has fractured her mind. She's losing it. She's not simply bipolar—she's developing schizophrenia.*

"Dani?"

She swallowed, mumbled something.

I recalled a dream: Dani's Easter Island stone facade and the sound of chanting growing louder and some enormous presence expanded behind that stone face and I didn't want to see it but there it was: an enormous wasp with a curved, black stinger, dripping venom—a monster from a black-and-white horror film about enormous, mutated bugs.

"Worship," I said.

"The Cowan," she said.

"What?"

"Cowan, Cowan."

I sat up. Beyond the bedroom window, night was thick black. "Dani?"

Whispered s-sounds slipped off her lips. I grabbed her shoulder, shook her hard. "Dani! *Wake up!*"

Her eyelids slid back to reveal creamy white eyes, and I screamed her name again and again, my own horror worsening my panic. "*Wake up! Wake up!*"

She sprang upward at the waist as if shoved from underneath, and turned toward me so quickly I didn't see her arm cutting through the air. Her hand slapped my face hard, and her nails, jagged from her nibbling at them, tore into my flesh. One finger caught the bump of my scissor-injury and ripped it wide. The pain was startling. Warm blood slicked over my cheek.

"Stop!" I yelled. "*STOP THIS!*"

Both of her hands, fingers hooked into claws, went for me, and I batted them back. Our bodies tangled on the bed, mattress thumping, and she hissed and growled, and I kept screaming for her to wake up, and somehow I snagged both her wrists in my hands and yanked her arms across her chest and shoved her flat against the bed.

Heart hammering, sweat slicking my skin, I stared down at her, heaving for air and completely horrified.

She stilled, and when she spoke it was dreamy and sad but clear. "It's no use, Mike. Even if we left now, it's too late. We belong here. Forever."

"I'm taking you to the hospital," I said between breaths.

She shook her head and laughed, not the girlish laughter this time but a throaty smoker's cackle. "I know how it happens. How we die."

"Stop this." I pressed down on her arms.

She laughed. It sounded crazed, awful. "The Cowan didn't come back. You did. And you brought me." She twisted her neck in a serpentine-like wobble. She opened her eyes—clear and sharp. "Do you want to know how it happens?"

"Shut up," I said. "Stop this." I was barely projecting, fear clamping my throat.

"The child dies, too," she said, and laughed, louder and louder.

"*Shut up.*" I slapped her across the face.

Her head snapped to the side—and she was completely still.

I thought I'd killed her, but she was still breathing, slow and easily. Asleep. I was as horrified of her as I was of myself: I'd never slapped anyone before.

Slowly, cautiously, I let go of her and got out of bed. She didn't move. Was she asleep—finally, really, actually asleep—or was she pretending?

I waited.

Waited.

I heard something.

My feet took me backwards toward the hall, but I kept my focus on Dani. Not moving. Breathing slow and shallow. Had to be sleeping. Had to be.

Voices. Coming from downstairs.

I walked backwards down the brightly-lit hallway, and wanted even more light. Any moment Dani would leap from the bed and come charging down the hall, screaming or laughing or both.

She *was* possessed. Maybe it was mental illness or something far more outlandish, but it came down to the same thing: she was no longer herself.

I'm not me.

Halfway down the stairs, I heard the voices more clearly and froze. I knew what it was. The old Sony TV was plugged in, and playing a movie through the built-in VCR. I recognized the sounds and chaotic images without needing to see the cardboard VHS cover of a man in a wife-beater undershirt glowering at himself in a mirror.

CHRIS DILEO

Henry: Portrait of a Serial Killer. The movie, which was a loose retelling of serial murderer Henry Lee Lucas and his co-killer, Ottis Toole, was already past the scene scarred in my memory: Henry and Otis invade a woman's house in the middle of the day and brutally rape and kill her. The sound of her ripping clothes and throat-grating scream had never faded for me, and when they murder her young son, while recording the whole scene to later watch and laugh over like friends enjoying an old sitcom, I felt the terrible images searing into my psyche.

There was a social critique intended in the depiction, but my young mind couldn't process anything but the awful horror, and my older self felt that childhood fear, as fresh as it'd been years ago.

How long had my father watched the movie on Halloween while wearing the two-headed mask and waiting for me to come home from school?

I hit the power button and the screen went black as actor Michael Rooker, in the role of the deranged title character, brooded dark thoughts and the music trembled on the verge of chaos.

Someone was behind me.

I spun around, expecting Dani, the pair of long scissors raised high in her hands, but there was no one.

No one I could see, anyway.

CHAPTER 71:
NO ONE SLEEPS

UPSTAIRS, DANI HADN'T MOVED.

I set a dining room chair against the far wall and sat there to watch her. She didn't flinch. She didn't whisper.

But I was sure she wasn't sleeping. Not in the normal sense.

Hours stretched and stretched, but eventually sunlight brightened the room, and the day went on while she lay there and I watched her.

Hours.

"Dani," I said. "It's time."

"I know," she said, her words clear and immediate, as if she'd been waiting for me to speak.

It was time for my mother's funeral.

CHAPTER 72:
COWAN ARISE

I WALKED TO the front of the room at Ferguson's Funeral Home and stood next to what remained of my mother—reduced to ashes in a silver urn. Two large bunches of flowers stood on either side of the urn, and a kneeler was set before it.

Dani sat back-stiff in the front row, head straight, eyes boring into me. We didn't say anything to each other after we were up and moving, but she'd left the toilet un-flushed, her urine deep yellow, almost brown, and smelling pungent, acidic. She'd showered, though, and I'd scooped out a soggy mess of hair. It dropped into the garbage with a seaweed slap.

It seemed like a lot of hair to lose.

She's deteriorating, I thought.

Randall was losing his teeth, too. Dropping right out of his head.

"Thank you for coming," I said.

Twenty or so women, and a few of their obliging husbands, sat in the chairs facing me. The women had thin, dyed hair permed to varying degrees, their faces pancaked with flaky, mismatched makeup, and their pantsuits and blazers baggy and wrinkled. The husbands wore grey or brown suits with clashing ties.

"You each knew my mother, and I know each of you meant a great deal to her."

Heads nodded and bifocaled eyes blinked.

"After my father died, my mother raised me by herself. She was working, too, and I can't imagine life was easy for her. I was a kid, so I wasn't much help. But she had each of you. As her friends, you kept my mother going. Thank you."

Someone sniffled, and several people opened pocketbooks to hunt for tissues.

I had no eulogy. This was to be quick. A few brief, sincere words, and then I was taking Dani directly to the hospital. She didn't know that, of course, and part of me hoped I could fool her into thinking we were going out to eat and simply pull up to the ER entrance where burly men in white shirts and pants would restrain her—for her own safety, and mine.

Several rows back sat Rom in a grey suit. His hair was combed, but beginning to spread in porcupine quills. We didn't say much to each other, but we sat side-by-side for a few minutes during a lull of visitors. I watched Dani, and from the corner of my eye Rom could pass for my father—or, at least, a certain conception of my father.

At one point, Rom reached into his pocket and held out his open palm to me: a round blue pill. Valium. I declined, and the pill returned to his pocket.

Farther back, and off to the side by one of the end tables, where an ancient lamp cast pale light onto boxes of tissues, Nina Calla sat wrapped in a thick coat, as if it weren't ninety degrees and humid outside.

She was the only one of Ned's disciples to visit. She'd taken my hand—hers chilled as ice—and said how grateful she was I'd tried to help Isaac. I nodded. What could I say? I wanted to ask about her husband. I wanted to ask if she believed someone killed her son. I wanted to know what Officer Koryta had said to her. I wanted to know why she was one of Ned's followers. But I had bigger concerns at the moment.

"Your mom is here with you," Nina said. "Death is not the end."

Someone coughed, and someone else honked a nose-blow.

Dani shifted in the front row, black dress and stockings, matching shawl pulled over her shoulders. She stared at me, unblinking. Did she know what I was up to? Did she at least sense I was going to do something? Air conditioning rattled in the vents; sweat slicked my collar.

I smiled at the crowd, and regretted it immediately. I touched the small Band-Aid on my cheek and winced. "My mother would be upset there are no brownies or cakes here for us to enjoy."

A few people chuckled. In the front row, Dani's lips were moving. Whispering.

"I'm just going to talk for a while and—"

"I'm sorry, Mike," Dani said. "But I warned you."

"Dani, what're you—"

"*Cowan*," she said, loud and clear, throwing the word at me as an accusation. Her cheeks speckled red swirls.

"Dani, sit down."

"*Cowan*," she said louder. People murmured to each other, looked around nervously. "Cowan COWAN COWAN COWAN COWAN *COWAN!*"

Dani stood, still shouting that one word. Her voice wavered and warbled, peaked in high pitches, and bottomed out in deep baritones. She was a mad preacher, caught on repeat, and no one made any move to stop her, me included.

"*Cowan! All die here*," she shouted. "*All die! All die! All—*"

Her frantic, insane words cut off—and she started screaming.

CHAPTER 73:
WHEN MOLOCH SPEAKS

IT WAS THE cry of a hawk screeching across the sky. The sound carved along Dani's throat and echoed through the room. Her scream stretched and stretched, its volume rising even as it began to die in a grinding, metallic howl.

The subsequent silence was palpable, the air jellied, clogging every ear and gluing everyone in place.

Dani snapped backward, falling into the wooden chair and tumbling backwards. Her legs kicked up, a flash of skin shone above her stockings, and she crashed into the row behind her. No one sat there, though a woman in a blue blouse and red blazer was directly beyond in the third row and she straightened up as the empty chair thwacked into her knees, her arms wrapping around her pocketbook, and her face crimping in shock and offense.

On the floor, Dani cried out. It might have turned into another hawk screech, but she either didn't have enough air in her lungs, or her throat was too raw to produce anything above a hoarse croak.

One of her black flats had fallen off her foot, and the other one dangled on her toes. Her legs scissored back and forth. The chair shook with her tremors and another chair toppled to her right and it careened into the next, but then her movements slowed to a stop-motion crawl. Her body jilted and stuttered in lethargic blinks, puppet-like.

I was eleven again and my father stretched one arm and his fingers touched my face and tapped a secret code on my cheek as if it were a telegraph.

From my angle at the urn and flower display, I saw Dani's arms flail out and her head snap side to side, audibly cracking, all movements torpid, a flip book slowly paged, but it was the lengthy stretches where I couldn't see her face that scared me the most. How much redder would her face be on the next sideways snap? How much farther could her eyes bulge? How far could the veins in her temples pulse before rupturing through skin?

Cowan, I thought. *Coward. Cowan. Coward. Cowan. Coward.*

After that, things moved very fast.

The women were up and moving toward the open door and the hallway beyond, or fleeing to the back of the room. More chairs fell. A woman in a green dress tripped and snagged another two women with her on the way down. Their cries of surprise were almost childlike, but instantly lost in shouts of pain. Someone's bag fell and its contents tumbled free: pocket tissues, lipstick, a checkbook, an emery board. A white shoe kicked the lipstick across the room, where it ricocheted off the wall.

"*Mike!*"

Rom's shout knocked me out of my paralysis. He was shoving his way through the crowd.

I tossed a chair out of my way and dropped to my knees beside Dani. She was shaking—*seizing*—arms and legs spasming, chest rolling up and down, and with every convulsion her head thunked against the carpeted floor.

Smack. Smack. SMACK.

"Dani!" I yelled. "Dani, stop!"

Blackish saliva slipped across her lips and bled down her cheeks into a morbid smile. I grabbed her head and the tremors rippled up my arms, an electric current of vibration prickling my nerves. Not natural. Not a seizure. This was something else. Something much worse. Something was speaking through her. A thing not sane.

"*Dani!*" I shouted.

Her eyes rolled back from milky whites to gray, but she didn't see me, didn't focus on me.

"I'm right here," I said, softer but still insistent.

Rom was beside me, hand on my shoulder, leaning down. More black liquid bubbled between her lips. "Turn her on her side," he said, and as I did, a violent tremor flopped her like a dying fish on land and she puked a slop of rancid bile. The smell stung my eyes and made me gag.

"Call 9-1-1," I said, but I wasn't sure if I was telling him or myself.

Dani's head pushed up against my grip, slipped free, and slammed down into the floor. The hit was so strong and sudden it trembled through the floor into my knees. I cringed. A hit like that could fracture her skull.

Heavy, erratic pounding echoed all around. It wasn't an otherworldly presence or a hallucination, just the chaotic footfalls of fleeing mourners knocking chairs into me and shouting to get out—all of it magnified through the adrenaline-charged blood pumping in my ears.

Dani's head flung forward again and she found me, honed in on me, and I saw one word in her desperate face—*HELP*—and her head snapped backwards out of my grip. The smack was hard, rock hurled against asphalt, and the hit was powerful enough to concuss her, strong enough to make her black out, deadly enough to do permanent damage.

"Jesus . . ."

Rom wedged past me onto his knees and cradled Dani's head. I'd been gripping her so tightly my fingers ached and she still slipped free, but Rom held her as he might a ripe melon and he stayed with her as she rocked forward and snapped back. His hands padded her head from each successive hit.

The hits lessened in strength. Her legs slid off the upended chair and quivered on the floor. Her arms dropped away.

Her eyes closed and her head shook with only the slightest vibration. Her chest eased into gentle breathing rhythms. Blood trickled from her nose, and black gunk smudged the corners of her mouth and up her cheeks in a demonic clown grin.

This was too much. How had the doctors not sensed Dani was ill? She'd tricked the doctors—skillfully pretended to be normal—and now she was going to be hospitalized for a long time, months and months.

I had my cell out, but Rom grabbed my wrist. "It's passed," he said. "For now." He was working his fingers into Dani's mouth. "A little Valium will help. Some." I tensed, thinking Dani would bite right through his fingers, but they slipped free unharmed. He held her mouth closed and massaged her throat and, a second or two later, she swallowed.

I started to dial, and Rom grabbed my wrist again. "Before you do, let's get her home—"

Dani howled. The sound wasn't the hawk screech but a throaty, painful bay of an injured animal. It surprised both of us and, in our surprise, Dani slipped onto her stomach, her shawl falling around her like drooping wings, her skirt bunching up near her waist, and she launched herself between us. Her arms flung out to knock us back.

Rom tumbled sideways into the few chairs still standing in the front rows, and I grabbed Dani around the waist. She hit me harder and broke through, but I snagged her bony hip and knocked her off balance.

Dani fell sideways into the display at the front of the room. Her shoulder hit one of the flower bunches and her arms came up, seeking something to grab, and she found the stand holding the urn. She took it all down with her in a haphazard crash.

The silver urn cracked against the wall. The top popped off and a black plastic box containing Mom's ashes tumbled to the carpet.

Dani reached for it, seized it, lifted it.

Rom grabbed Dani's wrist and yanked one hand off the box. She lashed out at him with her other, fingers hooked toward his face. She hissed at him. Spittle spotted his forehead.

Her legs swung around to hit him, almost knocked him over, but he snapped her arm hard, hard enough to dislocate her shoulder.

Her cry was genuine pain.

"*Stop!*" I yelled.

Rom eased his grip, and Dani quieted.

Her mouth opened and closed in a slippery, uneven way, and whispered words billowed out in a sustained single breath. They were nonsense sounds, sibilants and sharp-edged consonants that might pass for some ancient, long-lost language.

Speaking in tongues, I thought. *Possessed.*

Dani's words slipped and punched from her mouth without a break: an endless supply of oxygen on a single breath.

But she was calming. The outburst, the episode, was over.

It had happened so fast that only now was my heartbeat speeding up. My pulse throbbed in my temples. "I'm going to get you help," I said.

Dani screamed almost as loudly as her initial hawk screech. Her eyes gleamed. Her lips stretched white across her teeth. Blood clouded her right eye.

How much more could she take? How much could I?

I was right there in the moment, front and center to the horror, watching the woman I loved suffer a cruelty without parallel—or so I believed then.

Adulthood had a few lessons left to teach me: things can always get worse.

She rolled over and snatched up the black plastic box again. Her fingers tore open the plastic bag within. A cloud of ash plumed free. Rom grabbed at her and she growled and yanked from his grip.

She scooped out a handful of grey ash—Mom's Remains—and threw it at us. The ash scattered in a cloud. Rom turned his head, but I was so surprised I didn't move in time. Ash hit my face, tickled my nose, dusted my lips.

I wiped at my face frantically, felt a sneeze building.

Dani lifted the box in both hands, a priest raising the chalice at Communion, and dumped the ash on her upward-tilted face. It covered her, blanketed her dress.

She tossed the box aside and shook her head. Ash swept out from her hair. Her face was a gray mask, crumbling off to reveal the living thing buried beneath.

They're coming to get you, Baaarbaraaa!

Her tongue flicked out and lapped across her lips. Ash stacked on it, and she ate it. Her jaw worked up and down in exaggerated chomps. She wasn't growling, but the sounds rattling from her throat were animalistic and dangerous.

A woman in the back of the room screamed, and someone else expelled lunch in a heavy splash.

Dani clawed the ash from her eyes and turned toward me.

Her bladder let go. Urine soaked her black underwear and gave off an awful, noxious, sulfuric stink. She pushed upward against Rom's grip. I grabbed her ankles, and she kicked at me so wildly I lost my hold.

"Mike, Mike, Mike," Dani repeated, but her eyes were unfocused, empty as if she were blind. Perhaps she was—hysterical blindness brought on by whatever this was.

That's all it is. A fit. A spell. She's not possessed, not—

"The woods," she said between heavy, liquid pants. Spit bled through her ash-coated chin. "The woods. *It's in the woods!*"

CHRIS DILEO

"It's okay," I said. "It's going to be—"

She jolted upright into a sitting position. I had her ankles, but Rom lost his hold, and as he went for her again she elbowed him in the throat. His eyes went wide, his hands groped at his neck. He couldn't breathe.

"Dani, please—"

Her head snapped sideways with a chiropractic crack and albino bug eyes stared at me. "Wrong," she said in a painful rasp. "*Wrong*! **WRONG!**"

"*Stop it!*" I shouted.

"Mike, there can be no child. It must *not* be born. *It must die!*"

Rom finally managed to inhale. I leaned forward to ease Dani back to the floor, but her arm flung forward and she punched me in the nose. Something snapped and hot pain flushed my face. Too surprised to even make a noise, I dropped back. Blood was already flowing from my nostrils. My sinuses bulged, stuffed.

Dani lurched forward on all fours and scrambled past me. Skirt still yanked around her waist, her butt was rigid and bony, and there was something so ugly about this, something primitive and bestial, that I wanted to look away but couldn't.

Her hands slapped onto the spilled flowers. She batted them out of the way and seized the floral pick that held the tiny card—*For Mom, Love, Mike & Dani*—and clenched it in both fists.

The cardholder wasn't one of those flimsy plastic ones with the trident top: this one had a circular end for securing the card, and it was made of metal. The pointy end was wedged into a block of green floral foam inside the vase, but now light gleamed along it, as it had the scissors in the kitchen.

Dani flopped on her back, yanked her underwear from her crotch, flashing me. "*It can never live,*" she said in that grating rasp. "*It is wrong!*"

The sharp end of the floral pick passed between her spread thighs and entered her. She growled against the pain, spit popping around clenched teeth, but she pushed the metal wire further, deeper.

Someone in the back of the room screamed and someone else shouted, "*Oh, God!*"

I launched toward her. Rom tried to say something, but nothing came out.

I grabbed Dani's wrist, squeezed. "*Stop!*" I yelled. "*STOP!*"

She hissed at me. Black spittle dotted her ashy cheeks. I should have been able to pull her arm back easily—she was never very strong, and she'd lost weight she couldn't afford to lose—but her arm was strong now, her grip vise-solid.

"**Dani, STOP!**"

She didn't. She pushed the thing deeper.

Her nonsensical chant, all s-sounds and fractured noises, fell from her mouth, her lips worming around them as if birthing every sound, and still she forced the metal wire deeper.

DEAD END

I clamped on her wrists and pulled. Her bare ass dragged against the carpet. She thrust her pelvis, pushed the wire deeper, and screamed with her determination.

My own scream battled hers, and I pulled on her wrists, but it brought her closer and now we were almost face to face, with the wire between us. I wedged my right foot on her bare hip—black dress shoe against pasty white skin—and pushed her back while pulling her wrists.

Finally, I overpowered her, but she didn't relent. The wire slid slowly out. Blood dripped off and blotted Dani's thighs. My own blood salted my mouth.

Dani's eyes were huge white orbs, and blue veins squirmed through her temples, and her entire body shook.

She's going to detonate, I thought wildly, but I had enough leverage now and the wire fell out of her. It might have gone in seven or eight inches. She struggled against me, grunted. Pulled against my grip.

The wire neared her again.

"Dani, no! ***LOOK AT ME!***"

She blinked, and there was the dark-eyed woman I'd fallen for while slow dancing to "The Way You Look Tonight," the woman before whom I'd knelt on one knee and asked the ultimate question, the woman who said yes.

"Dani," I said. "*Please*."

Her grip loosened. I pulled the wire away and tossed it aside. A string of blood wet the carpet.

"It's okay," I said, though I could hardly catch my breath. "It's—"

Her hands curled into claws and she slapped my face. A finger snagged my lower lip and pulled. Another poked my right eye, and the flash of bright pain immobilized me.

She pushed me back, climbed over me. Blood gurgled into my throat and I choked on it. I shoved her and her knee thwacked my groin, and her hand tunneled into my open mouth. Her fingers scraped at my tongue. I tasted gritty ash. I gagged and that opened my mouth wider and her fingers stabbed the back of my throat—

"*Be still!*" It was Rom, finally able to speak again. "***COWAN!***"

Dani froze. Rom stood over us.

"***Cowan***," he declared in a booming voice, "***be still!***"

In his hand he held the glass flower vase. He swung it sideways, and it thumped against the side of Dani's head. She collapsed in an awkward sprawl.

For a moment, mercifully, nothing—only breaths.

He dropped the vase.

I went to Dani. My body ached, and blood ran from my nose and burbled out my mouth. I was sure he'd killed her.

Her eyes were closed, but her lips were moving, silently whispering.

"You could have killed her." I wiped an arm across my mouth, and blood smeared the entire suit sleeve through a coat of ash. I spat ash. It crunched like sand between my teeth.

Rom stared down at me. "Did she feel like someone who could die so easily?"

One of the morticians finally pushed his way into the room. His face was white, his suit pulled crookedly. He gasped, open-mouthed. "I'll call an ambulance?" He said it like a question.

"No," Rom said. "It's under control."

The bloody floral pick lay nearby. Mom's ashes were everywhere.

The mortician looked to me, and I looked to Rom for a long beat—yet another chance to make the right move—before glancing back up.

"No, it's okay," I said. "I'll take her to the hospital myself."

CHAPTER 74:
IT'S NOT GOD

"WE'RE NOT TAKING her to the hospital," Rom said. "Not yet, anyway."

"What?" My voice was muffled, a wad of tissues stopping up my bleeding nose.

Rom was driving, and I was in the backseat with Dani. She was asleep, or at least appeared asleep, body slack, slumped across the seat, head on my lap. I slowly caressed her hair.

When we were first dating, I would do that for hours, slowly trace my fingers through her smooth black hair and curl it around her ear. For hours more, my fingers would carry the perfume of her sweet-smelling shampoo. I'd touch my face to get a whiff of her smell.

"You saw what happened. No hospital can treat her."

"You hit her in the head with a vase," I said.

"She might be concussed, but that's not the issue."

"Oh, no?"

We turned onto Heintz Hill, and Rom exceeded the twenty-five miles per hour speed limit by almost double. "It's no use playing dumb, Mike."

I opened my mouth and closed it again. I wanted to play dumb, he was right about that, but Dani still needed medical treatment. She could be quite hurt. Who knows what damage she'd done to her insides with that wire? *The child dies, too.*

"How'd you know the word Co—"

"*Don't say it!*"

Rom's words were loud and panic-tinged. He stared at me through the rearview, and his expression left no doubt to his seriousness. "How do you know that word?" I asked.

Rom didn't respond.

"You've been talking to Ned," I said. "I know what you're thinking. We're not doing it. She needs a doctor, maybe a whole bunch of them."

"You believe in God?" he asked.

"It's not God," I said.

"Yeah. Exactly."

"That's not what I mean. You want to believe God is all-powerful or has some predestined plan, but it's bullshit, Rom, and you know it. I'm sorry Lee died, but God had nothing to do with it."

"No shit," he said, and we turned sharply onto Mullock.

"She needs to go to the hospital."

"You don't want to hear this," Rom said, "but doctors can't do much for Dani except pump her full of drugs. It's all doctors ever do. They don't heal. They don't cure. They medicate."

"We don't even know what's wrong," I said. My fingers tangled in Dani's hair.

"We can heal her," Rom said.

Head on my lap, Dani mumbled something.

CHAPTER 75:
THE WAY YOU LOOK

AFTERNOON SUN GLAZED across Dani's face. She was so pale and sickly. "Hey," I said, calm as I could. Her lips teased into something close to a smile, she said, "Hey," and her face fell slack.

I carried her inside, my nose finally relenting its gush so I could use both hands. She was a jagged bag of bones, perhaps not even a hundred pounds, and her knobby edges gave me the queer sense of actually carrying a skeleton, and if she tumbled from my arms onto the driveway she might scatter in fractured shards.

"Mike," she said in a voice almost lost in shallow breaths.

"It's okay," I said. "I'm going to fix this. I'm going to get you well."

"When the world is cold," she said, soft like a lullaby, "I will feel a glow just thinking of you."

"And the way you look tonight," I finished.

We were halfway up the stairs and she passed out, head lolling in my arms.

I folded the sheet across her neck. She breathed slowly, head sunken into the pillow. The comforter was bunched at the foot of the bed. Far too hot. The windows were open, and I thought of closing and locking them, but dismissed it. I'd keep one ear toward the room and the door open.

Did I accept Dani might be possessed, as in by an actual demon? Wasn't that what people used to believe before psychology and medical science stepped in to explain away the beasties?

Maybe it was schizophrenia, or some form of madness exacerbated by her bipolar disorder. There had to be a logical explanation, right?

Rom stood in the doorway. "She's okay. At least for now. Let's talk."

I kissed Dani's forehead and turned to him. "Fifteen minutes and I'm calling an ambulance."

CHAPTER 76:
SOMETHING BAD

"**W**HEN LEE DIED,** did you sense anything?" Rom asked. He sat at the kitchen table, the ivy wallpaper all around, the glass door behind him.

"Sense?" I stood in the doorway, one eye drifting again and again down the hall.

"A presence."

"What're you trying to say?"

"Mike, you saw my wife die, humor me, okay?"

"What do you want me to say?"

"I want you to be honest. Did you feel anything?"

"No."

"You're sure?"

"I . . . don't know." I saw Ned backed against the wall, heavy face paling, chubby hand going to the cross hanging from his neck. He was scared. Had there been something, a subtle though distinct . . . What, spirit? Ghost? Certain presence? *Had* I felt something? *She knows,* Lee had said, staring toward Dani. *Wrong, wrong.* It can't all be a coincidence.

"Maybe," I said.

"Definitely," Rom said. "I sensed it, and so did Ned."

"It was your wife. Of course you—"

"Don't give me that. I know what you're thinking, Mike, but I'm telling you: there was *something.*"

"You felt her spirit. It left her body, and you felt it linger before it ascended. Billions of people would agree with you."

I hated how callous and cruel I sounded, but I couldn't help it. What did he want from me? He'd lost his wife, but I was thinking about Dani. This discussion was not, in any way, going to help me figure out what to do for her. "You have thirteen minutes."

"Not *her* spirit," Rom said. "Something else."

"Something else?"

"Yeah. Something bad."

"Bad?"

"Play along, Mike."

"Fine. You mean some sort of nasty spirit or ghost, right?"

"Not nasty—*evil*."

"Okay, evil. You know this because?"

"I told you: I felt it, and so did Ned."

"Ned! He's a religious nut. Of course *he* felt something."

"Jesus, Mike, stop being so naive."

"He's a leader of a cult, but I'm the naive one?"

"Yeah, you are. There was something bad in the room when my wife died, and whether you felt it or not I need you to accept it was there, it was real, and it must be dealt with."

"So you're saying there was . . . something inside your wife and—"

"Not my wife," Rom said. "It's in Dani."

She knows.

We're going to die here.

I opened my mouth and closed it again. I could keep playing dumb if I wanted, as if feigning ignorance would somehow make all this go away, but of course I'd had Rom's same thoughts, these dark ideas that maybe something had gotten hold of Dani. An evil spirit? A demon? My twin out to avenge his death? The Cowan? Moloch? No matter how ridiculous it might seem, I couldn't outright dismiss any possibility. Not after what had happened at the funeral home.

I was shaking my head, but I was also thinking: If I took Dani back to the hospital, the doctors *would* pump her full of drugs, recommend a longer stay at the mental facility, and then what? Suppose she didn't get better. Suppose it *wasn't* a chemical imbalance in her brain. Suppose she descended into genuine madness and nothing could be done.

During ancient times, through the medieval ages, and all the way into the beginning of the twentieth century, people believed in demons and devils and Satan's imps, and in their ability to inhabit humans and scramble brains, all in service to the Dark Lord's wishes of mass anarchy.

Then psychology saved the day. People who might have been treated cruelly and even tortured in mental asylums (torture being the best method for driving out malevolent parasites, of course) were seen in a new, illuminating light. These people weren't victims of black arts. They were suffering from real phobias and anxieties and actual brain disorders, chemical imbalances, things that could be treated through therapy and medicine.

Yet, what if those bad spirits *were* real, and psychology merely gave them a better cover story, the perfect disguise under which they could keep doing their heinous work?

How conveniently plausible, no matter how absurd.

I glanced down the hall. "I don't know," I said.

"There is something," Rom said. "Back of the beyond, as Lee said. She saw it."

"Saw what?"

"More things in Heaven and Earth than are dreamt of in your philosophy."

"Shakespeare? Seriously?" I asked.

"You want to help Dani?"

"Yes."

"Then open your *fucking* mind to what I'm saying."

The sudden force of his words startled me. His eyes burned with palpable intensity, and some small part of me was afraid of him. As afraid of him as I was of my father when he stabbed little scissors into his face.

"Okay," I said. "Okay."

"Believe it or not, like Ripley's used to say, there *is* more to this world than what we see around us. We all know it, even if we won't admit it. It's why people go to church. Why they knock on wood or hold their breath when they pass a cemetery. Superstition exists because part of us knows there's truth to it, or at least some truth. We laugh as we do those superstitious things, yet we still do them."

"A fear of the unknown," I said. "It's—"

"We *should* fear the unknown," Rom said.

"Fine," I said. "Then what?"

"We do something about it."

I waited. He stared back until I relented, knowing exactly what he was thinking.

"No," I said. "We're not performing some half-assed exorcism. It's ridiculous and dangerous."

"What's dangerous is doing nothing."

What did you people do? I'd asked Del.

Drove out the Cowan. Tried to, anyway.

"No," I said. "Your wife just died, and God knows what Ned has been pouring in your ear. I get you want to believe—"

"It *is* there," Rom said. "You were there. You heard me tell it to be still. *It* responded."

I was shaking my head. "She responded to your voice, a child cowering before a screaming adult."

He sighed. "Remember when I told you about the Lenapes?"

"I remember you saying I was evil."

"You want to call an ambulance? Go ahead. You really think some doctors are going to be able to help her?"

"You're down to six minutes."

"You need to meet me halfway on this, Mike. Accept a basic premise—there is weird shit in this world, unexplainable by science or logic, and though most people don't want to think about it, our reality is *thin*."

"Our sanity is what's thin," I said.

"With all our knowledge and understanding, all we've learned about this planet, this Earth, this life—wouldn't you agree there is much we still don't fully grasp?"

"Tick tock."

"The Lenapes who lived in the woods around here might have had a simplistic comprehension of the universe, but they didn't shy from the unknown. They didn't try to bury it beneath textbooks. They named the unknown, but they also respected it. We don't respect what we don't understand. We fear it, and we marginalize it. We belittle when we should revere."

"You want me to revere some unknown mythological being a few Indians believed in?"

"Not a being—a *beast*. A monster."

I opened my mouth to dismiss him, but couldn't do it. I'd felt the presence of something back (*of the beyond*) among the trees. A large, looming, hulking something.

Was something back there?

"The Mul Lok," I said.

"Eater of dead souls," Rom whispered.

"I think it's my brother," I said quickly. "Maybe he was murdered and his spirit is—"

Rom's raised hand stopped me. "Not the case. Whatever happened to your brother—and I honestly don't know—his soul is long gone, off to what waits beyond or . . . " He made an uncertain gesture.

"Eaten," I said.

"Listen," he said, "I don't know, not for certain, but after what I felt when Lee died and what happened at the funeral home, I believe that whatever tormented Randall followed Ned and Del and your father here to Mullock. Maybe it's a demon or something without a name, but it has Dani now."

"Ned told you about Randall, about what they did?"

"Yes."

"They killed him," I said.

"You want Dani to die, too?"

"They tortured that boy."

"I'm not talking about torture."

"An exorcism. Same thing."

"Mike. Hear me out. It may be the only way."

"Indians and demons and a soul eater called the Mul Lok. That's what you want me to believe? *That's* the goddamn answer?"

Rom looked out the sliding glass door. Mount Munacy looked as large as it had in my youth.

"What if the Lenapes used this land as a burial spot?" I asked. "What if all this is because some white settlers forced out the natives? Angry spirits seeking vengeance? I can almost believe that."

Rom shook his head. "You forgot something very important."

"Which is?"

"The Lenapes—the faction who lived around here, anyway—didn't believe in death. So the rumor goes. There are no bones. Burial or not, no bones. The dead simply rose again."

His face left no doubt to his seriousness.

"And this beast—this *monster*—it ate the souls of those people?"

"And other spirits trying to inhabit the reborn."

"Because only one spirit can be in one body?"

He tilted his head; *who knows?*

"Where are these souls coming from, Hell?"

"Do Indians even believe in Hell?"

I was close, teetering on the edge of acquiescence (close to toppling off the mental cliff into the abyss below), but sanity pulled me back. Dani was sick, and she needed help—real medical and psychological help. "No," I said. "I'm not going along with any of this."

I fished into my pocket for my cellphone, and Rom moved fast to seize my wrist. We were almost nose-to-nose. "You *have* to help."

"Why's that?"

"Because your father started all of this."

CHAPTER 77:
WARD BELIEVED

WE STOOD THAT way for several seconds, lovers hesitant to move in for a kiss—or enemies challenging the other to strike first.

"I haven't been honest with you," Rom said.

"About what?" My throat was tight, my words thin.

"I met your father and mother when they moved into this house almost thirty years ago. I knew you as an infant, as a toddler. For a while, you called me Uncle Rom."

"Why not tell me that?"

"To protect you," he said, and finally released his grip. He stepped back and looked at me with sad eyes. "After what happened to Ward, I didn't want to watch you go the same way. Didn't want to be part of the cause."

"Cause of what?"

"Ward *believed*. In all of it. Monsters, demons, curses—everything. Belief drove him insane."

"But you're telling me he was right to believe."

"I should have told you, but it had been so long and nothing had happened, not anything out of the ordinary, anyway. People get sick, people die. That's life. You came back and woke it up."

You're evil! "Woke *what* up?"

"I was foolish to think I could conceal the truth," Rom said. "There's something much bigger than us orchestrating events."

"God?"

"Bigger."

"What does that mean?"

Rom took several seconds to respond. "When our child was stillborn, Ward was so sympathetic. We sat in my garage and toasted my dead child. I expected him to console me like most people would—offer condolences, and some vague notion that the body must've sensed something wrong with the child, better for the baby to die in the womb than be born and die, or say something even more childish about my child being in a 'better place'—but he didn't say that."

Rom was staring at his hands. Veins wormed across his knuckles. "He asked if I believed in curses."

"How considerate of him," I said.

"Ward loved horror stories. Always had, I think. He had issues with his own father; never spoke about it much, but I picked up on enough. Maybe there was abuse. Something. Your father found escape in stories of haunted castles and marauding demons and blood-sucking vampires. They were a release valve for him, I think. Helped steady his mind. He had that coffin built to keep his collection together. It was important, more so than he maybe realized. Without that outlet, without those stories, he would've been like a furnace, where the pressure keeps building and building until it explodes. And maybe he was more open to the possibility of weird shit happening because of those stories, or maybe because he was open to the possibility of the unexplainable, he was drawn toward the macabre."

"Yeah," I said, "and it drove him crazy. You said so."

"But look, just because those books and movies he so enjoyed are fictions doesn't mean they aren't true."

"Actually, that's precisely what it *does* mean: fictions are made up."

"I'm talking about truth, Mike, not fact."

"More things in Heaven and—"

"The evil is real," Rom said. "It's ancient, was here long before the Lenapes."

"You expect me to—"

He cut me off: "Your father summoned that evil. He's caused all of this. You want to know why he tried to help that boy who was hit by a truck? Because it was Ward's fault the kid was possessed."

"Did you help with the exorcism?"

"No. I wasn't a Mason. You have to be grandfathered in or something. But Ward told me enough."

I swallowed. "What do you mean, he 'summoned that evil'?"

"Ward was the one who did all the research on the Lenapes. He discovered their beliefs about life and death. He had a giant map—set it up in my garage, actually, to keep it from Beatrice. It was a topography map of Warrenville. Red lines all over it. Little notes in his neat penmanship. He thought he'd found where the Lenapes might've lived. Deep in the woods, behind your house."

Stay away. Stay away. It's heavy with life back there.

"When your brother died, I knew what your father was going to do. I should've talked him out of it. Should've followed him, stopped him, something. Anything. I didn't." He chuckled in a terribly awful way. "He believed so strongly, and part of me started to believe, too."

"In what? What're you saying?"

"I don't know what happened to your twin. I have no idea. But I know what Ward did with the body."

CHAPTER 78:
POISON BACK THERE

"**No.**" It was all I could say. The kitchen felt hot. The ivy looked thick, like an entrapping jungle.

"He exhumed it, carried it beyond your house deep into the woods, and buried it back there. He showed me on the map, best he could, anyway."

I felt the pickaxe and shovel in my hand, the squeeze of my shoulders as I swung and dug. "Did he . . . kill my brother?"

"I don't . . . know. I don't believe so. He was so grief-stricken, and your mother was not herself. Postpartum depression, maybe."

Standing in the bathroom, razor pressed to her flesh.

Suspicions against her husband and her surviving child.

"Did you help him?" I asked. "You know, dig up the body?"

"He did it himself. He never told me straight out he was going to do it, but after it was done, he confessed. Said it was a lot easier than he'd imagined. He wrapped your brother in a sheet, drove him back here in the trunk of his Pontiac, and walked him into the woods."

"Where'd he bury him?"

"Somewhere far back."

"You're saying there's some sort of Indian burial ground back there?"

"Not that you'd find any bodies."

"You actually believe . . . " I began.

"It's way too late for me to suffer any more doubts. Ward believed. He didn't say it, not in so many words, but he spent a lot of time in those woods. I think he was out there all night sometimes."

"Doing what?"

"Visiting his son."

"As in, resurrected?"

Rom shrugged. His shoulders were bony, his face pale. "'It's like an addiction,' he told me. 'I must go back there. Must go to it.' He felt something calling to him. A thing impossible to resist. He was obsessed, as he was prone to be. He said time was 'slippery' back there. He claimed he'd be in the woods for hours, but when he came back out only a few minutes had passed. I never really believed that, but I might as well believe it all now.

"He was okay for a while, but then he started to change. Grew paranoid. Scared. Stopped sleeping. I was worried. He stopped taking care of himself— eating, bathing. Got this crazed look in his eyes, beard all ratty, hair tangled. He stank of the woods, too, like rotting earth. I wondered, when it was late and I couldn't sleep, if Ward had died back there and the man I knew as Ward was actually something else."

"As in resurrected?" I asked.

"Infected with a different spirit."

"I don't believe that."

"I don't know if what you believe matters. 'It's wrong back there,' Ward told me. 'Wrong, *wrong*.' He said it was cursed back there. He said the curse was coming to get him."

"You're telling me this now so I'll go along with some deranged plan to stage an exorcism."

"Is there any truth to what the Lenapes who called themselves the Mul Lok believed about resurrection?" Rom asked, musing to himself. "I don't know, but I'm willing to believe. Your father said the ground was poison was back there. Not 'poisoned,' but 'poison.' He believed all the animals back there were, too. Birds, squirrels, wasps."

Wasps, I thought. "Where's that map?"

Rom went back to the table and sat. He looked so tired and very old. "When Ward died, I burned it. I hoped to never talk about these things ever again. Heart attack was lucky for him. I was genuinely afraid he'd go into the woods and never come back."

"He didn't die of a heart attack," I said. "Not solely, anyway. He killed himself. Jumped off that damn cliff, landed right at the bottom. Where we buried Dusty."

"And you saw it happen." It wasn't a question.

"Yes."

"I don't want you to be next, Mike." His voice cracked with genuine emotion.

"You think some exorcism is going to solve anything? It didn't help Randall. Didn't help my father."

"It will help if we're successful."

"How would we even know if we are?"

"We have to try."

"Why?" I said. "If something infected Dani, poisoned her, then even forcing it out—the Cowan or whatever the hell we call it—won't matter, because there's still that *thing* back there. That *beast*. Right?"

"Was the ground always poison, or did the Mul Lok poison it?" Rom asked.

"You want me to answer that?"

"There's no way to know the answer. Your father woke that monster when he buried your brother back there. Or maybe he didn't. Maybe it was always there. Watching. Waiting."

"We do this, drive out the Cowan, and what if *that* other thing is the real cause?"

Rom's hands were flat on the table, and he slid them off into his lap. "If the Mul Lok is responsible, there may be nothing we can do."

"Burn the fucking woods down," I said. His expression said he'd thought of the same option. "Dusty's gone. Something dug him up. Took him away."

It's too late, Dani said. *We're going to die here.*

"Please, Mike. I need to make this right. For Ward."

For a moment, the idea almost took hold, but this time with the world teetering, I made the right decision: I shook my head. "I'm sorry, but this is stupid. I don't believe any of it. I don't care what my father did. That's on him. Not me. I'm calling an ambulance. Your time's up."

Rom's anger deepened and retreated all at once. His face smoothed into sympathy and his shoulders sagged. He stood and approached.

"Time's up," I said.

He looked at me, red-eyed. "If I could have done something, anything, to help my wife, I would have. *Anything.* No matter what it was, no matter the risk, I would have done it. Cure her cancer? Save her life? Extend her life even a single day? *Anything.* Give up my own safety and health? I would have done it—gladly."

This from the same man who'd said home can be a place of death, and death can be welcome.

But something ice-hard splintered inside me, and began to crack in spreading spiderwebs. I wanted it to stop, wanted to stand on solid ground, but there was nothing I could do except wait to plummet into the icy water. "I . . . don't want Dani to suffer."

He gripped my shoulder. "That's why she needs our help. She's suffering now, and we can help her."

Words cracked in my throat, and Rom hugged me. I hugged him, arms gripped tightly around him, and it was like being in his garage again, with Dusty's body on the table.

It felt good, that hug. Reassuring. And, yes, standing there in that kitchen, I could imagine it was my father hugging me back, the way I always wanted.

"I'm going to get Ned," Rom said, "and I'll be right back."

I started to object, but stopped.

He left, and I creeped down the hall outside the bedroom. Dani was still (*pretending to be*) asleep. She looked peaceful. Could she really be possessed? Was it worth at least humoring the idea, or should I call 9-1-1 right now? But then what, doctors medicate her, observe her, study her?

Possessed? Like the girl in *The Exorcist?* Was it possible?

She isn't simply going to bounce back. This is going to linger.

I fished out my phone.

CHAPTER 79:
HELEN TELLS ALL

DANI'S MOTHER ANSWERED on the third ring.

"Hello, dearie," she said, voice jubilantly oblivious.

"I never got your letter."

"Oh, yes. My fault entirely. It's been so busy here. The days get away from me. Always have, and out here, well, California sunshine keeps you moving. I'll sit down this moment and write—"

"Tell me now."

"Can't do, sweetie. It would take too long and I have to be going. I shouldn't have answered the phone. Force of habit. Amazing, isn't it, how Pavlovian we become?"

"*Tell me.*"

She paused. "How is Dani?"

"You suddenly care?"

"For someone who wants information, you're being awfully uppity."

"*Hey,*" I said and stopped. I almost shouted it. Dani didn't stir, but I walked back down the hall to the kitchen. The fluorescent light hummed. The wallpaper glowed. "Dani is not well. She had a breakdown at my mother's funeral. A very bad breakdown."

I paused to give Helen a chance to express her condolences, but she waited for me to continue. I told her, more or less, what happened. I didn't mention how my mom's mortal remains stuck to Dani's tongue, or how the blood dribbled off the metal floral pick onto her white thighs, though it was picture-clear in my mind.

"I need to know if she has a history."

"We each have a history, dearie."

"Of this behavior," I said.

"Has she ever shoved a metal wire into her privates? No, I can't say she has."

"*Enough.* What aren't you telling me?"

"Did you ask her?"

"Yes."

"What did she tell you?"

"She was bullied in high school and snapped one day at soccer practice. Beat the hell out of a teammate. Bullying went on for years after."

"Sounds right."

"Tell me what really happened."

"One truth is as good as the next," she said.

"No, it's not. Truth is truth."

"You'd like to believe that, wouldn't you? I'll tell you something, because you sound a bit frayed around the edges: truth is relative. We each define our own. There is no one truth—there are all sorts of truths, each as real as any other. Dani chose hers, as you chose yours. But sometimes, things come back to bite you."

"Meaning?" I was being haunted by truth. Why couldn't life be simple, black-and-white?

Helen's breath erupted static in my ear. "I will write you that letter. Now I have to—"

"*No*," I said. "You tell me right now. I'm not fucking around. Tell me what you know or I swear I will track you down and—"

"What?" she said. "Hit me? Break my arm? Run me over? Please, elaborate."

Now I sighed, deflating. "I want to help her. *Please.*"

The silence dragged out.

"Dani wasn't bullied," Helen finally said. "She *was* the bully."

In my sideways glance, the ivy on the kitchen wallpaper was almost crawling.

"Doctors wanted her to stay at a facility, but I wouldn't allow it. They said she'd repress the memories, or shape new ones to fit however she chose to see herself. I helped her through it. A bad patch."

"What happened?"

"What did Dani tell you about her father?"

"You two divorced when she was five. He drove off, never heard from again."

"He came back when she was twelve. Drove right up in his piece-of-shit Ford truck with the bumper hanging by wires, and rust flaking off. Not that I lived in some high-class place. The sidewalk out front was crumbling, the roof sometimes leaked, and the water was sulfuric, but we had a good life, and now here was Christian, driving right up like he'd been gone five minutes instead of seven years."

"What happened?"

"Dani was reserved at first, not sure of him, you know. I didn't push it. If she didn't want her father back in her life, fine by me. But then I'd come home and they'd be in the kitchen laughing, or out in the yard playing tag, or even sitting in the den having a conversation. Him talking and her nodding away like a ventriloquist's dummy. Things seemed okay, but don't they always?"

I tasted metal, heard Rom's voice in my head: *Probably molesting him.* "What did he do to her?"

"There were bruises—little ones at first, speckling the skin green and brown like mold. Then small cuts. Went through a whole box of Band-Aids in a week.

I assumed Christian was using again—cocaine, his choice drug to make his life seem rosy—and I scoured the house for his stash but didn't find anything. Dani seemed okay. My good girl."

"Tell me what he did."

"*He* didn't do anything."

"What?"

"I came home one afternoon and found him unconscious on the back patio. Sprawled on the chaise. First, I thought he'd gotten drunk and passed out. Even OD'd. Then I saw the blood. Good-sized puddle of it on the cushion, and dripping on the white stone. It was coming from the side of his head, right above his ear.

"Took me a moment to shake him awake. He was disoriented. I asked him what happened, and he stared at me with this horrified expression. It was so surprising. I'd never seen Christian Tremblay scared like that."

Helen's drifty, reverie-tinged voice sounded a little scared now, recounting what happened. Maybe it's why she wanted to write this in a letter and also why she never got around to writing any of it.

"I asked him what happened, but then there was Dani. She was in the backyard, watching us. I hadn't seen her. She could do that sometimes, hide in plain sight. Used to scare me up the damn wall when she was a toddler. She'd vanish, and then she'd be right there beside me as if I'd been temporarily blind.

"Dani walked right up to me. Face empty, like she was sleepwalking, and in her hand she held a chunk of broken concrete from the sidewalk. Her fingers were raw and bloody.

"I went to her, and it was like she wasn't there. She stared off. I shook her, and she blinked, and there she was: my little girl. The chunk of concrete dropped beside her, and she stared at it like she didn't realize it'd been in her hand."

Down the hall, Dani was still sleeping, presumably, but it wasn't some demonic presence slumbering along with her. She'd always had problems, and they were never dealt with properly. Emotional problems. No supernatural explanations necessary. She needed real medical and psychological help.

"Christian had to have twenty-four stitches, and while we were at the hospital, Dani turned to me and asked, 'Why are we here, Mommy?' She didn't remember anything that happened."

"She did it to protect herself," I said. "He was hurting her."

"A week later," Helen went on, "I woke in the night to the sound of Chris screaming. Dani stood over him, her hands tangled in his hair. She was yanking his head back and forth. Snapping it. Violently. I thought she might actually break his neck.

"I grabbed her, and she collapsed in my arms. Chris was crying and trying to be angry, calling Dani a 'psycho.' I should've kicked him out right then. Dani wasn't psychotic. She had fits, yes, but they weren't intentional. She never realized what she was doing."

DEAD END

"You believed her?"

"Why wouldn't I?"

I'm a marvelous pretender, Dani had said. "What happened then?"

"After that incident, I kicked Christian out. Dani was fine before he came back. Unfortunately, as I warned you, her condition lingered."

From down the hall, the faintest sound. A mumble? Was Dani whispering in her sleep? Was she sliding out of bed? I started back down the hall.

"I shouldn't have let him back in, but when I kicked him out it was for his protection, not hers."

"You believe that?"

"I asked Dani if she wanted Christian to stay. You know what she said?"

I stopped halfway down the hall, waited. A rustle of sheet.

"She said, 'If he stays, I guess I'll end up hurting him again.'" Helen laughed in a sad, frightened way.

From where I was, I could see the edge of the bed. I couldn't see if Dani was still in it. She might be hiding somewhere in the room. Hiding in plain sight.

Helen's voice crackled. "She had such capacity for aggression. Maybe it was a puberty thing. Either way, she needed an outlet. Sports provided it."

I stepped closer. My angle on the bed widened ever so slightly. The edge of rumpled sheets. The corner of a pillow. "You weren't concerned at all that maybe she might hurt you?"

"Her own mother? No. I was a little concerned she might hurt other people, and maybe herself, but I was never afraid for myself. *Never.*"

"I'm concerned," I said. Another step and . . . Dani lay still beneath the lump of comforter. Was she breathing faster, the way someone might who'd hurried back into bed?

"Sounds like you should be." Helen paused. "I think it was the nightmares. She suffered the worst night terrors. Screaming and crying. Sometimes, though, I'd wake in the middle of the night and she'd be staring down at me, sobbing silently. Crying and watching me sleep. She said something was chasing her. All her violence was born out of her needing to face those monsters.

"When she took the field, she played fierce. Dani targeted her teammate. Dani wants to believe she was bullied by Erin and the other girls, but Dani was the bully. Erin started dating this boy Dani had a crush on and during a game, Dani laid Erin out on the field, hard elbow to the chest, knocked her down. She stopped, turned, and stomped on the poor girl's face."

"Unprovoked?"

"She did so much damage, the girl needed a half-dozen reconstructive surgeries."

"Shit."

"It was awful. After that, I home-schooled her. She went to college, and she seemed good. Occasional nightmares, a few sleepless nights, nothing abnormal. A bad patch, like I said."

"That's putting it lightly."

"Adolescence is no easy experience, and for some it's a living hell."

"This is a little different. She was hurting herself, too."

"She suffered, yes, but she coped."

Dani shifted with a faint moan.

"Did you take her to the doctor?" I asked.

"Of course I did. A mother, however, knows best. I helped her."

"*You* helped her?"

"She needed love. That's what you must give her—if you can."

"What's that mean?"

"Dani loves you, but she was worried about how closed-off you are."

"Dani is in serious trouble."

"It's another bad patch."

"Bullshit."

"So," Helen said, and paused, "can I assume the wedding is off?"

CHAPTER 80:
THY WILL BE DONE

DANI WHISPERED SOMETHING. Or was I hearing things?

The floor creaked beneath me. I edged into the room. It was hot—humid and over eighty degrees—and an unpleasant curdled-milk smell fattened in the room.

She *was* whispering. Sibilants slithered off her lips. The words—if it's what they were—rose and fell in recognizable inflection, as if she was asking a question. Then childish giggles bubbled free, and even as damn hot as it was in that room, my back prickled with cold.

She's possessed.

No. Ridiculous. Dani had relapsed into the severe emotional challenges she endured as a teenager. A relapse. A *severe* relapse. She needed medicine and intense therapy.

Still, I didn't raise the phone to call for an ambulance. Dani snored in a congested crackle. Her dark hair stuck out in all directions on the pillow like a large ink spill.

"It can't be real," I said. "Possessed?"

Dani kept on sleeping.

"Cowan." The word was soft and strange in my mouth.

No response.

Possession was for horror novels and B-movies. True, certainly, but there must be authentic cases, right?

The fear exists, my rational mind (what I hoped was my rational mind) said, *because people needed an explanation for erratic, disturbing behavior. It wasn't until the twentieth century, after all, when people realized there were germs in the air. They didn't understand the common cold, so how could they grasp multiple-personality disorder? Or viruses? Or tumors? Or bipolar disorder?*

My thumb hovered over the phone.

If I could have done something, Rom said, *anything, to help my wife, I would have. Anything. No matter what it was, no matter the risk, I would have done it. Cure her cancer? Save her life? Extend her life even a single day more?* Anything. *Give up my own safety and health? I would have done it—gladly.*

Possessed, though? She was a troubled child. *What if,* my mind offered, *she's been possessed her whole life?*

Maybe I should have gone ahead and dialed. I didn't. Even now, after all that happened, I'm not sure it would have made any difference. The world was hanging in the balance again, I made my choice, but maybe it didn't matter. If there is such a thing as fate or destiny, it is inherently cruel. There is no way to avoid the outcome. What happened would have happened no matter what choice I made. Or at least, that's something I need to believe.

Thy will be done.

CHAPTER 81:
THE LAND OF UZ

ROM SET AN open beer before me on the kitchen table and clinked his against it. The beer was sharp and hoppy. I resisted the urge to down the whole thing.

Ned stood huge in the doorway, as if he'd gained even more weight in the past dozen hours. His gold cross flickered fluorescent light, and red spots patterned his wide cheeks.

"We want you to listen," Rom said. He sounded completely genuine. "If you don't want to do what we're proposing, we'll accept that and go along with whatever you want."

"Dani has a history of this behavior," I said.

"There could be a reason," Rom said.

"Yeah. Mental illness."

Outside, night had come, and with it, a thickening darkness hugged the house. No moon or stars. The whole world condensed to this kitchen with its ivy wallpaper that sometimes creeped. Was the little man in there, watching me, hoping I would finally tear all of the wallpaper down and set him free? Or did he want me to find the way in there with him?

"Mike," Rom said, "we'll listen to what you have to say, but please listen to us first. Hear us out. Then you can decide what's best."

"I'm bringing her to the hospital. With your help or without it."

"Fine. Okay. I'll help. I will. But first, let's finish our beers and talk. *Please.*"

I didn't say anything, simply lifted my beer and drank a good gulp. Both men watched me, afraid I might chuck the bottle at one of them.

"Dani is possessed. There, I said it. Now what?" I was starting to get a headache and the beer tasted like metal, but I took another sip and a laugh burped out. "I mean, shit, it's what you want me to believe, right?"

Ned removed a blue handkerchief from his pocket and blotted sweat off his forehead. For a crazy moment, I imagined snatching it from his pudgy grip and stuffing it into his mouth. I thought of a roasted pig with an apple wedged in its jaws. "Are you familiar with the Book of Job, Mike?"

"He's the one who suffered, right?"

"Oh, yes, indeed." Ned sounded pleased, almost giddy. Was it because I knew who Job was, or because he enjoyed stories of suffering? Maybe all preachers were sadists in robes. "Job lived in the land of Uz, and he was a faithful, devout man. He was blessed. A loving family. Wonderful, verdant lands and healthy livestock."

"Verdant?" I said, and burped another chuckle.

"The Devil claimed Job only worshipped the Lord because his life was so blessed. The Devil challenged God: remove from him your protection, and let me test his faith.

"God agreed. The Devil could do anything, God said, except kill him. So the Devil killed off Job's children, diseased his livestock, destroyed his home, riddled his body with painful, seeping boils."

"And let me guess," I said, "Job didn't tell God to go fuck himself."

Ned didn't recoil from my vulgarity as I hoped. In fact, he smiled and all those tiny white teeth gleamed from the pocket of his catcher's-mitt mouth. "His faith did not falter, even when his wife begged him to turn against God. And for his steadfast resolve, God restored to Job all he lost and then some. He lived long and happily. Job refused to break when all he loved and cared for was taken from him. His faith sustained him, and it saved him."

In his other hand, Ned held a black leather Bible. He lifted it, rested it against his chest over the cross.

"Sounds like bullshit," I said.

"It's love," Ned said.

"Why would Job love a god who willingly, even eagerly, allowed the Devil to ruin his life?"

"Same reason Abraham brought his son up Mount Moriah to sacrifice him at the Lord's command—*love*."

"That's not love. That's fear." My father's arms reached into the sky and stretched and stretched. And in my head over and over: *Mount Munacy Mount Munacy Mount Munacy.*

"*Mike*," Rom said, like he had to snap me out of a daze. "Hear him out."

"You *are* Job," Ned said. His voice dropped and rolled in a funny way. "You are scared. I understand. You have suffered greatly, and you suffer still, but I want to offer you a chance for something else. A chance for love."

I stared at him. A chance for love? I'd been entertaining the idea of an exorcism, or at least a few prayers or something similar—certainly nothing like what Del, Ned, and Dad did to Randall—but now that it was right there in front of me as a real possibility, I couldn't go with it. "You want to do an exorcism or something on Dani, but it's not going to happen. She's not *puh-zest*." I stopped. My last word sounded so strange. What was I saying? I concentrated. "She needs help."

"We are that help," Rom said. "I get this isn't easy to accept, but you were there when Lee died. You felt it too. I know what happened at the funeral home."

"Ashes," I said. I meant my mom's. I'd left them at the funeral home. How had they cleaned them up? Vacuum? I made a mechanical-suction noise and chuckled.

"Focus, Mike. I saw it," Rom said, and clutched my wrist. "The *demon*."

The air left the room, as if it were sucked out instantly through invisible cracks, and the heat increased so rapidly I thought I might not be able to breathe.

The feeling worsened. Rom and Ned watched me, curious. I registered the cold beer in my hand, and breath filled my lungs. My stomach had soured, though, and I didn't want any more beer.

I concentrated. "What does the monster want?"

"What does cancer want?" Rom asked.

I nodded and couldn't stop. My head was so heavy.

"You okay?" Rom asked.

"*Mul Loook*." The word slurred out of me, long and slow.

"I've seen it before, Mike," Ned said. "That *thing* was in Randall. It is here now, in your fiancée. A demon."

"Satan's *imp*," I said, spitting the last word.

"Yes, absolutely. We will drive it out—together."

I opened my mouth, but it took a moment for the words to come, and then it felt like they were slipping past my mouth without being pronounced. "You two ate—*hate*—each other."

Rom leaned close. "Lee wanted me to make amends, and I did, but it was more than that. When she died, I lost everything—but I discovered truth. You'll discover it, too, and it doesn't need to come at Dani's peril. I saw it. You saw it. We're going to help her."

I had to think of each sound I was trying to make as I spoke. "That's *swilly*." I sounded drunk, and my heart fluttered in a strange, lopsided way, as if loose inside my chest. "More things in Heaven and—"

"Think of my wife," Rom said. "I told you: if there was anything I could have done to help her, I would have done it. *Anything*."

I was shaking my head again and couldn't stop. I grabbed my chin before I was so dizzy I'd fall off my chair.

"I think it has been here for years," Ned said. "It followed us. After that poor boy succumbed, the demon came here. It latched on to your father. Tormented him."

"Remember what we discussed," Rom said. "Who's responsible."

"We will cast out the Cowan for good," Ned said.

"No coward," I said, but that wasn't right, of course. The word didn't want to be said, at least not by me. "*Cowan*," I said. The floor was slick beneath my shoes.

"If Dani has emotional issues," Rom said, "it makes sense the demon went for her. Psychosis made her vulnerable. An easy target. Someone it could manipulate, like a marionette."

"Bird," I said, and flexed my hands as if Rom might understand. "Eats the flesh."

Ned stepped forward. The floor shook. "I underestimated the beast the first time. I know better now. Its time on Mullock Road is over. It killed Isaac. It drove my wife away. It robbed Suzanne of her memories. It corrupted your father. Maybe even killed your brother. Your mother was a terribly depressed woman. *This* is why. It infected her with disease and despair, made her ill, as it did to Lee. The demon must be cast out permanently. No exceptions."

Somewhere far off: the front door opening.

The ivy crawled up and down and across the walls. A little man so much like the Jolly Green Giant danced behind those snaking vines.

"Do you know the story of the man possessed by many spirits?" Ned asked. "He declared his name Legion, for he was many, and he begged Jesus to heal him. Jesus cast out all those demons into a herd of pigs that stampeded off a cliff to their deaths. It is what we must do. What we *will* do."

"Whhh . . . ?" I couldn't form the words.

Rom's hand squeezed my wrist. The beer toppled, and liquid spilled across the table and splashed on the floor in an amber pool. "But listen, Mike, maybe she isn't possessed. Maybe it is in her head," he said. "The power of suggestion, right? She responded at the funeral home when I said, 'Cowan, be still.' If she only *thinks* she's possessed or infected or whatever, the ritual will still work. She'll cure herself. She only needs the opportunity to do it. That's what we're going to give her."

"Whatever it is," Ned said, "it killed Isaac. He died while Dani suffered her breakdown, yes? Doesn't it make sense that whatever is controlling her also controlled him?"

My face screwed into the question I couldn't form. The air was Jell-O wobbly.

"What can't a demon do?" Ned said.

It took forever, but my arm rose and rose and my finger pointed at Ned. His cross glowed whitish yellow, somehow directly through the black Bible.

He watched me, that curious look again. "Did you give him too much?" Ned asked.

"He'll be fine," Rom said. He slipped sideways in front of me, but somehow didn't fall. "He's going to have one hell of a hangover."

I reached toward him, and he was five miles away and floating farther into the ceiling. The Ivy Man was up there dancing. His legs kicked up and his arms bounced above his head. A ritual dance.

"I'll get Del," Rom said. "It's a shame we don't have Ward. Your father would be a big help right now, Mike. But, then again, we do have you."

Someone else was in the kitchen. Many someones. Their feet stomped, the sound like distant thunder. The room stretched and warped and rubber-banded back again. A tan canvas bag thwapped on the floor. White fabric bunched from the opening.

DEAD END

"Sheets?" I asked, only the word came out "*Shhhhhh.*"

Call 9-1-1. Watch out for the Ivy Man who dances when the BAD THINGS happen. I opened my mouth and the room slanted steep and something thunked hard to the floor.

Beyond the door to the deck, a sickle of moon shone through the clouds and sliced across the cliff edge where my father long ago tried to kiss the sky.

PART THREE:
THE RITUAL OF ~~TAUROBOLIUM~~ COWAN

"Oh, my God, no, please, no."
—Ward Munacy, "The Ritual of Taurobolium"

───·∾∾·───

"Hell is empty and all the devils are here."
—William Shakespeare

───·∾∾·───

"Even in the grave all is not lost."
—Edgar Allan Poe

CHAPTER 82:
IMMENSE POWER AND TERRIBLE REVULSION

THESE SOUNDS: a clack, and then a clicking, metallic-rolling, followed by a *ffoomp* and a hard, sharp snap. It repeated. And repeated.

The floor spread out before me. Boxes and bags rose all around, but they'd been pushed farther aside to provide more floor space. The box of my father's stuff (*His Remains*) was an arm-length away. The copy of *Pet Sematary* was splayed open facedown, and next to it the VHS cover of *Henry: Portrait of a Serial Killer*.

Those works were haunting me, too.

I was on my side, cheek against the cool and dirty floor, and my arms were pulled back behind me, something wrapped tightly around my wrists, binding them together.

Across the room beneath the grey windows, the TV was on mute: Henry was decapitating his girlfriend in a bathtub. A staticky line shook across the screen.

The rocking horse's decaying face stared.

The *clack-clack-clack* of the Underwood was above and slightly behind me. I shifted—clenching my jaw against a surprise of pain that ripped along my spine and throbbed between my shoulder blades and echoed a thudding in my temples—and saw someone in all white sitting at the typewriter.

Suzanne?

The typist twisted around. A two-headed monster grinned at me with two mouths. A thick crease warped the middle of the old mask and the rubber was cracked in places, the color peeling off in flakes.

"Dad?"

Not my father, of course, and the laugh that echoed through the mask was the higher pitch of a teenage boy mocking my confusion.

He held the copy of *Popular Delusions* and now read from it, voice echoing inside the mask: "'Many priests encouraged the superstition of their parishioners by resorting frequently to exorcisms whenever any foolish persons took it into their heads that a spell had been thrown over them.' Blah blah blah."

He threw the book at me. It hit my chin and something metal clattered loose. It was the six-inch straightedge my father used for annotations. The one I'd cut my thumb on.

My captor peeled off the mask. A youthful, boyish grin emerged, but one full of knowledge and maturity beyond its years. A zit pulsed nasty red on Theo Loller's right temple.

"Well, there you are," he said. "Welcome back."

His robe was the same one he wore the morning Ned and his sun-kissed believers ascended Mount Munacy, and the same one he wore during Isaac's funeral.

"Help me up," I said. My voice sounded strained, weak.

"You've had a long nap," Theo said, "you should have the energy."

I lifted up, got the edge of my elbow under me, and discovered my feet (stripped of shoes and socks) were not equally bound. Once I got up, I could make a run for it. Run where, I didn't know. My insides felt loose and my head fat.

Rom had drugged me.

The demon must be cast out permanently. No exceptions.

I got to my knees, and Theo's foot found my throat in a quick dress-shoe kick. I thunked back to the floor, gagging, unable to breathe. My throat was a rubber hose smushed shut.

Heat flushed through my face and tears leaked. Theo planted his foot on my shoulder, shoved me down.

When I'd met him, I was struck by Theo's maturity. I'd expected some ignorant Bible-thumping fool who walked lockstep with daddy, but he'd slapped my biased expectations back in my face, and now he was holding me prisoner in my own home and seemed younger than his age, juvenile. Should I be amused by the irony?

A thumping sound came from somewhere. Upstairs.

From my bedroom.

Dani.

I growled against the pain in my throat and tried to push up again. Theo's foot slipped, and I was up at the waist and tucking my legs under me, but then Theo was down beside me on his knees, one hand tangled in my hair to yank my head back and the other seizing my neck. He stared into my face like some crazed lover—or a vampire about to feast.

"It's going to be okay, Mike. Everything is under control. The ritual is going well. There's no reason for you to worry. We're going to cure her."

His words were calm, but his eyes were wide, crazed with bottled mania, like he might start screaming or chanting. The mask had fallen next to me, the empty eyeholes staring.

"Let go of me," I said in a tight whisper.

"Oh, don't worry, Mike. I will. I will. They're going to need you upstairs. You're a vital part of the ritual . . . just not yet."

Another heavy pounding from upstairs.

"*Dani!*" I screamed.

Theo's hand vise-pinched my throat, severing the cry the moment it left my mouth.

He leaned closer, smelled of cologne, a little kid playing dress-up. "Save your voice. You're going to need it."

"Let. Me. Go."

He considered, and released me. For a moment, I wobbled, an infant learning to walk, and then Theo shoved me hard in the chest and I fell back to the floor. My elbow took most of my weight, and pain ice-cracked up my arm into my shoulder.

Before I could roll away or try to spring back up, Theo stood and dropped his foot on my chest. He pushed down, and I relented. He was a weakling reveling in his moment of power.

Behind my back, my fingers groped at the restraints. Thick rope, but not quite—*bungee cords*, I thought. The cord had been wrapped several times, very tightly. Blood throbbed at my wrists.

Another sound, outside and distant, but nearing: thunder. That was why the windows were grey. Not dusk, as it'd been when I was drugged. It was the next day. "How long have I been down here?"

"You mean, how long have you napped while we good Christians toiled to save your lover's soul?"

I wanted to curse at him, to spit, to shake his foot off my chest, leap to my feet, and railroad him backward. My forehead itched with the sensation of crashing into Theo's, and I could see how his head would snap backward into the wall, knocking him out or even fracturing his skull.

"What time is it?" I asked.

Theo made a show of looking at his bare wrist. "Forgot my watch."

He pushed me back down, and I stared at his foot as if I could will his ankle to snap. My fingers felt at something on the floor.

Theo loomed over me. His face cut the dusty lamplight into shadowy angles. "This is how God must feel," he said. "Immense power and terrible revulsion."

His arm snapped up, something flashed in his hand, and there was the familiar sound I'd heard: the click, the metallic roll, and the puff-sound of air.

He held a metal Zippo. A fat flame flickered.

"You killed Isaac," I said.

"No, I did not. Why would I? I was training him. He was my protégé." Theo's gaze fixed on the single flame, admired it. Little flames swayed in his eyes. Was he remembering how the boy's flesh turned soupy and charred? He laughed. "Or maybe I did."

The lighter closed with a hard clack.

I nodded. "It's not your fault. You were raised by a religious zealot."

"Believe what you want," Theo said, "but we're battling something real up there."

I pushed up, and he shoved me back down. My fingers grabbed at the thing on the floor.

The straightedge.

"How's the rope? Too tight? You have really slender wrists. Like a girl's."

"And you're probably a goddamn virgin."

Theo grinned, but it sagged almost immediately.

"You're warped, deranged, unstable, and psychotic," I said. It felt good to say those things, and it also distracted him from what I was doing behind my back.

"Would you like a thesaurus to find a few more synonyms? Must be one around here somewhere." He kicked his other leg behind him to knock my Father's Remains. The books inside shifted.

Beyond the windows, the grey light darkened. Thunder crackled and rolled, still distant. But it wasn't nighttime—it might be the middle of the day. What were they doing to Dani? How long had their ritual been going on?

"I read your *book*." Theo said "book" with a marked note of amused disgust.

A finger wedged under the bungee cord, pried it up, and it rolled down the top of my hand. The pressure eased a bit around my wrists, but the cord was wrapped several times. Now, however, I could get a good angle for cutting.

"It reads like you *wanted* your wife to go crazy."

"She's not my wife." The words were cold steel and vibrated along my teeth.

"Lucky for her," he said. "You know, I was going to write a suicide note for you, maybe a confession, but the words didn't sound right. Then I read your book . . . Whew, you did it all for me. I mean, the story of a young couple, the wife going crazy, but let me ask you this: it's really the husband who's crazy, right? That's the twist ending you've got planned. I see it coming a mile away. Pretty lame."

He leaned down, his foot pressing harder.

"Fuck you." He was, infuriatingly, correct—it was the ever-so-clever ending I'd imagined.

My fingers clutched the ruler.

"A real literary tongue you have." Theo chuckled. "And these creepy books and that sick movie. Shit, Mike, who the hell watches stuff like this?"

The movie was over, the credits rolling.

"And is that a coffin over there? Jeez. Your father built that?"

"He didn't build it."

"It's weird, either way. Who owns a coffin?"

"You're the one playing dress-up," I said.

"You know," Theo said, "if this goes bad, you'll take the blame."

A shout erupted from upstairs. I wanted to get up and attack, but I needed to free my hands first. "Let me up."

"I want to tell you something first. You'll appreciate it, I think." Theo's arrogant smile spread his lips. "I'm going to give you a Bible lesson."

"Not interested."

"Only take a second."

My finger on the ruler, gentle, straining against the pain and trying to press down hard, and it slid, slightly. But it was moving, beginning to saw.

"You recall the story of Abraham and Isaac," Theo said. "My dad recounted it at the funeral." He paused. "Can I get some confirmation here? You remember, don't you?"

His foot slipped up to my neck again, and air caught in my throat. I nodded, and he raised his foot—eyeing me, *challenging* me—and set it back on my chest.

"Good. See? Now I can proceed."

The ruler's sharp edges bit into my skin, but I pressed the blade hard against the cord and worked it slowly back and forth. My shoulder popped. Theo didn't notice. Was the cord splitting, or was the ruler simply sliding on it? What was a bungee cord even made of? What if I cut through fabric only to feel wire?

"When offerings were made to God, those animals, a lamb or maybe a ram, were not simply sliced across the throat"—he dragged one finger across his neck—"to bleed out. No, that wouldn't be enough. God demands a burnt offering. So Abraham cleaved the wood and made Isaac carry it up the mountain."

The ruler slipped, almost fell.

"They climbed the mountain for three days. Think of that: Isaac carried the wood to be used for his own burning death, and he had no idea, and he did it for three days." Theo laughed. "He even asked his father what they would sacrifice, and Abraham said, 'God will provide.'"

The ruler was slippery with sweat, only, no, not sweat—blood. The ruler's edges sliced me even as I used it to cut the cord.

A groan from upstairs and the immediate rumble of thunder. Closer now.

"Isaac—Calla, not Abraham's son—loved this story. He probably liked that he had the same name as the kid, but there was more to it. When I reached the part where Abraham grabs his son, ties him up, and throws him on the stacked wood and raises the knife to kill him, our Isaac would stare at me big-eyed, smiling, and even shiver. He was excited."

"Horrified," I said.

Behind my back, the cords loosened. It was working, cutting, severing, faster and faster.

Hard, smacking steps on the stairs. Someone coming down.

Theo bent over like he might spit on me. "He loved that story. Loved it too much. You think he took his own life? Favor me with a theory."

"No," I said through clenched teeth. "You killed him."

His smile was completely genuine. "You know what the bitch of it is? About that story, I mean—Abraham was one hundred years old when Isaac was born. A hundred! He lived to almost two hundred. You believe that? But what's really crazy is that Isaac wasn't some little kid when they ascended the mountain. No, no. He was in his twenties, a strapping young man. So how the hell did a hundred-year-old man tie a strong twenty-something to a sacrificial altar?"

"He didn't," I said. "The story's bullshit."

"It's completely true. So let me ask you again: How was Abraham able to do it?"

Life, as I've pointed out, has echoes. I knew the exact answer he wanted. Like father, like son. "Because God willed it so."

Theo clapped his hands together and cheered. It sounded loud and utterly insane. He picked up the mask, admired it. "Precisely. I knew you weren't a total idiot. And that brings us back to our Isaac. The police say it was suicide, but we know better, don't we? He didn't kill himself, but no one else killed him, either. God *willed* it. God willed the demon to kill him. *It was the demon.* The Cowan. The one your father brought here. The one upstairs right now ravishing—"

Dani's shout echoed through the house, a quavering, aching holler, crazed and pained, and I wanted to scream because I couldn't do anything, couldn't get these damn bungee cords off my wrists, could only lie here and listen to some psychotic teenage boy ramble on in his deluded fantasies about God and demons and—

"But God has willed us to cast out the demon." Theo glanced toward the stairs.

I screamed, pulled my legs under me, pushed off the floor, my fingers tenting beneath me, and Theo lost his balance, tumbled backward, and then I was up, finally standing, knees straining, and he was falling back into the Underwood, hitting it with a metallic jangle. The pages of my book spilled everywhere.

The whole room listed sideways, a ship rocked by a monstrous rogue wave, and I stumbled and hit the wall. My legs wobbled, and my head kept falling to the side, as if separate from my body. My bare feet slapped on the floor.

The ruler fell, but the cords were nearly cut through, and I snapped them off. Had the room not been careening hard to the left, I might have reveled at my own Superman-like moment.

Theo stared, stunned. A scared boy.

I went for him, and he flinched, arms coming up with my father's mask dangling from one hand, but the floor slid out beneath me, and I sidestepped foot over foot like I was doing some stupid comic-dance routine. I crashed into the TV. It fell off the box and smashed onto the floor with a plastic thunk and an electric pop.

I grabbed the closest box to steady myself. Metal baking tins clattered. I grabbed the top one—a Garfield cake pan Mom used to bake me a cake for my tenth birthday—and raised the pan overhead and charged.

He didn't run, didn't even try to turn away; he stood there peering in surprise at me through his raised arms. Even if Theo didn't murder Isaac directly, he'd corrupted the kid's mind so much the difference was negligible, and here he was cowering from a cake pan.

My legs felt far away, and the floor slippery, but forward momentum kept me upright. I swung the pan down.

Someone grabbed my arm.

The pan flew from my hands and bounced off Theo's forearms to clatter on the floor. He didn't lower his arms, too afraid to move.

A mad chuckle slipped out before I realized it was my laughter.

The hand yanked me backward.

"Mike," a man's voice said.

The man's other hand caught my back to keep me from falling. My father glowered down at me. *Coward*, that face said.

"Dad?" I said incorrectly for the second time.

The hand gripped my arm tighter, pulled me up straight. "Get yourself together, Mike. We need you upstairs."

Rom's face rose from my father's. The hair was darker, the beard not as full, but the eyes were as wide and bright with erratic life. *Crazed* life.

"Come on," he said, and tugged me toward the stairs.

CHAPTER 83:
DETAILS AND THE DEVIL

Lightning danced across the upstairs walls.

The temperature was at least ten degrees hotter up here, and the humidity thickened the air into something I had to push through. I smelled incense, sharp and acidic, and the ripe stink of body odor, potent enough to taste.

Halfway down the hall, my feet tumbling beneath me, Rom stopped and shoved me against the wall. The same white robe Theo wore draped over Rom, with the collar of his yellow polo jutting out. He was also barefoot. His forearm pressed across my chest.

"You need to focus, Mike." Rom spat the words at me—sharp and energized with an erratic mania. "There is something going on in that room. I've seen it. It is evil. Genuinely *evil*." This wasn't a joke, not a reference to a horror film: Rom was completely serious. He looked like he hadn't slept in days. His right eyelid twitched repeatedly, tugged by invisible strings.

"You drugged me." I even sounded drugged, words slurred and tripped out behind my thoughts, which slipped Shakespearean again: *This is the most unkindest cut of all.*

There was a moan from the bedroom and a flurry of heavy, rapid knocking seemed to erupt from everywhere.

"Mike—*focus.*"

"*No!*" My hands finally came up and I shoved him in the stomach. He stumbled back the few feet into the opposite wall.

I headed for the bedroom. Rom shouted for me to wait, yelling it because the knocking was thundering through the walls, but I ignored him and kept going, my hand on the wall for balance, and the bedroom door ahead vibrating inside a flickering light—and the door swung open and a white-draped figure was silhouetted against shaking light.

"Dani?"

The figure ran toward me. The white robe pulled tight against a narrow frame, but it wasn't Dani. It was Nina. She passed me, her face screwed into a painful grimace, her hand clamped over her mouth, her naked feet slapping rapidly across the floor. She banged into the bathroom door and shut it behind her.

Rom seized my wrist, yanked my arm.

"I gave you a mild sedative," he said. "Something to take the edge off, but you passed right out. You needed the rest. We had to get started right away, and we couldn't let you stop us."

I yanked my hand free.

The bedroom door was shut. Dani was behind that door. The woman I loved.

"The Devil is in there, Mike."

I ran the rest of the way down the hall and into

CHAPTER 84:
A NIGHTMARE

IF I'D HAD any air in my lungs, I would have screamed.

Dani squirmed on the bed. Her long hair was gone, cut off with scissors so jagged spikes of black hair jutted out in all directions. *It'll get caught in the branches*, she'd said. Was it her idea to cut it, or theirs? Her white robe, the same as Theo's, Rom's, and Nina's, was soiled, piss-stained, spotted with blood and ugly dark blots. It twisted around her, hugging her chest tightly so her ribs were the creased folds of a paper fan and her nipples were small bumps on an almost flat chest. The robe pulled high across her thighs. Purple bruises were starbursts on pasty flesh. Her bare feet pedaled into the exposed mattress. There were no sheets, no pillows.

Yellow and black bungee cords wrapped Dani's wrists to the headboard—crucified in place.

The woman who was to be my wife writhed and gyrated, body twisting and rising and collapsing back into the mattress, her arms pulling up and snapping down with the elastic restraints.

An IV tube dangled from the crook of her elbow where it was taped in place and looped to the metal stand that'd been in Rom's garage. The tube wasn't connected to anything.

Her face was pale and bruised along one cheek, as if she'd been hit with something. Fat beads of sweat rolled down her face, and her skin glistened with perspiration. Did they even give her any water? Saline? Anything? Her mouth opened in a wide yawn and clacked shut hard. She might bite through her own tongue. Her dry lips crumpled beneath yellowing teeth. Blood dribbled down her chin and she blinked frantically and tossed her head side to side and groaned and someone was saying something, or several people were, chanting, reciting, praying, calling for God's mercy and help and challenging the dark presence to show itself.

Ned Loller hunched over her on the opposite side of the bed. His gold cross reflected the flickering flames of the candles each person held. The people were gathered in a semi-circle around the bed. Around Dani. White robes and bare feet.

I shoved between two of the white-cloaked—Warren and Steven—and reached for the cord strapping Dani's right arm. I smelled the ripeness of piss and vomit and sweat and incense and the stagnant, bloated rot of humid air.

"*Dani!*" I shouted. "I'm here! I'm—"

Warren's long arms scooped around my chest and pulled me back before I could begin to loosen the cords.

Terrifically bright and blinding lightning flashed through the room.

Dani's eyes opened wide—completely white. Another unrealized scream failed to escape my chest. Her eyes rolled down from maggoty white to red-veined and oily.

"Mike?" She sounded lost. "Mike? Mike? Mike? Mike? *MikeMikeMikeMikeMikeMi—*"

Ned's meaty arm swung down and his fat hand slapped Dani's face. Bloody spittle fanned across the mattress. She blurted a nonsensical tangle of sibilant hisses.

"*I command thee, Cowan, to release this soul!*" Ned's voice boomed in an echoey baritone.

He slapped her again—harder.

She spasmed and cried out and the robe snagged up along her waist, exposing her nakedness. Red slashes scored Dani's inner thighs. These people had stripped her—the woman I was to marry and was supposed to protect—and they had had been doing who-only-knew-what to her while I was passed out downstairs. Hitting her. Torturing her. Violating her.

I tossed myself side to side, trying to get out of Warren's grip, but Steven clamped his hand onto my jaw and squeezed. "You've got to play nice," he said, "or this is going to end badly for both of you."

We're going to die here.

Logan and Edgar loomed behind him.

There were syringes with long needles scattered among blood-spotted gauze pads on the nightstand, and a glass vial of red liquid.

I screamed in rage and horror and disgust. They let me scream until it thinned to a throat-screeching cry.

Another hand grabbed my shoulder. "Mike," Rom said into my ear, "it's almost done. You have to help us finish it."

"You're insane," I said, my voice weak and cracking, but still fighting.

Thunder exploded overhead.

Someone raised a small black book. My father's Masons book.

"We need your help," Del said.

The sky opened and rain without equal fell in a torrential, angry deluge. The world outside became a battlefield erupting with liquid gunfire. Everyone stared at me, even Dani.

I fell back, scared and panicked. "What do you want me to do?"

CHAPTER 85:
EXORCISM GONE WRONG

DANI SHIFTED HER body rapidly side to side. She slid in her own wetness. Her lips rubbed together hard enough to peel dead skin away and reveal the bright rawness beneath. She made odd hiccupping and clicking noises that seemed to come from around her instead of out of her.

Warren kept his arms around my chest and Steven stood beside me, hands at the ready. In one hand, Warren's white candle flickered a flame near my chin. Had I a beard like my father, I'd already be on fire.

Someone slapped the Masons book into my hands, opened to the "Ceremony for Ousting Disease." *The final euphemism*, I thought.

"*Read*," Del said.

Dani chomped her mouth up and down, a hand puppet with no voice. How long had she been strapped to the bed? How long had she been their victim? I had to call the police, had to get her help, had to stop this madness.

"It's okay," Rom said behind me. "It's going to be okay."

"Why do I have to do this?"

"It must be the closest blood relative, or one who has known the victim intimately. It's why we failed with Randall. It should have been his mother or father who cast out the demon. *You* have to do this, Mike. It's the only way."

If I didn't do it, did that mean one of these men would force himself upon Dani, be intimate with her so he could drive out the Cowan? Rape out the Cowan?

I wanted to vomit. Warren gripped me tighter.

"Now, Mike," Rom said. "*Read.*"

"In this post I stand guard against all Cowans," I read, "human and otherwise, and I beseech all in the brotherhood to stand strong against all evil."

"Mike?" Dani said, small and child-like. "Mike, what are you doing? Why are you doing this? Why are you hurting me? Mike? *Please.*"

A sickening plunge hollowed my stomach.

"Let go of me," I said. I struggled, but they held me tight. "Dani, I'm going to—"

She spat at me. A long, yellowish-red string of phlegm splattered across the mattress.

"Keep going," Del said.

Massive thunder erupted and the rain fell and fell. It pulverized the ground.

This was a nightmare beyond comprehension. I could not participate in this. Rage boiled inside me, and it was enough to push aside the fear and horror. It was my father's anger—Ward Munacy, who knew a thing or two about madness, also knew something about anger and aggression: *Ward has a temper rivaling even the most aggressive of larger men. I have witnessed Mr. Munacy terrify a room full of muscled men with his startlingly dramatic rage. Ward tends to be quiet and reserved, an introvert, but I wonder if this is a disguise he wears to conceal his true, bellicose nature. He may have learned to hide his real self at a very early age.*—and I felt the same empowering capacity for rage. I let it flood through me. Let it drown me.

Let it possess me.

I fought against them, managed to get an arm free. "Let her go!" I shouted. "*Let her go!*"

Del saw the fury in my eyes and stepped back, and that only stoked the fire hotter. I yanked my other arm free. Warren stumbled back into the dresser.

"*This ends now!*" I shouted. "*This is all over*—"

Something hard and sharp pressed against my esophagus. A blade. "You will continue," Del said. The thing pressed to my throat was the small, curved knife he'd used to open the bourbon. "You will read or I'll cut your goddamn throat. *Read.*"

Warren's arms hooked around me again. His candle was gone.

Anger sharpened the words into crystal focus. My hands were steady. Blood gathered around my jaw in a pulsing neck brace. "Oh, Worshipful Master," I read, "we consider the great luminary of nature, which diffuses light through all spectrums and into every heart, and which hereby casts out the darkness."

Del took the knife from me and watched Dani, as if expecting her to burst into flames. "Do you feel it?" he said, but I didn't know if he was asking me or himself. "It's there. *Inside* her."

"Our days are as grass," I read, my words tight, strained. "It flourishes and rots. We each dwell in the shadow of death and sojourn through darkness."

At my feet, Warren's candle flickered a dying flame.

"*Keep reading!*" Del yelled. "*Louder!*"

"And in that darkness," I shouted, "we must endure and carry forth the gleaming light. For the light of the world is God and God is perfect and right. He is plumb and square, and His will dictates our sovereignty and—"

"I never loved you," Dani said. Her voice rang with a grating springiness, as if it came from coiled metal. "You did this to me! You brought me here!"

"Dani, no, I—"

"*Do not talk with the Cowan!*" Del shouted. "It will trick you!"

Dani hissed.

"Dani, I'm sorry, I . . . "

She replied in a warped string of wobbling s-sounds slipping between her lips as easily as the blood leaking from them. Nasty, blood-filled mucus slid onto her chin.

"You want to fuck me, Mike?" Dani's words were soft now, almost her own voice, but the tone was wrong, vile and foul. "You want them to watch?" She thrust her pelvis up and down, bouncing on the springy mattress. The robe was tangled up above her sunken stomach and her bare sex was gruesome.

I reached for her, to at least cover her up, but Warren yanked me back.

"Keep going," Rom said.

I read, shouting the words louder and louder as I went. My anger—and maybe my hope, too—energized the words. Could this actually heal her? It was too late to stop it now. They'd gone too far. The only option was to finish. "You the unholy, the unsanctified, the unrighteous, the unworthy, the un-noble, the unadmirable, the undignified, and the unpious, you are hereby cast beyond the gates and bounds of this Mighty Lodge of Honorable Men, cast forever out into the most desolate of all forlorn *despair!*"

"*Ohhh,*" Dani said, "I can *feel* your cock inside me. It's so deep. I worship it! The Bald God! The hairless cock! Oh, Mike. *Yes! Yes!*" Her body flailed from her pelvis outward as if she were a flimsy doll yanked by a giant invisible hand. Or a marionette on strings. The bungee cords pulled tight and rubber-banded back. Her hands and head smacked the headboard. She tangled her legs and rubbed her thighs together, sticks trying to make a fire. She moaned loud. "Yes, fuck me! Fuck me hard, Mike! Oh, I'm coming! I'm coming! I'm—"

She saw me watching her, my mouth hanging, my thoughts a blur of *WorshipWorshipWorship*, and burst into a glass-shatter of laughter.

"It's all fake, Mike! Everything is fake!" She laughed and laughed and laughed. It sounded like dozens of overlapping cackling voices.

This was how Randall died—squirming in his own waste while people chanted meaningless words over him. He hadn't been possessed, and Dani wasn't either. Not possession—psychosis and delirium.

"God, the Father in heaven," Ned said and made the sign of the cross. "Have mercy on us."

Ned lifted a tall glass jar—it was half-filled with clear liquid, and a large white label showed a 1-800-number. Slimy black worms squirmed inside the water.

Del stabbed one gnarled finger at the page before me. His hands were shaking. "Keep going."

"Come on, Mike," Dani yelled in a hysterical, fevered pitch, "hop on and show these old bastards how a real man does it! Only you can make my cunt this wet!"

She threw her body up and down wildly. Her legs bounced high and her foot cracked Ned along the jaw.

"Hold her down," he said.

Edgar moved to the other side, and Del grabbed the closer ankle. His blade was pressed flat to her skin. Dani rocked her body against their grips, but they held her in place.

"*Read!*" Del yelled.

My anger had fallen away before the escalating horror. This was wrong, wrong, so terribly, horribly wrong.

"*DO IT!*" Del screamed. The knife jutted from his hand.

I read. "Let us all take heed at this solemn warning: the Cowan must be uprooted and destroyed or else it will reroot and regrow and infect the soil of man."

Dani watched me, flicking her tongue out snake-like, and grinning whenever I glanced up from the page, and Ned recited gospel and thunder cleaved the sky and rain bombarded the house. It was so loud I thought the roof might collapse.

Ned raised the jar of worms and nodded at Rom, who raised the glass vial of red liquid. He uncapped the tube as Ned unscrewed the jar lid. Some echoes are too awful to consider.

"The Ritual of Cowan," Rom said.

"The body and blood," Ned said.

Rom shook the liquid over Dani. It splattered on her face and chest. He leaned forward and poured the rest of it directly into her mouth. She slurped at it greedily. It splashed across her cheeks and onto her chest.

"Animal blood for the beast," he said.

"And purification of the body," Ned said, and tipped the jar.

A moment before the water sloshed onto her neck and chest, I saw the label with the eight-hundred number again, and beneath that in a blue logo: LEECHES USA.

Was there actually a company that sold leeches? For a moment, I held on to that question because it gave me somewhere to focus my fear—were we living in the goddamn Middle Ages?—but when the water hit Dani's skin and seven or eight black slug- and serpent-like worms squirmed on her chest, I knew only terror.

The ugly things slithered on her. A fat one hooked along her neck above her collarbone and latched on. Another one appeared to tunnel into her skin above her right breast.

Not the Ritual of Cowan, but of Taurobolium. A bloodletting.

"*NO!*" I screamed.

"Read," Del said, "or we kill her."

Ned spoke fast, words hopping on each other, and I read from the Masons book and our voices overlapped into a cacophonous tumult.

"*—the beginning was the Word, and the Word was with God, and the Word was God—*"

"*—the omniscient Judge gives forth the invitation to all who seek brotherhood and peace—*"

"*—the same was in the beginning with God. All things were made by him—*"

"—*here before this Free and Accepted Counsel of Masons in deepest fraternal brotherhood, we expel and expurgate*—"

"—*without him was not any thing made that was made. In him was life; and the life was the light of men*—"

"—*all sinister spirits and roosting Cowans are banished and obliterated through the power*—"

"—*the light shineth in darkness; and the darkness comprehended it not*—"

The temperature had plummeted and the humidity was gone, as if the world's fever finally broke into a frigid chill. Dani's skin mottled into lizard hide. She yanked her legs free from Del and Edgar, rubbing them together again, crossing her ankles, and *thwapped* them down against the mattress over and over. She screamed through clenched teeth. A leech latched on beside her belly button. Another one slithered toward her crotch.

"Oh, my God," Rom cried. "Do you see? *DO YOU SEE?*"

Something. It held no distinct shape, and yet it carried weight in the room. Some presence. Some *thing*.

"Keep reading," Del said. He sounded weak, scared.

Ned stumbled over his words and kept going, shouting the gospel as loudly as he could.

Thunder cracked with millions of scattering reverberations, and it kept going, pounding, thumping, knocking through the walls, shaking the house, rumbling with furious life. It chattered into a frantic, heavy knocking of an approaching train that got louder and louder and louder and louder and—

"*WORSHIP!*" I hollered.

"We should be in my church!" Ned shouted.

"You fat fuck," Del yelled, "the kingdom of Heaven is within!" And he laughed madly.

Ned stared as if slapped, and for a moment, silence, or deafness.

Something on my hand.

A wasp.

Poison, poison, poison.

It perched on my finger at the edge of the book. I knew what it was and yet I couldn't believe I was seeing it. A wasp? It was large. Its stinger was several inches long, hanging across my thumb.

Along the baseboard, a glass Ball Mason jar was broken in a jagged crack. Wasps jittered along the fracture.

I put that in here, I thought without any doubt. *I found the jar of wasps in the pantry and instead of throwing it in the garbage, I placed it under the bed.* This was immediately followed by the certain fear: *I'm possessed too.*

Del stabbed a finger at the wasp. "*Cowan*," he said.

I stared at him. The wasp? Did he mean—?

He lunged for me. The knife was still in his hand. I threw myself backwards and this time Warren was caught off guard. His grip slipped enough, and he had to turn to keep his hold, so Del stumbled not into me but right into Warren, who cried out in surprised pain as the knife pushed into him. I stumbled into the nightstand. The syringes spilled onto the floor. My hand caught the IV stand and it fell over.

On the bed, Dani was choking. She made awful, clogged, gagging sounds. Her throat swelled, a snake bulging with fresh kill. Her eyes rolled to alabaster white, and veins throbbed through her cheeks and along her temples, and her skinny arms shook with the tremors vibrating her chest and hips.

I pawed at the bungee cord. It was wrapped several times and knotted.

"*We must continue!*" Ned shouted.

My fingers slipped and regrouped and slipped again. Ned tried to stop me, but I batted his doughy hands away. I'd break those fingers if I had to. Break his goddamn face open.

Dani hacked a garbled and sharp bark, and thick black gruel oozed from her mouth. It poured off her tongue in a slow, molten crawl. Her entire body rocked with the effort. The vomit—or whatever it was—coated her chin and painted her throat and kept spreading.

"Hold on," I said. "Hold on."

My fingers dug into the cord and I pulled it loose. Dani's right arm crumpled to the bed.

I swatted at the leeches and helped her sit upward and bent her head forward, my arms around her. She kept vomiting, hard and slow. The black puke stank of feces and rotting meat. It plopped onto the bed. More and more of it.

Ridding herself of the disease. Of the Cowan.

The ceremony had worked.

"Where is it?" Del said. He sounded crazed. He was looking everywhere. "Where did it go?"

"What are you—"

He grabbed at me, tugged at my hands, pawed at my neck. "It's here. It's here. It wants you. It had your father and now it wants you! I knew it! *I KNEW IT!*"

He seized my ear and yanked it hard. The pain was immense.

I fell back off the bed, leaving Dani there bent over and puking, one arm still tied, and Ned towering over her.

On the floor, Warren tried to reach for the knife stuck in his back and Steven was beside him trying to help.

Del was shoving me back, down, down, and still gripping my ear. It felt like he might rip it off. My hand smacked onto the nightstand, grabbed something, and slid off.

The wasp, or another one that'd squeezed free, floated between our faces. It moved so slowly, languidly, as if struggling to fly through water. Its buzz was slight, a minute vibration we couldn't hear among the chaos but one we felt.

Fear magnified Del's face, and he punched forward.

But not before my hand came up and smacked him as hard as I could in the face.

The syringe my hand fell on a moment before now protruded from Del's right eye.

He howled. The syringe quivered, the plastic stopper-end shaking. I'd buried the damn thing as deep as it would go. He stumbled backwards, tripped over Steven, and crashed to the floor. His hands shook before him, unable to do anything else.

A lick of flame caught the edge of Del's robe, and the fire leaped along the cloth as if it were soaked in lighter fluid.

WHOOOOOOSH!

The old man's scream screeched into pure fear.

Across the room, Edgar stood back from the scene, his face a perfect, shocked thousand-yard stare, but Ned was groping at Dani, trying to push her back down onto the bed even as she kept vomiting vile gunk.

"It's not done!" he yelled. "*We must finish!*"

Dani quivered with the last of her puke. It was thick and rancid and appeared to be moving. No, that couldn't be right. Trick of the light. Yet it was moving. *Creeping.* Alive.

Ned towered over her: "The power of Christ compels—"

Dani hopped up, black mush crumbling off her lips, mouth huge, and clamped her teeth onto Ned's fat cheek.

He was too shocked to even scream. Dani snapped her head back and forth, a Rottweiler's fury, hard, strong yanks, and flung backwards. She fell onto the bed with a springy bounce. Ned Loller's flabby cheek dangled from her mouth. I thought of my father's story, of the doomed woman walking into the darkness with something chewy in her mouth. She spat out Ned's cheek and turned to her other bungeed wrist.

Ned stayed on his feet a moment, shocked without comparison. Half his face was gone, a paint-slop of blood. His little white teeth shone through the stringy, tissuey hole in his face.

He stepped back, and his legs gave out. His collapse shook the floor.

"*Dani!*" I shouted.

She stopped, completely free now, half on and half off the bed, and stared at me. Blood and piss and black slop sagged off her robe. A leech was still stuck on her neck.

She yanked the IV tube from her arm. It ripped free with a tape screech. Blood dribbled. It looked black.

Behind me, fire raged and Del screamed the last noises of his life: a blubbering, jangled mess of "*Erk . . . GAK . . . OW!*" I turned, and the flames leaped higher. Del had fallen into the dresser, the wood beginning to char, and Warren was still on his knees in the corner.

Smoke covered the window and gathered over the ceiling.

The fire jumped onto Steven's robe and raced up his front to veil his face. He couldn't even scream before his lips melted.

"Dani, we have to—"

But she was already gone.

CHAPTER 86:
WE ALL FALL DOWN

I CHASED AFTER her down the hall, and my thwacking feet followed hers through the kitchen and out onto the puddle-strewn deck. The rain had stopped, the day smelled sour and damp, and the dark clouds were thinning, dissipating, summer sun slicing through in narrow arcs to flicker light in all those puddles.

"Dani!" I shouted.

"I've got her, Mike," someone called back.

Down on the patio, Rom held Dani in a reverse hug, the way Warren had been holding me. Her arms were pinioned, but she was kicking her legs and throwing her body side to side, a wild animal, and Rom kept his head back to avoid a skull-smack. Even as thin, exhausted, and delirious as she was, Dani thrashed and squirmed and made barking, growling noises. Her jaw snapped up and down in hard teeth-cracks.

I descended the stairs. "It's okay, Dani," I said. "Everything is going to be okay." My phone wasn't on me. Inside the house, someone was screaming. Several someones. "Rom, do you have your phone?" I sounded perfectly calm, reasonable even.

He didn't register the question. "We need help," I said, almost unnaturally calm.

"The ritual didn't work, Mike."

I paused, toes curling over that last step. "She's not possessed," I said. "You've let yourself be tricked."

He dodged a head-fling from Dani that would have knocked him unconscious. Her legs beat at his. "No, Mike. I saw it. In the room with Lee. It was there. It's *real*. It *is* inside her. After what you've seen, how can you doubt it? We have to finish the ritual."

I stepped onto the patio, edged closer. The concrete was wet and grainy. Ten feet or so separated us. Beyond him, Mount Munacy rose high, sopping, a beast emerging from a stagnant lagoon.

"Listen to yourself," I said. "There's no demon. She's delusional—*delirious*— because of what *you people* did to her. For God's sake, there's still a leech on her neck."

I cut the distance by half, but now Rom was backing up. He stepped onto the grass. It squished. "This isn't the movies," he said. "Demons don't follow scripts."

There was no furniture on the patio, no stray garden tools lying around—nothing to grab as a weapon.

He backed up, farther and farther. He was only a foot or so from where we'd buried Dusty, from where I'd spilled my father's ashes and punched the ground until my knuckles bled, from where my father looked at me for the final time, his fingers tapping my cheek.

"Listen to me," I said, hard and cutting. "I'm sorry your wife died. I'm sorry you watched her die slowly over weeks and months. I'm sorry there was no way to help her. I'm sorry there's nowhere to place blame. There is no Cowan. No Mul Lok. No demons. No goddamn monsters. You don't want to face the truth. Bad shit happens. You're only making it worse."

Something crashed, and fire tongues licked out of my bedroom window. If anyone was still screaming, I couldn't hear it.

"We have to get help," I said. "Let go of her."

"No," Rom said. "We have to force out the Cowan."

Dani hissed and snapped her teeth at Rom. Two more steps and I would charge him.

Dani looked at me. It was her, the real her, seeing through all the hysteria and mania and madness. I was sure of it.

"I'm sorry," she said, so tired and sad. "I warned you. It's too late. I have to go. I belong to it."

"No," I said. "There's nothing there, Dani. You're unwell. I'm going to get you help. Real help."

She shook her head. "I must go to it."

Someone was behind me.

I turned in time to see the metal slope of a shovel careening directly for my head. I ducked, but the shovel bumped across the top of my skull. Pain vibrated down my neck and through my spine. Pinhole-sized black dots peppered my vision.

I stumbled sideways, arms up to shield myself from another attack.

Dani's mouth unhinged wide and a primal howl barreled loose.

She flung her head back, and Rom wasn't quick enough—her skull crashed into his face and he let go, stumbling back, blood unleashing from his nose in a vivid gush. He reached for her and stepped into Dusty's open grave. His leg twisted and he fell.

Dani ran for the woods. Her bare feet splashed through the grass and flashed around the flap of robe. She could've been floating.

CHAPTER 87:
GOD'S FIRE

THE SHOVEL CUT through the air.

I backed up, fell.

Theo raised the shovel over his head. He was so young—just a kid, screwed up by a religious zealot for a father—but he was fueled from his own well of rage.

The shovel, the same one I'd used to dig Dusty's grave, swung down—and I rolled out of the way. The blade hit the ground, and I seized the wooden handle. I yanked it from Theo's grip and he tumbled forward, lost his balance, and fell beside me.

He tried to get up, and I shoved him down, hard, and held him there.

"*Getoffame!*" he screamed, no more than a child caught in a tantrum.

"*Hey!*"

Someone from above.

Wes the bus driver stood at the peak of Mount Munacy. His curly hair spiraled every which way. Unlike Theo, he wasn't in a white robe, but wore a long purple one with a matching stole slung over his neck to hang down onto his thighs like a super-long scarf. It featured a cross on one end and a rising sun on the other.

Sun-kissed disciples.

Dani was slumped on her knees beside him, her body slouched in an awful way, his hands tangled in her short hair, keeping her upright.

He killed her.

This thought was perfectly clear and unquestionable. I screamed, snatched up the shovel, and charged up the path, the shovel held across my chest.

Wes was grinning, but the smile faltered as I ascended the hill and kept coming. The rocky ground gouged my feet but the pain was far away, a distant echo.

Wes turned to face me and snapped Dani sideways. She resisted. Weak, but still alive.

"Dani!" I screamed.

"*STOP!*" Wes shouted.

In his other hand, he held a bottle of lighter fluid. He squeezed the contents onto Dani's face and chest. She thrashed as if the liquid burned.

He raised a metal Zippo, flicked it open, and thumbed the wheel.

The flame stopped me. I was fifteen feet away, panting, every inch of my body alive with buzzing, quivering adrenaline.

"Move and she dies," Wes said. "A burnt offering."

Near him were the bound stacks of yellowing newspapers. They were soaked. Maybe from the rain, and maybe from the lighter fluid. I didn't want to guess which. The box of my father's books and movies—*Remains*—was tipped onto its side, all the contents tumbling out. My father's story was in there, and I saw the pages of my novel strewn about.

Reddish-yellow flames bloomed high along the side of the house and onto the roof. The white siding had melted near the fire and was charring in fat, angry blobs.

The whole world is burning, I thought.

"In the name of God," Wes called out.

My hands tightened on the shovel. "Let her go."

The lighter flame flickered, fat, eager.

"Fire is so perfect," he said. "It is forever hungry. It eats everything."

"Drop the lighter."

"I intend to," Wes said. "I am sorry about your cat, though. If we'd been able to catch it, we could have had a proper sacrifice. But it's okay. Your girlfriend will have to do."

"She's not my girlfriend," I said. "She's my wife."

I ran toward him, screaming.

And someone else—a woman—screamed too.

The sound came from the woods. It was desperate, frantic, crazed.

Wes turned, and I swung the shovel.

Another figure in white darted from the woods. This woman's face was screwed in a crooked rictus, her arms out, hands curled into claws.

The shovel caught Wes's chin, and his head kicked back in a hard snap. He stumbled, releasing Dani, but didn't fall.

The lighter flung from his hand. It hit a corner of the stacked newspapers and fire immediately surged over the ancient paper in a powerful, hot burst. Along with it went my father's story and my manuscript.

I swung again, and Wes ducked and somehow his hands caught the shovel blade. I was too surprised to pull back quickly enough, and he yanked the shovel out of my hands. The wood pole splintered through my palms.

The screaming wraith from the woods went right for him. He turned quickly, swinging the shovel like an extra-long baseball bat.

The wood thwacked the woman's face. She collapsed as if instantly dead.

Wes went for Dani, but she'd already taken off—*into the woods*—and then I was throwing a punch at Wes as he swung the handle end of the shovel at me.

The pole hit me in the side, and a rib cracked.

I punched him in the face. He staggered back. Blood gushed from his nostrils and he scowled at me. Blood rimmed his mouth, outlined his teeth.

I punched him again, only this time he stabbed me with the end of the shovel handle. It hit me square in the chest and I thought, *He broke my breastplate*, and my feet slipped out and I hit the ground.

Wes spat a glob of blood and approached. Mud sucked at his boots. No bare feet for him. He adjusted his grip on the shovel so the digging end was toward me. One thwack to the head and that might be it.

He raised the shovel. Fiery arcs spun across his eyes.

"I see it in you," he said. *"Cowan."*

He swung.

Half of Wes's face exploded in a sleet of bone and blood. He wobbled and fell.

Down below, Officer Koryta stood with his gun aimed.

All I could do was stare back.

Bright blue wedges fractured the sky, and the sun found me.

CHAPTER 88:
INTO THE WOODS

IT TOOK A MOMENT, but I stumbled onto my feet. I lumbered a few steps and a hand snagged my ankle.

Suzanne glared up at me, her face in a terrified scowl. "Don't go back there. *Not safe.*" She couldn't focus. Blood slathered her cheek.

"*DON'T MOVE!*" Officer Koryta shouted.

I stopped, reflexively raising my arms in surrender. Koryta approached along the sloped side, gun poised on me. His partner stayed on the patio, gun drawn as well. Theo lay flat, and Rom was kneeling with his hands laced behind his head.

Flames stretched out of my bedroom window and hooked onto the roof. "*There's people in the house!*" I yelled.

Koryta slipped, kept his balance. "Help is on the way. I need you to get on your knees and put your hands—"

"*No!*" I said. "My wife is in the woods. I have to find her."

"Do *not* move."

Suzanne squeezed my ankle. "*Wrong, wrong,*" she said.

"*Get down!*" Koryta yelled.

"Please don't shoot," I said—and ran for the woods.

CHAPTER 89:
THE MUL LOK

I **WAS LOOKING** everywhere at once and still moving, all the trees and their gnarled branches spinning, clawing at me, and it was getting darker. Sunlight glowed high above and behind me, but the darkness among the trees was even thicker than I'd always feared it would be.

I thought of my detective character still languishing in an unlit corridor somewhere between the covers of a dog-eared composition book, and I thought of my father bent over me while I slept, whispering warnings to me, and I thought of the nightmares that roughed up my sleep—the dim worlds, the panicky need to flee, the fear it was no dream but a real hell from which I'd never escape.

Worship. Worship. Worship.

Was it in my head, or was the word panting from my mouth in a drum-beat chant?

Sounds gathered in a rising tide of noise: rain dripping off leaves in staccato plops, a warbling, a humming, and a clicking, and a high-pitched screech, and a scrabbling of claws, the stomp of hooves, and a coyote's lonely howl, and a deep-throated huffing, and the thick, papery flap of wings, and a clacking of sticks or bones, jangling in a death rattle, louder and louder, bloating the world and crushing in all around me.

From the trees, hundreds of crows took flight at once.

Everything shook as if the air itself was about to explode. The thunderous, beating flap of a thousand or more wings quaked through me, and I feared I might rupture, crack wide open in a gaping crevasse. I stopped, tried to catch my breath. The air was thick and slimy, a jungle, ripe and fecal.

Was an ancient power controlling the birds?

Poison, I thought. *The birds, the squirrels, the wasps.*

How many of those birds had been dead at one time, and yet flew once more?

I had to find Dani, and at any moment Officer Koryta was going to tackle me, arrest me, but the world—this forest dimension I'd avoided my whole life— closed in until all of it was where I stood, a damp plat of soil chilling my bare feet.

DEAD END

The sour stink made me gag. The smell of decay.

Above me, in the crow-less treetops but not beyond into the sunny sky of day, an owl took flight. It was enormous, ten or more feet from wingtip to wingtip.

The owl flapped its giant wings and flew off into the darkness. Light flickered around it, and the bird screeched a territorial cry. A primal, prehistoric call.

Fog whispered out of the ground and floated over my feet.

Something furry brushed my leg, and I looked down ready to scream and there was Dusty. He was alive. Somehow, he was alive. His eyes glinted with life. He'd been run over by a bus, I'd carried his corpse in a sheet, buried him in the ground, yet here he was, alive and rubbing back and forth against my leg. Purring.

From somewhere came the thrumming rhythm of chanting voices. Those voices didn't speak words—they repeated the primitive jungle sounds of tribal ritual.

No, not jungle—Native American.

The Lenapes.

I didn't move, unsure I even could, my thighs completely rigid, and I struggled to see: the darkness deepening, encroaching, concealing.

The chanting, moaning incantation grew louder, closer. Would spirits soon surround me? Would they be ghosts of the Lenape tribe, or perhaps the risen, reincarnated dead?

I reached toward Dusty, not believing, my fingers trembling . . .

A child's giggle froze me. It was close, within twenty feet.

On a crumbling rock wall stood a child of maybe two, or perhaps a few months younger, closer to eighteen months old, perhaps. Completely shadowed, the child was only an outline in a world of amorphous darkness.

Was that child my brother? Had he been back here all this time, running around, giggling, playing with the animals, searching for Dad, waiting for me?

Poison. The birds, the squirrels, the wasps.

The living dead.

I opened my mouth to say his name—

Something was coming.

A twig snapped underfoot and whatever it was *rushed* for me. Dusty ran off; the child laughed again, a warbling giggle, and jumped off the rock wall into the thicker dark. The air cleaved, sliced open so quickly I couldn't even get my head around before a hand clamped onto my arm.

My stomach squeezed into my throat.

Hunched over, face streaked with dried blood, a man twisted his neck to glare up at me. Not a spirit. Not anyone I knew.

Yet someone I recognized. Someone whose face I'd seen only a day or two earlier. "Bud Calla?"

Theo showing me the picture of Isaac's father and two of his AA pals, the three of them leaning into each other, and me saying it sounded far-fetched a father would murder his own son and Theo saying, *Because no father has ever committed prolicide before?*

"*Ak!*" Bud Calla said.

"What're you—"

"*Erf! Rawk! AK!*" His fingers dug into my flesh.

Even as dark as it was, I recognized his smug, lassitude-laced smirk, although now his lips stretched thin across teeth slathered in muck, like he was eating mud. And he was clearly insane. His skin was moon-pale and quivering, as if bugs were squirming just beneath.

Theo was right: Bud Calla had been hiding in the woods and maybe he killed his son and maybe he didn't, but either way the stress of something had broken his mind.

"How long have you been out here?"

"*Of! Furk! Ru*—" He froze, head cocked, ear up.

There was a hole in his temple the size of a nickel. A bullet hole. A smudge of blood was dried beneath it.

He killed himself, I thought. *He came into the woods after killing his son, and he got lost back here and he put a bullet through his head. He died back here but something brought him back. An eager spirit, or several, gave his body renewed life, but it didn't matter because the bullet scrambled his brains and he may be alive but he's completely insane.*

Was Dusty insane now, too? And my brother? *With eyes like those,* Del had said of his daughter.

Another sound: not the tribal, ghostly voices, but an actual thing—a solid, physical presence—something huge, a giant beast with plodding, heavy steps that vibrated through the ground.

The Mul Lok.

Branches snapped and a tree cracked and groaned, timber-splintering, until it thunked to the ground. Close, fifty feet away—maybe closer.

Fear chiseled through my skin, liquified my insides, and split my mind into two chunks of gleaming black, lifeless rock.

The ground shook. Branches snapped.

Bud made an awful keening moan, the helpless cry of an injured animal, and he ran off, turning away from me, and there was the other side of his head, not a small hole on this temple but a gaping wound of sagging, ruined skin and stubs of fractured bone. Even dead as he was, he moved fast in a haphazard scurry, jumping roots and swatting aside low branches. The darkness swallowed him, or whatever had become of him.

I immediately wanted his hand back on my arm, back and squeezing even harder. Its absence reminded me I was alone. No way I could face whatever was coming by myself.

It would drive me insane.

Don't worry, a sweet, silky voice whispered, *it won't hurt a bit, love, not a bit. Come to me. Let me hold you.*

DEAD END

Another tree yawned its way to the ground. All other sounds had ceased—no animal noises, no chanting—nothing but the sound of the monster approaching.

Let me feed.

I prayed Dani was somewhere far off, hiding.

To my left, and fewer than twenty feet off, something loomed. It hulked there. Heaving audibly in a throaty huff, the creature that once ate the dead souls of the resurrected Lenapes watched me. It had no eyes, because it needed none to see. It had found me, smelled my fear perhaps, and it could get me if it wanted. And it did have a mouth. Oh, yes, I was sure, an enormous black hole of a mouth crammed with fat, sharp teeth, and if I saw it I would go instantly mad just before it attacked.

"Mul Lok," I whispered.

The monster rose larger and larger. I couldn't see it, but I felt its presence expand. Displaced the air. It might be as tall as the trees and as wide as Wes's bus was long.

It wasn't the Cowan, not some demon—it was something far worse.

And it was right there.

Studying me, determining my fate. This unspeakable thing was going to put an end to all the misery, one way or another.

We're going to die here.

I felt it there, looming, mammoth and hulking, and I felt something else too—its anger and pain. And I saw what it saw: stalking, tromping through dense woods—*these* woods—a long, long time ago, a beast with sentience but not self-awareness, a predator by nature (be it natural or supernatural), hunting and being hunted, always hungry, always hurting, always scared, and now something else, many somethings, were coming for it, their noise echoing and cascading all around, chants full of incomprehensible meaning save one: *KILL.*

The Lenapes hunted the Mul Lok. They tracked it through these woods and surrounded it, and bombarded it with arrows, piercing its thick hide and—

It saw the attack, the onslaught, and then it saw nothing and never would again. At least not with eyes.

But without vision, the Mul Lok transcended its physical limitations and was much more dangerous, much more than mere beast—it was a monster.

I learned all that in a flash and stood there vulnerable and somehow violated. The Mul Lok could kill me easily. There was no defense.

My jaw was tight, but not frozen stiff, and though my heart seized in a block of ice, I found my voice—and the courage to use it: "Are you God?"

The Mul Lok's breath pushed branches toward me in a sharp wind. It smelled of rot and meat and wet earth.

Yes, that sweet voice said. *I am God.*

My skin was tight and cold. "Then come on and let's be done with this."

The monster lurked and time stretched and stretched, and tremors licked up my back and down my arms.

You will come to me, the voice said.

Dusty was dead and alive. My long-dead twin lived eternally young back here. Bud Calla had killed himself and yet lived.

You will live, too, the voice promised. *Come to me and live forever and ever and ever.*

I stepped forward—this beast had promised my father the same, an everlasting life, and Dad could resist only so long before he had either to go to it or take his own life, and it had almost driven him insane, and now it wanted me— but I stopped. It would be so easy to go to it, as easy and right as slipping into cool water on a hot day, and I wanted the lush relief of that promise, wanted it badly, but I didn't give in.

I resisted—I refused.

The beast exhaled and the branches bent toward me again in dozens of skeletal arms. The stink was a graveyard of decomposing matter: slimy mushrooms and moldy leaves, and corpses softened into sludgy blobs with loose skin.

"*You want me?*" I yelled.

The Mul Lok growled. The sound hurt my teeth.

"*COME ON!*" I screamed. "*COME GET ME!*"

The ground shook. The monster was moving—*THUNK. THUNK.* The ground quivered with its enormity.

The smacks of its steps were all I knew. This was it. The creature was coming for me. I'd refused its bait, stood up to it, and now it would prove how god-like it was.

How, perhaps, it even *was* God. At least in this world, among the trees.

THUNK. THUNK. Thunk. Thunk. Thunk.

The steps fell farther and farther away, only the faintest vibration in the ground now, and soon that too was gone.

The sound of summer crickets rose all around, and water dripped steadily from the trees.

"Mike."

Dani's voice was so small, but for me it was louder than all I'd heard before.

She was ten feet away, huddled in a fetal position at the base of the white birch, the tree I once believed was magical and called the Keeper of the Dark. She reached for me with a grotesquely skinny arm.

CHAPTER 90:
KILL THE COWAN

THE GROUND SUCKED at my feet with cold, wet mouths. For a moment, Dani was a few steps away, and then she was farther, much farther away—as if this were a trick, an illusion, a *delusion*, and perhaps I was trapped in another nightmare I couldn't scream my way out of.

Dusty was dead after all, not scurrying around back here through the underbrush. As for Bud Calla . . . Had he even really been there?

"Mike," Dani said again. She sounded so sad and so exhausted.

But she was there, right in front of me, and I dropped before her. "I'm here," I said.

I cradled her against me. She was cold and shaking and crying soft, steady tears. I ripped the leech off her neck. Had I let this happen? Was it my fault? It was my idea to move into my mom's house so we could save money. Dani had wanted us to stay in our apartment. Sure, it would take longer to save up for a down payment on a house, but we'd still be in our own place. Dani had said as much, and the rest was implied: moving into the house where I grew up would wedge us apart, because there were so many memories there, so many ghosts— ghosts of all kinds.

I squeezed Dani. Jagged bones poked at me, and her rapid heartbeat took over my own.

"I'm sorry," I said.

There was more to say, but a terrible thought stopped them: *Why didn't Dani say anything when Bud grabbed me or when the Mul Lok neared?*

Because, a cold rational voice said, *she was dead. She ran back here with the last of her strength and died, but as with Bud, something brought her back. Something was eager to call her body home. She's not the Dani you know. She's someone else.*

I'm not me.

No. That was ridiculous. *She didn't speak up because she's exhausted and scared. She didn't die. She's right here, alive.*

Just like Dusty was a moment ago, and my brother.

Dani's frigid fingers curled around my neck, and her breath tickled my ear. "It's right here," she whispered. "Above us."

Slowly, not breaking our hug, I looked up.

Sunlight flickered through the treetops, and directly overhead in the crook of two fat branches was a giant, grayish mass, as if the tree had sprouted a tumor. Which, in a way, it had.

It was the largest wasp nest I've ever seen. Easily the size of three or four basketballs crammed together, the papery nest was a genuine nightmare. Fat wasps flew back and forth from the curled hole at the bottom, and one or two wasps slowly crawled on the outside of the nest.

Poison. The birds, the squirrels, the wasps.

"Cowan," Dani whispered. "Kill them."

In her hand, she held the Zippo. She'd snagged it off the ground after the newspapers caught fire.

"No," I said, calm, quiet. "Dani, they're just wasps."

Her fingernails dug into my flesh. "You have to kill them. Burn them. Please, Mike."

Went on a killing spree. "Dani, there is no Cowan."

Her lips pressed against my ear. *"Please."*

I tore enough fabric from Dani's robe to wad into a soggy softball. Lighter fluid leaked over my hands. "They're only wasps," I said.

"No," she said.

She crawled several feet from the tree and flicked the lighter. She reached the flame toward me.

I shouldn't humor her fantasy. That was bad, wasn't it? She was delusional, exhausted, perhaps badly injured, and going along with the conjurations of her madness wasn't going to help her recovery. "I don't—"

"Mike, *please.*"

Rom's words: *If she only thinks she's possessed or infected or whatever, the ritual will still work. She'll cure herself. She only needs the opportunity to do it. That's what we're going to give her.*

Was belief enough? Could belief alone make things real? Could belief alone cure the sick? Was any of this real? Did it matter? I adjusted my grip and brought the ball to the flame.

Fire consumed it, and I threw it hard as I could at the nest.

The nest ruptured inward, wasps springing free, and fire engulfed it. The mass charred instantly, and it crinkled and crumbled and blackened. Papery fragments shed free in ashy wisps that floated among the trees.

My fingers were on fire, and I beat my hand against my shirt, wrapped it, and smothered the flames. Blisters reddened my skin that had barely healed from putting out the fire on Isaac's arm.

Wasps fell to the ground. Some were on fire, spasming with life.

I grabbed Dani under her arms and dragged her farther away.

"Mike. Do you feel it? We belong here. It won't let us leave."

DEAD END

Something with us in the woods. Not the Cowan possibly burning to death in the wasp nest, and not the Mul Lok that saw without eyes—there was something larger than those things, a presence as grand as God and as coldly menacing as the Devil. Whatever ancient thing it was, sentient or unconscious, it had us in its grip.

Almost.

"Dani, we do *not* have to stay here." I took her face in my hands. The flesh was chilled, the bags under her eyes heavy, but her vision was clear, perhaps more so than it'd ever been. "We can leave this place."

She started to respond, lips parting, and stopped. She saw what I meant—*all* I meant.

A wasp buzzed near my hand, and somewhere far back in the woods, a giant beast paused.

I caught the wasp in my burned hand and squeezed. It squirmed, vibrated against my skin, struggled, tried to sting me, tried to burrow into me. Pulpy slop slipped between my fingers and dripped to the ground.

Far off, the beast continued on its way.

Dani touched my face. "Let's go."

I picked her up in my arms. I hurt, and with every breath I felt a sharp stabbing pain in my side, but I could manage. We could leave. We didn't have to be slaves to powers as grand as the Universe Creators, be they God or something else. We could challenge those forces, ancient and omniscient or leviathan and evil. We could find our own way.

We headed into the light.

CHAPTER 91:
AS GOD SEES

IN THE WOODS, time was different—slippery.

Dani sagged in my arms, legs dangling off my left arm, back curled against my right. Her head rested beneath my chin. She cried gently.

Officer Koryta stumbled back from the tree line and lowered his gun. He stared at us incredulously while, behind him, my mom's house burned.

"Ambulance," I said.

He nodded and couldn't speak for several seconds. There was no explaining what had happened. To him, it appeared I had stepped into the woods and immediately turned back around with Dani in my arms. I'd been back there at least several minutes, yet no time out here had passed.

"It's on the way," he said.

I walked past him onto Mount Munacy and toward the cliff edge. Wes's ruined body lay nearby, and Suzanne stared, mesmerized by the crackling flames.

I went to the edge and stepped off: I flew—soaring high above against an azure sky, I lifted higher and higher with Dani in my arms, and there was Rom on the grass near Theo and higher and there was Nina on the front lawn weeping before another cop, her cellphone clutched in her hand, and Ned Loller barreling out the front door, his robe singed and smoking, his hands clamped on his mutilated face, blood seeping between chubby fingers, and I flew higher where the chaos below fell away, distant, and the air's chill refreshed me, and Heintz Hill carved through the trees, and there was another cop car, lights spinning, siren a soft wail from up here, and the fire truck pulling out of the station on Main Street, and there was all of Warrenville—its serpentine roads and thick clusters of trees—and there was Blackford Court where a young boy was long ago hit by a truck, and then it too fell away as we rose higher, cresting the Shawangunk Mountains, and then there were clouds and quiet and sun and an endless vista of sky, and I saw as God sees.

CHAPTER 92:
A NEW LIFE

DANI WAS MOVED to a top care facility in Vermont for patients with mental complications. My mother's life insurance paid for the move. I rented a blue house by the beach when she was moved there. The ocean was frigid, and the breeze that rolled off it could freeze you instantly, but it was nice to sit at the wall of windows overlooking the ocean and admire a world that was endless.

The facility didn't need to keep Dani restrained, though the leather straps dangled from her bed as a reminder that this patient had the potential to lose her calm and hurt herself or others. Someone had placed a plastic cross on her nightstand. It glowed in the dark.

"Hey," I said.

At the facility's recommendation, I always called an hour or so before visiting so the staff could assure me Dani wouldn't be under heavy sedation. They still had to keep her in a near-coma because of her "terrors," as the doctor called them. But she had come a long way; I should take comfort in that. She might be able to function without tranquilizers within three months.

Dani's head lolled on the pillow; her eyes struggled to open. I caressed her hand. Aside from being in a place for people with troubled minds, Dani looked healthy. Her face was smooth and clean, full of vibrant color. She'd gained some weight. She was rested and peaceful.

I had been visiting every day, but of those daily trips how many times had Dani realized I was there? How many times did she grab me and whisper in my ear, "The Cowan lives. There's no escape"?

That's not something I cared to think about. Why dwell on the miseries of the past or even those of the present? Hope springs eternal, right?

I squeezed her hand, and she reciprocated. She groaned something that might have been a word struggling to break free from her throat. I prayed it wasn't a slippery, whispered s-sound.

"What is it? You okay? I'll get a nurse."

Her grip tightened. Her eyelids rose slowly like a curtain, gently lifting to build suspense for what lay behind. Her eyes gleamed fresh and bright the way they always did after we had sex.

"Hey," she said.

"Hey." My eyes watered.

"I'm sorry."

"Don't . . . "

"It was supposed to be so wonderful. Our perfect little life."

"We can still have it," I said. "We can."

Her smile tweaked my heart in a funny way. "I love you," she said.

"I love you."

We kissed, and it was sweet and perfect and magical.

Sometimes that's really all it takes to make everything better. Things wouldn't immediately go back to normal, to the pre-Mullock days, but in time we would fight our way to somewhere close, if not better. Over the next few days, Dani underwent seemingly endless tests, but in the end the doctors offered me cautious optimism and wished us a long and prosperous life together. We packed up the car and headed down the coast. The calendar drew closer to Christmas, but each passing mile gave us a warmer climate and a sweet promise that everything would work out.

At first, we drove in silence, our minds reeling. We would never be able to make sense of all of it—there was no way. At a rest stop in Virginia, Dani began to cry while eating a hamburger. People stared at us while I took her in my arms and told her everything was going to be okay.

"You promise?" she asked.

"I do," I said.

She didn't cry again until we rented a house on the coast in Georgia and enjoyed our first meal there out on the deck. It was Christmas Eve, but we each only wore sweatshirts and the sun started to make that too hot for me. We didn't have any gifts for each other, but that didn't matter. We were the gifts. We were a family. We dared to believe happiness might yet find its way into our lives.

Time passed, as it always does, and we found a way to laugh again. We didn't mention New York or talk about what happened. We each saw a therapist, and at some point I came to terms with my father's death. I accepted him for what he was, and that I wasn't him and didn't need to be, and I left him in the past.

Dani got her Georgia teaching license and started teaching at Pembrook High School the next September. A year later, she was voted Teacher of the Year by the Georgia Association of Educators. Soon after that, Dani started giving lectures at schools about inspiring students to love literature. She even got to meet the governor at a special reception for Georgia's premier educators. Somewhere along the way, we found pleasure in the bedroom as well. We made love slowly, sweetly, maturely, and fell asleep in each other's arms.

Thankful doesn't begin to describe how I felt.

We were nearing happiness, but enjoying contentment.

Dani and I tried to get pregnant and even had a false positive or two that got our hopes up, but in the end, it wasn't meant to be. It didn't matter. We had each other. Every once in a while, I drank a beer and toasted my old friend Roman Fort, forgiving him because for a little while he was the best father I ever knew.

I could have joined Dani and gotten my teaching certificate too, but my heart wasn't in it anymore. We didn't need the money, so I returned to writing—not my poor detective trapped somewhere in a dark hallway, and certainly not *Dead End*, a manuscript that burned up on Mount Munacy, but a different type of story. A few hundred words a day that led nowhere became a rigid two-thousand-word daily routine, and I was outlining a coming-of-age novel in methodical detail.

"It's just a lark," I told Dani. She kissed me on the forehead and let me write.

My first novel was published two years later by Random House. It was called *Just a Lark*. It was about a young couple who fall in love after both of their parents die in a tragic accident. It earned good reviews and made it to number seventeen on the *New York Times* Best Sellers list.

It's too much to take in when I think about it like that—one bright moment after the other. How could we be given such an amazing second chance? What made us so special?

I'd think of Ned Loller and wonder if he ever found peace. I was Job, I'd suffered, but now I was blessed.

"I never thought I'd say this," Dani said, "but it was worth all the shit we went through just to get here. I love you so much."

We were on the deck, overlooking the ocean, more welcoming here than up North, and I leaned toward her, the warm water off the coast of Georgia twinkling starlight beyond.

A spark of electricity jumped between our lips when we kissed.

But none of those things happened.

A PLACE OF DEATH

LIFE IS NOT a fairy tale, and one kiss alone does not contain enough magic to set the world right.

Dani stayed for ten days in the hospital, it took two days for her to completely recover from severe dehydration. Her stay included psychiatric observation, and she was released in stable health with diagnosed bipolar disorder and PTSD. She was told to meet with a psychologist weekly. The nightmares were nightly enemies at first, but they gradually lessened, and she began to sleep in four- or five-hour sessions, and then all night.

That went for both of us.

Sometimes she would wake crying, and I would pull her close. I'd tell her it was going to be okay. We were going to find happiness, and somewhere in the novelist's part of my mind, there was a house in Georgia overlooking the sparkling ocean.

At break of day, dreams they say, are true, so wrote the poet John Dryden.

My father believed that.

So do I.

Last night, the bathroom door was closed.

I pressed my ear to the door, strained to hear . . .

Ned Loller and his sun-kissed disciples, Del Summer, Rom Fort, and Ward and Beatrice Munacy: each person nourished his own insanity and this collective madness hot-wired all of them to a bomb that had to detonate eventually. It led to violence and death. We suffered with them. We were each possessed in our own way.

If a theory must be offered, I think it's the cruelest one of all: bad things happen without explanation. Precisely because what happens is illogical and so horrifying, we commit ourselves to probing for secrets, but in the end there are none. Pain thrives. Misery multiplies. We all suffer. Some of us suffer a great deal. That doesn't make it fair; it's just how things go. Sometimes there's no reason for anything that's happened. There's no greater truth. There's only life and death. We must make of that what we will.

That answer doesn't please me or even placate me, but it's the best I've got, and I have to either live with that or die with it. I don't care if Mullock Road was cursed because, when you get right to it, the whole world is cursed. Each of us is cursed. Right from the start. Make peace with that or die trying.

Even so, the tears still come at night and the pain is always fresh.

But there are dark nights still when I can't sleep, and I wonder if there's greater meaning in all that we went through. In those dark, quiet (and, thankfully, whisper-less) hours before daybreak when time is no longer linear, I wonder if there was truth in what happened. Was the Cowan real? The Mul Lok? Perhaps even Moloch the Demon who demanded sacrifice by fire? Are there more things in Heaven and Earth than are dreamt of in my philosophy?

That was all bullshit. There may be things beyond our understanding, but demons and soul eaters? No. We're always so desperate for answers to the mysteries of life and death, to why bad things happen, that we are willing—even eager—to latch on to explanations, no matter how fanciful or unlikely. Those beliefs become (*absurdly*) convenient lies, and people accept them willingly, gladly, because the alternate view of a cold, indifferent universe is too horrifying to consider.

She's hurting herself again. There are little purple bruises on her thighs.

Maybe the real curse is that the old self we once were, the one we want to shake off, to bury, to be rid of forever, we can't escape.

Dani is forever the teenage girl stomping her cleats onto a teammate's face— or perhaps the younger girl with a chunk of broken sidewalk clutched in her hands, her dad's blood dripping off the jagged edge, faceless monsters tormenting her nights.

And I am forever a young boy in blue shorts screaming at the trees to stay back, forever the little kid on his knees in the grass bearing witness to his father's death, witness to the blood he chokes on, the final word he dares speak.

Cowan. Not *coward.*

DEAD END

But maybe there's no difference.

We are always and forever, no matter how much we wish it otherwise, our worst selves. When we try to be better than who we are, our old selves drag us back down. They return like ghosts to haunt us, just as the worst traumas haunted and created those versions of ourselves and—ultimately—they possess us so we can never be free.

※

She's biting her nails again.

※

Two months after she got out of the hospital, Dani tugged me close and kissed my cheek. She was holding something behind her back, and smiling ear to ear. Her hair was short, styled like Mia Farrow's in *Rosemary's Baby*, Dani's black instead of red. I found it rather sexy.

"Hey," she said.

"Hey," I said.

She brought her hand out from behind her back. It was a pink-and-white pregnancy test stick. "Guess what."

※

Last night, she was whispering. It was faint, and only lasted a moment. I'll have to tell her therapist. She probably needs a higher dosage of her meds.

※

Three months after the events on Mullock, we returned to the house where I grew up. It was the day after Thanksgiving, grey and cold. Dani and I were living in an apartment in Middletown again. Our holiday was quiet, just the two of us.

I was worried about coming back here, but even Dani's therapist thought it might be helpful. *A chance to square off against the demons of the past*, she said, managing to say it without any trace of irony.

Rom was sitting on the front porch steps, arms across his thighs, face tilted to the sky as if expecting something to appear. The face of God, perhaps.

Dani and I stood on the driveway and Rom stared at us and no one said anything for a while. Somewhere in the trees, a trio of crows cawed.

"How are you?" I finally asked.

"Alive," he said, and started to add more and stopped. Deep wrinkles grooved his face, and his hairline had receded to make his forehead noticeably larger. Rom stood and approached. "You two look good."

I didn't know about me, but Dani had gained weight, and her complexion was healthy, the pregnancy glow radiating off her. There were bruises on her thighs, and her nails were jagged, though.

313

"How's that cat of yours?" I asked.

"Had to put her down. Blood infection."

I saw Rom in my boyhood bedroom, glass vial in hand, tipping it to splash blood on Dani. "You killed your cat for the ceremony." It wasn't a question.

He squinted toward the sky.

"When's the renovation begin?" I asked.

Rom made a show of looking up at the house. Deep black fire marks scarred most of the second floor on the bedroom side. The roof had even collapsed over my old room. A big red sign posted to the front door declared the house a hazard, unsafe to occupy.

The deed was to be signed over on Monday. I'd sold the property to Ned for far less than its worth, but he was paying cash and I wanted to move on.

The First Church of Jesus Christ the Empowered was ready to expand. *What will happen*, I wondered on those nights when I couldn't sleep, *when Ned and his sun-kissed followers trek into the woods? What will they find back there? Will they call it God?*

"I'm not part of his cult," Rom said.

I glanced toward Ned's house, expecting to see him outside, perhaps even with his deranged son, who'd spent thirty days in psychiatric care before being released, but no one was there. No yellow school bus, either. Theo never confessed to anything, and Detective King ruled Isaac's death was "by misadventure," with Wes listed as a person of interest in the boy's demise.

The last I heard, Wes had skipped town. Perhaps he's driving for a new priest somewhere.

Outside Del's house, a Herrera Realty sign hung near the mailbox. Ned would buy his house next, and then he could rename the road Ned's Way or Sun-Kissed Street or Cowan Corner.

I didn't care. I was never coming back.

Suzanne spent what days she had left under constant supervision at Warrenville Golden Years Home, an all-purpose eldercare facility. She was downstairs in the dementia ward and continually expecting her dead husband to show up with flowers, the way he did when they were young.

"There's something we have to do," I said, and hooked an arm around Dani's waist. Soon it would be expanding. I could barely believe it. I was completely petrified to be a father, to bring a child into this fucked-up world. But I was also exhilarated, and filled with real hope for the first time in a very long time.

"Sure," Rom said, "I was thinking . . . "

I let the unsaid apology hang there, and walked with Dani behind the house, Rom watching us disappear.

I paused and glanced back, though Rom was out of view. Maybe he wasn't about to apologize. What if he came here to see how Dani was because he and Ned believed the exorcism had worked? Dani wasn't possessed anymore, after all. Right?

"He's wrong," I whispered. "Wrong, wrong."

"Mike?"

"Nothing," I said. "Let's go."

We continued around back to Dusty's grave. I'd filled in the empty hole. "Do you want to go up?" I asked.

"Yes," she said.

Hand in hand, we ascended Mount Munacy one more time. Our wedding rings slid against one another. We'd cancelled the wedding, and were married at the Warrenville Town Clerk's office a few weeks after Dani got out of the hospital.

The walk to the top of Mount Munacy took no more than thirty seconds, but it felt longer, much longer; an entire lifetime long, in fact.

The woods held the darkness—the branches skeletal—and we kept our backs to what might be there. The police had searched the woods, but Bud Calla was not found. *You must have imagined him*, Koryta had said. I didn't tell them about Dusty, or my brother.

I tugged Dani into an embrace. "Sometimes I feel like I don't know anything, except that I love you. It'll be enough. I promise."

We kissed.

"We should've brought some of your mother's ashes to scatter," she said.

She had no memory of what had happened at the funeral home, but some nights when she startled herself awake and crumpled into sobs, I could swear she was reliving the moment, the madness, the terror.

"Every death is meaningless," I said.

I'd started writing a new book. It wasn't about a serial killer or a cursed house—it was about a young man who finally steps out of the shadows of his past. I didn't know if it was any good, but it felt good to write it.

"Hey," Dani said softly.

"Hey," I said.

Life has echoes, and some of them are beautiful.

Some, though, are too terrible to even imagine.

"Mike," she said as I was about to kiss her. "I know what it all means, and I'm sorry."

Sunlight cut through the clouds and flickered across her face before shadowing again.

"It's okay. You don't need to—"

She kissed me.

"Yes, I do," she said slowly, confidently. "I warned you. I told you. It was too late. We belong here forever. I must go to it."

My hands slid down to her wrists, squeezed. "No, Dani. *No*. We came here to say goodbye to this place, and to all the awful shit that happened. There's no demons. No monsters. No Cowans. It's just us, okay?"

She looked down a moment and then back up. Her eyes were clear, focused. "The child dies, too."

She kneed me hard in the crotch, and I fell back, surprised and burning with pain through my groin and stomach. My hands let go.

Had she tried for the woods, I would have had her, falling as I was in that direction. I could've snagged her elbow or the loose flap of her blouse. I would've been able to knock her off balance, and I would've grabbed her and clutched her against me, no matter the pain inside me or how hard she might fight back. "We'll get through this," I'd promise. "Together." The sun would push through the clouds and I'd dare to believe.

But she didn't run for the woods.

I think I can fly, she'd said.

She sprinted toward the cliff, and when she leaped, feet kicking up dead leaves—arms out, crucified, legs stretching in full sprint—a scream barreled from my throat and followed her all the way down.

ACKNOWLEDGEMENTS

I knew about the coffin, of course, but it wasn't until after my father died that I dared take something from it. A heart attack killed my father when he was fifty-one and I was eleven. I saw it happen and maybe that's why I write horror (all you armchair psychologists can agree on that), but it's really the coffin—and what was inside it—that seduced me into the world of the macabre.

My father loved Halloween, and every year he decorated our front lawn with hand-inscribed gravestones and mannequins dressed as monsters, and he donned a costume as well (his favorite: a two-headed monstrosity, very much like the one Ward has in this book, that he wore with bloodied clothes, a severed head in one hand and a sickle in the other), and with strobe lights flashing and horror-movie soundtracks blasting, he emerged from a custom-built coffin to horrify and delight trick-or-treaters.

That is the image of my father I think of most often—a man embracing his monstrous side in full, public spectacle on Halloween night.

During the rest of the year, while my father worked as a textbook editor, that coffin stood in our downstairs, crammed with horror novels. I'd sneak down there and peek inside, but I was too scared to take one out.

After my father died, I opened the coffin and the books were not so scary anymore. They were a reminder of the father I'd lost, and an opportunity to connect with him through something he loved.

The first book I chose was by Stephen King—*The Waste Lands* (I dug the cover of a ghostly runaway train)—and when I read it, my life changed forever. The entire world opened up to me in a way I couldn't have anticipated. I read and read and read, one book after another. Those books were not the bland, safe *Hardy Boys* tales I'd been reading. These were books where kids and adults had hidden thoughts and fears and didn't behave the way the Hardy Boys did. These were real people, people like me and my friends and my teachers, and I wanted to discover as much of that reality as I could. There was a distinct revelation that through these stories I was granted the privilege to know what the adults didn't want me to know.

Reading King's works and the other horror novels from that coffin was an electric charge, thrilling and scaring me, and it was all the more exciting because it felt taboo. None of my peers read such books. Their parents wouldn't let them if they tried.

When my mother discovered I was working my way through my father's coffin collection, she did not tell me to stop, did not advise me that those were adult books too mature for my pre-adolescent mind. She gave her approval, her permission, and her encouragement.

Parents are scared to let their children read books and watch movies targeted at adults, and perhaps in many cases they are right, but I am absolutely certain that if my mother stopped me from reading those books, or discouraged me from writing the horror stories I scribed in high school, I would not be who I am today.

That is why this book is dedicated to my parents. Without those books, and without the freedom to read them, I wouldn't be a reader, a writer, or a teacher, and this book certainly wouldn't exist.

Thanks to everyone who came to my book signing for *The Devil Virus*, and my heartfelt thanks and gratitude to the following people for their encouragement and support: Marian O'Neill, Brenda and Jack Carter, Jean Bolton, Arlene and Bob Riemann, LeeAnn Doherty Van Koppen, Lucas Kane, Chris Piazza, Marissa Rantinella, Karla Herrera, Gabrielle Esposito, Sage Higgins, Chris Ransom, Michael Marshall, Scott Nicholson, Michael Koryta, Kelly Braffet, Owen King, Scott Miller, Pete Kahle, Mark Williamson, James Rogulski, and Robert Lyon.

And Stephen King, too, of course.

This book would not exist without the following books: *The Exorcist* by Peter Blatty, *Pet Sematary* by Stephen King, and *A Head Full of Ghosts* by Paul Tremblay.

I am indebted to Scarlett Algee and Chris Payne and everyone else at JournalStone/Trepidatio for publishing this book, Sean Leonard for copy editing, Lori Michelle for formatting, and Don Noble for his cover art.

Finally, thank you to my wife, Jenn, who has been endlessly supportive, and thanks to you, dear reader, for giving this book a chance. Horror is the most truthful of genres: it forces us to reconcile with our mortality and confront our fears of things both known and unknown, and in horror there is also hope that when the monster comes we might stand strong and face whatever calamity threatens to disrupt our lives.

Chris DiLeo
January 2020

ABOUT THE AUTHOR

Chris DiLeo is the author of *The Devil Virus* (published by Bloodshot Books), *Meat Camp* (co-authored with Scott Nicholson), *Blood Mountain*, *Calamity*, and *Hudson House*. He is a high school English teacher in New York. Connect with him @authordileo and authordileo.com.